joyce carol oates

Unholy Loves

A NOVEL

THE VANGUARD PRESS, INC.

NEW YORK

Library of Congress Catalogue Card Number: 79-64396
ISBN: 0-8149-0813-6
Manufactured in the United States of America.

Designer: Ernst Reichl

Other Books by Joyce Carol Oates

NOVELS

Son of the Morning
Childwold
The Assassins
Do With Me What You Will
Wonderland
Them
Expensive People
A Garden of Earthly Delights
With Shuddering Fall

SHORT STORIES

Night-Side
Crossing the Border
The Goddess and Other Women
Marriages and Infidelities
The Wheel of Love
Upon the Sweeping Flood
By the North Gate
The Hungry Ghosts
The Seduction
The Poisoned Kiss, Fernandes/Oates

CRITICISM

New Heaven, New Earth:
  The Visionary Experience in Literature
The Edge of Impossibility:
  Tragic Forms in Literature

PLAYS

Miracle Play

POEMS

Anonymous Sins
Love and Its Derangements
Angel Fire
The Fabulous Beasts

ANTHOLOGY

Scenes from American Life:
  Contemporary Short Fiction (EDITOR)

Masks are arrested expressions and admirable echoes of feelings once faithful, discreet, and superlative. Living things in contact with the air must acquire a cuticle, and it is not urged against cuticles that they are not hearts. Yet some philosophers seem to be angry with images for not being things, and with words for not being feelings; words and images are like shells — not less integral parts of nature than the substances they cover, but better addressed to the eye and more open to observation. I would not say that substance exists for the sake of appearance or faces for the sake of masks, or the passions for the sake of poetry and virtue. Nothing arises in nature for the sake of anything else. All these phrases and products are equally involved in the round of existence.

— Santayana, *Soliloquies in England*

for Lois Smedick

I At the Byrnes', 1

II At the Seidels', 97

III At Albert St. Dennis's
     and At the Housleys', 165

IV Hour of Lead, 243

V In the Founders' Room, 289

At
the Byrnes'

September 11.

The hour is late, the hour rings with confusion, the voices and laughter of strangers, and something is happening to Albert St. Dennis.

Something is happening to Albert St. Dennis and it is happening, as he has always dreaded, in public; before strangers. At a wild windy improbable edge of the world, quite new to him.

"Something is happening—" an elderly voice murmurs.

Everyone stares. Everyone listens. It seems to him suddenly that an entire continent is his audience. They are greedy strangers, they are memorizing him, storing up anecdotes to be repeated after his death. Tales of the great old poet. Tales of his last days. Final words. Had he wisdom to pass on to the young? Had he visionary calm, authority? The enigmatic utterances of a Blake, the sprawling rhapsodies of a Whitman, the finely toned, bitter, beautiful pronouncements of a Yeats . . . ? But he is only Albert St. Dennis. Only Albert St. Dennis in the frail trembling outraged flesh.

He holds himself stiffly upright as usual. His public posture. His posture before strangers said to be "admirers." He is wearing his good-luck ring — bought at a bazaar in Cairo decades ago, in the company of Maria Huxley — whom he *did* love, as he loved many women, but who did not, contrary to Harriet's accusations, and contrary even to Aldous's sly encouragement, find the time to love him in return: a large old garnet, darkly red, brownish-cherry-bloodstained red, in an ostentatious silver setting, now badly scarified; he is wearing the new green vest (bought at a "men's boutique" on the Kings Road just last week) with the wild aqua designs stitched into it, brave and gaudy, pavonine, like something tossed off by Beardsley in a benevolent mood, mysteriously soiled now but still very attractive, in St. Dennis's opinion. Of course Harriet would not approve; she would say he was descending into "elderly youth" like certain of their friends. (Like Graves, for instance. But then, gossip perhaps exaggerates. . . .) Harriet, however, does not know. There are many things now that Harriet does not know: even St. Dennis's whereabouts must be a mystery to her. (Thirty years ago — or was it forty — St. Dennis spent a surprisingly agreeable evening in the company of Carl Jung, whose theories he had always found rather implausible; but they had talked at length of the dead, of the beloved dead, and Jung had said, it would seem quite seriously, that the dead depend upon the living to give them information — for they know only what they learned while alive, and after their deaths the world continues, knowledge is accumulated, knowledge they require for whatever salvation is to be theirs. But was Jung in earnest? And what sense could one make of all this? Perhaps St. Dennis's skepticism is keeping Harriet from communicating with him.)

In this part of the world strangers listen eagerly to everything he says, and nod with approval. So many faces! So many eyes! Can one be crucified by the simple *attentiveness* of others, St. Dennis wonders. He sputters with laughter. A forthright merry old man, not at all pompous. He wipes spittle from his mouth and realizes suddenly that he will not survive his year in the United States.

Another drink?

The walls of the Byrnes' living room are rosy with smoke and distance. They are fading back into the night, into the wind-tormented foothills of upstate New York. St. Dennis knows where he is: they have told him. They have been very kind, very solicitous. It is all part of the American flummery, perhaps, but helpful nevertheless. Lodgings; apartment-, building-, and office-keys; "group insurance plan"; telephone installed; a list of services — laundry, shoe repair, pharmacy, The Woodslee Market, even Woodslee Liquor & Wine — and of course a plethora of information about the university, including detailed maps. Back in London, back in the old flat, a slightly trembling forefinger traced his westward route for him, for it would not do to wander about lost, to slip into the vast empty spaces of the New World. Nor would it do, he cautioned himself, to think of the size of the North American continent, for it staggered the mind, taxed the brain, frightened up spirits of confusion and distress. He had known Englishmen decades younger than he who returned from visits to the United States and who spoke of the ineffable terror of the continent: the terror, that is, evoked by one's knowledge of its size, which no map could ever quite adequately suggest. One had to be here, one had to journey to the West Coast, St. Dennis was told. (But he would not journey to the West Coast. Thank you, but no. And some supremely silly woman here tonight has told him he *must* see Hawaii while he is in the States. . . .)

Your first visit here?

And how do you like it?

And how was your flight?

Now that he is over seventy years old he has the right to brush aside such inconsequential gnat-like questions. He knows what he wants to talk about, and he will talk about it. Poetry. The discipline of poetry. The sacrifice. Service. Pilgrimage. He needs only a few intelligent faces about him, he is always stimulated by intelligent faces that are also youthful, and attractive, and the

Byrnes have provided him with a small circle of such faces, and he will talk, he will talk. He has sold himself quite shamelessly — and with necessity — to an institution of higher learning some two hundred and fifty miles north of New York City where he will be expected to perform, monkey-like, dancing-bear-like, chattering-parrot-like, and it will give him a kind of perverse pleasure, it is already giving him a kind of perverse pleasure, to speak his mind directly and frankly on all subjects, but particularly on poetry, while people stare curiously at him and listen with concentration, strangers with keen eyes and earnest, innocently cruel faces, storing up anecdotes. Albert St. Dennis. Oh yes. The great poet. The great English poet. Poor man, he seemed somewhat befuddled, he drank too much at the very first party of the year, a party in his honor; yes, to begin with the poor old dear was two hours late and everyone was imagining the worst, yes, and it was *almost* the worst, thank God he hadn't died somehow in his apartment, he had only arrived here, what a scandal it would have been for the university! But he did arrive by cab, already fairly sozzled, and didn't even apologize to his host and hostess but launched immediately on some sort of tirade — about poetry, about Eliot and Auden and Yeats and someone named Bridges and someone named MacNeice — and an old friend of his, Stevie Smith, of whom no one had ever heard — while Marilyn Byrne tried to round us up and herd us into the dining room, futilely, comically — poor gallant Mrs. Byrne, the dean's wife — and there sat as if immobile the great poet himself ("Since Auden's death," says the *TLS*, "the incontestably finest of living English poets") chattering away as if he were at home, and gesturing wildly and nervously, and flicking cigarette ashes (at his age, St. Dennis is a chain smoker) over Marilyn's brushed-velvet love seat, poor dear eccentric withered creature, his eyes a pale washed-out vacuous blue — focused on no one at all. The walls of the living room fell away and we crowded near, a blurred mass of leggy strangers, all of us robust and healthy and marvelously young, taking note of the great man's slurred voice and doughy skin, which soon went dead white from all the alcohol; taking note and applauding everything he said no matter how incoherent it was, no matter how mad or spittle-flecked, for isn't this our role in the comedy? — and isn't that *his* role?

He speaks: Alone among men the poet creates himself. As Yeats knew. Through the strenuous activity of his art. Through the cruel, heart-straining pilgrimage of his art. He risks despair and madness and exclusion from life's feast in order to create his own soul. Alone among men —

And now to the dining room? To dinner? It is about to be served —

Another Scotch, St. Dennis says sharply. If you please.

The chunky icy glass soon trembles in his hand. They cannot refuse him, cannot deny him any whim. He has sold himself for a rather stunning sum of money — stunning by his frugal standards, at any rate — and he will play the comedy as he wishes, in the style of, say, Auden or Frost or Oscar Wilde: yes, back to Wilde, why not? In the style of the elderly Isak Dinesen with whom, once, he was unfortunate enough to have dinner, an interminable evening shrill with the vain old woman's monologue. Now it is his turn.

He is arguing with someone. He is defending Yeats, of all people. A long thread of something clings to his fingers as he wipes excitedly at his mouth, and imagines that his new-found admirers are inching in closer in order to stare and memorize. Blind in one eye, growing deaf, embittered by the body's betrayal of the soul — why should Yeats *not* be forgiven anything? Unlike the hypocrite loudmouth Pound, he was an artist. An artist! Incomparable!

St. Dennis interrupts an objection (who *is* that hoarse sweating fool in the corduroy jacket, have they been introduced, will he be a colleague of St. Dennis's, will St. Dennis really be expected to know the names of these people, this horde?) with a brusque

motion of his beringed hand, and simply raises his already strident voice, declaiming, in a manner meant to resemble and very
gently and skillfully to parody Yeats's own singsong reading voice:
*The soul's own youth and not the body's youth/ Shows through
our lineaments.*

Something about Fascism. The usual. Impertinent spread-
bellied opponent, a "professor" of American literature no doubt,
challenging St. Dennis in a manner meant, presumably, to be
courteous; but really intolerable. The fool! The idiot! Excited, St.
Dennis waggles his foot. Old habit. Harriet will scold. Excited,
craning his head forward on his skinny neck, dropping ashes. He
has drunk too much, he is making a spectacle of himself, he has
no shame. Even his accent fascinates these barbaric people, yet
he must quarrel — *must* triumph.

So he interrupts and silences his opponent. Crushes him.

Yes, Mr. St. Dennis, the creature says, but —

Crushes him, declaiming fiercely:

> . . . Poets, learn your trade,
> Sing whatever is well made,
> Scorn the sort now growing up
> All out of shape from toe to top,
> Their unremembering hearts and heads
> Base-born products of base beds . . . !

Of course it is an insult — a deliberate insult. But will these
people have the wit to grasp it, to interpret it?

Someone over to the left murmurs something about "Irish
poetry" but St. Dennis does not hear. He cries triumphantly:
"Base-born, base-born, base-born. *Base*-born. Do you see? Eh?
Do you follow?"

Base-born, indeed. Base beds. Base. Scorn. His vision narrows
swiftly. Someone hands him another drink through a long qua-
vering tunnel. Distant, distant. What time is it, where is he? Far
from home? His fingers close greedily about the glass. He remem-

bers: he has bested the squinting staring horde of them with his insight and his passion, he has crushed the paunchy smirking gargoyle-faced opponent, blushing and sullen in defeat but still "smiling" like all Americans . . . wanting to be thought good-natured.

Whoever they are, Americans, strangers, hosts, they are slowly flattening out and shifting into two dimensions. Like wallpaper. The colors of their party costumes are oddly faded. St. Dennis's own hands are remote, and his fingernails — what, is that dirt? — dirt black as tar lodged 'neath the nail of his left thumb? — too far away to maneuver. A smudge on his white cuff? Another stain on his handsome vest? His admirers shift uneasily in the glare of his genius, are not accustomed to confronting genius head-on. Diffracted, the light of *their* faces goes flat.

Must speak more calmly. Give others a chance, even the women. Otherwise Harriet will scold.

Must allow a "conversation." "Give-and-take" of ideas. Must appear to listen, even to be impressed. . . . Ah yes. An excellent point.

Is this drink watered? (The stewardess on Pan American played an insidious trick: poured liquor into a glass and then poured it out again and filled the glass with soda and ice. He'd been told they sometimes did this, the clever bitches. He suspected but couldn't prove. Lipsticked smile, typically American, eager to "please." Hypocrite. Their method, an acquaintance said, of controlling undisciplined drinkers. Undisciplined! He, Albert St. Dennis! . . . And she had been so pretty, so easily effortlessly cruelly pretty.)

Is *this* drink watered as well?

Something is happening. Has been happening. Perhaps he made a blunder, accepting this appointment in North America; perhaps the gods are displeased. He had halfway thought as a younger man that he must never leave England . . . and Harriet had supported him in this vague superstitious nonsense . . . palaver about needing his homeland, English soil, Antaeus, that sort of thing. Perhaps there is something to it, he *isn't* altogether himself any longer. The feverish poetic activity a year and a half ago in Rottingdean . . . the sense of being possessed and used, brutally used, and then abandoned . . . ah, so *that* is the secret meaning behind Yeats's famous Leda and her swan-lover . . . ! *That* is the secret, perhaps, behind all art: the violent use of the flesh, of any flesh, and then its abandonment. But he had survived Rottingdean. Whatever was happening to him continued to happen, continues even now to happen; life itself is the "untranslatable speech" the poet confronts. (But what will Harriet say about his behavior tonight? He has been rude, insufferably rude. For shame! And he so honored, so admired. Very nearly a sacred relic.) . . . The frenzy at Rottingdean, the protracted astonishment of his travels, the bomb that fell from the sky that day, that afternoon, in Paddington, decades ago, which he had not deserved to escape but had nevertheless escaped: these mysteries are with him even now, in the New World.

There will be a season of festivities, they have promised him. Parties, celebrations, rituals in honor of poetry. In honor of *him*. (But he dreams nightly of rewriting his poems: book by book by book. Patiently. Cunningly. Rewriting the book of himself and changing not only the private history of Albert St. Dennis but the public events of history as well. He dreams, he cannot help dreaming. Even now, awake, laughing sociably, the dreams of rewriting the world.) He is warmly drunk. He is really quite happy. The mysteries churn inside him, their dreadfulness is familiar, he can live with them as one lives with arthritic joints and a chronically aching knee and eyes that have not been quite right for several years now: he can live with practically anything. Even the persiflage of these silly people. . . . Should he clear his throat noisily and command them to be still, should he speak to them of the sacred mysteries of his life: not only the agony of creation that August in Rottingdean, when he came so close to death, but the agony of survival during the bombing of London, and the agony of love that has discovered itself sterile (for either he or Harriet was at fault: and too protective of each other and too cowardly to determine the exact nature of the problem), and the earlier vaguer rather comically melancholy agonies of boyhood that seem now to have belonged to another person, a child costumed in the quaint outfits of 1912 . . . ?

Certainly not. They would only misunderstand. They would listen eagerly enough but they would misunderstand and in the end they would denounce him. ("Such beautiful poetry — such an ugly man! An impostor! How has he managed to deceive so many of us?")

Is the drink watered? Its effect is paltry. He waits, he waits for something marvelous to happen. Instead the wallpaper trembles, loses its color, goes flat. Seen through the wrong end of a telescope. He takes off his glasses and rubs his eyes. He remembers having been so powerfully impressed by his hosts' house some hours ago that he exclaimed aloud: Is this your private home? This? (Surprise rather than envy; some resentment, perhaps; thinking of the miserable flats he and Harriet rented year after year in London, thinking of the dismal sunless perpetually chilly "maisonette" he now owns in Chelsea.) Such lavish furnishings! That enormous fireplace! Mirrors, a small grand piano, rugs, surfaces that gleam — polished, brilliant, blinding — drapes of pale saffron, silken wallpaper of rich roseate hues. Upon entering the Byrnes' small mansion he felt a thrill of something akin to pure dismay. It was not simply that he was unaccustomed to such elegance, and not even that he rather resented it: he felt instead that he would not be equal to it. As if England itself, the English people as they were now — humiliated, impoverished, frightened of the future — could not possibly be equal to it.

Nevertheless he performed his part, and is performing it still. He is, after all, English. An Englishman. Which means, in the eyes of his gregarious well-intentioned hosts, that he is any num-

ber of things they believe they admire, and respect, and even
envy. An English poet: the very sound of which calls to mind, to
the educated, Milton and Chaucer and Keats and Pope and
Shakespeare, of course! — how could one forget Shakespeare
even for a moment — and Jane Austen and Dickens and — and
the man who wrote *Tom Jones*, and the man — woman? — who
wrote *The Mill on the Floss*. And of course many others. Many,
many others. Kipling, for instance. The British Empire. (On
which the sun never set — or so it was boasted.) England and
the English and the Tower of London and the Thames and
manor houses and castles and ruined cathedrals and churchyards
and Stratford-on-Avon and Yorkshire pudding and pence and
pounds and shillings and Big Ben and Hyde Park and the Queen
and Mr. Pickwick and unheated homes and high tea and Parliament and trade unions and the dole and Piccadilly Circus, which
always turns out to be not a circus at all but simply a very busy
and very dirty square in the heart of an astonishingly busy and
dirty city. Ah, yes. England. Englishman. Poet. Famous? (Someone has told them he is famous — not only in England but
throughout the world. And they evidently believed it. And so he
must perform his part.)

The ordeal of shaking hands. So very pleased to meet you. And
you. Yes. So very pleased. The ordeal of straining to hear: why
do these people mumble, is it a sign of awe or of simple bad
breeding? The ordeal of smiling. One *must* be courteous, at least
at first. Oliver Byrne seems a halfway decent fellow. His wife is
quite gracious, despite her almost oppressive desire to please. But
there are so many guests. Must he remember them all? Their
mumbled names? These strangers who appear before him as if
paying homage to an elderly dignitary, declaring their admiration
of his work, even insisting upon it (as if sensing his courteous
disbelief). Strangers, strangers. And their wives. The dean and
his wife. Couples. Affluent and handsome and hopeful. With
such remarkably good teeth, on the whole. (*His* teeth — the ones

he had suffered with for so many wretched decades — grayish-green, and rotting in his jaws, and the source of such anguish and humiliation! — if these people could have gazed upon his teeth, before they were all wrenched out and replaced with a handsome though extraordinarily awkward set of dentures, how they would pity him, and pass by him in sympathetic silence.)

But of course they don't know, they cannot guess, they are touchingly childlike in their awe of him. And only children, St. Dennis thinks irritably, could be so direct, so crude in their flattery — one of the women told him, her eyes shining, that it was a scandal he hadn't been awarded the Nobel Prize this past year, when everyone — *everyone* — knew he deserved it. Oh yes? Really? How very kind of you to say. And he continued shaking their hands. They were surprised, perhaps, by the strength of the old man's handshake. By his gay good humor. His rather dandyish clothes. He was to be, evidently, a "good sport." Though he had believed he would stay at the Byrnes' only an hour or so, and then beg off, he somehow found himself enjoying the party after all; enjoying the harmless if rather silly adulation; and the dean's excellent Scotch.

After all, these Americans were so eager to honor him. The educated and articulate and well-to-do members of a nation that barely tolerates the serious arts, and is frankly contemptuous of poetry — how touching that they were eager to isolate and honor *him*. He was a single individual, of course; and it is far easier, and far more pleasurable, to honor a single individual, to award him prizes, prize after prize, than it is to take his discipline seriously in any wider sense, and to be attentive to what others are doing in his field. Yes, he understands; he understands the motive. And in a way he can sympathize with it. For Albert St. Dennis is famous. "Famous" in the narrow hothouse world of letters — whatever letters are — whatever people imagine they are. We can't possess your sensitivity, they murmur, we're practical pragmatic heedless citizens, we skim the surface of life and do it with considerable skill, we don't probe, we don't poke into corners, we never commit suicide, or fall into despair, or into ecstasies — we leave all that to you; and now we're at such a point in history that we won't make you a god and devour your heart, we won't even bother to persecute you; all that has changed, we're quite friendly now, we're no threat. . . . Mr. St. Dennis, do you hear?

He *wants* not to think such things. He detests skepticism, cynicism. After all, these good generous people have offered him the title of Distinguished Professor of Poetry. And they are demanding very little of his time, it seems: he has been assigned no formal classes, he is expected to give only two public addresses or readings for the entire academic year, and to be on campus only two days of the week. So he *is* grateful. And he *does* like them. But something has been happening as the hours have passed, one drink following another, and these strange uneatable things meant to whet the appetite — mushrooms stuffed with something like liver, tiny fat sausages wrapped in bacon and pierced by festive toothpicks — and the sound of his own excited voice, and the keen frank staring faces that surround him, and the astonishing fact that he is the oldest person in the room, perhaps in Woodslee itself, perhaps in all of New York State; and that he is very far from his Chelsea home.

Dinner? Food?

Isn't it time — ?

Another drink?

Mr. St. Dennis was saying —

Quiet, quiet!

What time is it?

He blinks and sees that everyone is still watching him expectantly, like children. Perhaps they *are* children . . . ?

His?

Closest to him, in fact sitting on the floor near his feet, is a most extraordinary young man. St. Dennis cannot quite believe in him: he must be a poet, a flamboyant young rival. His name?

His name? Can't recall. Something rather archaic. Hellenic. Heroic. The young man is very young and very blond. Early twenties perhaps. His hair is shaggy, charmingly unkempt, streaked as if bleached unevenly by the sun: predominantly a very light, platinum blond, with streaks of brown. Outrageous. Long straight Roman nose, a firm chin, rather full, sensual lips, striking eyes. The eyes are so brown as to seem red, blood-red, like St. Dennis's garnet. Classic profile. Flawless. Fearless. Beauty. And such chilling confidence — ! For the past hour he has been sipping at a drink and staring coolly up into St. Dennis's heated face as if not terribly impressed with the old man's palaver. He sits gracefully, casually, one arm draped about his raised knees, his chin thrust forward. He too is listening, listening closely. But not uncritically. St. Dennis wonders if the young man is being rude, sitting there on the floor like a boy, assuming a kind of intimacy with him that is totally unjustified. And is it appropriate, in any case, that a young person should sit on the floor of the dean's living room, on this special occasion? Or is it a queer American custom? The boy seems too self-possessed to be a student, and yet he is too arrogantly casual, too blatantly glamorous, to be a member of the faculty. He is wearing what appears to be a suede suit, fawn-colored, with a silky green shirt open at the neck; there are several rings on his fingers, and his wrist watch is a solid gold bracelet with a black face and no numerals that St. Dennis can discern. From time to time St. Dennis's foot twitches involuntarily, with the violence of his passionate words, and comes close to touching the young man's knee. But the young man does not draw back, does not flinch; supremely contained, perhaps even a little contemptuous, he sits hugging his knees loosely against his chest, a drink in one hand, eying St. Dennis calmly. Gawky old well-intentioned fool! Let him perform.

A few yards away, facing him, is a young woman who reminds St. Dennis of a beautiful young cousin of his — no longer young, of course, and no longer living. Agnes: two years younger than he. Like this woman, slender, black-haired and black-eyed, too intense, perhaps, too highly wrought. He had always feared that Agnes might kill herself. Might — suddenly — over a weekend, perhaps — kill herself. Of course it was nonsense. Of course he had not mentioned it to anyone, certainly not to Agnes herself. She had died, however, just the same: dead at the age of thirty-two, in a bombing raid in London. The poor girl! She had wanted so much to live, had wanted so passionately to love — and it had not worked out for her, love had failed, loves had failed, she had been bitter and disillusioned while still in her twenties. . . . Yes, this young woman has Agnes's pale glowing skin, her look of being nervously restrained, almost angry. But Agnes had been rather more beautiful. This woman — her name is Brigit, Briget something — St. Dennis seemed to recall she was married — and she was an artist, perhaps? — or a writer? — this woman's fine black hair was beginning to go gray in patches, and her thin, faint eyebrows were raised too sharply, as if she were waiting for the right moment to interrupt, to protest. Introduced to her earlier in the evening, St. Dennis had liked her well enough, squeezing her tiny hand in his, noting its damp coldness: ah, she was nervous, as nervous as he! But in fact she does not seem nervous any longer. There is something annoying about her dark, glittering stare. Why are her lips pursed so tightly? — so primly? She too is judging him, she too finds him wanting. Silly old scarecrow, old coat-upon-a-stick! Her occasional smile is perfunctory, her low, throaty laughter is merely conversational. Has she been drinking too much? Where is her husband? He can't recall having been introduced to her husband.

Food?

Ah yes: food.

Mrs. Byrne and a young woman in a white outfit are passing plates around. Be careful, this is quite warm . . . ! The young woman is swarthy-skinned, with thick eyebrows; must be a servant. Somehow St. Dennis did not expect his American hosts to have servants; he did not expect them to acknowledge their servants. Food. Plates. Silverware. Linen napkins. Yes yes yes. Of course. No appetite but one must go through the motions of eating, of pleasing one's hostess. Be careful, Mr. St. Dennis, this plate is quite warm. . . . Can you manage? Let us set this tea table up, it will be more convenient. How's that? Can you manage? Mrs. Byrne with her good-natured smile, her display of gum and strong white teeth, wonderfully American; a woman in an advertisement. He has forgotten her first name. A robust handshake, though, and a good lemony soapy smell. Undisguised pleasure at meeting him. Albert St. Dennis! What an honor! Woodslee's guest for a year, what an honor for Woodslee and for all of us! Ah yes: her name is Marilyn. The dean's wife. Open and sweet and hearty and helpful and motherly, though she is thirty years younger than he, and daughterly too, her eyes filling with tears when they met at the air terminal in Champlain. Tonight he has been a bit naughty, hasn't he, ignoring her timid requests that everyone come into the dining room, refusing to budge, so that no one else budged, and she has been forced to serve her dinner in the living room; naughty old Albert St. Dennis of whom it has been said: *One of the unparalleled poetic geniuses of our time.* . . .

Still, he is naughty. He is capricious. He peers over his eyeglasses at one of his interrogators, as if the man's words were incomprehensible. Yes? Yes? Speak more distinctly! — A question about Eliot. So banal, so predictable. So annoying.

"Tom Eliot . . . !" St Dennis says slowly. He means to shake only his head but his entire body shakes, as if in revulsion. "He himself dismissed his work, you know. Swept it aside. As indeed he should have. Adolescent grousing and nothing more and yet you Americans have always taken it so bloody seriously."

The tea table is wobbling. No one speaks, and for the first time St. Dennis notices the watery blood easing from the hefty chunk of beef on his plate. Though no longer a vegetarian, since his doctor told him to forget that foolishness some years ago, St. Dennis eyes the meat with distaste. Can it be that these people expect him to eat what they are eating . . . ? Do they expect him to eat at all, while they gape? The brute in the corduroy jacket brings up another subject, he is tireless, now asking about experimental poetry, High Modernism, Eliot and Pound and Yeats and Joyce, wasn't their era long finished, wasn't the word itself more or less finished? Carefully wrought art — wasn't that doomed in the Electronic Age? Aren't we in an entirely new world, nearing the birth of the twenty-first century? Things are happening much too rapidly for them to be assimilated and interpreted, even by artists. And if that is so —

St. Dennis is staring at him. Lewis, the man's name is. He smiles at St. Dennis tauntingly, eating his beef without pause, handling knife and fork with skill. It's remarkable, St. Dennis notes, how the man switches his knife and fork from one hand to the other, not losing a beat in his chewing or in his bullying attention. Close-set gray eyes, a rodent's eyes, fixed steadily on St. Dennis, awaiting his reply. But what can St. Dennis say? Is his craft indeed doomed, is he already extinct, have they brought him to North America as one of the last surviving (and elderly) members of an endangered species . . . ? An aged man is but a paltry thing. And Harriet, could she see, would sharply scold.

Then the dark-haired young woman begins to speak. Her voice is low and cool and throaty, not at all like Agnes's soft girlish voice. She says bluntly: "Mr. St. Dennis, don't feel you must take Lewis's remarks seriously. It's generally known that he says anything that flies into his mind. Sometimes it's brilliant, sometimes it's merely shit. And it's very difficult to distinguish between the two."

Everyone laughs. A few people are startled by the woman's choice of words, and St. Dennis himself is gravely shocked. What on earth did she say! That frail-boned attractive young woman! He finds it hard to believe that he has heard correctly, that she has really spoken such vulgar words in company, unblushing, unhesitant. The comely young blond man grunts his amused approval. Lewis himself flushes a deep angry red but does not reply.

Mrs. Byrne is asking once again if St. Dennis can manage his food.

"Oh my God," he whispers, "leave me alone. I beg you."

"Mr. St. Dennis . . . ?" she says, not hearing.

"Leave me alone," he says, his words slurred, his eyes moist. And then, raising his voice: "You're very kind, Mrs. Byrne. But I can manage very well, thank you. I can manage quite splendidly on my own."

And can she love him, after her days of lurid and humiliating anticipation? She cannot, for St. Dennis is simply too old.

Not merely old but oldmannish. Peering over his spectacles like that . . . his lips loose and wet and his teeth so obviously and so painfully not his own: ceramic-white, too perfect. No one would ever make teeth like that in North America, Brigit thinks.

She had wanted to love him — to fall in love with him — but it was to be a failure. In spite of the liquor she has had. In spite of her tractable and desperate spiritual condition. Still, his voice *is* beautiful. Papery thin and delicately modulated, the voice of the BBC broadcasts and the single recording she has heard, Albert St. Dennis reading selections from *Hecate* and *Lovesounds*. Perhaps she can half-close her eyes and lose her footing gradually and fall in love with his voice . . . ?

Talk. "Serious conversation." Poetry, the arts, technological America, the future of civilization, the lost *mana* of the poet, the circumscribed condition of the humanities in general, the fact that suicide among young people has increased nearly a thousand percent in the past decade — a fact that St. Dennis appears not to grasp though it is repeated for him. (That none of the rest of us are shocked any longer, Brigit thinks, is a bad sign. But then we've been badgered so much by statistics meant to shock.) . . .

St. Dennis's face is frail-boned, tremulous. His skin is soft, softly puckered beneath the eyes, discolored with age and fatigue. The whites of his eyes have gone yellow. The water-color blue of his eyes looks transparent, as if he were really blind; Brigit finds it discomforting to meet his gaze. Suppose he knows, suppose he can guess, her anxiety? — her naive half-angry wish to love him?

Brigit Stott is thirty-eight and Albert St. Dennis is nearly seventy-one, but that should make no difference. Other, odder matches have transpired. She has known of a few; she has heard of many others. He is a widower, and lonely. She is a recent divorcee, and very lonely. And there is something to be said for the eerie depthlessness of those eyes. Imagine sinking into bed with him! Being embraced by him! His hair is thin but unruly, charmingly unruly, and perfectly white. Absolutely white. Colorless. A look of fastidious purity, bone-dry, beyond mortality. (Mortality, Brigit thinks, is the unattractive gray hairs sprouting on her own head. Hairs that are wiry and brittle, unlike the others; unlike what she thinks of as her own hair.)

In her imagination she had already loved him with a sinking-heartedness, a swooning girlish asininity decades outgrown, resurrected now as if to spite her better judgment. But what to make, in the Byrnes' handsome living room, of this skinny old English bird with the potbelly and the trousers with their frayed cuffs and the ragged dirt-edged nails and the clumsy job he did shaving and the querulous drone of his voice and the fact that he is evidently half deaf, or pretending to be so . . . ? What to make of the wattled throat, the trembling hands, the sharp creases in the cheeks, the skull so prominently ridged above the forehead and speckled with liver spots that show evilly through the thin white strands of hair . . . ? The disappointment! The dismay! For she knows, swallowing another large mouthful of her drink, that nothing in her life will be altered. She had hoped for another of her unholy loves — or perhaps it would have turned out holy? — but it will not transpire. Nothing at all will happen.

Brigit Stott had been anticipating this party for weeks. You must come, you are first on our list, Albert St. Dennis will be delighted to meet you, Marilyn Byrne said. Shameful to admit, but Brigit had been thinking of little else. Her course preparations — she would be teaching three courses, one of them an immense section of American literature that would require lectures three times a week — were done hurriedly, early in the day, so she might spend the evening hours thinking and speculating and brooding, sipping a drink, rereading St. Dennis's books. Oliver Byrne had expressed surprise that Brigit owned most of St. Dennis's books, which had irritated her. She told him that St. Dennis's poetry and travel journals and essays and novel (his only novel, dense and all but unreadable, a sort of extended prose poem with a *fin de siècle* weariness, set on a Greek island) were very important to her: genuinely important: she wasn't fabricating enthusiasm like everyone else. She did not tell Oliver how desperately grateful she was to be included in his invitation, nor did she temper her usual coolness toward Marilyn, whom she likes well enough — as she is fond of declaring — but whose inane babble drives her wild.

Surely it must mean something that the Byrnes' party is on September eleventh, a Saturday; and it was on March eleventh, a Saturday, that Brigit was married. Of course that had been some time ago. And the marriage did not turn out as she had anticipated. But Brigit Stott is superstitious, despite her intelligence and her locally famous skepticism; dates are very important to her. As are certain colors (apricot, pale blue, cream), certain odors (lilac, toast, the crass fishy smell of harbors and seashores, new leather, new lumber), music (her mind is clogged with trivial trashy popular songs from her young girlhood, which she sings when safely alone: she *is* ashamed of this weakness), articles of clothing and cities and names and numbers. She is eccentric enough to believe that her superstitions point to a benevolently organized universe; she is willful enough to wish to believe in destiny, but not in fate. When coincidences occur that have an ominous tinge — a lover attired in a fashionable new blazer that is precisely the blazer her husband wore in court, her mother telephoning long-distance to announce, in her plaintive accusatory voice, that an aunt of Brigit's had just "passed away," not an hour after Brigit found herself thinking unkind thoughts about that woman — she brushes it all aside, declaring it folk nonsense, Virginia hillbilly metaphysics.

But she is superstitious, there is no help for it. And despite her hyperborean calm, her somewhat indifferent grooming, her studied look of simply *not caring* about the impression she makes socially, she is really eager, even anxious, to do well socially. She has written novels, she has written innumerable critical essays, she has a small, mild reputation, and is evidently a successful teacher — though she flinches from discussions of teaching and nervously brushes aside all compliments — for if one speaks of something treasured, might it not be lost? — though she is, in others' eyes, an enviable person, it is nevertheless the case that the Woodslee parties are her only solace, her only hope. No one can guess at her loneliness. No, it is more than loneliness: it is a raging ravenous despair, a sort of philosophical despair, as if the drawn-out divorce and the reversal of certain emotions ("love," "tenderness," "compassion") allowed her to see into the depths of the universe itself, and to find it distinctly inhuman. Camus ended his curious little novel *The Stranger* with his psychopath hero's rhapsodic words about the "benign indifference" of the universe, which felt to him brotherly, and comforting; but Brigit, peering into the blank lightless unsubtle abyss outside the human sphere, found nothing benign there, and certainly nothing brotherly or comforting. She wonders: Did Camus himself, dying entangled in a wrecked auto, his blood gushing deliriously free of its confinement, come round to thinking that there might be something malevolent in indifference after all?

Marriage. The deterioration of love. Separation. Reunion.

Separation. Divorce. Certain consequences of divorce, unforeseen. No one in Woodslee can guess the degree of Brigit's exhaustion. She has felt, at times, with a remorseless logic, that it might be a good idea for either her or her former husband to die: simply to cease to exist. How cleansing that would be, how generous. . . . As "love" turned inside out to something resembling a furious unremitting "hatred," nearly infantile in its intensity, Brigit, like a stunned onlooker at a disaster, wondered at times if she were losing her sanity. It was enough, it was more than enough, that Stanley should turn so passionately vicious: but then she was confronted with her own viciousness, which threatened at times to overleap *his.* And there was the possibility, with which she pricked herself often, that she had made him into what he was now. Certainly he had not been so unjust, so unstable, so mean, in the first stages of their marriage.

A storm of emotions, roused into life and now beyond control. It is true that Stanley seems to hate Brigit more consistently than she hates him, but perhaps that is simply a consequence of her inadequacy as a human being — her infamous anemia, her "frigidity," of which, as their relationship deteriorated, he spoke often in a bitter aggrieved tone, both in private and in public. If he now hates her more wildly than she hates him, perhaps that is to his credit: Stanley would certainly say so. I am a man of deep, intense feelings, he would claim, though he never claimed such nonsense years ago.

But there are parties. There will always be parties. Woodslee is a very social university — detractors might say it is desperately social, because of its isolation, and the long dark merciless winters. Without social life one would simply freeze to death here. Without friends (or the semblance of friends) one would simply die. The Byrnes' party will be followed by another, perhaps at the Seidels'; and then there will be another, and another, and yet another, stretching deep into winter, warming Brigit, keeping Brigit alive. (She will give a party herself this year. Now that the divorce is behind her.) What need to die if there is a party next weekend? So much can happen at a party! Gregariousness dispels all dark somber joyless thoughts. It is, perhaps, our natural condition: and the soliloquies of aloneness, the mere phenomenon of *thinking* itself, are less than natural.

She would like to take St. Dennis aside and speak quite frankly to him. This gibberish about poetry, art, civilization — very impressive, of course — but what about human feeling, what about despair, the utter blankness of the soul? Could he talk her into wanting to live? Surely — if he tried — this golden-tongued potbellied oracle, gaily drunk, could talk her into anything. If they were alone together she might take his hand, or he might take *her* hand, to comfort her. If he would stop quibbling about old, dead rivals — if he would stop waggling his foot — she might even recite for him a certain poem of Emily Dickinson's, that has been plaguing her for weeks: *This is the Hour of Lead* — / *Remembered, if outlived,/ As Freezing persons, recollect the Snow* — / *First* — *Chill* — *then Stupor* — *then the letting go* — .

(Must decline the next drink. But perhaps no next drink will be offered.)

(Must try not to say offensive things. "Vulgar" things. An innocently contemptuous remark about Anglicanism made last spring at a party given by Lewis and Faye Seidel, uttered within earshot of Vivian Hochberg — whose grandfather is, or was, a bishop in Boston — evidently offended the icy Mrs. Hochberg considerably; and she is, after all, the wife of the chairman of the English department. And once in a crowded place — the foyer of the university theater, in fact — Brigit referred to the president of the university as a *quidnunc*, simply because she liked the word — she liked it, and wanted to use it. But because no one knew its meaning it flew about and could not be recalled, and was, in one of its transformations, the ugly and inexplicable word *queer* — inexplicable in this context, since poor President Garrett has not the imagination for sexual adventures of any kind. Your mouth will get you into trouble one day, missy, people in her family said, and this has already been the case.)

(Must remember to *seem happy*.)

(Must make an effort to be civil to Marilyn Byrne, out of consideration for Oliver.)

(Must draw the conversation, sometime this evening, onto St. Dennis's *The Explorers*, which she wants to ask him about. Not out of flirtatious idleness but out of a genuine curiosity: Has St. Dennis really lived through such experiences? And she should tell him, he will be amused, of her first encounter with *Love-sounds*. Eighteen years old, a freshman at Smith, reading the volume of poetry in the college library, blushing and gasping aloud, shocked into incredulous laughter. She had never come across poetry like this, she had not known that poetry could say such things, do such things. The remorseless cataloguing of the lovers' parts, their mating galumphing parts, as a kind of music-hall song; and the voices of their dismayed spirits as a kind of accompanying dirge. Witty and precise and frank and, yes, vulgar, richly and comically vulgar, even obscene, *Lovesounds* had shocked and offended Brigit at the time (as a girl she was puritan-ical and is still inclined in that direction), and she remembered thinking how she disliked the poet for his poems and wanted to meet him, to tell him so.)

And now they are together, and he has been looking at her strangely. Dividing his attention between her and Alexis Kessler, sluttish foppish Kessler, the aging *Wunderkind* of the music de-partment, sprawled like an odalisque at the famous man's feet. The conversation is now lively — race relations in America, in England; the situation in South Africa; the scandalous folly of the United Nations — and St. Dennis seems to have given up on his prime rib.

Oddly, Brigit was an hour late to the party. For some reason she had fallen asleep at five, and hadn't awakened until after seven; and then had to shower, shampoo her hair, dress herself, contrive some sort of appearance, snatch desperately for some sort of reasonable face. In a fury of self-loathing, she cursed herself, and chased the cat out of her bedroom and wondered if her stupor-like sleep was a sign of some new illness or a sign, simply, of her spiritual slovenliness. Nothing mattered to her except tonight's party: and so she comes close to missing it. Is it the first step to suicide, after all . . . ? Though she knows herself too cowardly to commit suicide, perhaps the psyche plays tricks, arranges pranks and accidents, and one day death, the unthinkable, comes with the ease of a letter through a slot, or ice cubes bouncing into a plastic container. Suicides are angry people, Stanley once said, reading in the *Times* with grim satisfaction of the suicide — by hanging — of an old classmate-rival. They must be angry to hurt themselves so.

Brigit was an hour late. But St. Dennis was two hours late.

He arrived listing on his feet and mumbling insincere apologies in what sounded like a BBC announcer's voice. Ah, is *that* the great man — ! A stubbly chin, unevenly shaved, that reminded Brigit for a moment of her grandfather, long dead; the stale denture odor; watery squinting eyes behind thick lenses; an utterly ludicrous bright-blue vest.

They had all worried about him. As soon as Brigit arrived she realized that no one had missed her, no one had even thought of her, they were all earnestly discussing Albert St. Dennis. Marilyn Byrne wanted to telephone him. But Oliver thought it unwise, for St. Dennis was known to have a capricious temper, and sometimes flew into a rage if he believed his private life was being invaded. Lewis Seidel was arguing in his Bronx voice that it would be no trouble at all for him to drive across town to St. Dennis's apartment; but he would like to call the old man first, and would need his number (which is unlisted, and which the Byrnes have). I could even say, Lewis went on, that we'd arranged ahead of time for him to be picked up. He's probably somewhat absent-minded like most poets his age, he wouldn't really remember.

But Oliver as the Dean of Humanities was irritated by this suggestion, which smacked of frivolity; though Lewis, pacing about and jiggling his car keys, was hardly joking. (Oliver Byrne and Lewis Seidel had quarreled some years earlier over an "ideological" matter: their rivalry was presented to Brigit as having sprung out of an intense, passionate difference in their philosophies of education. But they rarely quarrel now in public, and the issue remains somewhat mysterious.)

Marilyn Byrne's eyes brimmed with tears. Her house was so lovely, there were flowers, there were hors d'oeuvres about to be slid into the oven, all her guests were here, everyone was drinking, her husband was gravely worried, that awful Lewis Seidel was bullying him and Oliver was too courteous to reply. . . . Fortunately, Faye Seidel talked her husband out of his plan. Then someone said that Albert St. Dennis might simply have forgotten the date. He might not have marked it on his calendar. Hadn't he a reputation for being somewhat vague about things. . . . But, no, he knew about the party, Gowan Vaughan-Jones stated in his prim brusque voice. He'd run over to St. Dennis's apartment yesterday with a copy of a first edition of *Hecate* for him to sign, and St. Dennis had seemed quite pleased, "almost boyishly pleased," at the prospect of the party in his honor. He had even said something about buying a gift for his hostess, to show his appreciation. What would be appropriate for the charming Mrs. Byrne, he'd asked Gowan.

Then it was said — in fact by Brigit, who dreaded the worst — that something might have happened to him. After all, he was alone in that apartment. He might have slipped in the bathtub, or fallen and struck his head against something hard. . . . Gladys Fetler joined in to say that the poor old gentleman hadn't looked well when she met him the other day. He had been coughing, and spitting into his handkerchief; and for some reason he insisted upon smoking. Lewis Seidel said that he'd heard from friends of friends at Oxford that St. Dennis had had a series of cataract operations not long ago, and was prone to accidents since his wife's death. Which meant that someone should certainly telephone; *he* would be happy to do it.

Warren Hochberg then said in his slow pontifical calm voice that they were being unreasonable. A man of St. Dennis's stature could be as late as he pleased. They could not expect him to contort himself to fit their Woodslee conventions. His wife Vivian added that close friends of theirs at the University of London said that Albert St. Dennis was sometimes late even for poetry readings, and that no one really objected. He was a genius, one must remember.

"Yes, I believe he is a genius," Warren Hochberg said. "I have recently reread all his books and I believe he *is* a genius, somewhere above Auden but below Eliot, and far below Yeats of course." He made this pronouncement in his characteristically ponderous manner, a thumb and forefinger gripping his lower lip, his eyes fixed upon the floor; a picture that stirred Brigit to wonder. As chairman of the English department, Hochberg was an indecipherable personality whom everyone feared, or enjoyed fearing, but Brigit thought perversely that he was rather charming. If one viewed him from a certain angle. She liked it that Hochberg, the author of several well-received scholarly books, and a past president of the Council of Learned Societies, should deliberately impersonate in public a slow-thinking country-headed good-natured oaf.

"Well, we're all geniuses here," Alexis Kessler said. His voice was raw and rude, he meant only to antagonize Hochberg. The Byrnes' guests laughed nervously. One never knew with Alexis whether his acerb comments were genuine, or whether they were a droll form of self-mockery. Brigit stared at him, not liking his outfit. He was resplendent in a taffy-colored suede suit with a green silk shirt open to mid-chest (the sickly pallor of the man's chest was all the more striking in contrast to the frizzy dark curls that sprouted in the V of his shirt); he wore all his usual rings, but had left off, at least, his heavy gold necklace that, rumor had it, was solid gold, a gift from an admirer in Italy; he was drenched in some sort of cologne that smelled like mouthwash; his hair was going dark at the roots because he had neglected to bleach it for some time. Brigit was appalled at the Byrnes' error in judgment in inviting Kessler, of all people, to meet St. Dennis. She would say nothing to Oliver, of course; but she thought it an egregious mistake. She was herself a writer — a failed writer, in her own estimation — but a writer nevertheless, with a small reputation — while Alexis Kessler was a former musical prodigy, long burned-out, long exposed, now a spoiled child whose disdain for his colleagues at Woodslee was notorious, and whose jealousy of their successes was legendary. Seeing him there in the Byrnes' living room, Brigit had felt her heart sink. Oh that bastard, she had thought. She detested men with pretty faces.

And then she was somewhat disoriented by having slept so long, and by the manic haste of the past hour. How odd, how very odd, that she should have fallen asleep, and should have found it so difficult to wake up. . . . These bouts of sleep were becoming disturbingly frequent. She might teach a most agreeable class, manage to intercalate all the small clever "casual" details she'd hoped to during the course of the fifty minutes; she might feel gloriously alive, alert, invincible; and then, back in her office or back home, the drowsiness would sweep upon her. . . . At first it was warm and comfortable, like inhaling the smell of fresh-baked bread (another of her cherished odors); but then, quickly, it became overwhelming. She was suddenly exhausted, deathly exhausted, and must lie down at once, without even taking the time to undress. And in sleep she was pitched down, down, far down. She did not dream, or did not remember dreaming. Sleep struck like a blow, a sword. It was utterly blank and featureless, though when she tried to describe it she spoke of it as muddy. The muddy floor of an unfathomable ocean, where nameless faceless bodies are rolled gently over and over, helpless and mute and perfectly at peace. But it was not really the sleep that terrified her, but the difficulty with which she woke. She had always been an insomniac — she had rather prided herself on her insomnia, imagining it betokened a pristine sensitivity.

Perhaps St. Dennis could give them a little lecture on sleep? There was a poem of his. . . . What was its title. . . . A chilling sonnet that drew together Plato, and the gardens of Adonis, and the dead of World War II. Brigit had been reading about sleep and death and the soul and consciousness a great deal recently, and hurriedly too, as if time were running out for her. She had become fascinated by the phenomenon of consciousness itself. She read books by neurophysiologists, she reread *De Anima*, and even Schopenhauer, and Erich Neumann, who described in such detail the labor of consciousness, of becoming human: the gravitational pull each individual feels toward sleep, the unconscious, the original Uroboros: the cessation of all conflict. In the end, though, more than the others Neumann succeeded only in making her pathologically drowsy.

And so it was 8:30 and then 8:45 and then 9:00 and then 9:20 and Brigit consoled Marilyn Byrne, hearing herself say banal reassuring false things, feeling herself stretch her lips into a smile. The mask, the cuticle, the necessary gesture. She isn't quite willing to admit that she envies Mrs. Byrne — envies the woman her attractive husband, and her settled position in life — how relaxing it would be not to be fired by a compulsion to "create" — simply to live, to consume, to decorate rooms and plan dinner parties and blink tears out of one's eyes when the guest of honor fails to appear! — but she is willing to admit that Marilyn has been extremely helpful and generous to her. During the worst months of Brigit's disastrous marriage she had telephoned several times a week, she invited Brigit to the City Women's Club for lunch, asked her for sisterly advice about clothes and furnishings and other claptrap, and which people might be invited along with which people to parties (for, as the dean's wife, she was con-

stantly entertaining; and as the dean's wife she was somewhat
sheltered from, or deprived of, the delightful claver everyone else
trafficked in); she invited Brigit to join her at meetings of Am-
nesty International, Planned Parenthood, the Woodslee-Cham-
plain Environmental Commission. Brigit declined these invitations but was grateful for them. Had Marilyn Byrne saved Brigit's
life? It would not do to think so.

Waiting for Albert St. Dennis. Who must have left his apartment, who must be en route to the Byrnes', for Oliver finally
weakened and telephoned; but there was no answer. Waiting for
the great man, and drinking too much, and breaking into peals
of unaccountable laughter. Twenty-five people. Most of them
were familiar to Brigit, a few of them — Lewis Seidel, for instance — rather too familiar, since their offices in the Humanities Building were adjacent, and they were invited to the same
parties. But two couples were new. They were also young, dis-
mayingly young. Brigit was introduced to them but mixed up
their names immediately, and for the rest of the evening could
not remember who was who, or who was married to whom. Barry
and Ernest. Carol and Sandra. The Jaegers, the Swansons. The
men were both assistant professors in the department, new appointments whose vitae she had evidently studied, though she
could remember nothing. Barry Swanson, Ernest Jaeger. Or was
it Barry Jaeger and Ernest Swanson? Both wore glasses. Both
were quite nicely dressed — the taller of the two in a herringbone
suit with a vest, the kind of outfit Brigit's husband liked to wear
when things were really bad with him; he believed, as Brigit had
come to believe, that the more wretched one felt, the more con-
spicuously elegant one dressed. What was distressing was the
youth, the actual boyishness, of the two young professors. . . .
One of the wives, Carol, was vivacious and rather intimidating in
her snug white dress; a moderately pretty girl with a jarringly loud
laugh, evidently of Italian or Greek descent; Brigit might envy
her spirit, her zestfulness. But the other wife, Sandra, was strik-

ingly beautiful. Really, there was no one like her at the party tonight, no one like her in Woodslee. Fine cool unperturbed features, silky blond hair expertly cut to swing loose at the level of her chin, large gray eyes, lovely mouth. She was beautiful and knew it, and Brigit could not help glancing at her, like certain others — Lewis, for instance — and even Alexis Kessler, who might have sensed a rival. Ah, to be that age again, with a kind tender intelligent promising young husband! — to be that age again and to look like *that*. Brigit could not help herself, she did envy the young woman. In fact she envied all four young people.

A world of married lovers.

Might she have another drink . . . ?

No one watching. Bar set up at the far end of the living room, French doors opened onto the flagstone terrace, a pleasantly cool September night. There was Oliver Byrne laughing uneasily at an anecdote spun out by Lewis Seidel (an anecdote not about St. Dennis but about another year's distinguished professor, the sculptor Myron Tyne, who had presented some grave problems to the administration, and who even — so gossip had it — was roughed up by the Woodslee city police); there was another colleague of Brigit's, Gladys Fetler, deep in conversation with someone's wife. Miss Fetler was one of the senior members of the department, a popular teacher, a Shakespeare scholar, of whom it was said — invariably — that she made Shakespeare "come alive"; she was sixty-three years old and gracious and ladylike and kindly and youthful, and from the start she'd been extremely friendly to Brigit — who had drawn back from her, not wanting intimacy, not wanting maternal compassion. When they meet, Gladys is always hearty and Brigit is always shy, and nervously guilty. She *should* allow Miss Fetler to befriend her. . . . But somehow she always eases adroitly away, and feels ashamed of herself afterward. . . . What a marvelous person Gladys Fetler is, everyone says. Students love her, she's still publishing (her most recent publication is a note on the staging of Webster's *White*

Devil, in *PMLA*), she has these wild wacky hobbies — moun-
tain-climbing, bird-watching treks into the Everglades and into
the Arctic Circle, canoeing in the White Mountains. And she's
reticent about her religion, which is also something odd: Sev-
enth-Day Adventist or Christian Science: she's such an obviously
good person.

I can't bear good people, Brigit said. Afterward she wondered
if her remark made its way back to Miss Fetler.

Brigit found herself in a conversation with Oliver Byrne but it
was disappointing — about the university senate, quarrels over
budgets, parking-lot assignments, library privileges. Then he
asked if she were going home to Norfolk for Christmas. (So soon?
Questions about Christmas so soon?) The youngish Dean of Humanities possessed a golden smile, a toothed charming glow;
his suits were impeccably tailored; if he turned discreetly aside to
wipe his nose, it was a white linen handkerchief with which he
wiped it — no lurid pink or yellow Kleenex for Oliver Byrne. He
has the air, a jealous detractor once said, of yet another Kennedy
sibling. Brigit told Oliver curtly that she certainly was not. Five
days last December were quite enough, as she might have mentioned to him — for she and Oliver were friends, of a sort — it
flattered her that he appeared to be mildly and half-mindedly
attracted to her, and she tried to make herself feel something,
feel anything, in the presence of a handsome man, if only to
assure herself — contrary to her husband's accusations — that
she was a normal woman. But though Oliver initiated "personal"
conversations with his faculty, behind his encouraging smile and
the intelligent blandness of his blue gaze he often mixed people
up; and Brigit saw that he simply could not remember the evening
he and Marilyn had consoled her. But then, perhaps, they consoled so many Woodslee misfits.

Someone else joined them, ice cubes clinking in his glass, and
the subject was the discouraging fall enrollment: perhaps if publicity had gone out earlier on the new fine arts program, and the

work semester in South America, and the poet-in-residence St. Dennis — ?

Brigit pretended to listen. She could pretend as well as anyone, she was quite skillful at parties, and knew that all one had to do was stand near people who were talking animatedly; one could then daydream or brood as one wished. . . . How annoying, that Oliver had asked her about Norfolk. Brigit's mother, Brigit's father, Brigit's younger sister Janet (who has been married now for fifteen years, a mother twice over, and altogether content — *Look at Janet*, Brigit's mother whines, *she made a success of her marriage without even trying*), too many Stotts who had nothing to do but drop by the house and inquire after Stanley. Stanley who had always "seemed so courteous." "Seemed so gentlemanly." Brigit's was the first divorce in the family since someone's great-uncle back in 1923 sued his runaway wife for desertion — she had fled to Texas, family legend had it, in the company of a dusky-skinned, suspiciously thick-lipped itinerant photographer; in El Paso, the tale went, she had died of food poisoning before the divorce had even been settled. So the Norfolk Stotts eyed Brigit, seeing not the thirty-eight-year-old university professor and novelist, seeing, in fact, not a thirty-eight-year-old woman at all, but just Brigit, Hannalee's older daughter, the "strange" one, the "bookish" one (Janet was the "popular" and "pretty" one, of course) who had insisted upon going North to school and who had rashly married a New Yorker after only a few months' acquaintance and who had written two or three peculiar books — what kind of books would you call them? — fiction? — or was it poetry? — and who had separated from her husband and was divorcing him, for reasons not made clear — but then Brigit was always headstrong and mouthy and wouldn't have the first idea of how to make a man happy.

A world, Brigit notes bitterly, of marriages. Yes, everyone has declared himself — or herself — liberated: and so they were "liberated" for a few years. In the mid-seventies. It felt good for a

while, it felt exquisite, why hadn't anyone known about this before? But then, after some years, it no longer felt quite so good;
couples were discreetly forming once again, newer couples, new
combinations, surprises. One by one people were hooking up
with mates again. Taking refuge in each other. The most astonishing combinations, in fact. . . . Brigit, however, does not want
to marry again. She loathes the very idea of it. And her divorce is
not *quite* final yet — there is still the vestige of a union — as if
part of her soul were in bondage to a stranger. As if someone, his
name unknown, his face unknown, someone in this very room
perhaps, were staring at her secretly, staring right into her head
and discerning her thoughts. (As Stanley once boasted of doing.
I can read the thoughts rising like bubbles in your brain, he said,
plagiarizing Pope; which had exasperated Brigit all the more.)
She does not want to marry again, not in any conventional
way. . . . Yes, but: but perhaps in another way?

So her mind turned and turned upon Albert St. Dennis, stimulated by the several photographs of him she owned, on book
jackets: not a handsome man but attractive, very attractive indeed. Deep-set eyes, a thin-lipped calm smile, not a smile so
much as an indentation, a gesture. Of course the photographs
were dated now, the most recent one had been taken in 1952, but
perhaps. . . . And then Brigit has never been the sort of woman
to admire physical appearances. . . .

She does not want to marry again, she has said so, frequently
and passionately; and yet some sort of alliance with a man like
Albert St. Dennis. . . .

He would be one of her holy loves. She has had holy loves, and
unholy loves. Very few of the former; too many of the latter. And
then, quite inexplicably, certain of the former — notably her
husband — evolved into the latter. But Albert St. Dennis is in a
sense immortal and she can see herself as his bride. Made young
again, or young-seeming. Albert St. Dennis and the American

novelist Brigit Stott. Why should it *not* happen, when preposterous things happen so routinely these days . . . ?

(It is because of such adolescent fantasies that Brigit has come to dislike herself sharply these past few months. She knows better, certainly; she *knows* a great deal; and yet her imagination swerves to such idle hopes, such pathetic aspirations. Of course she isn't drifting into madness. Madness has always struck her as slovenly and exhibitionistic, and a great deal of trouble for other people. If one had concern for others one would *not* go mad; it seems to Brigit as simple as that: a moral choice. Instead she fears that she is becoming weak and callow and sentimental. Stanley had knocked certain daydreams out of her, and she knows herself well rid of them. Yet now new dreams threaten. It would be quite in order for Brigit Stott to fantasize about her career — completing a lengthy essay on Henry James she had begun eighteen months ago, completing her novel and delivering it to her publishers by next May (she promised this novel to them in May of four — or is it five — years back); she might even fantasize shamelessly about its being well-received in the press and read by numerous sympathetic people, a few of whom would take the time to write her — the only really pleasing consequence of her first two novels, published long ago. (By now, Brigit supposes, the people who had liked those novels are dead, or inoperative.) She does not dare to fantasize about the novel's being widely acclaimed, since the acclaim attending the first (an austere girlhood novel, obliquely autobiographical), and to a lesser extent the second (an analytical first-person narrative set inside a doomed marriage), backfired on her in certain dismal ways, some of which she has yet to comprehend. She might, however, fantasize that the completion of the novel — she has come to think of it as wretched — that wretched novel — might bring to an end this unhappy phase of her own life. All these fantasies, while silly, would be at least respectable.

Instead, her imagination turned about the figure of Albert St. Dennis. And as she drank, awaiting the famous man, no longer listening to the edgy conversations surrounding her, no longer bothering to seem interested, her imagination took on feverish energies: here, in this very room, before a small crowd of university people, she, Brigit Stott, was to be introduced at last to Albert St. Dennis. The way they grasped each other's hand, the way they smiled — startled, pleased — as if recognizing each other — though of course they had never met before — would be keenly noted by all. The Byrnes and the Hochbergs and the Seidels and the Haases and the Tomlinsons and the Housleys and Gladys Fetler and Gowan Vaughan-Jones and the Ryersons and the Swansons and the Jaegers and whoever else was present — ah, yes, Alexis Kessler — would all be witnesses. St. Dennis would be very like his photographs: a beautiful old man, white-haired, with fine, noble cheekbones, a warm and gracious manner, surprisingly quick to laugh, however, and witty, and energetic, and obviously in superb physical condition for a man of his age — rather like Picasso, people would say afterward; or Pablo Casals; youthful but certainly dignified, with a steady, sometimes stern gaze — he had no patience with fools, not this old gentleman. Beautifully dressed, again as his photographs suggested: watch chain, vest, full resplendent necktie, interesting ring — was it an antique, had it any sentimental or superstitious meaning? (Brigit would find out.) A remarkable man. A genius. A kind of saint, in fact. His innumerable honors and awards meant nothing to him, it seemed; he dismissed them with an embarrassed wave of his hand; he was (so he would confide in Brigit) at work on the only significant poem of his life — a sequence even greater than *The Explorers* — a work that would rank higher than *The Wasteland* in the estimation of future lovers of poetry. (But would so modest and self-aware a man as St. Dennis actually say such things to Brigit . . . ? Perhaps not.) A kind of saint, in any case. Generous with his time, his money, his attention. But lonely, since his wife's death. (When had the wife died? Brigit seemed to think it was only a year or so ago: she had come across a tiny obituary somewhere, *Harriet Arnold St. Dennis, 65, after long illness, London, England. Married to the poet Albert St. Dennis. A poet herself, having published several books in the thirties. . . .*) Yes, lonely since his wife's death. Very lonely.

Introduced to Brigit Stott, he would be struck by her face, by something in her face. Her fine dark eyes, perhaps. Her enigmatic expression. He would be bringing with him warm greetings from the president of the English publishing house that brought out both their books in England, and possibly from Brigit's editor as well. (Though she was not certain that the young man who had worked with her novels, years ago, was still with that house. Everyone moved around so much in English publishing circles; and she had heard a rumor, a while back, about his having been fired.) . . . St. Dennis would have been anticipating their meeting, perhaps, as she had anticipated it. Perhaps a friend had given him one of Brigit's novels to read, perhaps it had been his wife, even, who had discovered this quiet, slender, impeccable talent, and who had pressed upon him *Worlds Elsewhere* or *Melodies*, insisting he must read it: it was so exquisitely beautiful, so classically restrained and yet so moving. Very likely it was *Melodies* he had read, since that had sold a little better than *Worlds Elsewhere*, which had been misconstrued as a sort of low mimetic science-fiction work, though it was, in fact, about genteel life in Virginia. Yes, it would be *Melodies*. He would have been struck by the dust-jacket photograph, perhaps, Brigit in her late twenties, wan but quite lovely, undeniably lovely. . . . And of course the Byrnes would have told St. Dennis about her. One of Woodslee's outstanding talents.

"I'm very honored to meet you, Miss Stott," he would say softly. "Very honored. . . ."

Everyone would be watching, everyone would be listening.

A historic meeting, in a sense.

Albert St. Dennis and Brigit Stott.

Seated beside her at dinner he would pay attention to no one else. Utterly fascinated, charmed, as only a distinguished man might be, willing to make his interest in a woman quite public, since he is so confident of himself. Unashamed of emotion. Lesser men would deny their interest in a woman if it swept upon them so violently, since they would be alarmed by it; but St. Dennis, the author of *Lovesounds* and *Hecate* and *The Brides of Rain* and *The Explorers*, was equal to his own passions. Like the heroes of his long poem, he was an explorer of his own fate, his own destiny, and did not draw back from a love affair with a woman so very much younger than he. . . .

He falls in love. Tonight.

In the days that follow he pursues her, with the self-conscious, mildly ironic gallantry of old age. *Why should not old men be mad?* He will quote Yeats. He will quote Yeats desperately, laughingly: *Because I am mad about women/ I am mad about the hills. . . . A young man in the dark am I,/ But a wild old man in the light. . . . I forget it all awhile/ Upon a woman's breast. . . .* But no: why would he quote Yeats to her? He would compose his own poems. A sequence of poems, perhaps. For her. For Brigit. For my love, Brigit. For my darling Brigit. For my wife.

But now events accelerate: he pursues her, writes the poems, marries her, they return to England. They are a devoted couple. Everyone is amazed. Brigit Stott puts aside her own work and dedicates herself to Albert St. Dennis. She wishes to make his old age as comfortable as possible. She helps him with his manuscripts, types for him, does proofreading for him, reads galleys, meets with agents and editors and interviewers and professors, protecting him, her own work quite forgotten. An exceptional marriage. Noted by all. The envy of everyone. She entertains in their charming Chelsea maisonette; she is a tireless hostess, bringing a certain American vivaciousness, a certain Southern flirtatiousness and combativeness, to these famed social evenings. All of literary London attends. New Yorkers fly over, simply to visit. St. Dennis's new poem is finished, parts of it have been appearing in the *TLS* and elsewhere, and it is immediately acclaimed as his major achievement, and one of the great achievements of the twentieth century. He is praised everywhere. Translated into many languages. He gives readings, lectures, addresses. Accepts more prizes. Accepts a knightship (if that is the word — Brigit groggily isn't sure). Of course his young wife accompanies him everywhere. It is rumored that she helped him compose his brief but memorable Nobel Prize address. How astonishing that she should abandon her promising career for him, that she should so efface herself in the service of his art. . . . And there is no question but that the two are genuinely in love. "Behind Albert St. Dennis stands Brigit Stott," people will say. "She saved his life, you know. A remarkable woman. . . ."

"Sometimes it's brilliant," Brigit hears her drunken voice declare many hours later, "sometimes it's merely shit. . . ."

Too late she sees the old man's displeasure; but she cannot stop; despite the subtle change in the atmosphere about her (others are displeased, not just St. Dennis) she must follow through with her point.

Lewis hardly minds. In fact it delights him to be publicly attacked. Now he has an excuse to launch into a fifteen-minute lecture, a noisy swaggering harangue, sweeping all "consciously wrought," "aristocratic" art into the abyss, naming names with the zest of a triumphant guerrilla leader: Proust and Valéry and Nabokov and Mann, and of course Virginia Woolf, Henry James, Joseph Conrad, Yeats and Eliot and Pound and Auden and Lowell and Stevens and Faulkner and Hemingway and — Modernism is dead, faith in literature itself is dead, absolutely dead, even *Finnegans Wake* came too late, for hadn't Joyce realized — as Lewis had himself realized, irrevocably — that literature ended with the publication of *Ulysses*, with the publication of — nay, the very conception of — such episodes as "Wandering Rocks" and "Cyclops" — ? No, no, it does no good to argue, no good at all! Literature is dead. Exhausted. We have now a kind of meta-literature, shoulder shrugs and vaudeville routines and grimaces, schoolboy stuff, but honest just the same, willing to acknowledge its fatuity, its futility. He, Lewis Seidel, had been a Modernist without knowing it, an elitist, grimly faithful to the Word, to the intellect, refusing to acknowledge the fact — which the young had acknowledged so blatantly in the sixties — that the Word has been replaced by the Sound or the Image, the soundless Image or the imageless Sound, sheer sensation, and the intellect has been replaced by the instincts, and in the future there would be no "art" at all in the sense in which we know it, only random improvised experiences, bits and particles of sensation, brute sensation —

Lewis speaks passionately. St. Dennis, gray-faced, one eyelid drooping lower than the other, appears to be listening; he sits with his liver-spotted hands meekly in his lap. Most of the others, who have heard Lewis's ideas before, are waiting patiently for him to finish. He usually finishes by quoting Wittgenstein, though sometimes he quotes Heidegger, in German. Faye Seidel, plumper than Brigit remembers, and looking as distressed and apologetic as usual, is going to try to calm down her husband; Brigit can see the poor woman's hand twitching — she wants to touch his arm, wants to reach over and touch his arm, lightly, but does not dare — it was said that he had once struck her for trying to quiet him, in a similar situation, at a party in Myron Tyne's studio. Marilyn Byrne, hovering hostess-like behind St. Dennis's chair, is waiting for the proper — the exact — moment: when Lewis pauses to catch his breath she will lean down to whisper in St. Dennis's ear, to ask him — not whether he'd like more wine, surely? — not more food, he has simply messed about on his plate Marilyn's superb dinner — perhaps if he'd like to stretch his legs, walk out onto the terrace with her — ? And there is the prospect of some music, to change the situation entirely. (Brigit was told earlier that Alexis might be persuaded to play one of his compositions for them. Though Brigit is not looking forward to hearing a Kessler extravaganza, she hopes for Marilyn's sake that he will play and save the evening.)

Poor Albert St. Dennis! Trapped there behind the wobbly tea stand, a quite ordinary-appearing old man, shabbily English, his hair poorly cut and his oversized spectacles slipping down his nose. He has not been following Lewis's argument, just as the others have stopped following it, but for reasons of his own: he appears to be nonplused, annihilated. Brigit hopes he hasn't *believed* Lewis's remarks. . . . He is a terrible disappointment to her, of course, hardly the lover-savior she had anticipated, just an old man, a sick-looking old man. Genius, no doubt — or had been once. And possibly nicer, kinder, than he has appeared tonight. (So blustery and bullying and oldmannish earlier, shouting people down, defending Yeats needlessly, chanting *base-born* at his hosts and new colleagues as if he were chanting a curse against all Americans.) He is not the lover Brigit's feverish imagination contrived, but he is likable, she likes him, she hopes they will be friends. And now he really must be rescued from Lewis. . . .

But Marilyn misses her opportunity, her own husband interjects a comment, as if he were taking Lewis seriously, and so the discussion continues. Gowan Vaughan-Jones is drawn in and is easily rebutted by a prankish Seidel; Alexis Kessler mutters something that sounds vaguely concurring; the beautiful young woman, Sandra, whose last name Brigit has forgotten, stares at Lewis open-eyed, her slender fingers actually closed upon — ah, how Brigit is pierced by envy! — her husband's wrist, as if she felt him threatened, yet could not resist his opponent's massive satyrish charm.

Brigit finds herself studying Alexis Kessler. She must ask Oliver why on earth he was invited; hadn't there been rumors last year that the dean was maneuvering to ease him out on account of some small scandal or other: students and drugs and missed classes and outrageous impertinence (Kessler was the one who turned in to the University Committee on Promotion, Tenure, and Status a blank sheet of paper on which he had scrawled an obscene imperative in red ink, instead of a dutiful listing of his activities and publications during the preceding academic year). There are rumors about everyone at Woodslee, of course; Brigit even suspects there may be a few about her, but since she leads so conventional a life the rumors must be dull indeed; but the rumors about Alexis are particularly savage. And he does nothing to refute them. Look at those epicene features, that outrageous bleached hair, not even *well*-bleached. Look at the tight trousers, the exposed chest hair, the innumerable gold-glinting rings. His idle contemptuous expression. . . . Brigit, sipping her drink, stares at him. If he notices she does not care: she too can be rude. He *is* a very handsome man. A boy-man. In his late twenties. A *Wunderkind*, a prodigy. One of those very young debuts (as a pianist), and afterward it must have gone to his head, all the attention, the admiration and applause and fuss. . . . His first compositions were performed in public, and even recorded, before he was in his twenties. Quite by accident Brigit had seen a ballet of his in a Village theater once — talked into going by friends of hers and Stanley's, though both she and Stanley disliked avant-garde art — and she had been impressed, not altogether negatively, by the outrageous demands Kessler's music had made upon the dancers. (The ballet had been a grotesque satire of some sort about contemporary American life: Brigit remembers immense ugly papier-mâché masks, and plaster heads and shoulders, and people tottering on built-up shoes like drunken giants, a great deal of percussive sounds, whistles and drums and horns and hissing noises and sudden startling blackouts. The ballet had been fairly controversial. At least the *New York Times* Arts and Leisure section had treated it as controver-

sial. Brigit could not recall whether the production was successful
or whether it failed miserably and closed after a few weeks.)

So he is prodigious, and talked-about. Brigit has heard people
refer to him as a genius. That he is talented she has no doubt,
that he is a genius she refuses to acknowledge; no one younger
than she could possibly be a genius. . . . And he is in retreat up
here at Woodslee, which suggests that things haven't gone well
with his career. Like Brigit herself he is, perhaps, in hiding. (But
Brigit, unlike Alexis, leads a quiet life, a near-monastic life.)

The rest of the party dims; the others become two-dimen-
sional. Even Lewis's voice fades. Alexis Kessler with his shaggy
blond mane, his lean body, his slender arms and wrists . . . his
somewhat sullen expression . . . the affectation of his watch,
which glows a sinister purple-black and seems to have no numerals or hands. . . . Tight-fitting suede trousers, stylish custom-
made shoes, bared chest, rings (one of them is a topaz, Brigit
notes suddenly: rather like a ring of her own, a precious, sentimental piece of jewelry bound up with her girlhood and a friendship that had meant a great deal to her) on several fingers, fingernails fastidiously manicured. He is dandyish, sinister, silly,
frightening. Not male and not female. A purely sensual being:
frightening. His body seems to exclude personality. His body *is*
his personality. She is attracted to him in a way. From time to
time he glances at her, as if sensing her interest. In a moment
Marilyn will lean down to St. Dennis and the scene will be altered, they will be freed of Lewis's overheated intensity, everything will be changed. Brigit stares quite frankly at Alexis now.
She is not really attracted to him — she feels, instead, a fascination for him, a curious impersonal revulsion. He is so glamorous
and yet so sleazy. He is so handsome a young man, and yet so
unmanly. Affecting a kind of childlike innocence, and yet the
rumors that fly about his head — ! Someone in New York, a
dancer with the Martha Graham Company, had evidently com-

mitted suicide over Alexis a few years back; or was it a prominent director in the theater . . . ? A man, of course. And Alexis had fled, had had a breakdown of some kind, had disappeared and then reappeared, not very changed, a little quieter, perhaps, a little less brazen. He had come to Woodslee a year before Brigit. Again and again they have met each other, at innumerable parties they have been thrown together, have even been seated beside each other at dinner. Two artists, after all. A failed novelist and a musician-composer who is — perhaps — not quite a failure, not yet, but not a success either. Staring at him, Brigit tries to recall why she dislikes him in a specific, personal way; had he insulted her once . . . ? She dislikes him as a being, as a creature, as an appearance: his deliberately sensual manner, his presentation of himself as an arrogant, self-important artist, a pretty face, accustomed to arousing emotion in others without being required to express any himself. . . . She sees in him an earlier form of herself, the petite and almost pretty Brigit Stott of Norfolk, a high-school girl, rabidly self-conscious, vain, desperate to be admired. She sees in him something that defies her, as not even Lewis Seidel defies her, or her own husband with his wild charges of infidelity and his promises to make her "regret" everything defies her — and she feels inexplicably moved, stung, annoyed. He glances at her unseeingly. He is being *seen*; he has no need to see anyone else. There is no one at the Byrnes' tonight worth Alexis Kessler's attention except, in a way, Albert St. Dennis, at whom he has been gazing for a very long time.

Brigit recalls having studied Alexis in the past, at one or two other parties. Always she was repulsed, disturbed. She has no interest in younger men, for one thing, and has always been mildly baffled at the fact that any woman could be attracted to any man younger than she — wouldn't it be a kind of incest, like brother and sister? And then, he is not really a man; not really. There have been occasional rumors about his involvement with women, even with girl students at the university; but Brigit is inclined to discount them. She doubts that a normal woman would be attracted to Alexis Kessler.

As for his music. . . .

She really should not judge because she knows herself unmusical. She can barely grasp the musical logic of Bartok, and is quite at a loss to comprehend such radical and odd-sounding developments as twelve-tone compositions, and electronic symphonies, and the discomforting silences of John Cage and his protegés. She should not judge and yet she cannot resist: Kessler's music *sounds* unmusical to her ears. Like objects falling off a shelf, she once said wittily, glasses and plates and pots and pans. . . . It crossed her mind that the remark must have been repeated to Kessler, but she did not regret having made it.

Most of the time, when they meet, Alexis greets her vaguely and then ignores her, but tonight Brigit is struck by the hostility in his face. There is a sharp unattractive line between his eyes — he had better be careful, she thinks, he will lose his looks. Their uneasiness with each other began some time ago. As a new member of the English department Brigit was introduced to the rest of the faculty at the president's reception, always held near the start of the academic year, and by accident she drifted into a group that included Alexis Kessler. She had not known who he was — she hadn't remembered the name — but the occasion was exhilarating, she had had several glasses of excellent champagne and was feeling quite hopeful about her new life; and so she had found herself talking animatedly with Kessler. She had *felt* like an attractive woman that night. (She and Stanley were living apart at the time, but he had not yet become hateful.) And of course Alexis was capable of being extraordinarily charming when he wished.

They went to a buffet table together. He handed her a plate. She happened to notice his hands — how filthy they were — actual webs of dirt between his fingers. The nails were clean enough, even polished, and his outfit was fashionable and probably quite expensive. But his hands were filthy. Brigit, unthinking, had exclaimed, "Oh, look at your hands — do you know your hands are dirty?" and Alexis, unhesitating, had smiled coldly at her and said, "If you think my hands are dirty, lady, you should see the rest of me." He had spoken in an utterly calm, jeering voice.

The bastard.

Remembering, now, she shivers with dislike of him.

Brigit touches Lewis's arm. "Enough, enough," she says, her voice hoarser than usual, "too much," and she gets to her feet and stretches, rather rudely, not caring what anyone thinks. This party is not going to change her life after all: what does she care any longer what anyone thinks? — even the guest of honor?

Once he was beautiful; now he is merely pretty.

Once a probable genius — now, merely talented.

Still, he is playing this difficult piece for the Byrnes' guests as if his reputation depended upon it, as if his very life — his life as an artist — depended upon it. He is playing and they are listening. Music: the rapid, percussive notes: the sudden deep chords: a kind of triumph that might redeem him.

And Albert St. Dennis is here tonight.

Alexis plays, hunched over the keyboard of the Byrnes' baby grand, beginning to perspire. The room is too warm, and his outfit is too warm. He has been nervous for hours. Not simply the prospect of meeting St. Dennis, after all these months, but the prospect of the party itself had unnerved him: he dreads these Woodslee evenings, these hearty gatherings in one or another couple's home, hour after hour of amiable trivial chatter in which he can't successfully participate. He is well aware of the veiled stares of his colleagues and of their courteous dislike of him. Several of these people frankly hate him — he knows that; he would swear to it. There was a move of some kind to fire him not long ago and only the dean's humane intervention saved him. Alexis isn't sure, but he believes it was the president of the university himself, Garrett, who wanted him fired. . . . Why? He

didn't know. Deosn't know even now. Matt Ryerson, the head of
the music department and a supposed friend of his, has never
explained the ugly situation satisfactorily to Alexis. He suspects
that Garrett listened to lies told him by certain rivals of Alexis's
in the music department (Bannon, an aging fop, professor of
composition, is especially jealous of Alexis), or by people like
Gowan Vaughan-Jones or Warren Hochberg, who have never
quite managed to disguise their loathing of Alexis — pedantic
bastards forever talking of scholarly "standards" at Woodslee,
self-appointed fag-haters — or perhaps it was Roger Haas, the
university's chief attorney, or Brigit Stott, who stared at him so
rudely a few minutes ago — as if that bitch hasn't acquired quite
a legendary reputation herself — or Lewis Seidel, despite his
forced display of admiration for Alexis's work ("I played your
sinfonietta the other evening — dusted the record off and played
it for some students who had dropped in — and it's really quite
good, Alexis, it's still *alive* — a pity it seems to have disappeared
from sight —") and his even more forced display of casual cama-
raderie — or perhaps it was that fantastical cow Mrs. Garrett, all
bifocals and wispy bangs and cruel hard joyless grandmother
smiles, listening greedily to gossip told her by faculty wives. Ryerson called in Alexis one dismal winter afternoon and told him it
might be a good idea for him to cast about for another position;
he had been very embarrassed and seemed genuinely stricken.
He *seemed* concerned for Alexis's position. But he refused to
explain the issue, who had complained about Alexis or brought
charges against him, who wanted him to leave Woodslee and
who wanted him to stay. . . . Alexis's hysterics alarmed Ryerson
but he did not explain, and though the issue blew over, after
several weeks of the sort Alexis hopes not to endure again, during
which he was drunk much of the time and too sick to meet
classes, there is the distinct possibility that his enemies will strike
again. . . .

All this is stirring, exciting. In a strange way invigorating.

Is he playing for his enemies tonight? At this very moment? And for Albert St. Dennis, at last.

The piece is difficult, quite tricky; a virtuoso piece; showy in a subdued way. Not very long. His own composition of some years back, written out in Aspen, not yet recorded but admired by several pianists of his acquaintance: echoes of Cowell, Cowell of the twenties, and echoes of Ives. A tiny heartbeat of a moment lifted — lifted playfully and with gratitude — from *Thoreau*. But the work is Alexis's, all Alexis's, and no one else's. Tone clusters, outrageous percussive hammerings, and then a teardrop of a break, and a moment of silence, and on, on, into the powerful last section. . . . They are listening. They are being forced to listen. Marilyn Byrne claims to have had the piano tuned just that morning, hoping Alexis will play, and Oliver Byrne is standing just a few feet away, absorbed, watching the incredible feats of Alexis's hands. Does he really admire Alexis, is he really as supportive of Alexis as he appears to be . . . ? Arguing in the university senate that more money must be allotted to the fine arts program, that the university match the state's grant for a Woodslee Center for the Performing Arts . . . not afraid to speak of his hope to make Woodslee a true community of artists, scholars, teachers, and humanists. . . . He hired Alexis some years ago, against the wishes of other administrators and, certainly, against the wishes of most members of the music department, and he has supported him since, though he would not tell Alexis the details of the attempted purge last winter. He does not *tell* anyone anything; beneath his social manner he is taciturn, perhaps even secretive. Balding but handsome, always nicely dressed, something military about his bearing but a lover of culture, rumored to play the piano himself and to have been an amateur actor before coming to Woodslee — rumored, even, to write poetry — Byrne is an exceptional administrator and one of the few people at Woodslee whom Alexis admires. But his wife, that perennial Girl Scout — ! Thick ankles, overearnest smiles, totally unconvincing in her "interest" in Alexis. . . . Perhaps Mrs. Byrne is one of Alexis's enemies: it wouldn't surprise him in the slightest.

It was through Byrne that Alexis made contact with Albert St. Dennis last spring, and through Byrne that Alexis received a small, token grant from the University Arts Council to enable him to take a semester off from teaching and to compose a cycle of songs based on St. Dennis's *Lovesounds* — those remarkable, chilling sonnets of the thirties. Alexis had come across the poems some years before and had been struck, at the time, by their resemblance to a certain kind of music — sly, coy, and yet melancholy — the word-sounds eerily musical — haunting — the sort of music he sometimes heard in his own head but could not quite transpose into notes. The words, disguised as bearers of meaning, were, in fact, ingeniously arranged constructs of sound. Alexis had read them aloud. He would write a musical accompaniment — he *must* do something with the sonnets — must translate them into his own art: otherwise they would be lost to him. But years passed, other works intervened, his life went ragged and frail and he came close to dying (or so he realized afterward: at the time he had existed in a kind of trance, detached from his own actions and his own physical pain), and the sonnets were temporarily forgotten. Then, last fall, he came upon them again, by accident; and not a week later he heard that Dean Byrne was trying to get Albert St. Dennis to come to Woodslee for a year — one of those remarkable coincidences, the sort that seem to occur in Alexis's life at regular intervals. He is not crudely superstitious but these things *do* happen. (Just as "Albert" and "Alexis" resemble each other, and even "St. Dennis" and "Kessler" have some of the same sounds.) So Alexis had run over to Byrne's office and spoken excitedly to him about the project — allowing Byrne to know, or to assume, that the song cycle was already begun — wasn't that a marvelous coincidence? — and that he would like very much to write to St. Dennis himself, to urge him to come here, and of course to ask formal permission for use of the poems, which he had not yet done. Byrne had seemed pleased. He too believed it was something of a coincidence.

Hurriedly, Alexis had put together a package of materials for St. Dennis: a cassette of certain pieces of his, and some photostated reviews of his work, and a photograph taken when he was about twenty-seven. (He is now thirty-two, though he looks, of course, a decade younger.) And a lengthy, handwritten letter, in which he spoke quite nakedly of his deep admiration for St. Dennis's work, especially *Lovesounds*. That cycle of hallucination, pain, despair, ecstasy — and recovery! St. Dennis was, Alexis claimed, a genius in his poetry, his art, but a genius, as well, in his life. For how many people knew what he seemed to know . . . ? How many had survived the sort of catastrophe he described, from the inside, in that sonnet sequence . . . ? The letter had been fifteen pages long. Alexis had written it late one night in a kind of delirium, tears in his eyes, his lips moving silently. The poetry was so beautiful, so powerful — it demanded to be translated into music — it *must* be metamorphosed into Alexis's art. The project meant so very, very much to him. It was all he cared to work on in this phase of his life. If St. Dennis would be kind enough to give him permission, he would be grateful the rest of his life. He would never forget St. Dennis's generosity. And the song cycle would be his gift to St. Dennis, one artist's homage to another.

I am entering a period of rebirth, Alexis thought.

I am not finished with my life after all. So he thought.

So he thought then, last spring, and so he thinks now, as he plays his *Vivace* for St. Dennis and the others, hair in his face, perspiration running down his sides. They are listening: they are being carried along by the music, by his music, by him. How can they resist? He knows the piece is exquisite, he knows he is playing as well as ever. No matter what the condition of his nerves, Alexis is capable — usually — of playing the piano well. He

began, after all, as a small child. One and two hours a day, and
then three, four, five. . . . At the height of his obsession with this
particular instrument he was practicing (though he did not call it
"practicing" to himself) between eight and ten hours a day. The
power in his fingers — ! The joy of the music itself, of music
regardless of its emotional tone — ! It is the *fact* of art that matters, not the art itself, not, surely, the message or the theme or
the effect it has upon others. Mystery. Magic. The one incon-
testable good. Never-failing beauty of art, of music, no matter
who creates it or performs it, no matter what they think of him
— staring at his back as if they wish to see into his skull, into his
very soul — cagey with him, disapproving of his life (though they
know nothing of his life — his "private" life) and even of his
physical appearance. Never-failing beauty: the cascade of notes,
the stubborn crystal-bright clusters of sound, pricking, painful,
gliding, hammering, liquid, fluttering, serene, cataclysmic. . . .
Is St. Dennis listening? He remained seated in his chair; he didn't
get to his feet as a few of the others did, to gather nearer the
piano. Of course he is an old man. Not very well, it seems. And
rather drunk.

Alexis hears his music as if it were somewhat detached from
him, a miracle that springs from his fingertips, and yet is clear of
him, uncontaminated by him. He is — he knows — not the person he had wished to be. There is — he knows at such times,
when he is deep in his music — something wrong: something
wrong. But what . . . ? Why . . . ? How . . . ? He knows, he
knows. He cannot say. Wordless sounds assail him. The music
springs from him, streams through him, uses him to find its way
into the world, and it does not matter that he is Alexis Kessler
— flawed, failed, aging, doomed, spiteful, childish, in debt —
most of all in debt — it does not matter who he is: only the music
matters. That is his triumph.

But the music moves so quickly!

The evening has moved so quickly!

Tonight, introduced to St. Dennis, he had squeezed the old man's hand and smiled his dazzling hopeful smile and received, in return, a rather puzzled half-smile. . . . "We know each other, we've been corresponding," Alexis said, still smiling. St. Dennis glanced at Marilyn Byrne, as if appealing for help; Marilyn, jumpier than usual, stammered something about "composer-in-residence" but failed to say that her husband had put Alexis in contact with St. Dennis and that Alexis was the young man working on a song cycle based on St. Dennis's sonnets. Alexis was forced to explain, himself, and it seemed to him that St. Dennis recalled the project . . . it *seemed* the old man had caught on. . . . He recognized Alexis, that was certain. Recognized his face. *That* was certain.

He had been surprisingly rude to a few of the other guests — barking and jeering and more or less shouting them down — but quite charming to Alexis, though he said little. His glances were friendly, even rather paternal. He *did* recognize Alexis. . . . Of course he arrived at the Byrnes' fairly drunk; that had been something of a surprise. Alexis had heard the old man was a vegetarian and a non-drinker. Or was that another distinguished English poet? No matter, no matter. Albert St. Dennis has come to Woodslee, to Alexis Kessler, he is here tonight, a man of genius, in this very room, tonight, not far away, listening, absorbed in Alexis's music. . . .

A stir? Something wrong? Alexis does not hear; he will not hear. The piece is nearly ended. He is hunched over the keyboard, his strong, perfect fingers in control. Nothing has gone wrong. He has never played more beautifully. Making love does not demand of Alexis such exquisite control, such deep affection, such respect. . . . Making love is something technical, a mere skill, at best a kind of talent; making music is something impossible to fathom. The one is a diversion, the other is life itself.

He is very warm, flushed, transported out of himself: yet detached. The music is impersonal in its beauty. It insists upon its own motion, it shapes itself, flowing through him, accelerating his heartbeat —

What is wrong? Is something wrong?

The piece is nearly ended —

But there is something wrong, a commotion, a muttering in the room. Alexis stops playing. His fingers stop. He turns on the piano bench, shaking his hair out of his eyes, astonished, his face burning — How *dare* anyone disturb his playing? —

A sudden gagging sound. It is St. Dennis. On his feet now, at the other end of the living room, the old man seems to be in distress. Brigit Stott is beside him, her arm linked through his. "Mr. St. Dennis!" she cries in a throaty, incredulous voice, "why — what's wrong? What's wrong?" He staggers, his knees buckle, the poor woman is practically holding him up. While everyone stares he stoops over suddenly and begins to vomit. Marilyn Byrne cries something unintelligible, a shout of sheer angry despair — and in the next instant presses her hand over her mouth. But no one has heard: all are staring at Albert St. Dennis. Something light-colored and liquid flows from him, splattering his vest and trousers, splashing onto the Byrnes' handsome Oriental carpet. He gags and chokes and retches, helpless, bent nearly double.

My God, my God, Alexis thinks, his hands still poised over the keyboard, *this cannot be*.

But it is, it happens, it will not be undone.

The Byrnes' party is ending abruptly.

By Monday — no, even by Sunday — people will have spread the word, laughing richly at Alexis Kessler's humiliation. He can imagine their sneers, their satisfied grins. Albert St. Dennis was sick to his stomach listening to a piano sonata of Kessler's! Yes!

Yes, really! *Yes.* In full view of the Byrnes' guests. It will be reported in the Phoenix Heights area by the Haases and perhaps by Marilyn Byrne herself, and up on the Old Armory Road by the Hochbergs, and along the Valley Mills Drive by the Housleys, and around campus by Gowan Vaughan-Jones and Brigit Stott and Gladys Fetler, and in the residential area just east of the university, where everyone lives, by the Seidels and the Tomlinsons and the Ryersons and the others, the young couples whose names Alexis has forgotten — and by Wednesday the entire university community will know about it. Alexis writhes in despair, thinking of it. Another Kessler tale! Another Kessler defeat! His enemies will gloat, his rivals will repeat the story and embellish it, even his friendly acquaintances will spread it across town and back. When police raided an apartment two floors down from Alexis's last autumn and arrested several people on marijuana charges — which were later dropped — the story leaped across Woodslee that Alexis Kessler had been arrested, that he was in jail along with a number of other drug users, that he would certainly be fired from Woodslee. In some versions of the story Alexis was dragged out by police naked except for his jewelry; in other versions, he was completely unconscious and had to be carried out. Some said that his bail was set so high — $100,000 — that he had had to telephone numerous relatives and old friends to raise bond. Some said the judge refused to let him go at all. A corruptor of youth! A degenerate! . . . While the stories wound their way through the university community, becoming ever more outlandish and artistic, colliding with one another, sometimes joining one another, Alexis was forced to meet with his classes as usual, and with his colleagues, who eyed him with great interest but never mentioned the scandal. And so it went. . . . And the stories were never exactly refuted, because they were not public and not available to Alexis. It simply happened that they reached a peak and then declined and faded and disappeared, to be resurrected when another "Kessler" scandal came along.

What good does it do, Alexis thinks dully, St. Dennis apologizing now so passionately . . . ? The old man is so sorry, so very sorry. Clutching at Alexis's arm. Practically weeping. (He, too, is worried about his reputation, Alexis suddenly realizes. St. Dennis, of all people!) What good does it do, this expression of regret? Too late. The party is ending, the party is over, most of the guests have escaped. Only midnight and the party is over.

"I . . . I . . . I simply can't express, Mr. Alexander, how ashamed I am," St. Dennis says, leaning toward Alexis, his head thrust forward in a way that is both cringing and aggressive. "How very, very sorry. . . . Simply can't think what happened, what seemed to . . . suddenly . . . come over me."

"That's all right," Alexis mutters.

"I was enjoying the music so much," St. Dennis says eagerly, "I was sitting with my eyes closed and listening, utterly transported . . . utterly charmed . . . Wasn't I, Mrs. Stott? Weren't we both? Such a very, very fine . . . such a very fine little concert. . . . Simply can't think what happened to me," he says, shaking his head slowly. "I do hope you will accept my apology."

"Fine," Alexis says.

". . . And Mrs. Byrne, your rug! What a shame!"

"No, no," Marilyn says at once, "it's nothing, really; really nothing. It's already cleaned up — you see? Nothing to it! The stain will disappear by tomorrow."

"I hope you'll send me the bill if —"

"Mr. St. Dennis, please, there's no need to apologize, there's no need at all," Marilyn says warmly. "We're more concerned about *you*. We only want you to be happy here. Don't we, Oliver? I think that — all the excitement —"

"Yes, the excitement — the turmoil — The shock of landing on this planet," St. Dennis says vaguely, trying to smile, "I mean this continent — among strangers — I mean, among — among — The strangeness of it, don't you see, the heady excitement of — a new life — new vistas and adventures — Simply too much for my shaky old system."

"No, Mr. St. Dennis, no, really, it's just the late hour —"

"I behaved inexcusably," he says, touching Alexis's shoulder, turning to Brigit Stott and smiling sadly. "I wonder if these two young people will ever forgive me. . . ."

He reaches out for Brigit Stott's hand; he grasps it firmly in his own. Alexis feels, for an instant, a prick of jealousy.

The Stott woman looks surprisingly attractive, as if given a kind of perverse energy by St. Dennis's distress. Woodslee is sharply divided on the subject of Brigit Stott's charm: a number of people find her strangely appealing, even rather beautiful in a soiled, depraved way, and others — the majority — find her very odd indeed. The rumors of her promiscuity! Her desperation! Her drinking! The mess of her apartment, where she lives with five or six cats — the ugly tales that circulate freely about her behavior during her marriage — her cruelty to students and to friends — her habit of forgetting people entirely, simply erasing them from her consideration. A vicious woman, Alexis has heard. Supremely self-contained, egotistical. Eccentric. Doesn't she carry a revolver in her purse, or at least a knife — ? Tonight her eyes are ringed with fatigue and her unfashionable dark lipstick is partly eaten off and she seems vulnerable, very human. Not at all formidable. Her graying hair has gone limp; there are several large stains on the skirt of her severe black dress — stains from St. Dennis's vomit, most likely. She is saying something about St. Dennis having been no trouble at all — he shouldn't be distressed — not at all. Everyone assents. But St. Dennis continues to squeeze her hand, staring at her. Alexis is suddenly quite annoyed.

He makes an impatient move, as if to leave; and St. Dennis looks around at once and takes his arm. "And you, my boy, you most of all — I've offended you irreparably, haven't I — Mr. Alexander, is it? Is that your name?"

"It doesn't matter," Alexis says at once. But his voice is raw and young and hurt. There is a childish whine in it that alarms him.

Someone tells St. Dennis Alexis's name and St. Dennis nods slowly, blinking. The name must mean nothing to him. Old fool! Drunk! Once a genius, no doubt, but now a doddering ruin; not even a very intriguing ruin. Alexis would push past these boring people and escape, but St. Dennis is holding his arm. . . . He had missed his chance for a dramatic exit some time ago: when his sonata was so rudely and stupidly interrupted, he should have risen from the piano bench with no sign of the outrage he felt (for signs of emotional weakness are taken up at once by one's detractors), he should simply have walked out of the Byrnes' house and into the night. His apartment building is a considerable distance away but a hard, brisk, self-punishing walk would do him good. Now it is too late.

Everyone is offering to drive Albert St. Dennis home.

Lewis Seidel is the most aggressive; he has his car keys out and is rattling them. Alexis can see that St. Dennis's interest in Brigit Stott and in himself has annoyed Seidel. "It *is* late for Mr. St. Dennis, who isn't used to our way of life yet," Seidel says. "Faye and I will be only too happy to drive you home, Mr. St. Dennis. Shall we go — ?"

"Yes, I think that — If —"

Oliver Byrne interrupts. "I had thought I might drive Mr. St. Dennis home myself. Isn't it out of your way, Lewis?"

"Out of my way? In what sense?" Seidel says, staring. He and Byrne contemplate each other. Alexis recalls a rumor he had heard a while back — that Seidel wants Byrne displaced as dean, that he wants the position for himself, that he and several other powerful members of the faculty are planning a move to "dethrone" Byrne this fall. The two men had seemed friendly enough tonight, in Alexis's opinion, and of course the wives seemed friendly — Faye was always "friendly" and Marilyn really had no choice — but now it appears they are not on good terms at all. Seidel can hardly manage his characteristic insouciance, his wide-eyed frank sincerity, and Oliver Byrne, unusually pale, can hardly control his voice, which trembles slightly when he is upset. ". . . You know very well that Faye and I live on Strathmore, and Mr. St. Dennis's apartment building is right out on Phoenix Boulevard. Isn't it? Right on our way home," Seidel says gaily. "And even if it weren't — would *that* matter? Mr. St. Dennis's comfort comes first."

"Thank you," St. Dennis whispers. "I think that —"

"It's still quite early," Byrne says weakly.

But he has lost, the party is over and he has lost, it's hardly midnight and the evening has come to an abrupt end. Marilyn Byrne looks drained and disappointed; her forehead and nose are shining, her smile is unconvincing, her upright, self-conscious posture seems ludicrous and strained. Poor woman! Alexis feels sorry for her. Oliver Byrne, usually so confident, usually so much in control, looks boyish in defeat — rubbing his hands together — trying to regain his magistral smile. St. Dennis was *his* accomplishment, his *coup*. Everyone has been saying of him that he has done an excellent job as Dean of Humanities — a truly superb job — and for months people have congratulated him on the acquisition of Albert St. Dennis. Now he must surrender him to Lewis Seidel. And the old man's grayish, deathly look isn't very encouraging.

"If you'd like to spend the night with us, Mr. St. Dennis," Byrne says, "we do have a guest room — in fact we have two — and — I mean, if you're feeling unwell — It would be no trouble —"

But this suggestion is absurd, and no one takes him up on it.

"Thank you for a fine, fine evening," St. Dennis says weakly, "but now I really must say good night. *Enough? — too much!* As this lovely young woman has said. You understand, I hope — ?"

It happens that Alexis and Brigit Stott are swept along with St. Dennis, squeezed into the back seat of the Seidels' car; St. Dennis will not surrender them. Alexis protests that he can walk home — he would really prefer to walk home — and Brigit says, in her hoarse, almost inaudible voice, that she could very easily call a cab. But St. Dennis grips each by the arm and holds them fast and has assumed, now, an odd sly grandfatherly air, a rakish, conspiratorial manner. "Thank God for fresh air! Thank God for freedom! American hospitality — it's really quite amazing, isn't it?" he murmurs. The three of them squeeze into the back seat of the Seidels' car though Alexis knows very well that Lewis doesn't want him, and probably doesn't even want Brigit; he wants St. Dennis to himself.

Phoenix Heights, where the Byrnes live, is only a fifteen-minute drive from the university area, where an apartment has been rented for St. Dennis in a handsome old building; during this drive Lewis Seidel tries to ask St. Dennis a few questions, glancing into the rear-view mirror, but the old man ignores him, chatting away companionably with Alexis and Brigit, their hands in his. Somehow he has gotten onto the subject of Auden: an old rival, no longer in the competition, whose lust for the Nobel Prize was legendary. Did they know? Did they *know* the degree of the poor man's craving? It was, St. Dennis says with relish, positively embarrassing.

Alexis says he doesn't know — mumbles that he knows very little about poets.

Brigit says she had heard Auden was quite a kind, generous man; but of course he had had a drinking problem. . . .

St. Dennis ignores her remark and for the rest of the drive talks

of Auden's undeniable but limited gift, the folly of his personal
life, the fact that the poor man had been nowhere near the Nobel
Prize — how deluded he had been! Alas! How deluded so many
of them were, St. Dennis's contemporaries! And so many of them
had fallen by the wayside, it was really quite pitiful, quite . . .
frightening. He names names, mumbling, sniffing. Alexis doesn't
recognize most of the names. He glances over at Brigit Stott,
who is looking at him. An alarmed smile? A conspiratorial smile?
Poor old St. Dennis is muttering and sniffing loudly and he seems
unaware of his surroundings, his eyes half shut, his jowls sagging,
lips loose and damp. Auden and folly and the vanity of human
wishes and the litany of the dead, the poor pathetic helpless dead,
the world filling up with them, being appropriated by them, the
earth and the air and the streams, the dwelling places of the
dead, the Mothers and Fathers, the Hosts, Yeats knew, Auden
knew, St. Dennis knows, he can smell them and taste them,
hadn't he written of the plunge of life in *The Explorers*, which
must, alas, lose its energy and its sacred, proud beauty and come
to rest . . . come to rest as the Explorer-heroes came to rest,
ultimately, in the arms of the Mothers . . . hadn't he written of
it already . . . must he live it out now in the flesh? "My dears,
you've been too kind to me," he says, his voice broken and tearful. "I don't deserve it. You . . . you . . . you are so young and
beautiful . . . your love is so pure . . . so . . . so frightening to an
old man. . . . *The young in one another's arms:* ah yes! Yes! *That!*
It's true. Am I bitter? Are any of us bitter, old men poets, shaking
our bones? I think . . . yes . . . I think we are bitter but we are
also . . . we are also . . . we . . . also. . . . We celebrate, don't
you see, the plunge . . . the love . . . the young lovers. . . . Not
jealous. Not. Envy maybe. Quite natural, isn't it. And so I . . .
I . . . I want you only to be happy," he says, beginning to weep.

And then he does an incredible thing: he brings Alexis's and
Brigit's hands together, squeezes them together on his knees.

And they cannot resist. Staring at each other over the old man's sagging head, they exchange a look of sheer stupefaction. It is a moment they will remember all their lives. ". . . happy. Lovers. The young. The eternally young. In each other's arms. . . . And no bitterness. None. Only celebration. Poetry and celebration and. . . ."

That occurs at 12:20 A.M. By 1:45 A.M. Brigit Stott and Alexis Kessler *have* become lovers. In a sense.

The Seidels drive Albert St. Dennis home, across the river and south into the small city of Woodslee; the drive would be pleasant — there is a glaring half-moon in the sky, the river is dark and placid and lovely, Lewis inhales the fresh, chilly air in noisy gulps and proclaims it a tonic, a life-saver (he has been coughing much of the evening, a dry wracking painful cough) — except for the fact that Lewis can't interrupt the old man's babbling to ask him certain important questions. He glances at St. Dennis in the rear-view mirror, noting grimly the tear streaks on the old man's cheeks. Unbelievable. Drunken sentimental babbling. Perhaps what he says is valuable — Lewis can make out important words now and then, like "Auden," "death," "art," "fate," "Nobel Prize" — but it is an incoherent jumble, a terrible disappointment.

Lewis has been planning for months a highly original kind of critical work: by no means ordinary criticism, and not even speculative, experimental metacriticism of the sort being done by younger men who are scornful of old-fashioned structures and value judgments; but a dialogue, a duet, his own voice and that of a representative artist of the old order, locked together in ferocious combat. The artist is to be, of course, Albert St. Dennis. Lewis has read all his books, even the early, minor works and the embarrassingly bad propaganda prose poems of the thirties; he has always been a voracious reader, a tireless seeker of truth. As a young man at CCNY he had, for a while, spent so many hours in the library that his vision had begun to be affected; the strain had been so great he had thought he might go mad, his eyesight violated by tiny darting black specks that swelled and faded and reappeared whimsically. The most devastating attack had taken place while Lewis was plowing through Marx. He had actually whimpered aloud and rushed from his carrel in the library and out into the street, clutching at his head. . . . But he was, even then, a highly charged and aggressive person with no respect for weakness, not even his own, and so he had forced himself back to his books, eyestrain or not, headache and dizziness and fears of madness notwithstanding, and he had conquered Marx to his own satisfaction, as he had conquered, one by one, book by book, every important writer of the modern era. It had been necessary for him to abandon his early, boyish enthusiasm for books, for "liking" and "enjoying" were outmoded means of approaching literature; but in place of such simple-minded enthusiasm Lewis learned to experience the far more complex satisfactions of the scholar-critic who not only comprehends his material but, in a sense, overcomes it.

And so he has read all of St. Dennis's books; he even owns most of them, having ordered them this summer from various booksellers, in preparation for St. Dennis's residency at Woodslee and for his dialogue with him. A Nietzschean duet, a contest of sorts, the "old" and the "new" struggling together, so that out of their fierce death-combat a timeless truth might emerge. Of course the essay — or perhaps it will be a book, with wide margins and experimental typography — will be totally original, possibly not even about poetry at all, but about ways of perceiving reality. So-called "reality," that is: for Lewis knows very well that reality doesn't exist, not as the simple-minded nineteenth-century thinkers (Marx, for one) believed. A highly provocative, outrageous, stunningly original, baffling, exasperating, but brilliant contribution to literary thought. . . . A *highly provocative, challenging, sometimes outrageous and sometimes beautifully clear work . . . goes beyond even Seidel's earlier books. . . . A highly provocative, original mind, a critic who is really a poet himself. . . . Criticism is, perhaps, the highest art form; in reading the brilliant, provocative works of Lewis Seidel, one is continually forced to consider this odd, rather alarming proposition. . . .* Dialogues *evidently grew out of a historic series of confrontations between Lewis Seidel and the distinguished poet Albert St. Dennis (whom the dust jacket described as "close, loyal, affectionate friends") but it is, in this reviewer's opinion, a work that goes far beyond any ordinary debate as we know it. Seidel's most recent book, the highly controversial* Cul-de-sac *of 1959, a close study of the philosophical assumptions of Henry James's fiction, brilliant as it was, did not prepare us for the stunning originality of* Dialogues. . . . *A new form of criticism, iconoclastic and merciless and certain to be widely imitated by young critics everywhere: in every way a masterful creation.*

But: St. Dennis is merely babbling. And all evening he managed to avoid Lewis, as if he had taken, from the first, an irrational dislike to him. (And his rudeness to poor Faye — quite incomprehensible.) Of course Lewis has a great deal of time. Months. St. Dennis is certain to be impressed, when sober, by the fact that Lewis is the only person at Woodslee (with the possible exception of Gowan Vaughan-Jones, who is working on an immense study of twentieth-century poetics that will include a chapter on St. Dennis and his imitators) to have read all his books, *all* his books; he is certainly the only person at Woodslee to own these books. That, surely, will impress the old man. . . . Lewis has already told Faye they will have St. Dennis over for dinner as soon as possible, so he can show St. Dennis the books and ask him to inscribe them; and they will have the next big party for him, scheduled to follow his first public address in November. (The Hochbergs wanted to have this party but Lewis

argued Warren out of it, claiming that the Hochbergs' house —
some nine or ten miles north of the city — was simply too far for
St. Dennis to go immediately after his lecture on campus; it was
more reasonable, wasn't it, for the Seidels to be hosts, since they
lived only five minutes from the university . . . ?) As time passes
it seems quite likely that Lewis and St. Dennis will become
friends, intimate friends, despite the disparity in their ages.
(Lewis is now fifty-one, but looks no more than forty-five.) The
Seidels' home on Strathmore is hardly three blocks from St. Dennis's apartment, and since the old man hasn't a car, and won't
know his way around, it is altogether probable that Lewis will
drive him to parties this winter; the old man might want to go to
New York, to visit his publishers, or to Boston, and Lewis could
drive him there, and meet St. Dennis's friends, and perhaps introduce St. Dennis to friends and acquaintances of his own; a
former student of Lewis's, a beautiful girl now working at *Time-
Life* and living in the East Village, often invites Lewis to her
apartment when he is in the city, and has marvelous, rather crazy
parties that last for days at a time . . . it might be educational for
old St. Dennis to be exposed to such people. Lewis will be a close
observer, noting the old man's reactions, memorizing his remarks — which are certain to be sharper and more original than
those he has uttered this evening. . . . After the year is over and
St. Dennis returns to London, it is quite likely that Lewis will be
a regular guest at his Chelsea apartment, or flat, and that St.
Dennis will introduce Lewis Seidel to the London literary world.
(None of his books, thus far, have been published in England, a
phenomenon utterly baffling to Lewis and to his New York
publisher and to his many admirers in the United States.) Perhaps St. Dennis's next book of poems will be dedicated to
Lewis Seidel, "the American Socrates" . . . or "the American
Nietzsche". . . . No: simply "my American friend." A slim volume, the poet's last work; possibly a posthumous work. Lewis will
fly to England for the funeral. Lewis ("the only person of my

acquaintance to have not only bought all my books but to have actually read them") might even be mentioned in the old man's will. The *New York Times* might quote . . . might photograph. . . . The *Times Literary Supplement*. . . . *Time* and *Newsweek* and. . . . A photograph of the two men together, taken (perhaps) at Woodslee, during the poet's residence there. Taken at the Seidels' house, perhaps. St. Dennis and Seidel. (Must have the Polaroid on hand for that party; but mustn't be too obvious about it. Faye could introduce, maybe. Mid-party. Spontaneous.) And then, after a decent period of time, Lewis's memoirs of the grand old man will appear. . . .

Excited, Lewis glances in the rear-view mirror and asks St. Dennis if the night air has refreshed him a little, if he feels better? — but the old man doesn't hear. He repeats his question; but the old man doesn't hear. Faye whispers to him not to drive so fast; he's over the white line, hasn't he noticed — ? Lewis ignores her. He sees that Brigit Stott and Alexis Kessler are sitting close beside St. Dennis, their heads inclined toward his; opportunists, bitchy and pragmatic and ruthless, both of them . . . why did Byrne invite them to his party? The Stott woman had to be invited, perhaps, since she is in the English department and is a writer, the department's only novelist, but the Kessler creature makes no sense at all, no sense at all. A homosexual, flagrant and malicious and arrogant, attractive enough, no doubt, in a superficial way, but surely not fit company for Albert St. Dennis. It might be that the Byrnes are simply naive . . . ? Or is Oliver coldly and shrewdly scheming his way to the presidency by means of an odd assortment of people and events and interlocking relationships Lewis cannot hope to figure out . . . ? It is no secret that Byrne wants to be president of Woodslee; Garrett himself knows that, and though in public he seems to support Byrne, in private, it is said, he detests the man. (Byrne was an ambitious young dean at Swarthmore before being brought to Woodslee — that is, bought by Woodslee — some years before, when the university's reputa-

tion was at its lowest in seven decades; even Lewis has to admit
that Byrne has done an excellent job, has scooped up foundation
money and grants from the state legislature and loans for building
purposes and promises of still more money, has defended the
faculty's stand on tenure, merit raises, and annual salary incre-
ments based on cost-of-living scales, is crusading for a new graduate library, and for an expanded center for the performing arts,
and for. . . . He has done an excellent job, so far: even Lewis has
to admit that. And the *coup* of St. Dennis is certainly an enviable
one. (It was known that Cornell and the University of Texas were
both high bidders for St. Dennis, but that Woodslee came
through not only because of the amount of money offered but
because of the young dean's persuasive personality: he had flown
to London twice to talk with St. Dennis.) But the year is only
beginning and there are enormous issues ahead, and Lewis is
rather skeptical about Byrne's idealism, and not at all "hopeful"
— as he has said to innumerable colleagues and to President
Garrett himself — about Byrne's continued presence at Woodslee.) . . . Is it possible that Byrne actually *likes* Kessler? And Brigit Stott? Lewis cannot believe that: it's too absurd.

He and Brigit have known each other for three years now, and
Lewis had met her earlier in New York City, at about the time
her second novel came out and her marriage began to deterio-
rate. He had liked her well enough at first. She was so painfully
shy, almost mute at times, overwhelmed by large parties . . .
really an attractive woman, though too thin for Lewis's taste . . .
and curiously delicate, vulnerable . . . feminine. Her husband
Stanley Fifield, a man of Lewis's size, swarthy-skinned, with a
mustache and a quick busy joky manner and stylish clothes, had
been very protective of her; Lewis remembers a party on New
York's West Side in someone's big apartment where Fifield more
or less blocked guests from approaching his wife, who stood in a
corner sipping a drink nervously, her black hair down to her
shoulders at that time, glossy and much thicker than it is now,

and not yet streaked with gray . . . he remembers slipping
around Fifield and approaching Brigit with a wide, hearty grin
and a handshake, telling the frightened woman that he had read
both her novels and liked them very, very much and that he
thought she was the most promising young stylist of. . . . And
then Fifield had interrupted, with the sort of large loose good-
hearted manner Lewis himself had perfected.

Yes, Lewis had liked Brigit Stott well enough at that time. He
approved of shy, demure, fastidious women, though he tended to
be attracted — violently — to tall fleshy extroverted girls, of
whom there were many at Woodslee; and he had been the one
who pushed Brigit's appointment here, arguing Warren Hochberg out of his choice of an older, far more conventional woman
writer, a New England regionalist whose husband was related in
some tedious, complicated way to Vivian Hochberg. (The department had had to hire a woman that year, at all costs: Gladys
Fetler was their only woman professor, and though she was a full
professor whose salary was nearly at the top of the scale, her
appointment had been made in 1942 and there had not been
another permanent appointment of a woman since; the State
Commission on Women's Rights was investigating Woodslee,
and a federal agency was planning to block loans to a number of
universities and institutions that did not comply with certain
quidelines on the hiring of women and minorities. "Outrageous
sexism," someone had charged.) So Stott was hired and the commission got off their backs.

Is she one of your former girls? colleagues asked, winking.

Certainly not, Lewis said.

Come on, now, Lewis! — we won't tell our wives, and our
wives won't tell *your* wife. The woman's name is Brigit Stott and
she's a young novelist and you can vouch for her work, and for
her ability to get along with students, and — ?

Brigit and I are only friends, Lewis said. Old, good friends.

"Friends" — ?

And she isn't all that young, actually, Lewis said with a touch
of regret.

But though he insisted they had never been lovers, and had
not even slept together — Lewis used the expression "slept together" out of a real disdain for more contemporary slang, which
his students, even his girl students, used quite casually — his colleagues at Woodslee nevertheless believed there was something
between the two of them, some shared experience, some secret,
perhaps even a mutual contempt for the faculty at Woodslee and
for the faculty wives. Your Brigit Stott is quite an interesting
woman, they might say, with a faint emphasis upon the *your*.
Your friend Brigit has turned out to be rather eccentric in certain
ways, hasn't she? — though the students seem unusually enthusiastic about her lectures. What is her candid opinion of us, has
she told you?

It was difficult for Lewis to resist — indeed, he found himself
unable to resist — hinting that, yes, Brigit Stott did confide in
him occasionally; and, yes, they had been friends, quite intimate
friends, years before in New York. But privately he was disappointed in her. Disappointed and distressed and hurt and bewildered.

Betrayed, really.

From the very first she has shown little interest in Lewis; she
seems to have no time for him, no awareness of the importance
of his ideas in relationship to the art of prose fiction. She could
learn a great deal from him, but she resists; and she is not nearly
so shy as Lewis had believed. (She has declined several of Faye's
invitations to dinner over the years, though she usually accepts
invitations to larger parties.) Lewis loves to talk, to argue, to
harangue; he is the department's most popular undergraduate
teacher, and his students crowd around him after class and in the
coffee shop and at the Riverview, a tavern near the university,
eager to hear his ideas. Certain of his colleagues are very respectful also; tonight at the Byrnes' those two young assistant pro-

fessors, Jaeger and Swanson, Ernest Jaeger and Barry Swanson, were fascinated by his remarks on Borges and Barthes and Kafka . . . their wives, too, had been deeply absorbed in his argument. Mrs. Garrett claims to be an admirer of his; she sometimes audits his course in the American novel, sitting at the rear of the little amphitheater and taking notes like any student, coloring slightly at Lewis's ribald jokes — for he *is* outspoken, and often shocking; that is the Seidel manner. Other faculty wives attend his lectures from time to time. And he still receives compliments on *Cul-de-sac*, and invitations from universities to give lectures or attend conferences (he is a very successful speaker, in fact, once he manipulates his audience into laughter), and he is engaged in correspondence with nearly one hundred writers, critics, and scholars everywhere in the world, including Japan and New Zealand and Nigeria and Pakistan. His archives will be a treasure. It seems to him, at times, that he is taken very seriously by everyone except Brigit Stott — who, more than most, should be grateful to him, and respectful of his work. Her attitude bewilders him, and angers him, for isn't it a kind of provocation . . . ? Doesn't she know how powerful he is . . . ?

(Still, he is wary of her: for it is generally known in Woodslee that Brigit Stott is working on an immense roman à clef in which all of Woodslee figures — a merciless, venomous satire that might very well destroy careers and lives and provoke — so the rumors hint — a number of libel suits.)

Sometimes he likes her, and sometimes he hates her. It is she who is unpredictable — ungovernable. Appearing shy and even tongue-tied, she is capable, nevertheless, of coming out with extraordinary statements, especially when she has had a bit to drink. (The drinking *is* a problem, Lewis has come to believe; Faye has told him some unpleasant tales related to her by other faculty wives about Brigit's behavior.) She once said within earshot of the university's ambitious but sadly limited vice-president Clay Waller — whom everyone more or less scorns — that "lack of power corrupts": and the remark became famous at Woodslee. She cruelly undercut a pedantic discussion by Gowan Vaughan-Jones, of all people, on the subject of the history of the sonnet with a single disparaging remark, and she said of Gladys Fetler's highly respected scholarship that "no one reads it" — though she seems to be genuinely fond of Dr. Fetler and to have meant no harm by the remark or, indeed, by any of the remarks. They seem to leap from her without her conscious knowledge. Perhaps it is the effect of the alcohol on her delicate nervous system . . . ? Her remark tonight about Lewis's ideas was really rather unforgivable. *Sometimes brilliant, sometimes shit.* Yes: really unforgivable.

Though possibly it is the woman's way of flirting with him . . . ?

Not that it mattered in the slightest. Lewis is accustomed to being attacked in public, and he is adroit at turning even the crudest attack to his own advantage. All he requires is an audience! He had seized the issue gladly enough and acquitted himself well, impressing St. Dennis and the others with the range and depth and ferocity of his knowledge, and the rapidity of his mind; so it had turned out well. In a way he was grateful to Brigit for having stimulated him into speech. But she herself had appeared bored, turning a ring round and round her finger, refusing to look at Lewis though it was obvious he was really addressing her and cared very much for her opinion. Instead she had stared at Kessler for a long time until even Kessler, who normally craved attention, grew uneasy. A strange woman, not nearly so feminine as everyone had thought, rather disappointing, rather maddening. . . .

If she isn't careful, Lewis thinks, watching her in the rear-view mirror, he will force her out of Woodslee: it is in his power, after all, to make things so uncomfortable for certain people that they will give up and flee rather than fight. (He had successfully blocked the promotion from associate professor to full professor of a Victorian specialist who had aroused his antagonism over an issue too complicated to recall, and the man finally quit Woodslee and went elsewhere, without ever knowing — not *really* knowing — who was behind his repeated failure to be promoted; and he had eased out a young American literature specialist just the year before, when the man was up for tenure, having presented to the Promotion and Tenure Committee a very persuasive case against the man's ability to do original research. (In fact, Ernest Jaeger is the man's replacement, and he strikes Lewis as very promising indeed.) Along with several other powerful faculty members Lewis was responsible, some time ago, in forcing the old Dean of Humanities into premature retirement — a stubborn, unimaginative man, with a weak background in literature and history and a perverse distrust of "the arts," who had tried personally to destroy Lewis — but Lewis had not foreseen that Oliver Byrne would be the new dean and that he too, in his own way, would prove so unsatisfactory.) And then there was the unfortunate, rather silly Adrian Hogan. . . . It would not be difficult to force Brigit Stott out, if he put his mind to it. That bitch! So cool to poor Faye's attempts at friendship. . . . Though Lewis isn't chairman of the English department he is nearly as powerful as Warren Hochberg, who respects and fears him, knowing how skillful a politician Lewis has become; it was Lewis, after all, who herded Warren into office, during a tumultuous period in the mid-sixties when it looked, at times, as if the entire university were about to fold. Warren and Lewis are friends. In a sense. In a sense they are friends. . . . Lewis and Vivian are, oddly, friends; or were. In a sense, also. In a very special sense.

But then, it might be argued that everyone in the department is friendly with everyone else, in a sense.

The night air has revived him but Lewis, too, has had more to drink than he can comfortably handle — because of his nerves he always drinks too much at the Byrnes' pretentious gatherings. Now he realizes he has overshot Alexis Kessler's apartment building, that new high-rise on the Powhatan River, and since he wishes to get rid of Kessler, since he does *not* intend to allow St. Dennis to invite Kessler up to his apartment, he stops before Brigit Stott's apartment building on the corner of Strathmore and Linwood and asks if this is all right for both Brigit and Alexis? — pretending he doesn't know that Alexis lives more than a mile away. Alexis agrees quickly, however, and Brigit murmurs thanks, and despite St. Dennis's protestations — what *does* the man see in these two, anyway? — what perverse enchantment have they worked upon the old fool? — they get out of Lewis's car at last and he drives away, thank God.

Turning onto Linwood he glances back and sees the two standing close together near the building's front entrance; they seem to be talking earnestly. . . . But what have Brigit and Alexis to talk about? They have never seemed very fond of each other.

By the time Lewis parks before St. Dennis's apartment building on Phoenix Boulevard, the old man has somehow managed to light a cigarette. He is still babbling, now about a Russian poet, something about translations, or perhaps it is his own poetry translated into Russian, or a trip he once made to Russia that was evidently disastrous. Lewis and Faye maneuver him out of the back seat of the car; he drops the cigarette; it falls into his lap, then down along his leg, to the floor of the car; Faye, grunting, has to stoop over to retrieve it. St. Dennis is apologetic. He belches, and apologizes again. His fingers brush against Faye's cheeks as if he were blind.

"Who are you? So kind! Kind. Americans so kind. Food and liquor and cars and warmth and beds and money and good teeth and smiles . . . smiles. . . . Who are you? Dean? Good man. Kind. Talking. Too much talking. Kindness. Money. Cars. . . . Is this where they have lodged me? Do you have a key? Can't see. Glasses dirty. Oh, thank you so much . . . didn't see that bloody step."

They maneuver him into the foyer and into the elevator and upstairs to the fifth floor, and walk him along the corridor to his apartment, 508, that faces the boulevard and, across the way, the northeastern corner of the Woodslee campus. The apartment is dark; Lewis switches on the lights.

"Thank you," St. Dennis says with dignity, ". . . Very kind."

"Be careful of the rug," Lewis says, "it's bunched up here. . . ."

"Don't let him fall, Lewis," Faye cries.

". . . Very, very kind," St. Dennis mumbles. He has another cigarette in his fingers and is looking from side to side, blindly, as if for a light. "I'll be able to manage now quite nicely. No trouble at all."

"Should we take him into the bedroom?" Faye asks nervously.

". . . no trouble at all," St. Dennis says.

His legs buckle suddenly; they maneuver him to a sofa and he falls onto it; he begins to laugh quietly. From somewhere he has produced a box of matches that he holds in one hand, opening it upside-down, so that matches fall onto his lap and the sofa and the floor. "Harriet," he says softly. "Asleep and nobody's to know. Eh? Mum's the word! What you don't know doesn't hurt. Exactly. Cicero. 'Grace of delivery.' . . . Don't wish to disturb Harriet, you know; best idea, simply sleep here, sofa here, no trouble at all. Very kind of you."

"Should we just leave him here?" Faye whispers. "It doesn't seem right to. . . ."

"Of course we can't leave him here," Lewis says sharply. He glares at his wife: it is the first time he has looked at her in hours. The sight of her — the sad tinted-blond hair, the penciled eyebrows and dainty rouged cheeks and innocuous pearl earrings — annoy him for some reason. She is not so stupid as she appears, and yet she *appears* to be so stupid! Lewis Seidel's wife, of all people. He suspects people talk about their marriage, about Faye, wondering why he married her. She has gained at least thirty pounds since their wedding. Is it to spite him? To humiliate him in the eyes of his rivals? Of course she is a good mother to their three boys, a good housekeeper, a good cook, a good daughter-in-law, a good hostess, not so clever, perhaps, as Marilyn Byrne, or as confident as Vivian Hochberg, but hard-working and tireless and absolutely loyal to Lewis. . . . He wonders at his sudden anger; the mere sight of her tired, distressed expression makes him want to shout. "Of course we can't leave him here like this. Don't be so damn stupid. He's likely to start a fire, isn't he, in the condition he's in? Stupid cow. Get out of the way."

"No trouble at all now," St. Dennis says sleepily. " 'S nearly morning, isn't it? Church bells. Will wake. Harriet must sleep, must rest. No disturbance. Mrs. Byrne? Is it? . . . Where is my cigarette?"

"You'd better lie down," Lewis says, embarrassed. "You're very tired, Mr. St. Dennis, you've had an arduous day . . . evening . . . so much excitement, conversation. . . . You're far from home, you know. . . . Yes, just give me that box. Thanks! You don't want a cigarette at this late hour, do you, you're very sleepy, aren't you, yes, for Christ's sake, Faye, get his other shoe, will you? — take it off, please! — don't stand there so damn helpless. Get a blanket or a quilt or something from the bedroom. Hurry up. . . . No, Mr. St. Dennis, I think I'll take this box of matches with me . . . you don't really need a cigarette now, do you? . . . you were coughing earlier this evening . . . yes, you're very sleepy, yes, that's right, I'm going to put your glasses right here on the table, see, right here, by the sofa, that's right, that's fine, we've got your shoes off and I'll just loosen your tie a little and . . . and that should do it, that should be enough; are you comfortable? Yes? These old-fashioned sofas are nice and roomy, aren't they? . . . Okay, here's a blanket, we'll just tuck you in and you'll be quite safe here, as good as in bed, as good as at home, nothing to worry about, see? . . . you're already asleep, my friend. Already asleep! Fine."

Lewis checks the apartment quickly, poking his head into the bedroom and into the bathroom and into a small cluttered room that is evidently going to be St. Dennis's study. And into the kitchen, a surprisingly large, dreary room with an old-fashioned sink and worn linoleum. Not very attractive, really. The only decent room is the living room, which is rather small; and even in that room the ancient molding at the ceiling is gray with dust and the carpets are faded. A disappointing place. Lewis is annoyed and plans to complain: surely Woodslee University could have housed this distinguished man in better accommodations. Why did Oliver Byrne put him here? . . . This apartment building is generally considered to be one of the most interesting examples of Greek Revival architecture in the area; it was purchased by the university some years ago, and while Lewis has always admired its façade, its columns and ornamentation and stately, flaring steps, he has never been impressed by its shabbily elegant foyer and its pretensions to style. It might be necessary for him to locate another apartment for poor St. Dennis. . . . If the man is really disappointed with this place, he might possibly wish to live with the Seidels; they have a roomy, sprawling house, a late-Victorian monstrosity that is the envy of the university community, very nicely fixed up inside, warm and hospitable and attractive . . . and Lewis would charge nothing, certainly, for St. Dennis's stay.

"He's asleep," Faye whispers.

"He's unconscious," Lewis says.

Without his glasses the old man looks even frailer. His skin appears to be clammy; it is very pale, almost white. Breathing as if with an effort, he makes a wet wheezing noise, and his lips part in a grimace, revealing his false teeth, too white and too even and slightly large for his narrow chin. Poor man! Lewis pities him. On an impulse he touches St. Dennis's forehead as if blessing him, then, stooped over the sleeping man, he brushes back a strand of limp white hair. Sad. He appears to be older than seventy. Could be eighty, at least. Lewis's father is seventy-eight now and in excellent condition, except for his arthritis; St. Dennis looks older. The blanket is drawn up to his chin and tucked in around his shoulders. He sleeps, wheezing, obliterated by the sudden depth of his sleep, the plunge into sleep, its terrible necessity. Faye turns out the lights and Lewis remains, for a moment, bent over the sleeping man. Amazing, that this person is Albert St. Dennis! *This* person. Though Lewis is going to argue against the worth of St. Dennis's poetry as part of his contention that all such art, such consciously wrought art, is no longer valid for our era, he has always acknowledged the fact that St. Dennis's poetry is poetry of surpassing beauty and power — a remarkable body of work. And this person, this sleeping grandfatherly person, is the poet himself. . . . Or was.

"Lewis?" Faye whispers. "Is something wrong? Shouldn't we —"

"Shut up," Lewis says.

He is blinking tears out of his eyes.

By 1:30 the Hochbergs are asleep in their three-bedroom colonial house out on the Old Armory Drive, Warren in his own room, Vivian in hers; Vivian lies awake for a while, thinking of that new, young girl — Sandra Jaeger — whom she had introduced to Lewis Seidel, and of Marilyn Byrne's comically desperate attempt to salvage the evening; and of the dinner party she will give in a few weeks, Albert St. Dennis the guest of honor, and the Garretts . . . if President Garrett is in town . . . and the Haases, whom Warren finds tolerable . . . and Gladys Fetler, whom everyone likes . . . and the Seidels, probably: despite Faye . . . and the Housleys . . . though maybe not the Housleys, since Mina has been so distracted lately . . . a look, almost, of the convalescent about her . . . a married daughter dying of cancer, it is said, in a clinic in Buffalo; so sad! . . . but Mina's presence is rather depressing as a result. . . . Anyone else from the department? Not that foul-mouthed Brigit Stott, of course; and not the young people, not to so important a party; Gowan Vaughan-Jones, perhaps, though he says so little and hardly eats or drinks, merely looks from person to person, squinting and frowning, no doubt thinking of his work: one of the most brilliant men in his field, Warren believes, and only thirty-five years old. . . . Possibly Gowan, then. And Lewis, has she counted him? Lewis and Faye. Cannot avoid. Year after year after year, Woodslee a small town, thrown together, cannot avoid, might as well accept. Make the best of. Rejoice, even.

She falls asleep, a handsome woman in her late forties, married now for . . . how many years? . . . can't recall: seventeen, nineteen, twenty. Or more. She falls asleep, thinking of a party. Thinking of the table, the candles, the water goblets, the wine glasses, the floral centerpiece, the china and the silverware and the linen napkins and . . . and . . . . And. . . .

By 2 A.M. nearly everyone is asleep except Brigit and Alexis, and Lewis, and Oliver Byrne, and Sandra Jaeger. Brigit and Alexis lie in Brigit's bed, in the rumpled, damp sheets, stroking each other sleepily, in the aftermath of love, dazed by the phenomenon of what has happened, rather drunk, unquestioning, not even uncomfortable yet; not even self-conscious and embarrassed yet. By 2:35 both are asleep. Oliver Byrne walks about the downstairs of his house, quietly, putting things away, rinsing plates and glasses, setting them in the automatic dishwasher. Marilyn is upstairs in bed; she nearly collapsed when the last of the guests left. Oliver, too restless to sleep, rather enjoys these oases of time after the excitement of a party, during which he can walk from room to room, unimpeded, partly undressed, in his bedroom slippers, putting his house in order. *His* house, *his* party. *His* guests. Brushing cigarette ashes from the piano — checking rather anxiously to see if — no? — no burns? — he tries to recall Alexis Kessler's piece. Difficult, tricky music; perhaps a parody — ? Something meretricious about Kessler, unsettling. Ryerson saying of him he can't be trusted; can't take responsibility for his students falling in love with him; can't see how he invites infatuations, tragic misunderstandings. And that pouty swollen look of his. . . . Oliver draws his fingers lightly across the piano keys. Undeniable talent in Kessler. How did the piece go? Reminiscent of Bartok. Or Ives. Erik Satie? Puzzling. Seductive. Not for Oliver to grasp. Long ago he learned *Clair de Lune* and *Sonate Pathétique* and the "Moonlight Sonata" and certain manageable pieces by Chopin and Liszt and Rachmaninoff and Ravel, but years have passed since he has even attempted them, since he has even allowed himself to think of attempting them, and of the humiliation he would certainly experience; his mind snapped one day when he was working on Ravel's *Jeux d'Eau*. . . . (A piece he has heard Alexis Kessler play while semi-drunk, with a certain flamboyant contempt.) Music was not his primary interest anyway; he earned his degrees in English history of the Elizabethan and Jacobean periods, published his dissertation at the age of twenty-eight, and was drawn into university politics the first year of his first appointment, at the University of Pennsylvania. An assistant dean at thirty-one, a dean at thirty-five, Dean of Humanities here at Woodslee at forty-two, and a most promising future, as everyone keeps telling him. . . . How did Kessler's piece go? Oliver would like to ask him for a copy of it, but he knows Kessler would only be amused and sarcastic, imagining that Oliver is patronizing him. The boy's suspicious nature. . . . Oliver knows Kessler is unreliable, but he intends to keep him at Woodslee just the same: Kessler became an issue last year when a number of his colleagues in the music department wanted him fired, and Oliver defended him, and does not intend to back down. He never backs down. Any sign of weakness would immediately be taken advantage of by his enemies.

He walks from room to room, carrying ashtrays, glasses, plates. He is not very efficient. How pleasant to be alone after that crush of people, how marvelous to relax, no conversations, no pose to be maintained, no anxiety over certain of his guests and their disappointing behavior, no constant checking of his wife, to see if — ? To see if she is getting nervous. If her hands are trembling. He is cleaning up after a party, he is putting his house back in order. All is well. He will not think of Albert St. Dennis, of the man's ashen face, his broken voice, the tears that welled up in his

eyes as he stammered his apology. . . . He will not think of Lewis
Seidel's arrogance. Instead he relives the party as a series of tab-
leaux, frozen in the mind's eye. So perfect is his recall, and so
visual, that he can count his guests if he wishes. Count heads.
(He has a habit of counting heads — at parties, at meetings of
the university senate, even in stores or on the street.) His party,
his guests. His lovely house. He counts them now, the people
who came to his home tonight and helped to make his party a
success: his supporters, his friends, his admirers. He is very fond
of them. He wants only to be very fond of them. Someday Woodslee, New York, will be known as a center of the arts, a true
community of artists, scholars, teachers, humanists . . . a community unique in this part of the world, perhaps in all the United
States . . . a place where talented people from all parts of the
world will meet. Not an impossible dream, is it? Not too ambitious.

He rinses glasses. Rubs lipstick stains off with his thumb. Emp-
ties ashtrays into the trash basket beneath the sink. So many
smokers! Unfortunate habit. He throws crumpled napkins into
an untidy heap. Ugh, the napkins used to wipe up St. Dennis's
vomit. . . . Might as well discard with the trash. Too disgusting
to send to the laundry. . . . Poor Marilyn, her hysteria in the
kitchen after the last of the guests left. Good-by good-by good-by
Gladys, good-by Roger and Charlotte, so happy you could come,
so very happy, very very happy. Another vomit-stained napkin?
Throw out with the rest.

By 2:00 he has cleaned as much as he can, taking his time, in
no hurry. He can't, of course, plug in the vacuum cleaner or start
the dishwasher. By 2:30 he is asleep, in the twin bed beside his
wife's bed, suddenly exhausted, his spirit quite drained from him.
The day had begun, hadn't it, with an 8:30 A.M. emergency meeting at the university, so many hours ago, a small lifetime ago, the
Romance languages department in a state of chaos, the head of
the department in a fierce struggle with some of his senior men,

threats of violence, threats of actual murder, emergency meeting at 8:30 A.M. in secret, and what had he done afterward? . . . luncheon with the Dean of Men. . . . The hours, the hours. Falling asleep he hears Alexis Kessler's music. He hears his friends' voices uplifted. They are happy together, they are laughing together, he has made this miracle possible. His guests, his miracle. Continuing miracle. In rapid succession his friends' faces appear and disappear: last of all he sees Lewis Seidel's jocose, maddening smile, one eyelid twitching, as it often does. And then a person whose face is unclear. A vapor. Shadows for eyes, a gaping hole for a mouth. Who . . . ?

Stranger. Can't see. Lost.

He sleeps.

By 3 A.M. Lewis Seidel is asleep beside his wife, snoring fitfully. Because he perspires so much at night he is wearing not only his pajamas but a T-shirt and shorts. At about 5:30 he will probably awaken, soaking wet, shivering, and go to the bathroom, and change into a clean pair of shorts and another T-shirt; but now he is sleeping soundly. He stayed up for a while, downstairs, though Faye wanted him to come to bed. But no, he wasn't ready for sleep, his mind was too jumpy for sleep. He was thinking of. . . . But he did not want to think about St. Dennis; he wanted to relax. He opened a can of ale and sat at the kitchen table, leafing through last Sunday's *New York Times Magazine*, which he had already read. Driving back from St. Dennis's he had turned deliberately down Linwood to see if Brigit's light was still burning . . . and it was, she was still up . . . and he wondered suddenly if he might drop Faye off at the house and make some excuse about checking St. Dennis again . . . wondered if he might circle back and ring Brigit's doorbell . . . invite himself up for a nightcap. They are friends, after all. Have much in common. A department of thirty people and among them only three or four you could talk to; must be lonely for Brigit. He considered dropping in, giving her the opportunity to apologize for having been rude; possibly telling her how annoyed he often was with her, though he supposed she couldn't help it, she was quick and witty and did not suffer fools gladly, which was why . . . which was why he had always liked her . . . which was why, in fact, he had hired her at Woodslee. Oh, didn't she know that? — that *he* had hired her? He might tell her he was quite fond of her; might ask her what she thought of him. The late hour . . . the alcohol . . . the good cheer of a party . . . the loneliness of her life . . . trauma of divorce . . . need for affection, for touching, for sex. . . .

But he said nothing to Faye, he merely parked the car in the garage, suddenly too tired to drive out again. Enough for one night. A successful evening, he had acquitted himself well, had caught the respectful ear of St. Dennis, had driven him home, had initiated what would probably be a long-lasting friendship . . . enough for one night. He drank ale, he leafed through the *Times*, he waited until he was really exhausted before going up to bed (lying awake has begun to terrify him for some reason: he is too keenly aware of his own heartbeat and of his wife's presence close beside him, her small moans and twitches and sighs). Then sleep. Sleep. So much to think of, must sleep . . . ! St. Dennis and Brigit and Byrne and Alexis and Faye and Vivian and the others, the others, and his classes on Monday, two large sprawling adoring classes of undergraduates, lectures not yet organized, the thought of Sunday evening depressing, must telephone Brigit next week . . . must insist upon her understanding him. . . .

The bitch.

By 3 A.M. only Sandra Jaeger is still awake. She is sitting in the imitation leather chair bought only two weeks ago at a discount store downtown, in her blue flannel bathrobe with the rosebuds embroidered on the collar and the satiny belt, her long narrow pale feet, bare, tucked beneath her. She is too excited to sleep. She is more excited now than she was at the party. An almost erotic sensation courses through her; she has experienced it before, after other parties, and finds it halfway pleasant.

She sits in the black leather chair, turning the pages of a journal. It has a dull red cover; it resembles a ledger book. A diary, a disconnected series of impressions, random entries in Sandra Baird's life, Sandra Baird Jaeger's life. Begun when she was eighteen, a freshman at Boston University six years ago.

Only six years — ! Sometimes it frightens Sandra, to realize she has come so far.

She turns the pages, rereads her most recent entry — which has to do with the faculty wives' tea of last week, an event she had anticipated with excitement but that had disappointed her terribly, though it was not a total loss because she and Carol Swanson had gone together; she takes up a ballpoint pen, one of the many Ernest has left lying around the apartment, and begins to write about the Byrnes' party. Her make-up has been cleaned off carefully and she looks young and fierce and pure, and rather impatient. So much to record! So much to assimilate and comprehend!

The erotic excitement stays with her. It is not physical so much as mental. The desire to write down her impressions . . . to sort out, to analyze, to make clear. . . . From time to time she gazes at the wall opposite at the inexpensive Cezanne print framed in a simulated walnut frame, from Woolworth's; from time to time she finds herself staring at the orange shag rug, without seeing it; she is in a kind of trance. Her eyes are opened wide and unseeing, an unclouded depthless blue. Her skin glows with defiant good health. She can hear her pulse in the silence; sleep will be impossible for many hours. Going to bed, slipping in beside Ernest: impossible.

She hopes he won't wake, as he sometimes does, and call out for her. And come looking for her.

She relives the party. She sees herself there, in the Byrnes' living room, at the center of that group of fascinating people.

And how remarkable it was, as she and Ernest and the Swansons said repeatedly, their being invited to such an important function . . . a party in honor of Albert St. Dennis. (Ernest had found out, inadvertently, earlier that week, that the young man who shared his office — Bradley Keough, had *not* been invited.) It must have to do with the dean's interest in the younger faculty. They are so very fortunate to be here, at Woodslee, to have fled that dismal heartbreaking place in Trenton, New Jersey, that had almost destroyed Ernest; their good fortune makes Sandra tremble, it is so precarious, so amazing. And the Swansons are, if possible, even more grateful: Barry hadn't even had a job the year before, and Carol had worked fifty hours a week as a clerk-typist in Scranton. Now everything has changed. Their lives have changed. Their real lives have begun.

She sees again the handsome living room, the highly polished surfaces, the fresh-cut flowers, the lovely rug. The piano. The doors to the terrace open, a bright moon, everything marvelous, perfect. Mrs. Byrne speaking to her so warmly. Asking her and Carol about their impressions of Woodslee. About their apartment-hunting. Recommending stores in town, a grocery store out at the new mall. . . . Attractive woman. Early forties? Gracious, charming, kind. Expensively dressed. Allowed Sandra and Carol to help her with the food, passing things around. Dean Byrne so kind also. A little distracted at times, eyes darting about the room, handsome man in mid-forties, beginning to lose his hair, gray eyes, easy gracious smile. Remembered Ernest's name. Seemed impressed with Sandra — her master's degree in library science. (It has already been arranged, informally, that Sandra will have a part-time position at the library; when the budget is stabilized in another week or two, when the library determines how much part-time staff it will be allowed, Sandra will be working there. Ernest's previous college, that wretched extension in Trenton, had promised Sandra a job semester after semester but something had always gone wrong.) Was impressed, perhaps, with her looks also. Staring at her, smiling, smiling. Gray eyes. Dark gray. And hers blue, that startling pale blue. . . .

She knows she is pretty, how could she not know? She has been told for so many years. By so many people. Pretty blue-eyed Sandra Baird. . . . She must take good care of her skin and her hair, must be aware of her posture, her clothes. (Tonight the lavender dress with the long dipping skirt: perfect.) She is pretty and she is intelligent, how could she not be aware of her good fortune . . . ? The dean staring at her and smiling, asking about her background, Ernest's background, their impressions of Woodslee — the architecture is so striking, isn't it, Brandford Chapel most of all? Historic landmark. Built 1851. Dean Byrne shaking hands with his guests, introducing them to Sandra and Ernest as if they were equals, all of them equals. The odor of furniture polish, of cut flowers, of perfume. She is dizzy even now, remembering.

That sound? Her pulse. Heartbeat.

Impossible to sleep tonight!

She has been an insomniac since the age of fourteen. At first it alarmed her, and worried her parents, but now she hardly cares — now she is rather proud of it. Ernest worries; Ernest loves her very much. In a way, though, he is proud of her too — her sensitivity, her imagination. (What a contrast with Carol Swanson who, when the four of them met for dinner at a cheap Italian restaurant near the university, said something crudely sentimental about a man in a wheelchair, wheeled up to a nearby table — Sandra cannot remember the exact words, but they were mawkish and embarrassing, even Barry was embarrassed, and Sandra and Ernest exchanged a look of sheer surprise.) He has boasted within her hearing that his delicate little wife can get along on three or four hours' sleep a night.

The excitement is with her still; she writes as quickly as she can, covering page after page in the journal. Her handwriting is large and clear, girlish in its loops and dotted *i*'s. Ernest admires

it: his own handwriting is small and severely slanted, almost unreadable. Everything you do is so lovely, he says; so beautiful.
(They have been married a little over two years.)

In his eyes, that look of love.

In others' eyes, admiration . . . sudden interest . . . assess-
ment. At times, it must be admitted, jealousy. (One of the women
at the party tonight, middle-aged, rather plump, powdered:
whose wife? Looking at Sandra with a queer listless expression.
Not very friendly.) But she is accustomed to jealousy and envy,
even to spite. In high school certain friends of hers talked behind
her back, tried to hurt her feelings, tried to come between Sandra
and her boy friends, and all because they were jealous of her
good looks and her popularity. Now that she is married things are
different — young women don't feel she is competing with them
so directly — but there is still a sense of rivalry; in a way it exhil-
arates her. What Ernest said when they came home was true: *She
was the most beautiful woman at the party tonight.*

Again she sees herself in the lavender dress, her hair swinging
about her face, the thin silver chain about her throat. Mrs. Jaeger. Ernest Jaeger's wife. A clear, cool, melodic voice; long graceful legs; fashionable open-backed shoes. (The most expensive pair
of shoes she has ever bought — $29.98.) She sees, again, Albert
St. Dennis as he is being introduced to her: surprising, he is so
much shorter than she had imagined. An old, old man. Face
wrinkled but beautiful in its way. Must be eighty, eighty-five years
old? So famous. No longer quite real. Evidently a little deaf.
(Impossible to believe she will ever be that old — her skin lined
and creased like that — really impossible. She cannot even imagine herself Mrs. Byrne's age.) Albert St. Dennis shaking hands
with her, mumbling something she couldn't quite make out. He
seemed very sweet, though; wasn't rude to her at all. . . . And
Dr. Hochberg, head of Ernest's department, with his metal-
rimmed glasses and his peculiar downward smile, his nasal voice
— a little awkward with her but friendly enough, asking if she

and Ernest were settled in their duplex apartment yet; something
chilling about him, but Sandra is prepared to discover he is really
very sweet. (Like a shy, reserved sociology professor she had had
as an undergraduate.) He is certainly a brilliant man; Ernest said
of his book on Dryden that it is a masterpiece of scholarship. . . . Most surprising of all was Mrs. Hochberg's interest in
Sandra. Innumerable questions about plans for children, Sandra's hometown, Sandra's opinion of Boston. A woman in her
fifties, perhaps, with graying hair, stern good looks, a slightly
sardonic manner. Mole on upper lip: wonder why she doesn't
have it removed. Must have been quite attractive at one time.
Evidently charmed with Sandra, not at all jealous, taking her
around to meet other guests. So many people . . . ! Dr. Fetler,
tall and white-haired and grandmotherly; Dr. Seidel, moon-
faced, scowling and grinning, shrewd, rather forward — saying
playfully, with a wink at Mrs. Hochberg, that it was too bad
Sandra was married; Dr. Vaughan-Jones, with his loose,
strengthless handshake and his gray-green teeth and his slight
stammer — a young-old man whom Ernest admires very much
also. And Brigit Stott, the novelist. Strange angular-faced
woman, high cheekbones, messy hair, black dress falling below
her knees, something melancholy about her — and that low
husky almost inaudible voice — glittery-eyed as if on drugs —
but friendly enough in her queer, chilled way; she actually smiled
at Sandra, though she had nothing to say to her. Must have been
a friend of St. Dennis's: took care of him when he was sick. A
friend, too, of that bizarre young man with the bleached hair —
the pianist — who had not once glanced at Sandra or Ernest or
the Swansons. ("A homosexual," Carol said afterward, "wasn't
he — ?") Sweetest of all the guests was Mrs. Housley, the wife of
the Chaucer specialist, a woman in her early sixties who must
have weighed 160 or 170 pounds and who stood no higher than
Sandra's chin — they had had a conversation during dinner
about the town of Woodslee, about its handsome old Victorian

homes that were in danger of being razed, its mills and factories that caused such problems, downriver especially, its loss of population, the poverty of its French-speaking section, the poverty in general, financial crises year after year after year, as long as Mrs. Housley could remember. . . . The woman was passionate and quite articulate. Worst of all, she said, was the fact that the town of Woodslee was invisible from the university's point of view. It was really arrogant of the university people, wasn't it, to refuse to take seriously the locality in which they lived and worked—? Sandra agreed. She listened closely, she was very polite. Mrs. Housley must have liked her because she mentioned something about Sandra coming over for tea sometime soon. . . . Afterward, when the party was over and Sandra and Ernest and the Swansons were getting into the Swansons' car, parked a few houses up from the Byrnes', the Housleys were standing by their car, talking loudly, and Sandra thought perhaps she should ask if something was wrong — and it turned out (according to Mrs. Housley, who seemed quite upset) that someone had broken into the Housleys' car during the party; one of the rear windows had been broken, the door unlocked, and a few items of no great value stolen — an umbrella, Mrs. Housley said, and an old valise.

Fortunately the Swansons' car had not been broken into; there were only a few books in the back seat.

"We just don't have crime in Woodslee," Mrs. Housley said, astonished.

Sandra, writing, pauses to look up: does she hear something?

Someone?

No. Silence.

Only a car with a faulty muffler out on Van Buren.

What time — ?

Almost 3:30.

She is not yet ready for bed; she is still alert, excited, exhilarated. If only she could explain her queer, passionate yearning to

Ernest — her sense of things being almost too wonderful, too enormous, for her to grasp. She knows she is very lucky, for instance. Her marriage to Ernest Jaeger was a stroke of good fortune. Their coming here to Woodslee, Ernest's appointment as an assistant professor — it is almost too wonderful, it is almost unreal. Many of Ernest's former classmates from Harvard have not yet found positions, even in junior or community colleges, or in high schools, and no one of their acquaintance has a job as good as Ernest's. Of course Ernest is an outstanding young man. He worked for several years on his Ph.D. dissertation, which was nearly seven hundred pages upon completion, and which is to be published by the University of North Carolina Press; his professors think very highly of him; everyone thinks highly of him. He is an experienced teacher — twenty-nine years old — by no means a beginner. He is industrious, dedicated, brilliant. . . . Still, there are former classmates of his who have worked almost as hard, and who are almost as dedicated and as brilliant. Sandra thinks of them with pity. Some are bachelors, which makes their unemployment easier in one sense but more difficult in another, since they live alone; others are married, some even have children. When Ernest was offered that position of instructor at a university extension in Trenton everyone was envious, even a little bitter. He had not yet finished his Ph.D.; he had not seemed, on paper, so qualified as some of his friends.

In fact Ernest had lost a close friend at that time, a young man who had sent out two hundred fifty letters of application, without results, and who had come to think that his letters of recommendation were betrayals, that former professors were plotting against him, conspiring to ruin his career. His thinking was so twisted that he had convinced himself that his classmates — Ernest among them — stole his mail from his university mailbox and talked behind his back to professors. His grin became fixed, demonic. Another classmate of Ernest's, a brilliant young woman

with an M.A. degree from Johns Hopkins whom Sandra had
known fairly well and had liked, was still jobless after two years of
applying to innumerable universities and colleges . . . and Sandra had heard, only the other day, of a suicide attempt, and
hospitalization. Should she write to the girl? Dare she write? (For
the fact of Ernest's excellent position could not have failed to
depress her.) And there are other, wilder tales. Too improbable,
in a sense, not to be true. A married couple with advanced degrees — hers in English, his in political science — were reported
to have been seen in a massage parlor off Times Square (but who
would have seen them, who would have confessed to having seen
them in such a place?) where they were both employed. An attractive older student, a woman in her mid-thirties, was said to
have abandoned her doctoral dissertation and to have agreed to
marry into a harem — in Turkey, was it? — somewhere distant
and exotic; she had met a very attractive, wealthy Middle Eastern
man on a recent trip to England, and had been, so rumor had it,
"quite easily seduced." There was a former friend of a friend said
to be in jail, having been arrested for selling heroin to high-
school students; or was it marijuana, merely; or had he been
caught up in a police raid on a commune in Boston, and unfairly
charged with possession of drugs, and unfairly treated. . . .
There were outlandish and equally distressing tales of petty thiev-
ery, prostitution, gambling, and madness.

Sandra wonders: Should I feel grief for them. Should I care.

There are too many of us now.

Better not to think about the situation. Better to put it all behind her. After all, their lives have changed completely now.
They are no longer graduate students: they are adults, with a
genuine place in an academic community. Ernest is not a teaching assistant, he is an assistant professor of English, on what is
called the regular payroll; and Sandra is on a list, a marvelous list,
of names that belong to faculty wives. Some years ago, in the late
sixties and early seventies, it might have seemed inconceivable

that anyone, particularly bright young intellectuals, would have prized such things so highly, and so desperately; but it is no longer the late sixties and the early seventies.

Our friends wouldn't have cared about us, if Ernest and I had failed, Sandra thinks. There isn't time any longer to care.

A little sleepier now, she begins to think of a party. She and Ernest will give a party. In a few months, perhaps. A small party, because the living room here is so small. . . . A dinner party. She could prepare something special, something elaborate; beef Wellington, perhaps; she believes she might be an excellent cook if she tried. And Ernest could help her. And the other women would be quite impressed. And they would go away saying nice things about her. And their husbands, their husbands too, they would go away saying nice things about her, and about Ernest, and. . . .

A small dinner party for those people who have been especially friendly.

But — would it be premature? Would it appear to be presumptuous?

Possibly.

There was gossip, year before last, of an assistant professor's wife who had been too eager, too aggressive, who had made the error of inviting senior faculty members and their wives to her home far too quickly, and what had happened to her and her husband . . . what had been their fate . . . ? Even the graduate students had known, and had laughed.

Sandra will wait: she will be cautious, and observant, and she will wait.

At

the Seidels'

November 5, 8 P.M.

There he sits, on stage, diminutive, child-sized, so aged — by the glare of the lighting — as to seem no longer human, but a figure out of mythology.

In a navy blue three-piece suit bought for this occasion, in a starched white shirt with a stiff collar, a dark tie knotted tightly and perfectly at his throat and tucked down inside his vest, Albert St. Dennis sits, rigid and short-legged, very pale, staring out into the crowded twilight of the unfamiliar auditorium. His skin is luminous; his scalp gleams whitely through his thin fluffy hair; his glasses catch and reflect light in random sliver-like blinks. He stares at the crowd, the crowd stares at him. One abyss into another. What does he resemble, sitting there so properly? — a doll? His skin is pale, oyster-pale; it looks powdered. His mouth seems to have disappeared. His hands — which seem very small — are resting on his lap, motionless, atop a manila envelope. Feet also small: shoes that look new and are smartly polished. He is dressed properly and sedately, like an Englishman or a businessman or a small-town lawyer. His stomach churns with mild regret — he had only a small portion of his dinner, but perhaps even that was an error.

(Since 5:30 he has been herded about by busy friendly fussing bullying people, helped into and out of automobiles, an umbrella held ineffectually over his head to protect him against the sudden cold rain; he has been served cocktails, hors d'oeuvres, various courses of a lengthy and confused dinner at the president's house in the company of innumerable people, most of them strangers — President Garrett himself was unfortunately absent from the dinner, having flown to San Francisco to attend a national conference of university presidents only that morning.)

He is staring patiently at his audience, at the rows and rows of faces. So many people . . . ! Even the air is jostled and overheated. All the seats in Brandford Hall appear to be filled. Were filled, Dean Byrne informed him, half an hour ago. Students, professors, wives, people from town and perhaps even from nearby cities: row upon row extending out of sight. More are standing at the rear and in the aisles. Some are sitting in the aisles. Who are these people, St. Dennis wonders, quietly alarmed; what do they expect from him . . . ? So many, many strangers, all of them eager and watchful and curiously reverential. He wonders what perverse logic has assembled these people here tonight and brought him to sit before them, elevated above them like a minor, rather embarrassed god.

He blinks rapidly, scanning the first several rows. Familiar faces? Where? . . . His wife? No. He can't see beyond the first four rows.

8:00. 8:05. Still the hall is filling; doors at the rear are continually opening. A young man with shoulder-length hair approaches the stage and, twisting his body oddly, takes a photograph of St. Dennis. The flash of light is blinding.

His hands clasp each other firmly. Moist and cool. A secret handshake. He is frightened but he will manage to get through the reading as he has managed to get through many readings, and afterward people will congratulate him and there will be a party or a reception and then he and Harriet will leave together quietly and that will be that. A midnight reward: brandy, a few mints, and bed.

How many hours until then . . . ? Only four.

But Harriet isn't with him, is she; no longer with him. He has crossed the wide storm-gray Atlantic alone. He is alone. "Poetry and the 'Eternal Affirmation of the Human Spirit.' " Alone on this enormous continent with only a frail skein of words to hold his life together.

The microphone is being adjusted; there are aggressive coughing noises. Static that rises and becomes a high-pitched whine, and is then miraculously cut off. The audience quiets. Oliver Byrne is at the podium, shuffling through a half-dozen note cards. Dressed casually but impeccably in a sports jacket that is probably genuine camel's hair, a wide handsome striped necktie, shirt cuffs that are very white. St. Dennis has never seen Dean Byrne with glasses before; he looks fastidious and aristocratic, peering at the notecards as if he were entirely alone, absolutely at ease.

8:08. The evening begins.

A voice, many times amplified, fills the auditorium. It is grave and graceful and beautifully modulated. Its subject is Albert St. Dennis. "The most distinguished of living English poets." "A superb artist and craftsman, second only to Yeats himself in this century." How proud the voice is of its subject, how quietly triumphant it rings out . . . ! St. Dennis stares at his clasped hands and wills that his spirit not slip out of his body; not tonight. It is unreal, all of it is unreal, lacking even that jarring hellish reality of a nightmare, which, however unpleasant, is nevertheless one's own. The voice that trumpets his excellence, the crowded hall, the blinding lights, the rows of indistinct faces, the endless cocktail hour, the endless dinner, those well-intentioned people querying him about his "impressions" of the United States and his "opinions" of the federal government — about which he knows nothing — and filling his wine glass with wine despite his prudent entreaties: unreal, all unreal. Yet it must be confronted. It must be acknowledged.

Thirty-seven books since 1926, when his first volume of poems, *Harlequin*, was published privately in London; books that have been translated into countless languages. Awards and prizes and medals and grants and commissions. Honorary degrees from English and European universities. Said to have been (and to be) considered for a Nobel Prize. Most famous for his poetry but also the author of distinguished prose works: a novel, several collections of essays, a travel book, the first volume of his autobiography. A libretto in 1955 in collaboration with Ralph Vaughan Williams. A verse play produced in London to critical acclaim and modest commercial success. Translations and editing of Russian and Greek and Czech poetry; a much-praised translation of *The Divine Comedy*; a brief but excellent critical biography of Hopkins, written in 1931. And on and on. St. Dennis has lived a long full life, a most formidable life; it sounds enviable. It sounds unbelievable.

He is staring at his hands, now fussing with the manila envelope. A sheaf of poems, written in longhand, in pencil. Rather messy. Difficult to read. New poems — fairly new — written within the past year. The poems are real enough. The smudged pages are real. Each of the words is his own. A skein of words, a strategy not of survival but of the costs of maintaining survival. Who will understand? Who in this crowded hall will understand? Words, frail and mortal. Sacred. "Albert St. Dennis" no longer recognizable except as a voice, a mouth, a spirit composed of words. . . .

Oliver Byrne has shifted now, has backtracked to speak of St. Dennis's family history. His people were glassmakers in York in the eighteenth century; some of the family moved to London, gave up glassmaking and became merchants, small tradesmen, grocers. There was even a barrister or two in St. Dennis's branch of the family. St. Dennis himself was born in 1906 in Ealing. In public school and at New College, Oxford, he specialized in the classics. Married to Harriet Arnold, 1936. Co-editor of the avant-garde magazine *Proteus*, 1934–1939. Schoolteacher, clerk for an insurance firm in London, a year of medical school, British army (infantry), wounded in 1943. Travels to Greece, Egypt, Jerusalem, Persia, Russia, Australia. Controversial "Letters from Rhodesia" published in *New Statesman*, 1951–52. Many invitations over the years from the United States — many proffered awards — including a medal from the National Institute of Arts and Letters — but, until this year, St. Dennis had always declined to visit with his American admirers. Woodslee University is therefore very conscious of its good fortune, very honored to have been singled out by Albert St. Dennis for his first visit. The author of a number of modern classics, notably *The Explorers* and *Hecate*, the author of the tantalizing statement, "All art is absurdity," here with us tonight — here to give the first of his Woodslee readings — "Poetry and the 'Eternal Affirmation of the Human Spirit' " —

The voice concludes; the audience applauds.

Elderly, hard of hearing, short of leg and of breath, dim-visioned, uncomfortably warm, slightly sick to his stomach; peering with elfin solicitude into the cavernous hall, who is this person who has accomplished this lifetime . . . ? The strangers are applauding enthusiastically. Applause brings St. Dennis to his feet. He knows he is an impostor, he knows he is taking advantage of his American hosts' gullibility, but they are applauding as if eager for his poetry, his wisdom — "All art is absurdity," what can that possibly mean? — what could it have ever meant? — as if eager for his being itself. And so he rises as Dean Byrne turns to him, smiling, as the applause flows in waves about him. He does not know who he is, who they expect him to be, he has forgotten most of his life and does not care to summon it back, but the Dean's generous introduction and the audience's gener-

ous applause awaken him to his duty: he is to impersonate "Albert
St. Dennis" for the next hour.

He begins with a line from Keats: "The poetry of earth is never
dead."

At first his voice quavers. Then, gradually, it regains its fragile
strength. He hears himself speaking as if from a distance. Earth,
poetry, craftsmanship, labor, love, despair, joy, the necessary
restrictions of art. He is shuffling unobtrusively through his papers. He selects a poem — some relationship to the line of Keats?
— he can't quite remember the connection though he is certain
there is one — ah yes: poetry of earth never dead. Deathlessness
of the human spirit, that point at which art and nature converge.
Communion of mankind through language. Yes.

He reads his first poem, a soliloquy set in a garden.

An autumn garden, it is. Friends' home in Rottingdean. Allusions to Hardy's garden poems — will his audience understand?
Hardy a mourner and a survivor like St. Dennis, a widower like
St. Dennis. The kinship of loss. Brotherhood. Someone has died
— someone has always died. One by one by one: mother, father,
grandparents, cousins, friends, many friends, enemies as well.
Sunlight becoming ever more powerful, glaring, merciless, no
shadows remaining in the old, untidy garden, everything exposed
and broken. Someone has died. Wife? Forty years married. Forty
years. (The hushed amazement of the young: perhaps a little
embarrassed.) A poem worked and reworked innumerable times.
Torture, the refinement of emotion into art. As Auden spoke of
an estrangement between oneself and one's name, so there is an
estrangement between oneself laboring in the present and oneself laboring in the past; yesterday's triumphs are today's embar-
rassments. What was tragic becomes merely anecdotal. Is grief
that can be so ingeniously measured grief any longer . . . ? But
the cunning of the poet knows no limit. . . . He is reading the
poem slowly and again his voice quavers. (To his shame he broke
down once during a reading, in London; long before his wife's

death, however. Could never understand, afterward, why his own poetry, at that particular moment, had seemed to him too painful to be borne. But it had torn into him, had torn from him a sobbing cry.) . . . The autumn sunlight, a glaring golden haze; the parched earth; the hazards of love and survival. An old man scribbling in a ledger book. Secretive. Secretive as a boy of six, secretive as an old man of seventy. Character is fate, unchanging. Nothing changes. Scribbling the inexpressible until his cold blood heats. Whirlwind. Swirlwind. Endless teasing of sounds. Anonymity of art when one surrenders entirely to it, delicious privacy of perfection, inexpressible joy. He does not dare hope that anyone else can understand.

The garden soliloquy came to him as if dictated from without, from a source beyond him. Something to do with Harriet, perhaps — her poor pain-wracked spirit? Bodiless. Teasing. A poem of more than one hundred lines in its first version, a terrible pressure of words, flood of words, crowding one another in his small slanted handwriting until his fingers ached. Arthritic anyway, knuckles slightly swollen. A poem that forced itself out onto the page, gave birth to itself, as certain other poems of his had, over the years, flowing through him, animating him, using him. For some time before the writing he had felt extremely cold, chilled, yet in a state of impersonal euphoria. Time had stopped. There was no time. How, then, to burst into his own life, claim his own being again, give a legendary quality to his own commonplace grief . . . ?

An hour's feverish scribbling and then exhaustion. Upstairs to nap, a nervous fretful evening, no appetite for dinner, alone in his room with the challenge of the poem, the mad torrent of words, working and reworking it through the night. As if he were still a young man. As if his life were still before him. Monologue. Grief. Finding the right words, the perfect rhythm. . . . Trying to recall a poem already written, complete. . . . A voice not his. Superior to his. Vocabulary deliberately austere, pared back,

ruthlessly denuded of the gorgeous, the dramatic, the "poetic."
Memento mori. Untranslatable emotion. His masters Dante and
Shakespeare and Yeats cannot help him here. Experience of having lived — of having lived as himself — yearning now for anonymity, for peace —

He has finished reading the poem. Suddenly it is over. He
glances up, startled, timid, like an uncertain lover.

The applause begins immediately, then dies back: as if the
audience, though deeply moved, fears intruding upon his grief.
But then he blinks and manages a confused smile, and they take
heart and applaud again, rather more loudly than he recalls other
audiences having applauded in the past, back home. He stares
out at the rows and rows of strangers. They *are* deeply moved.
The poem does mean something to them. And they are grateful
for their own emotion — grateful to be allowed to show that they
possess emotion —

He blinks tears from his eyes, embarrassed, flattered, shuffling
through his messy papers. For some reason he had not expected
things to go so well, he had not expected such warmth, such
enthusiasm, perhaps it was not a mistake to come to North America, perhaps this will be a turning point in his life. . . .

He is, after all, "Albert St. Dennis."

Oh God, Brigit thinks, *I love you*.

It is Alexis she loves, it is St. Dennis she loves. The young man sitting beside her, scented, his thigh pressed against hers, his arms folded; the old man behind the lectern, peering out at his audience as if perplexed by their response. The rumors were false: St. Dennis is in excellent health and he isn't drunk and his voice is frail but authoritative and he reads his poems beautifully and the entire hall is under a kind of enchantment. . . .

"Thank God he's all right," Brigit whispers to Alexis. Her eyes have filled with tears and she hopes they won't spill and run down her cheeks; what if someone notices . . . ! People have been looking rather curiously at her this evening.

"Yes," Alexis says. "You shouldn't have worried."

They are sitting near the back of the auditorium, having come just before eight o'clock when most of the seats were already taken. It is the first time the two of them have appeared in public, in Woodslee, except for a few walks along the river and dinner one evening in a downtown hotel; their sitting side by side tonight has the look, Brigit believes, of an accident. No one can see how they are pressed together in the dark, thigh to thigh, knee to knee, or how Alexis has reached beneath his own arm to grasp her fingers in his, in secret, so that they are holding hands like children, undetected. Both are quite well dressed: Alexis is wearing a pale gold jacket of soft, fine wool, and a black turtleneck sweater, and Brigit is wearing a cashmere suit with a dark fur collar, and silver earrings that swing heavily against her thin cheeks; if people glance at her it is probably because they have never seen her wearing earrings before. Nor have they seen her so striking, so well groomed. *Is* that Brigit Stott . . . ?

With Alexis Kessler?

But it must be an accident.

For the past several days there were rumors that the reading would be postponed: St. Dennis had left Woodslee suddenly to fly back to London, having resigned his position; St. Dennis had had a breakdown of some sort; St. Dennis had had a heart attack, a stroke, a severe case of the intestinal flu now making the rounds of Woodslee, a quarrel with the administration, a failure of nerve. Brigit telephoned Oliver Byrne to see if there was any truth to the rumors and he denied them angrily, charging his "enemies" with slander. Over the weeks St. Dennis has made a varied impression on people. Some are struck by his warmth and kindness and his generosity with his time; others are hurt that he is aloof with them and interrupts their questions with rude questions of his own. One of Brigit's students, a young man named Todd Andress, who has committed much of St. Dennis's work to memory — he has a photographic memory, evidently — has visited St. Dennis in his office at the university and also in his apartment, and cannot stop praising him, rattling off St. Dennis's terse, gnomic remarks in a high excited voice; Andress is keeping a journal of his conversations with St. Dennis. Other students are uncomfortable with the old man because he so frequently murmurs Oh yes, yes, to their questions, nodding gravely, blinking at them through the slightly magnified lenses of his glasses. He is bored with them all, they say. No, but his mind is elsewhere — he is preoccupied with his own life, with his own work. Perhaps he is homesick for England . . . ? Or is he merely deaf? Nodding courteously, he gives the impression of both hearing what people say and not hearing. And then there have been times when he's been quite impatient and has cut short an interview, saying he has an appointment elsewhere. Warren Hochberg has declared himself immensely pleased with St. Dennis. Rumors of the old man's drinking, his probable alcoholism? — totally unfounded. A rumor that he had telephoned the airport at Champlain the very next morning after the Byrnes' party in his honor to inquire about flights back to England — ridiculous. He is very happy at Woodslee. Very happy. (Vivian Hochberg telephoned Brigit one morning back in October to invite her to a dinner party that very evening because, as she said — Vivian Hochberg being, as everyone knows, a remarkable woman — Albert St. Dennis, who was the guest of honor, had specifically asked that Brigit be included in the party; Brigit and that young man with the amazing blond hair, the pianist, what was his name . . . ? Brigit had declined the invitation, and Vivian had not troubled to plead with her or to disguise the subtle relief in her voice; Brigit and Vivian know each other as well as they care to, and there is no need for dissembling. But it was a surprising call and Brigit was quite moved by St. Dennis's interest in her.) Warren is officially pleased with his Distinguished Professor of Poetry, but Gowan Vaughan-Jones is rather hurt that St. Dennis hasn't much time for him — he had planned a series of taped interviews in conjunction with his study of twentieth-century poetics, and had even arranged with the editors of several prestigious journals for the publication of these interviews. But midway in the first session St. Dennis suddenly got to his feet and, coughing rather badly, cigarette in hand, told Gowan that he had nearly forgotten a luncheon date with an old friend — he was very sorry, but the interview would have to be postponed. (Gowan tells everyone the story, his expression mournful, his eyes moist as a dog's eyes, and receives their sympathy with a look of abject resignation; he is oblivious to the fact that, behind his back, his colleagues imitate his voice and repeat the story with extravagant variations and embellishments, and even Brigit, who finds Vaughan-Jones both pitiful and alarming (he is, after all, a widely published scholar, an expert in his field) cannot help but laugh at the Vaughan-Jones routines her colleagues do.)

Lewis Seidel has reported better luck, having taken St. Dennis to lunch at the Faculty Club a few times, and even down to the Riverview one Friday afternoon, where the old man was rather flattered by having been surrounded by young people, and where he had drunk innumerable glasses of beer as round after round was brought to the crowded table; but Lewis has complained that St. Dennis evades his questions and has fallen into the habit of talking without regard for his audience, of simply droning on and on . . . interesting monologues in themselves, sometimes fascinating, touching upon his mild friendship with the Huxleys, his boyhood interest in astronomy, his love of Agatha Christie and Dorothy Sayers mysteries, his old hobby of bird-watching, which he wished he might revive here in North America, if only his legs weren't so uncertain and his eyes so weak; his collection of biographies of Newton, which he regretted not having brought along to Woodslee; his love of jigsaw puzzles, of mushrooms and garlic and butter sauce, of toffee, of chocolate-coated biscuits, of Hollywood musicals of the forties; his hatred of travel by air and by car; his good-natured envy of American plumbing and heating and housing and salaries; his vehement hatred of the welfare state; his slightly slurred and perhaps, for that reason, not entirely serious expression of a wish that a "Stalin or a Hitler" might come along to "save" England; his love of Thomas Hardy's later poetry (which he recited at great length); his old quarrel with certain Krishnamurti disciples among his circle of friends; his old quarrel — a lover's quarrel, really — with the nominalists; his fascination with geology and the exploration of the earth and of space; his declaration that *The Explorers* was not only his own best work but the most important poem of the twentieth century, and that no one understood it, and that he intended to write a fifth section to extend the poem's metaphorical base so that it included space exploration — if only he were young enough, if only he were another person entirely, and might explore the "eternal silence of those infinite spaces" himself! Monologues sometimes delivered in a bright loose manner, a boy's smile raying across his face, but sometimes slow and dull and cold and slurred and really not very pleasant, so that his listeners shivered, wishing themselves elsewhere, while they nodded solemnly and made an effort to commit these strange words to memory.

It was said of St. Dennis that he began his day early, shortly after six, that he had fruit juice and coffee and a cigarette at his desk, that he worked steadily until noon — always writing: notes, drafts of essays, translations, reviews, prefaces, a journal, and of course poems, always poems, old drafts revised, new poems blocked out, even poems that were already published reworked and re-imagined; if he hadn't a luncheon engagement he made a simple meal for himself, usually soup (mushroom or vegetarian vegetable) and cheese (cheddar cheese of the mildest variety) and bread (rye or whole wheat), and then he returned to his work, to mail that must be answered, which he felt to be a necessity — an obligation. Always letters, most of them requesting favors of one kind or another, some enclosing poems for his comments: and he was courteous enough to reply to them all, or so it was said. Lewis Seidel remarked to him that his energies were being drained by these self-promoting strangers, these flatterers and con men; it would be wiser to hire a secretary to answer them and wisest of all merely to throw the letters away without reading them. St. Dennis had replied (or so it was said: Brigit got this story at many removes from the occasion) that, in *that* case, he would never have come to Woodslee University and would never have made Mr. Seidel's acquaintance.

He works an eight- to ten-hour day, either in his apartment or
in his office at the university (where he spends most of Tuesday
and Thursday afternoons); he is besieged by invitations for the
evenings and is forced — with genuine regret, it seems — to decline most of them. A gentleman, hostesses say; a typical English snob, say those whose hospitality has been rejected. After
Vivian telephoned Brigit it occurred to her that perhaps St. Dennis might really like to see her again . . . and so she wrote him a
note, asking if she and her friend Alexis Kessler might take him
to dinner one night; he had replied at once, warmly, but insisted
that they come to *his* apartment; and so they had, arriving sepa-
rately, elated and apprehensive and, as the curious evening wore
on, rather dismayed at St. Dennis's behavior — the dinner of
smoked salmon and caviar and marinated mushrooms and rye
bread with margarine was well-prepared, though oddly chosen,
and the wine — a white German Rhine — was superb; but St.
Dennis drank too much, in fact had drunk too much before Brigit
and Alexis even arrived, his monologues were sleepy, near-
inaudible, and it alarmed Brigit that he seemed to be addressing
them as if he knew them very well, as if they were old, intimate
friends who already knew most of what he was talking about or
alluding to; as if, in short, they were someone other than Brigit
Stott and Alexis Kessler. At the very end of the evening he had,
however, wakened sufficiently to apologize for having bored
them, and for the dinner, which he realized was somehow incomplete, lacking something — vegetables, of course! — there
were carrots and fresh spinach and broccoli in one of the com-
partments of the refrigerator but he wasn't accustomed to the
refrigerator and had overlooked them — would Brigit and Alexis
please forgive him? And allow him to make up for the evening by
coming to dinner again soon? Naturally they had protested that
the dinner had been excellent, the evening's conversation excellent, there was no need for him to apologize, and it was they who

wished to repay him, sometime soon, by taking him out to dinner or, if he preferred, by having him to dinner at Brigit's apartment, which was only a few blocks away. . . . St. Dennis appeared to find this a delightful suggestion; he accepted at once. They suggested a day in two weeks' time, a Wednesday evening, and St. Dennis nodded enthusiastically, and when the evening came he simply didn't show up and neither Brigit nor Alexis dared telephone him. It crossed Brigit's mind that he hadn't really heard the details of the invitation and so could not be blamed for having failed to come.

They ate the dinner themselves and finished the wine and made love in Brigit's bed and, for several hours afterward, talked of old age, of their mutual fears of senility, and cancer, and the gradual atrophy of the body; they talked of their work and of St. Dennis's achievement; of friendships that had blossomed and died; of past loves; of how much they liked St. Dennis without knowing exactly why — was it because he was so famous, or because he was a genuinely lovable person? — was it possible, really, to distinguish between the two? — and did he suffer because of this confusion? In her lover's arms Brigit spoke of fears she would never dare admit to in other contexts; she told Alexis that it had become painfully obvious to her, during the evening at St. Dennis's, how little people can do for each other, ultimately — how little they can do most of all for someone that age, who has already lived his life, who is wrapped about in a cocoon of memories, hypnotized by his own voice. "People talk and other people appear to listen. People talk to relieve their loneliness and other people appear to listen to relieve their loneliness. Isn't that it? One by one they die of loneliness, they're suffocating of loneliness, but they don't know it. . . . Or do you think they know it?"

Alexis murmured a sleepy reply, pressing against her. His breath was warm, his embrace warm, one of his legs was resting partway over one of hers, his penis stirred and hardened and ebbed again, pressed against her thigh; he murmured what sounded like *Yes* but Brigit could not be sure.

Now she sits beside him listening to St. Dennis's slow thin beautiful voice speak of love, of marriage, of death, of art. Her eyes are still stinging with tears. "All art is absurdity," St. Dennis has declared. There is a melancholy puckishness about the old man. Far from being shy before this impressive crowd, St. Dennis is addressing them as if he were speaking casually and frankly to a small gathering of acquaintances. Ah, a remarkable man! Perfectly in control. He is not the noble ruin Brigit had feared; he is clever, he is even a little theatrical, there is no mistaking his genius. Diminutive and appearing shy, he stands behind the lectern, reading poems of loss, of grief, of bitter despair; he is mortal in every syllable, utterly vulnerable, a widower confessing to his bewilderment at the cessation of his own despair; a man among men, questioning his own humanity. His poems are stark as exposed bone. They are almost too painful to be shared. (They appear to be new poems — in manuscript — evidently written here in Woodslee.) The absurdity of poetry: its risks, its possibilities, its necessary defeats. Its explorations. Its occasional beauty. (Brigit's own work is temporarily stalled. It is balked, stopped, stuck; it may never move forward again. She wonders if it was not out of despair at her continuing failure to write her novel that she fell in love with Alexis Kessler, and fell in love with him so helplessly.)

Brigit, pressing against her lover as if for consolation, inhaling his scent, squeezing his fingers between her own, listens as St. Dennis tells them of the death of passion and the metamorphoses of the human spirit beyond even the point of despair, and the need of the poet, if he is to survive, to impoverish his own youthful language in the service of a simplicity as utterly ruthless and inevitable as death itself.

Poetry is an absurdity but a gorgeous absurdity: like civilization, like love, like the adventure of human life itself. A risk that must be taken. A risk that must be taken again and again, as long as we live.

My God, Brigit thinks, *I love you. . . .*

It is Alexis she loves.

Her spirit seems to have shifted from her, her center of gravity seems to lie outside her, now, yearning outward, desiring only to plunge into this man, this stranger.

She thinks of him constantly.

He is close as her pulse beat, close as the interior of her eyelid, the roof of her mouth. Away from him she experiences at times a sensation of actual vertigo at the thought of him, the memory of him — his voice, his eyes, his mouth, his hands, his body, his love-making — the incredible fact of him, that he should exist at all and that he should love her. It seems at such times that the two of them have known each other most of their lives, and that everyone must know of their love; when in fact no one in Woodslee knows or could guess. They have been discreet, secretive and cunning and jealous of their knowledge of each other.

Since that night in September Brigit has come to think of Alexis Kessler as the center of her life — not only her life at the present time, but her life in its entirety. The past has become insignificant. Her marriage — her feeling for Stanley — her feeling for one or two other men — have become meager and anemic and irrelevant to her truest self. In a sense the past is a delusion, an error. She has never known anyone like Alexis.

Nor is it likely that there is anyone like him, another man quite like him. He is the center of her imagination no less powerfully than if she had created him herself. Beyond the small, tight, intense universe of their passion the rest of the world is transparent, not altogether real. Once or twice he has asked her about Stanley, about her marriage; is it true she isn't yet divorced . . . ? And she tells him hurriedly that the marriage doesn't matter, belongs to the past, she can't believe in it or remember her husband, not now, not any longer, not when she is with him.

"But you're married even now, even this minute. . . ." Alexis says slowly, as if bemused.

"No. Not really," Brigit whispers.

For years no one had approached her. She had allowed no one near. There were men, there were even friends of Stanley's, and even a few men here at Woodslee, but she kept herself from them, fastidious and virginal and rather hateful — she had felt a certain revulsion at the mere thought of men, of love, of being touched again. What had passed between Stanley and her had been a kind of love, after all, and she wanted no more of it.

("Why don't you die," Stanley had whispered once, lying beside her, the two of them exhausted and tranquil in the midsummer heat. "You're suicidal. You know you've always been suicidal. I promise not to lift a finger to stop you.")

She never thinks of her husband now. She thinks only of Alexis.

The edginess of early girlhood has returned and she finds herself anxious about mirrors — dreads glancing into them and yet cannot resist, needing to know how she appears to her lover. It no longer matters very much what she knows herself to be from the inside; her spirit has indeed shifted outside her body.

"I love you," one of them says.

"I love you," says the other.

No one had approached her for years. Yet Brigit and Alexis had risen as if their names had been called and, without knowing how it happened, they moved into each other's arms. She embraced him hungrily, he embraced her, they found themselves laughing with the surprise and the ease of it. Becoming lovers had been less difficult than having a conversation. . . . Alexis said to her afterward, "I would have been afraid to touch you," and she had said, "I would have been afraid to touch *you*," as if they had not, in fact, had to touch each other at all; as if neither had had to make the first move. Upstairs in Brigit's apartment, after Lewis Seidel had dropped them off, they had had several drinks and talked for a while about their lives here at Woodslee, their mutual dissatisfaction, their vague teasing hopes — they had not talked for very long, Brigit realized afterward — and then for some reason they had smiled strangely and rose and simply stepped into each other's arms.

And so it had begun.

The following weekend they left Woodslee after Brigit's class on Friday afternoon and drove to Montreal, where they stayed at the Sherbrooke Arms, not far from Mt. Royal. They walked for hours along the windy streets with their arms around each other, reckless and exhilarated. They were one hundred miles away from Woodslee, in a city of strangers. They were in a foreign country and in a very foreign city: the French spoken in Montreal did not resemble the French Brigit had learned in college and had spoken, with some awkward, minimal success, in France. Alexis, here in Montreal, speaking French rapidly and gracefully with waiters and shopkeepers and hotel personnel, seemed to Brigit a different person — less self-conscious than he was at Woodslee, less flamboyant and pretentious. There were many men on the streets near the hotel and on Rue de la Montagne, some not so young, and none so attractive as Alexis, who dressed as colorfully as he, and his raw, abrasive, delighted laughter did not seem so startling. She no longer flinched when he burst into laughter as he often did; she found herself joining him. She too had a robust, hearty laugh, a way of laughing with her entire body, that she had not experienced for some time.

She had forgotten how much she liked to walk. How much she liked to walk in cities. It did not matter where, it did not matter what she found to look at, or into — the mere fact of walking was a delight in itself, a joy. At Woodslee she had sometimes walked along the river or in the arboretum west of the university, but she had never cared to walk in the residential sections, however attractive they were, because she was likely to meet someone who knew her, who would invariably feel the need to involve her in a strained, pointless conversation about the university or the weather or the scandal of local politics; and she had not liked to walk in the downtown area, which was becoming rather shabby. The only thing she really missed about New York City, apart from two or three friends, was her habit of taking long aimless solitary walks to clear her mind, during which she had plotted her way to a new life, erasing her errors and beginning again, unhusbanded, virginal, innocent. These long hours of walking had cultivated her interior voice until it seemed to her, at times, that she lived only in that voice, in that constant harangue, and would be extinguished if it were ever silenced.

Alexis also took great pleasure in walking, and he expressed surprise that Brigit — who was so slightly built — should be able to walk for hours without tiring. (It had seemed to Brigit that Alexis would tire quickly: she had seen him yawn so often at parties.) He was fascinated by people, as Brigit was, drawing near them to overhear their conversations, taking note of the qualities of their voices. He did not pay attention to what they said, as Brigit did; he cared for their intonations, for the music of their words. At times he was rather blatant about eavesdropping and did not seem to notice that others were aware of him. He carried himself with a peculiar aggressive innocence that Brigit had never seen in anyone else; it was one of the qualities in him that had seemed to her so annoying in the past, and now seemed so powerfully enchanting.

Like a child, he was insatiably curious. He found nothing dull in a street of ordinary stores; he enjoyed window-shopping without regard for the sort of merchandise he was looking at. He liked the pretentious boutiques in the ghastly underground palaces that tunneled beneath the city, honeycombed with innumerable stores and restaurants and cinemas. He loved to browse in bookstores, as Brigit did, and in record stores, and he loved to shop — he bought a two-volume set of Mozart's letters for Brigit, and a recording of Elliott Carter's *Variations for Orchestra*, he insisted upon buying Brigit the suit with the muskrat fur collar and bought himself a winter overcoat with a near-identical collar; he bought hand-tooled leather boots for himself on Rue de la Montagne, and tried to talk Brigit into buying an immense purse for herself in the same store; he bought her the earrings at a silversmith's in a basement shop near McGill University and another ring for himself; he encouraged her to buy a new pair of shoes with unusually high, chunky soles — he did not like the more conventional shoes Brigit customarily wore — and to buy a forty-five-dollar blouse of silky beige, though Brigit protested it was impractical and not her style at all. He insisted she make an appointment at the beauty salon in their hotel to have her hair cut and styled — couldn't she see how unbecoming her hair was, grown out so unevenly about her delicate face? Didn't she care that she was not nearly so attractive as she might be? He suggested, too, that she have her hair tinted. Silver streaks in dark hair were attractive, but not gray; there was no need, he said, for her to look years older than she was. She accepted his gifts with some reluctance; she bought the blouse but not the shoes, and not the purse; she agreed to have her hair styled but not tinted. She insisted upon paying for half the hotel bill, which was considerable. In the end, back at Woodslee, he had to borrow fifty dollars from her for grocery money, to last until October 1.

They spent a lazy Sunday in the hotel room, in bed most of the morning, drinking tea and eating croissants, reading through newspapers. It was extraordinary, how little the newspapers meant to them. . . . Politicians whose names Brigit had never heard of, photographed in attitudes of self-righteous anger; the president of the postal union calling for a general walkout; Quebecers' demands in regard to something called the "bilingual" bill; a speech made by a Progressive Conservative candidate for Parliament; a scandal involving a provincial health minister; the charges made by an NDP candidate that mercury poisoning among Quebec Indians was not being taken very seriously by Ottawa. It was disturbing in one way and reassuring in another, that the headlines and the articles and the photographs related to so little that Brigit and Alexis knew. "We should move to Canada," Alexis said gaily. "Nothing means anything here — we could be alone, we could be ourselves. There would be nothing significant to think about here. It's like passing through the looking glass and coming into another world. Or like waking up in Lilliput."

There were several articles on the crisis in unemployment and inflation, which Brigit scanned but could not take seriously; apart from New York City, Montreal seemed to her the most demonstrably and ostentatiously rich city she had ever visited. The high-rise apartment buildings, the hotels, the expensive restaurants and boutiques and nightclubs, the numerous people like themselves, tourists like themselves, strolling aimlessly and happily along the hilly streets and into the center city. . . . Even Canadian money — two-dollar bills, saffron-colored bills, fifty-dollar bills illustrated like comic strips — seemed unreal, like Monopoly money.

"It's hard to take seriously," Brigit agreed. "But I suppose we must."

"Why?" Alexis asked.

They lay together atop the enormous untidy bed and talked. Brigit and Alexis. Registered under the name Kessler for the sake of convenience only; in an excellent room on the fifteenth floor of the hotel, with a lovely view of the lower city. They kissed, they stroked each other, they yawned and talked and lit cigarettes, and stretched lazily, and smiled, and found themselves inordinately happy. Alexis spoke of his plans for the song cycle based on St. Dennis's poems; he had completed one of the songs so far and was fairly satisfied with it, though he hesitated to show it to anyone. He spoke of his uncertain position at Woodslee. It baffled him that any of his colleagues should hate him enough to send him anonymous letters or make anonymous late-night telephone calls, as they sometimes did, or spread amazing rumors about him; worst of all was the knowledge that people wanted him fired — didn't they know how much he depended upon his job, not only financially but emotionally?

"Emotionally?" Brigit asked, uncomprehending.

"Yes. Of course. I require a job, a place to report to, colleagues, that sort of thing," Alexis said. "I'm very fond of my students. Most of them, anyway. . . . Why are you looking at me like that?"

"I wouldn't have thought you felt that way."

"But why not? Why shouldn't I feel that way?"

Brigit kissed him, and stroked his hair, and could not think how to reply. She believed he was telling the truth now — he spoke so simply, so directly — and yet it did not seem quite possible: Alexis Kessler saying such things?

"Don't you like the idea of a community too?" Alexis asked. "The sort of thing Oliver makes speeches about. . . . Of course I can't stand most of the people at Woodslee but the idea is superb and I have a kind of Platonic belief in . . . in some sort of essence. . . . Don't you feel the same way? I've given up on my family, I don't believe in marrying and having children, but I think there's something very real about people sharing certain values, certain beliefs — The community of art, of artists — Don't you agree?"

It had not occurred to Brigit in quite that way but she supposed that, yes, she did agree. When the frightening bouts of exhaustion had overtaken her — and now, now that she and Alexis were lovers, they had nearly stopped, thank God — it was the knowledge that she had to be somewhere, she had to meet with colleagues or students, she *had* to get up and get dressed and be presentable that drew her up, gave her the energy, however feeble, to return to the world. And she did like that world. She complained, like everyone else; but she liked it; she knew who she was in it; it may have saved her life more than once without her conscious knowledge.

But it was not a world, a community, in which Brigit felt altogether comfortable. Nor did Alexis. They could not speak openly of their feelings to their colleagues, since everything they said — especially if it was critical or abrasive or mildly "interesting" — was repeated and magnified and distorted. If Brigit expressed temporary despair over her marriage or her writing ("Your writing?" Alexis asked in surprise. "I would have thought your writing came easily to you, that's the impression you give. . . ."), in a few days everyone in Woodslee would be saying she was suicidal, or had even attempted suicide; more than once people approached her on the street or in the supermarket or in the university library with expressions of sober restraint, even of heartfelt compassion, wanting to take her hand to console her or give her courage or — or whatever — she had no idea what was going on most of the time. ("But I'd always heard that you did things impulsively, even bluntly," Alexis said, "even . . . well, brutally. That *is* the impression you give.") And of course her colleagues were quick to detect, and to resent, any indication of superiority on her part. ("Oh, we're both hated because we consider ourselves superior to Woodslee," Alexis laughed, yawning. "But what can we do, my love? — we *are* superior.") On the contrary, Brigit said emphatically, she was rather in awe of her colleagues, especially in the English department — the compromises they had made with mediocrity, both professionally and domestically. There wasn't a man in the department, with the possible exception of two or three of the senior staff members and Stanislaus Chung, who wasn't really bright — even brilliant — or had been, certainly, at one time: Brigit knew, she had made it a point of reading their books and essays and reviews. She *wanted* to know and to admire her colleagues. But something had happened to them. Something very sad seemed to have happened. In mid-career most of them had simply . . . stopped. Stopped reading widely, stopped thinking; stopped writing anything of more than routine academic importance. Certainly there were exceptions: Gowan Vaughan-Jones, Lewis himself, one or two of the younger people. But in general their professional lives were shabby suburban gardens in which, beneath an old strip of canvas, one found a discarded child's rake; in a clump of burdock and milkweed one found an old boot; the place hummed with activity and life, the incessant jumping about of grasshoppers going nowhere. And then their domestic lives: those brain-obliterating marriages! The men had married (Brigit hoped not deliberately) women distinctly less intelligent than they; women who did not, indeed could not, share their intellectual interests — who sometimes smiled wanly and said, Oh *that?* — it's all beyond me, what he does; or *That?* All that fuss about nothing? — women whose conversations about households, vacations, children, hairdos, recipes, local scandals, induced in Brigit jaw-wrenching yawns she tried gallantly to swallow. She *liked* these women, some of them were truly fine people, like Marilyn Byrne, and Mina Housley, and poor Faye Seidel . . . but she simply could not tolerate their company, and she sensed their dislike and disapproval of her life.

"You're lonely," Alexis said bluntly. "Like me."

"Is that it?" Brigit said, charmed.

She had fallen in love with Alexis because he was so vibrant, so attractive, so impetuous, so gentle: when he had kissed her, that first time, in her kitchen, he had half-lifted her from her chair and stood above her, gripping her thin shoulders, daringly, yet almost brotherly, with a physical compassion she no longer associated with men. How can people say you are sardonic and flippant and arrogant, Brigit wanted to protest to him, burying her face in his neck, hugging his sides, when you are one of the

most . . . the most congenial people I have ever met. . . . His
sexual grace, his sexual agility, were far less astonishing than his
simple frank unanticipated friendliness.

They lay about the hotel room, and then showered together,
and dressed, and went for a long walk, up to the mountain and
along the Rue des Pins, and back around again to Sherbrooke;
they stopped at the Ritz-Carlton and had a late lunch and several drinks; gripping their fingers together tightly, they hurried
back to their room, kissing in the elevator, flushed and breathless
and apprehensive. It was all so new; it seemed to Brigit experimental and provisionary; she supposed she was opening herself
to a great hurt, but there was no time, she hadn't even the breath
to draw back, to contemplate. . . .

Alexis reminded her of no one. No other man she'd known, let
alone loved.

And then there was his striking appearance: that beautiful face.

And his slim, well-proportioned body; his modest but strong
shoulder and arm muscles; his hard thighs; his slender pale hands
and feet. (Which were not grimy. Which were clean and nearly
as soft as her own.) She kissed him and caressed him and stroked
him almost with a sort of greed, a hunger she hadn't known was
in her.

When he told her she was a very attractive woman, when he
insisted upon the fact, fairly laughing at her refusal to believe
him, she felt, queerly, as if she were deceiving him: as if someday
he would find her out and no longer care for her. And at the
same time she could see herself drifting into vanity . . . outfitting
herself, acquiring the right make-up, the tricky little accessories,
that might flatter her appearance and make her seem younger.
"But what I really love about you," she said, quite sincerely, lying
with him naked on the oversized magisterial bed, "is the fact that
I can talk to you about anything, and you don't judge."

"Of course I don't judge," Alexis said. "At least not *you*, Brigit."

Their intimacy encouraged her: she began to speak, hesitantly at first, of her writing — which was after all the center of her life, or had been before she met him. Her novel. Her wretched novel. Which she had been working on for years, and which still seemed so far from completion. . . . She had labored at two separate drafts, and there were drawers filled with unused notes, hundreds of sheets of paper, brain-swirlings scribbled at four in the morning that were unintelligible at dawn and never again read but stuffed in the drawer along with everything else, all a great heartbreaking mess. Virginia Woolf noted in her diary that her work, her ceaseless mental activity, was like a strip of pavement over an abyss; Brigit felt she knew what the metaphor meant. The work was a triumph over despondency, but if the work itself became despondency, how could one be saved . . . ?

She wanted desperately to finish the novel, she told Alexis. Yet she couldn't write. It was easier to plan course lectures, to reread material she'd read a dozen times already, it was far easier to invite students into her office for "conferences" on their "major papers," no matter if they took up hours of her time drifting onto personal subjects: their parents, their current loves, their gripes about other professors. Even correcting examinations was oddly pleasurable. It was so definite, so real, so pragmatic, it had immediate consequences, it was after all a part of her professional responsibility. . . . Teaching was addictive, and so was the busyness, the fuss, the exaggeration of small things that characterizes the academic life.

But why can't you finish your novel? Alexis asked.

She had no idea. Her very desperation got in her way, made her anxious, weak. . . . The novel was to evoke the Norfolk of her childhood and girlhood, it was to be a feat of memory, an homage to the past, not sharply critical and analytical like her first two novels, but subtler . . . slower, less pointed, flowing and sprawling like life itself . . . something generous, something complete. A celebration, as St. Dennis said.

A novel about childhood, Alexis murmured.

Well — not really about childhood. About much more than that.

Alexis poured them both drinks. Straight Scotch, very powerful, very soothing.

After a while he said he hadn't any feelings about his own childhood. He was inclined to think all that was overrated — the so-called gifts of perception children possess. And then it had been so boring, to be watched constantly; to be under the thumbs of two adults from whom you had to hide, naturally, your most important thoughts. His parents were conventional people, his father was an executive with Prudential Life, his mother an amateur pianist and organizer of musical groups, that sort of thing. He rarely thought of them and they had long since stopped despairing over him.

At this point in his life, Alexis said, the music that excited him was more intellectual than emotional. Memories of his childhood in Waterbury, Connecticut, meant nothing to him because they had no application to his work. Anyway, he was temperamentally inhospitable to nostalgia — what was nostalgia but a sentimental slander on reality? "Music has had enough emotion, it has been drenched in emotion," he said.

"You sound very pragmatic," Brigit said slowly.

"I am nothing if not pragmatic."

"And yet everyone thinks. . . . You give the impression of. . . ."

"Yes, what?" Alexis asked sharply.

But Brigit could not say. That Alexis Kessler was thought to be reckless, slovenly, lazy, debauched, willfully wasteful of his talent and energy and youth. . . . It seemed no longer possible to her that anyone should really believe such nonsense. Brigit laughed and drank her Scotch and refused to consider it. Instead she asked him about his boyhood. If not his childhood, his boyhood. Tell me, she begged, about the first girl you fell in love with.

"Girl?" said Alexis calmly.

No, it was a boy; a boy of seventeen or eighteen; an assistant conductor at the New England Conservatory, a prodigy, sallow-skinned, already balding, with a pinched, meticulous expression, whose smiles were cataclysmic — Alexis was eleven or twelve at the time and lived for those smiles. Sick with love for the better part of a year, he was, and though it was a small lifetime ago he remembered vividly the humiliations and ecstasies of that infatuation; he dreamed of the boy sometimes, even now. . . . What had become of him? Oh, a quite ordinary career, a conductor with a Midwestern symphony orchestra, St. Louis and then Kansas City and then Alexis had lost track of him, no longer interested. He, Alexis, had been the real prodigy, a pampered darling, a little prince, and it had always seemed to him, in the years that followed, quite likely that the young man had been attracted to him . . . but neither had dared approach the other.

"If I saw him now I wouldn't even bother to cross the street to him," Alexis said slowly. He shivered. "It's extraordinary, isn't it, how we change. How passion fades. . . ."

Brigit's first love was a boy of about fifteen whose father was involved in city and county politics, as Brigit's father had been; she must have been twelve years old at the time she fell in love with him. He was a high-school student, she a seventh-grader. Ludicrous and pitiful, her fantasies of him, her prowling after him downtown as he walked along, oblivious to her, in a group of boys his own age. His name had been Ronnie. Ronnie Brooker. (That name had the power, still, to make her pulse jump — for a moment.) He and his friends had been loud and rather homely and exceptionally profane, even obscene; they had shouted filthy words at girls and at one another, laughing maniacally, and Brigit had excused it all — hadn't understood it, perhaps. She had loved him for over a year. He had worn a certain maroon jacket, a canvas jacket with *Norfolk JC's* stitched in gold on the back, and she had loved that jacket, had looked for it in the crowds that milled about the high-school steps and on the streets, on Saturdays, and at the roller rink, and. . . . She laughed, hiding her face in her hands. It had been hideous, that infatuation, but also rather wonderful. She had never forgotten him. Whenever she went back home she looked his name up in the telephone directory and checked his address and it was always the same — he'd married a girl in his senior class, they had several children who were probably grown up now, he didn't know the name "Brigit Stott" at all. He knew nothing of her, nothing.

But the most important person of her girlhood, Brigit said, wasn't that boy; it was a girl named Louellen. They had known each other from first grade to tenth grade, they had been best friends for nine years, and now — so many years later — Brigit sometimes dreamed of her. For a long time she had simply forgotten her. The youngest of seven children, her father an alcoholic, a former miner, always on relief, her mother — Louellen's poor mother — an employee at one of the canning factories. Her six brothers and sisters always in trouble. Louellen had been skinny and big-eyed and surprisingly funny, and though Brigit's parents had known nothing of the shoplifting expeditions the girls had gone on — mainly to Woolworth's and Grant's — they had sensed something dangerous in Louellen, and had disapproved of her family because of their poverty; so they hadn't encouraged Brigit to invite Louellen home. And they had never allowed Brigit to spend the night with Louellen. But the girls had been closer than sisters, they had loved each other very much, had exchanged innumerable gifts — purses, scarves, games, cheap bracelets — and were known to be inseparable. One Christmas, Brigit spent five dollars on Louellen, an extraordinary sum; she bought Louellen a pair of fur-lined gloves. Louellen in turn gave Brigit a topaz ring that had belonged to her grandmother. Topaz! The setting was rather cheap but the stone was genuine. When the parents discovered it they had wanted Brigit to return it to Louellen, but Louellen wouldn't take it back, and Brigit had not known what to do. There were many telephone calls. There was a great deal of weeping. The Stotts were upset and vaguely insulted, and Louellen's parents were angry. In the end Brigit had been allowed to keep the ring but she had not worn it, for fear of losing it, and for years it remained in her mother's bureau drawer, untouched; it was probably still there. "Sometimes it seems to me," Brigit said, "that I've never had another friend who meant that much to me. Something happened to Louellen's mother when we were in tenth grade and the family was broken up — she went to Baltimore to live with a married sister — and we wrote for a while but I never saw her again. Sometimes I dream I'm back in Norfolk, I'm a girl again, and Louellen is somewhere near, and it's very important that I find her — but I can't find her. We're at school, we're downtown, we're lost. I don't know where to look. I call her name but she doesn't answer. In the dream I start to cry, I make a wailing sound — like the wailing of an animal — I'm horrified by the sound of my own voice — but — but nothing happens, Louellen doesn't come. I wake up gasping for air. My body seems to be going through the motions of crying, of sorrow — but I don't know why — I don't understand it. I'm so upset that it takes me an hour or more to get back to sleep," she said, wiping at her eyes. "I really don't understand it."

Alexis seemed touched. "You wake up crying?"

"It's terrible," Brigit said. Then she laughed, not wanting to sound so plaintive. "But it hasn't happened for a while."

"I don't think I've cried for years," Alexis said slowly. "It must be something of an accomplishment. . . . Crying over a girl you haven't seen for so long, crying over a childhood friend: yes, it's an accomplishment. I've never cried over a friend. I don't even know what the word means: friend. Friendship. There have been lovers, of course; I've cried over them. But not for a long time and even while I was crying I think I knew how pointless it was, how futile and self-serving. Weeping for little Alexis, who can't have his own way all the time. . . ."

"You sound awfully hard," Brigit said uneasily.

"I'm not hard, not at all," Alexis said. He sat up and reached for his cigarettes. The new silver ring glinted on the third finger of his right hand, so large as to nearly cover his knuckle. He smelled of perspiration and cologne. "I'm realistic. I'm neutral. As you say, I'm pragmatic. . . . I'm much older than you are, Brigit."

St. Dennis in his dark three-piece suit, his white hair seeming to float softly about his face, his voice a little weaker now: a wry, convoluted poem about love, written decades ago, set in a run-down resort hotel in Southampton. Crabbed, cruel, jarring, astringent. Love's nostalgia. Yearning for the dark, for dark places, for paradise, for the mythic center of Schopenhauer's vast dream of a universe in which dreamers are dreamed and in turn dream — *must* dream or become extinct. The audience is quick to laugh at the satirical lines and Brigit laughs with them though her body wants to weep, her body is protesting, she is in love and cannot bear a slander upon love, not now, not now. And yet St. Dennis is witty and wise and she too will applaud him.

. . . Bucking, heaving, straining. Her heartbeat ferocious. She grasps at him, clutches at him. It cannot be happening to her, not after so long, so many years, she isn't certain she really wants it to happen to her: yet she is drawn irresistibly forward, her mouth open and twisted, saliva running down her chin. She loves him, she clutches at his hair, his shoulders, his back, she beats at him with a fist that breaks open, helpless, the fingers spread. . . . It cannot be happening. (Stanley, who loved her, who protested how he loved her, weeping as she wept, bewildered at his own cruelty, unable to comprehend his sudden outbursts of rage, derision, mockery, despair — Stanley saying she was tight-bodied, too shy, still virginal in her imagination, always resisting him — didn't she know how he loved her, how he wanted only to be certain she loved him?) With Alexis she is open and helpless and raw and heaving and it frightens her to know she must seem ugly to him, her mouth gaping, her eyes dilated, but she cannot stop, she does not want to stop, he embraces her tightly as if unaware of her terror. She is about to lose control of herself. Panicked, she falls back; she wants to escape; she does not trust him. She does not know him. Someone, a man, a stranger, a lover or a husband . . . someone is making love to her and she is frightened, she does not know him, does not know what will happen to her. With one part of her mind she dismisses it all as absurd: she has sloughed off any interest in men, in love, in enduring bouts of lovemaking and submitting herself to another person's judgment. She does not care for anyone's opinion of her and does not want to care. She is thirty-eight years old, she has been married, she has lived with a man for years and now lives alone and prefers to live alone and is happiest in the early morning when, alone, she looks out the window of her sixth-floor apartment and sees the sky lightening, sees the first of the birds — sparrows and juncos mainly — picking about the seed on her tiny balcony; she walks through the apartment, alone, rejoicing in her aloneness, she makes coffee, she considers working at her desk, she wonders if perhaps — if — perhaps today — if she might have better luck with her novel — if she dare attempt it — Alone, rejoicing in the quiet, walking about half-dressed, feeding the cat and unembarrassed at talking to it, isn't this Brigit who is independent of others' judgment, isn't this Brigit Stott as she knows herself from the inside, isn't this her truest self . . . ?

With one part of her mind she dismisses rudely even the proffered love of Alexis Kessler: she knows he is going to hurt her badly and she wants no new pain, not now. With another part of her mind, however, she is afraid that something will happen to her one day when she is alone, there is an overbright insistent elation to her aloneness, her emphatic independence; she is guilty of something — what? — and will be punished. Though a day might begin marvelously, she is always in danger of being

overcome by mid-afternoon by one of those spells of fatigue that
are so sudden and so profound as to seem, almost, blackouts.
Sleep during the day isn't soothing but very disturbing. She
knows there is something wrong with it, with her, she dreads the
heavy drugged deathly naps, she sinks into sleep as if into the
grave and has no faith, really, that she will wake again: and at the
moment of sleep it sometimes crosses her mind that she does not
care. Quick, fleeting, teasing, cruel. So cruel. You drink too
much, her mother might say; Stanley might say, aren't you taking
too many pills . . . ? You're suicidal. You always were. Die, why
don't you, I promise not to interfere, you know you can trust me.
Trust me. You know you can trust me. . . . Waking so brightly
but without any appetite, alone, guilty and uneasy and happy in
a perverse way, filled with a profound sense of unearned pleasure
if, among the birds on her balcony, she saw a cardinal or a gros-
beak or even a jay — there was a jay in the neighborhood with a
broken leg, poor doomed creature flopping about and flying with
difficulty — but unable to eat, unable even to think of food for
most of the day: so she drank coffee and smoked cigarettes, went
out to teach her classes or attend meetings, or stayed home on
the days she didn't teach, driven by a peculiar inexplicable energy, alert and attentive and perhaps a little edgy, hoping to avoid
the sudden weariness that called to her mind's eye the instant of
collapse of a piece of paper dropped upon a fire — at first whole,
white, complete, then scorched and blackened, and then, suddenly and irreparably, overcome by flame and destroyed. There
were days when she began to feel hungry only around eight
o'clock. Even then she prepared a meal only with reluctance and
an obscure sense of resentment, as if she were being forced to
cook for someone she despised. She often made scrambled eggs,
impatiently; the eggs scorched and stuck to the pan and she cried
aloud in vexation. If her black silky long-haired cat brushed
against her legs at such times she kicked it away. Damn it! Damn
you! But then she would be suddenly ravenous, she would sit at

the kitchen table and eat the eggs and two or three pieces of toast, her hands fairly shaking, her eyes watering, she would eat the entire meal in ten minutes after having eaten nothing in twenty-four hours; then suddenly she would feel bloated and sick, she would rise from the table, revulsed, again resentful, she would stagger to the sink and put the dishes and the pan in it to soak overnight, now she was reeling with exhaustion and wanted only to go to bed: nothing mattered except sleep. Her stomach was bloated, hard, her brain was emptied of blood, she went to bed and waited for sleep to overtake her at last, violent and merciful as a hammer blow. It seemed to her at such times that she was all stomach — the tight, heavy mass of food in her was all that remained of her, all that was vital and living. Her name, her personality, her work, her fate? — nothing mattered.

But Alexis mattered, Alexis matters; she does not dare tell him of these peculiar habits of hers though she has confessed other eccentricities (as he has confessed charming eccentricities of his own: a fanatic's sense of perfection in his work, for one thing). Since that night in September when they became lovers Brigit has believed herself changed, she is optimistic about changing, about becoming more normal, and she is not a person to take pride in quirky, self-destructive behavior. . . . He matters to her; he matters very much. With another man she would be self-conscious, but with Alexis there is no consciousness of self, there seem at times to be no self, no selves, at all. "I love you," he says, and she repeats, "I love you," and they clutch at each other, blind, eager, childlike, hopeful. Again, again, again. The first time they made love Brigit could not believe that it was happening to her, she wished to stand aside in despair, in hilarity, in awe, as she had sometimes stood aside with her husband, unable to remain in her body, unable to subordinate herself to him, to his strenuous exercises, his vexed and arduous will; but she found herself kissing and embracing and loving Alexis, absurdly grateful for him, astonished at his beauty — that a man should be so handsome, and not stupid! — she could not quite believe in him even as she loved him, writhing with pleasure beneath his body. No. Yes. No. She is terrified of losing control of herself; she is terrified that she will not lose control but will remain behind, unchanged. She knows she has felt pleasure before and has not been destroyed and yet it seems to her, each time, that she must stop — must not continue. That flurry of pleasure, spiraling upward suddenly and carrying her with it and throwing her body into convulsions: she will not endure it, she wants desperately to endure it, she clutches at her lover and cries aloud of her love for him, the madness of her love for him.

A horrible childlike wailing — she hears it, it fills the room, it cannot be disowned.

Afterward he wipes the tears from her face, sometimes kisses them away. But does not ask why she cries and why, afterward, she is so stricken, so mute.

Woodslee University, founded in 1848, with a chapter of Phi Beta Kappa established in 1879, is a private, richly endowed institution famous in the East for its high tuition, its liberal arts and fine arts departments, and its academic rigor; though much has been made in recent years of a lowering of standards. Students rejected at Harvard, Yale, and Princeton routinely come to Woodslee, as they come to Cornell, or the University of Pennsylvania, or Boston University, or even the state universities of New York. There are approximately six thousand undergraduates, two thousand graduate students, and a negligible number of part-time students. The majority are from New York City and its suburbs, though there are a number from the Midwest, and from California; there is a considerable foreign-student population. The university was built just to the west of the small town of Woodslee, New York, on the Powhatan River, and it covers more than three hundred acres of land, bounded on the east by Lake Champlain and on the west, irregularly, by the Adirondack Mountains. Much of the land is hilly and densely wooded and impenetrable. Woodslee is famous for its architectural beauty, the ferocity of its winters (porch thermometers in the area are equipped to register thirty degrees below zero), a certain ascetic zealousness among its most vocal faculty members and alumni, and a sense of uneasy privilege among its students, only minimally eroded by the "democratizing" influences of the sixties. It is an expensive school, how can one deny the fact? — despite a number of scholarship students (blacks, "the culturally deprived") it belongs to affluent America, and does that America justice.

The campus is impressive even to visitors who are not easily impressed. They marvel at the uniform Greek Revival architecture, the buildings made of limestone and granite from a once-rich quarry in nearby Kittyboro; and at the small marble chapel with an Italian rose window of stained glass; and the many graveled walks and curving graveled tree-lined drives; the old bell tower; the old Administration Building atop a steep hill; Brandford Hall with its innumerable columns; the new limestone-and-glass library, built in 1971 at a considerable (and controversial) cost, several hundred thousand dollars above the builder's original estimate; the palatial student union, overlooking a gully and a waterfall; Kerr Theater with its sweeping buttresses and startling peacock-blue glass; dormitories that resemble elegant old apartment buildings, on the outside at least; dining halls all plate glass and Italian terra cotta; the president's neo-Georgian home that rivals the White House itself in restrained splendor, and is in a far more attractive setting with the Adirondacks in the background, and blue spruce and enormous oaks and elms on all sides, and a garden of roses and ornamental trees and statuary nearby, open to the public. Even the graduate students' housing on the far side of campus, over by the physical education complex and the security division, is fairly attractive. There are bicycle paths, tennis courts, small lakes, granite benches, a monument commemorating the Battle of Powhatan in 1777. *Attendance at Woodslee University is a privilege that can be revoked at any time*, incoming freshmen read in their orientation week booklets.

A place of worship, Brigit Stott thought uneasily when she was first driven through the campus.

The 1977 census showed a population of approximately twenty-three thousand for the town of Woodslee, down several hundred from the previous census.

There has been an unemployment problem in the area now for some years: one of the textile mills was forced to close in the late sixties. The town is small and undistinguished; there is a fairly large park on the river with a Revolutionary War monument at its center; the new Bank of America is an impressive though rather small building; there are a single movie theater, a single downtown hotel, and a few motels at the edge of town, along Highway 9. There are a number of small factories — paper pulp; women's and girls' sweaters; fish packing; shoes. There is a single high school. Near the interstate expressway to the east is a new shopping mall — Powhatan Hills — and the usual gasoline stations and drive-in restaurants and motels, and several subdivisions featuring small modestly priced "colonials" and "ranch-type" houses.

Very few of the university faculty or administrators live on the east side. The most attractive part of town is just north of the university and across the river, Phoenix Heights. There, lots are wooded and sloping and usually quite large, lanes are unpaved, houses are occasionally hidden from sight behind massive stands of spruce and Scotch pine, there are fieldstone walls, there is a sense of privacy and great worth. The Byrnes live on Fairway Drive; their property is adjacent to the enormous lot owned by Judge Conroy, now retired, a prominent member of the Board of Governors of Woodslee University. (The Conroy house, a neo-Georgian mansion, was built in 1881 by one of the mill owners.) On the golf course of the Phoenix Hills Country Club there is an amazing house — owned by a Woodslee attorney, for whom it was especially designed by Frank Lloyd Wright — or one of his associates — consisting of numerous layers or slabs of limestone punctuated by panels of glass that appear to be blue-tinted; on their first Sunday drive north of town Sandra and Ernest Jaeger were much taken by this house, though Sandra came to feel, on subsequent drives, that it did not have the dignity of other homes in the area.

Just to the east of the university campus is another excellent residential area of two- and three-storied homes, most of them brick; it is here that the majority of the university people live. There are a number of extraordinary Victorian houses in the neighborhood, three or four Greek-revival houses, even an octagon-shaped house with a veranda circling it on its second floor, on Colfax Avenue, owned by Dr. Trevor of the fine arts department; the Trevors' house is of course coveted by everyone in the area. On Linwood Avenue a few houses down from the apartment building where Brigit Stott lives there is an exquisite Cape Cod, owned by the Haases; around the corner on Strathmore there is a possibly ugly but impressive old Victorian mansion with innumerable narrow windows and queer jutting angles and slopes of roof that appear to be rotting and a tiny sun porch whose window, facing the street, is completely clotted with plants whose leaves and tendrils seem to be growing flat against the glass — a home owned by the widow of the former Dean of Humanities, a woman who speaks of putting the house on the market every spring but then unaccountably, and maddeningly, never does: the house is so large, however, and the heating bills so high (it is speculated), that she will probably not be able to hold out much longer. At the other end of Strathmore is the Seidels' house, also generally coveted. Built in 1910, it is sprawling and asymmetrical and grandiose, a mixture of styles, Victorian and Tudor, with the customary small windows, and spires and peaks and turrets and stained glass in the stairwell, and wide oak archways, and high ceilings; a child's nightmare of a house, vaguely suggestive of Germanic fairy tales, its downstairs rooms always a little dark. The foyer, slate-floored, is overlarge and always chilly; it is impressive, however, like the wide staircase leading down to it. Faye

Seidel has placed a cobbler's bench just inside the door, and there is an antique coat rack with a cloudy mirror, and an umbrella stand picked up cheaply at a country auction — covered in deerskin, it is something of a curiosity. The house is agreeably shabby. Its rooms are smaller than one might suspect because of the wide archways and the oversized closets, and Lewis's study — just to the right of the front door — is almost tiny. Crammed with bookshelves, it is messy and shadowy, like a cave; it gives an air of being comfortable, however, and protective. The bathrooms were renovated when the Seidels bought the house some time ago — amazing, it has been fifteen years now — and the kitchen was completely redone, so that guests are moderately surprised, walking from the living room and the dining room into a kitchen of gay-colored surfaces, orange and lime counters, a floor covered with something slick as plastic, walls covered with tile suggestive of the Southwest. The stove and refrigerator are olive green; the big unsanded cypress table looks like a butcher's block; there is always an air about the Seidels' kitchen, during parties, of desperate good-natured merriment, a messiness that is somehow reassuring, as if part of the festivity.

It is partly the house, it is partly Lewis's marvelous exuberance, that account for the success of the Seidels' parties. They give a party in the fall, generally, and in the spring; occasionally they give a New Year's Eve party. Lewis has estimated that the house can hold one hundred quests if they spread out into all the downstairs rooms. A few parties have become legendary, having lasted throughout the night and into the morning; there are admiring tales still in circulation of long drinking bouts and dazzling repartee at the Seidels' when John Berryman came to Woodslee to give a poetry reading and stayed at the Seidels', and Lewis invited most of the university community to a party in Berryman's honor. There is always praise for Lewis's generosity with liquor and for the food Faye serves, which is more lavish and imaginative than the food offered by people — like the Housleys and the Hochbergs — who have considerably more money than Faye and Lewis.

Lewis loves parties. He is loud, merry, euphoric; it is only 9:15 and a half-dozen couples have already arrived, all friends of his, friends and colleagues, grateful to be invited to his party for Albert St. Dennis. He expects the old man himself at any moment: Oliver Byrne is to drive him over.

After the disturbing rumors of St. Dennis's ill health, the gossip about his drinking and his quarrel with someone in the administration and his threats to quit . . . what a marvelous surprise, the old man's performance tonight! Everyone is impressed. Everyone is pleased. The doorbell rings and Lewis hurries to the foyer, but his son, Harry, is already opening the door — who is it? — ah, just Gladys Fetler, pink-cheeked, her raincoat and plastic rain hat streaming wet. "You didn't walk all the way, did you?" Lewis cries, as much for the pleasure of hearing his own raised voice as for anything else; he takes Gladys's cold hand and grips it hard and introduces her to his son, who is seventeen, long-haired and shy, and already an inch taller than Lewis.

9:20. 9:25. The rain has turned to sleet; people hurry up the Seidels' walk, stamp their feet on the porch and in the foyer, shake their umbrellas, exclaim in high elated voices that driving conditions will be very bad tonight and it's only the first week of November. . . . George and Mina Housley, both out of breath. Joe and Mona Cuffe. The Bannons. Excited, Lewis shows them into the living room, asks them what drinks they would like. (There is a bar set up in one corner of the dining room, near the archway.) He is pleased to see them, pleased to see everyone. His friends. His colleagues. He squeezes Brad Keough's arm in passing and asks how he is and how he liked the reading? — excellent, wasn't it? Lewis's gray-red hair rises from his ruddy face in exuberant spurts; wide creasing smiles ray across his face, dis-

tending his nostrils. The time? Only 9:25. He is very excited. He
has been planning this party for weeks.

Already rather warm, he takes off his jacket and gives it to Faye
to hang up; he is wearing a dark blue shirt of some thick, coarse
texture, rather stylish, and a cream-colored necktie, and a new
pair of trousers. He carries a drink and a cigarette in his left hand,
so that his right hand is free. He squeezes someone's arm, he
slips his own arm around a friend's shoulder and leans into a
conversation — do you people all know one another? — does
anyone need a drink? — more ice? What did you think of St.
Dennis — wasn't the old boy superb tonight? Gowan Vaughan-
Jones, in a peculiar muddy-green corduroy jacket that is too large
for him, asks Lewis his opinion of St. Dennis's new poems and
Lewis can't ease away — Matt Ryerson is standing there, blocking the doorway — and so he lists the qualities in the new poems
that struck him as admirable, and those that struck him as egregious; as he has told Gowan in the past, the poems of St. Dennis's
he most approves of are those gray-lit sardonic *Motorway* sonnets, muted, mean, defiantly mundane: English poets are only
good, Lewis declares loudly, when they satirize their depleted
impoverished ludicrous tottering empire. The new poems were
moving, of course, and courageous, but the risks were too much
for the old man — didn't Gowan agree? — no? — but he must
agree the subject of bereavement is dangerous, and that St. Dennis — despite his characteristic control of language and those
brave brittle tricks he has mastered — faltered once or twice and
sank into sentimentality — ?

The doorbell rings. Lewis excuses himself and pushes through
the crowd. But Harry has opened the door and Faye is greeting
Pete Springer, who is alone, and Lewis rushes forward to shake
his old friend's hand, not wanting him to see he's disappointed.
Pete is a friend of ten or twelve years, a colleague Lewis's own
age, recently divorced; his breath smells of alcohol. What did he
think of the reading, Lewis asks. Pete shakes his head, embar-

rassed, and says he hadn't been able to make the reading; had been busy with something else. . . . Up the walk come two couples, at first Lewis can't even recognize them, then in the porchlight they turn into those new people, those young people, the Jaegers and the Swansons: he greets them himself and urges them inside, wants to make them feel at home, asks if they had any difficulty finding the house? — people often did. The girls are both very attractive. They are so young, and so eager to smile! The dark-haired one with the faint mustache on her upper lip and the lovely brown eyes is complimenting him and Faye on their house while she struggles out of her coat — a full bosom, full hips, a strong perfumy odor, a dress of purple zigzags that fits her snugly; the other one, Sandra, the blonde whom Vivian Hochberg has spoken of to Lewis, gives him a dazzling smile, her lower lip caught in her teeth, her eyes on a level with his. She is wearing an extraordinary outfit. The men in attendance — her husband and Barry Swanson — glance at her and at Lewis as if embarrassed. What is she saying? — something about St. Dennis being a little delayed? He was evidently besieged by people after the reading, admirers and autograph seekers. . . . Ah, is that it? Lewis says, relieved. He has been wondering where St. Dennis is. It's already 9:30. So . . . is that it? He's very grateful, he tells the girl, to learn that St. Dennis is all right, what with the sleet and the bad driving. . . . Would she like a drink? Why didn't they all follow him into the living room? It might be easier for them to introduce themselves to his guests, but let him make them drinks first, what would Sandra like, why didn't she just hang onto his arm and he'd escort her through the crowd . . . ? The girl is really striking. That platinum blond hair, that smile, that nervous flirtatious manner; and the outfit she is wearing — a tunic top, long floppy trousers made of a queer silver material, metallic and clinging. The tunic fits tightly across the girl's small hard breasts and tightly across her stomach and hips, and Lewis finds himself grinning at her body, distracted from her words, nodding emphatically. Someone bumps into him and his cigarette falls from his fingers. He stoops to pick it up, Warren Hochberg is apologizing, Lewis laughs and offers him a drink and asks where Vivian is; she *is* here, isn't she?

"Of course Vivian is here," Warren tells him. His smile is small and measured and gives the impression of turning downward. "You know she would never miss one of your parties."

Lewis escapes from Warren and uses the small lavatory beneath the stairs and goes out again to the foyer, where more people are taking off their coats. Among them are Brigit Stott and Alexis Kessler. Lewis stares at them for an instant before breaking into his hearty welcoming laugh. As he shakes hands with Kessler he senses the man's hostility; he notices that his son Harry is staring at Kessler too — having never seen a man with bleached hair and innumerable rings and filed, polished fingernails. And he smells of perfume, does he? — of cologne? Lewis would kiss Brigit on her cool cheek but he knows she may shy away, and this would embarrass everyone, so he merely squeezes her hand — quite hard, in fact — and tells her that he's delighted to see her; for some reason he had had the idea she wouldn't be coming.

"Didn't I answer your invitation?" Brigit asks, opening her eyes wide as she customarily does when she is lying.

Lewis is struck by her appearance. It is Brigit Stott his old friend and colleague — and yet it isn't Brigit, it is a strikingly attractive young woman, far younger than her age; she is almost beautiful. Her eyes are darkly emphatic, her lipstick is an unobtrusive pale fleshy-pink, there is something arrogant and radiant about her very being. So she is in love! And how obvious it is! Lewis would guffaw incredulously, but he is too moved, too strangely disconcerted, for hadn't there been from the very first a sort of understanding between him and Stott. . . . From their first lively meeting at that party in New York, when Lewis had penetrated her husband's defense. . . .

Brigit and Alexis. Lovers, pretending (in public) to be no more than friends. Lewis is tempted to wink at them and nudge them in the ribs. *He* knows. Why dissemble with *him?*

(The rumors Lewis has heard! For weeks tales have made the rounds of the university, coiling and doubling back on themselves, growing ever richer, ever more scandalous. The Stott woman and that Kessler walking brazenly along the river with their arms around each other; Kessler, never before seen in the Humanities Building, emerging flushed and disheveled from Stott's office on the second floor, carrying an armload of books for a prop. It was said that in a resort hotel in Sarasota, where the two had escaped for a weekend, Stott emptied a drink in Kessler's face, and the resulting brawl — in the hotel's elegant cocktail lounge — brought not only the hotel's detective but a city patrolman as well. A young instructor in the music department stopped by at Kessler's studio apartment to ask Kessler to return some music he'd borrowed (Kessler is notorious for neglecting to return anything he has borrowed, particularly money), but there was no answer when he rang the bell, and as he was about to leave he heard — he is *certain* he heard — a woman shouting angrily inside: Brigit Stott's voice without question. It has been said that the two of them smoke hashish together. Alexis flies back and forth to New York frequently (on an admirer's borrowed credit card), where he is supplied with hashish, and even cocaine; and the Stott woman has been sniffling of late, hasn't she, and is often red-eyed when she meets her classes — aren't the symptoms obvious? A depraved, debauched pair. Really quite demoralizing for the community. And what their impressionable students must think — ! Lewis heard from two different sources on the same Monday morning that Brigit's former husband — or are they still married? — tried to break into Brigit's apartment over the weekend, when Kessler was there. In one version Brigit fired her revolver into the door (it is said she carries a handgun everywhere, in her purse, though no one has actually seen it; and once, when Lewis wandered into her office next to his and she wasn't there, he took the opportunity to glance casually through her purse and was mildly disappointed to come upon only a much-worn wallet of imitation leather, some crumpled tissues, a comb with broken teeth, a cheap dime-store compact, a lipstick in a plastic tube, and loose pennies) and Stanley Fifield fled; in the other version he actually succeeded in getting the door off its hinges, but police were called. Lewis has also heard that Brigit and Alexis are planning to resign their appointments at Woodslee and elope to Greece; or is it Northern Africa; or Mexico? He has heard (this by way of his wife, who heard it from Vivian Hochberg at the Faculty Wives' Association luncheon the other day) that Brigit and Alexis are pursuing Albert St. Dennis shamelessly . . . dropping in at his apartment, inviting themselves over, doing errands for him. Lewis was a little upset to hear this; he half-wondered if he should warn St. Dennis that they were plotting to befriend him for selfish reasons. . . .)

He steers them into the living room, one hand touching lightly against Kessler's back, the other gripping Brigit's arm at the elbow. He asks Brigit how she enjoyed the reading, eying her closely, curiously, believing that he sees in her a certain arrogant confidence, the result, no doubt, of her alliance with Kessler. Lovers, the two of them! *Them.* He makes Brigit a drink and Kessler makes his own, ignoring Lewis's friendly chatter, actually turning away as if he were unaware of his host; the effeminate bastard. Lewis glances at his wrist watch without seeing the time and, nervous, knowing himself too excited, continues to address Brigit though he senses she wants to edge away from him. St. Dennis is going to be a few minutes late for the party, he tells Brigit. Did she know — there is a reporter here from the Albany *Post* to interview St. Dennis and take a few pictures? He's over in the corner by the Haases and he had expressed the wish to meet her too, he'd heard of her novels, wondered if. . . . Brigit says something Lewis can't make out, she has a bad habit of mumbling, and in this din it's impossible to hear her; he stoops and inclines his head toward her and she draws back, the bitch, with a foolish little laugh; at this moment Faye approaches, harassed and heavier than Lewis recalls, in a blue silk hostess gown, with a plea that he come to the foyer and help out — poor Leslie Cullendon needs help.

Lewis finishes his drink and sets the glass down. Leslie Cullendon. Leslie . . . ? He doesn't remember having invited the Cullendons.

9:40. The house is crowded. There are guests in his study and in the hall, sitting on the stairs, Rhoda Taylor of the black studies program — a willowy, very black-skinned young woman from Vassar — is laughing at something Vivian Hochberg is telling her, and both women turn as Lewis hurries past, smiling broadly as if *he* is their subject; he waves and grins in return, shoots Vivian a puzzled look, but there's no time, Barry Swanson and Todd Andress — had he invited Todd? — a student, invited to this party? — he doesn't remember — Barry and Todd are helping Leslie Cullendon with his wheelchair, lifting it up the front steps, while little feisty-chinned Babs Cullendon holds an umbrella over her husband. "Don't let go! Don't let go!" Leslie is crying drunkenly. "Watch out! Careful! *Care*-ful!"

Lewis helps; they get Leslie into the house; Babs's umbrella pokes Lewis in the cheek.

"It's stifling in here," Leslie says. "I want a drink. Which direction is the bar? Take this fucking coat off me, Babs, for Christ's sake. I'm stifling, I tell you. I'm suffocating."

Lewis mutters something about the unexpected numbers, apologizes for the stuffiness, agrees it is quite warm — he discovers he's sweating himself, his underclothes are damp, a droplet of perspiration runs down his temple. What time is it? Where the hell is St. Dennis? . . . Leslie pushes his wife aside impatiently and begins to wheel himself into the living room, a thin, hunched man with a very pale face and curly shaggy hair; he would have run into Gladys Fetler if Edie Ryerson hadn't warned her and pulled her aside. Lewis exchanges a look with his wife for the first time this evening. She too is warm; her eyes are glassy. Leslie Cullendon! A dying man! Dying now for over a year, slowly, an associate professor in the department, a specialist in modern British literature whose doctoral dissertation was on James Joyce — only thirty-four years old and weakening month by month, week by week, brazenly continuing with his teaching and never absent from any departmental or committee meeting: is it possible that Lewis mistakenly put an invitation into Leslie's mailbox at the university?

"He's been drinking since lunch," Babs is saying in her whining nasal voice. "Oh, Dr. Seidel, I don't know what to do, just look at him in there, it's terrible, it's just terrible, nobody cares, my so-called friends don't give a damn. Dr. Seidel, you know we used to be so close to the Cuffes and now Mona makes all these excuses, they just don't *want* to see Leslie any more and we used to be so close, we used to be such good friends. . . . Are they here? Is Mona here? Dr. Seidel, what am I going to *do?* Just look at Leslie! Pouring himself a drink! He's been drinking since lunch and he wouldn't touch his food and he's supposed to be on this high-protein diet, you know, they don't really know what's wrong with him — did I tell you? — did he tell you? — it's like multiple sclerosis but it *isn't* that — the diagnosis *isn't* multiple sclerosis — it's something to do with the spinal fluid and the brain, something about motor centers in the brain," she says, clutching at Lewis's wrist. "Dr. Seidel you don't know what it's like to live with him, you just don't know, as soon as he moves away from the bar I'll make myself a drink, you needn't bother. Dr. Seidel, it's so wonderful of you to have invited us," she says, wiping at her eyes, "you just don't *know.* If it wasn't for the university keeping him on like this and letting him teach his classes and work with his students — ! You just don't know, none of you *know* — Look, do you see that? Do you? Poor Leslie was heading for Brad Keough

and Brad pretended not to notice and he escaped out through
the kitchen — the son of a bitch! — I *saw* that myself — it's no
wonder Leslie is so sensitive and paranoid about you people in
the department — I *saw* that myself —"

Lewis has a fit of coughing. Little Babs makes her own drink,
Lewis pours himself some Scotch in a glass, no need to bother
with ice, he takes the opportunity of passing some chips and
avocado dip around to his friends, nervous, keyed up, anything
to escape from Babs Cullendon, a girl he had once found exceptionally pretty and had — hadn't he? — or was that another little
wife? — kissed for ten or fifteen minutes very early one morning
at someone's party a few years ago. He slides one arm around
Matt Ryerson's broad shoulders and inclines his graying shaggy
head into a conversation: Mina Housley in her piping voice,
something about rent control, welfare cutbacks in the county,
terrible poverty right in town a few miles away and all this agitation about expanding the highway, simply for tourists, and Woodslee wouldn't profit from tourism, as everyone knows except the
politicians, who are only pretending not to know, and what about
that shocking case of starvation or malnutrition reported in the
paper — there may be quite a number of families as poor as that
family living in the foothills — only a few miles away from the
university — from this very living room — Lewis coughs and
clears his throat and says that St. Dennis will be a little late;
evidently quite a crowd of autograph-seekers converged on him
after the reading. He sends his apologies and he'll be along any
minute now. . . . Mina Housley peers at Lewis through her bifocals. She doesn't seem to know what he's talking about, and even
Matt Ryerson smiles vaguely, and Ted Bannon cups his hand to
his ear: God, you can't hear yourself think!

"Great to see you all! Great evening for a party!" Lewis cries.

He escapes, circles back to the bar — where Pete Springer has
more or less taken on the responsibility of bartender — and fills
up his glass again; doesn't remember having finished his last

drink. So hot! All these people! Lewis's eye wanders helplessly from person to person, face to face. Colleagues. Friends. He knows them all and is fond of them all. He knows them all and. . . . A woman throws herself backward in a spasm of laughter, colliding with Lewis so that his drink spills (fortunately not onto his trousers: onto the rug), and all the while he is nodding at Pete Springer who is complaining in a bitter monotone about his former wife. A voice nearby rises querulously: it is Stanislaus Chung of the English department, already rather drunk. Dr. Chung's quirky bad temper is legendary and Lewis wonders why he invited him . . . oh yes: he invited Dr. Chung because the Chungs invited *him* to a dinner party last spring. The wife is small-bodied and unobtrusive, almost pathologically shy, and consequently not much of a problem; but Chung himself is bristly, loud and whining when drunk, really quite unpredictable. He has joined Matt Ryerson and the others, a stocky, swarthy little man with a broad grin, dressed in an ill-fitting plaid suit, curiously asymmetrical, as if one leg were shorter than the other. Lewis is still nodding in Pete Springer's direction, numbly but enthusiastically. He is really feeling quite good. He loves parties, needs parties. . . . He loves. . . .

Jesus Christ: out of the corner of his eye he sees a shape in a wheelchair approaching.

In frantic haste he looks at his wrist watch without seeing the time, mumbles something to Pete, turns and hurries blindly through the dining room and into the kitchen . . . where Faye and Charlotte Haas are taking a large casserole out of the oven. There is an odor of something burned, scorched. Lewis stares at the clock set in the stove and sees, sickened, that it is ten minutes to ten.

Ten minutes to ten.

The poetry reading ended just before nine. St. Dennis had finished his last poem just before nine. Nearly an hour ago. It means: what? . . . Faye is nagging him, pulling at his sleeve. Has

he been smoking again? How many drinks has he had? He promised, didn't he, it wouldn't be like the last time, at the Hochbergs',
when he drank so much he was sick all night, and where is Mr.
St. Dennis, isn't he here yet? There is a sharp line between Faye's
eyebrows, a vertical crease that fascinates and repels Lewis. . . .
Charlotte Haas tells Lewis in an excited, slurred voice, one hand
cupping an elbow and the other hand cupping her chin, that
she'd been telling Faye about the strangest thing that had happened to her today, this morning, this was Friday, wasn't it? — it
had happened just this morning. Well, Lewis knows where she
and Roger live, on Linwood, doesn't he, and there's an alley out
back, an alley for garbage pickup — is there an alley running
behind Strathmore? — no? — anyway — anyway she was home
alone as usual and happened to see, about ten A.M. it was, these
two men coming along the alley walking very slowly and stooping
over quite a bit — picking up something — and she watched and
watched and they came to her own back yard where there's just
a chain-link fence that isn't in very good condition any longer,
it's quite rusted, she has asked Roger about putting in a redwood
fence maybe at a height of about ten feet, and these two men
looked over the fence into her back yard and for a long terrible
moment she knew that something was going to happen: she
knew. In her bathrobe and bedroom slippers, standing at the
kitchen window, terrified, trembling, wondering if she should get
to the telephone before it was too late — ! One of the men had
straggly blond hair and the other was dark and swarthy, maybe
an Indian, she was quite sure he was an Indian, maybe from the
reservation at DeWitt, but what was he doing down here in
Woodslee? — what were these two men doing? Both wore lum-
berman's jackets and caps. The blond had a reddened face, the
Indian was very dark, the two of them kept staring into her back
yard and they weren't even talking but it was like there was a
communion between them — did Lewis know what she meant?
— like a scene in a movie, you know, where everything is un-

stated and you must *infer* — ? Oh she was terrified, just terrified, because of course there was that item in the paper about the rape out by the interstate the other night in the picnic area. . . . Anyway the moment passed: thank God the moment passed. The men continued on down the alley and she watched until they were out of sight, going from one window to another upstairs, never so frightened in her life; what if they had decided to leap over the fence and break into the house . . . ? They were carrying canvas bags, both of them, they were evidently scavenging around the garbage cans, but they were out of luck because the garbage wouldn't be picked up until next Tuesday and there was really little for them to take. What a terrible ten minutes Charlotte had lived through! She hopes, she says, touching Lewis's sleeve and managing a smile, she *hopes* nothing so upsetting will ever happen to her again. "It was as if my entire life flashed before me in that space of time," she says, blinking rapidly, "and I seemed to — oh, I don't know how to express it — *you* would know, Lewis, you're so articulate and — and verbal — I seemed to see how precarious and precious our lives are — our homes and our marriages — our families — And — And — It came over me like a revelation, like a vision, it was so powerful, so overwhelming: We must love one another while we have one another. I think that was it. I know I've had too much to drink, Lewis, and I've been taking antibiotics all week — fighting the flu — I know I'm not as articulate as you but I feel, I feel very deeply," she says, still touching his arm, holding his shirt sleeve, while he stares miserably into her putty-colored face, wishing only to escape, "I feel very deeply the truth of what was revealed to me and I will never, never forget — It's so precarious, you see, our homes and our marriages and the university and, oh you know, the books you men write, the meetings and the — the salaries and — Do you understand me at all, Lewis? Do you understand me at all? *We must love one another while we have one another.* We must —"

"The doorbell!" Lewis cries.

He hurries into the back hall and nearly collides with the Swanson girl, just coming out of the guest lavatory; he grips her broad shoulders and gives her a little shake, out of sheer excitement. She smiles dazedly: perhaps drunk? Lipstick on front teeth, a vague smear. Heady overripe perfume. He asks her if she's enjoying herself and she says yes, emphatically, a big happy grin, nice girl, healthy and uncomplicated and full-bodied, he asks if she and Barry know everyone, he hopes the party isn't too much of a crush for them, she says no, no, absolutely not: it's the most wonderful party she has ever been to in her life.

"You sweetheart," Lewis exclaims, squeezing her shoulder.

But when he gets to the foyer he's disappointed: Harry is taking the Bradys' coats. John and Frances Brady are old friends, very fine thoughtful cultured gentle people — John a professor of mathematics, Frances an excellent amateur cellist — but they are not, after all, Albert St. Dennis. Seeing them, Lewis groans aloud, involuntarily, but the noise from the party is such that no one hears, not even Lewis himself. He lunges forward to kiss Frances on the cheek and to shake John's hand. How good to see them, how *are* they . . . ?

Ah, the weather! This Woodslee weather!

He leads them into the living room and excuses himself and doubles back to the front door; he stands for a few minutes on the porch, staring at the icy rain, wondering what he should do. A car's headlights — but the car continues past. What has gone wrong, where is the guest of honor? He dreads looking at his watch. Must be ten o'clock by now. The poetry reading ended at nine and an hour has passed, has slipped by, what should he do, what is going to happen . . . ? He discovers a drink in his hand; he finishes it in one swallow. A slow dull burning sensation in his throat. A sudden attack of coughing. . . . His son leans out the door, asks him what's wrong, doesn't he feel well? Lewis waves him away. He loves the boy — lanky awkward sweet Harry —

Harry now seventeen years old, incredible as it seems — and he's grateful that his son is fond of him, as his friends' sons are not fond of *them*; but he doesn't want to talk with him at the moment. "Go help your mother set up the buffet," he says morosely.

Not long ago Lewis had an unsettling experience. He had been complaining at the Riverview about St. Dennis's aloofness — the old man had to protect his privacy, but he was being remarkably unfriendly. He declined most invitations and seemed rather uncomfortable around the department and had not — so far as Lewis knew — invited anyone to his apartment yet; one might reasonably expect an invitation for tea or sherry, certainly . . . ? Rumor had it that he spent a fair amount of time at the local library — the *local* library, not the university's. There, in that dismal tatty place, amid the shelves of murder mysteries and women's romances and science fiction, where a single work of Flaubert's — *Madame Bovary*, of course — was nearly crowded off the shelf by Hedda Stange Fleuve's oeuvre of fifteen novels (all Gothic romances), and where a shelf called, simply, *Poetry*, was less than an arm's length and consisted of several oversized "treasuries" of "best-loved" poems and did not contain Yeats or Eliot and still less Albert St. Dennis — there, sipping tea with the aged librarian, Woodslee's Distinguished Professor of Poetry was content to chat about gardening and birdlore and the Queen and memories of England in the twenties and thirties. (The librarian, a Mrs. Willard, had been born in Manchester and had come to the United States with her husband in 1938.) Rumor had it, Lewis had complained irritably, that St. Dennis wasted hours there and even had begun to cheat on his responsibilities at the university; several students had gone to see him with their poems and had found his door locked. Of course he was a fine man, Lewis said, and possibly a genius, but . . . but it was disappointing, after all.

"But you people are so bourgeois," a young man had said.

Astonished, Lewis had not known how to reply. The charge

was absurd, of course. But what about the librarian — ? Surely she was "bourgeois." And it was a ludicrous accusation to make against Lewis Seidel, of all people: hadn't the young man read *Cul-de-sac?*

He had, he believed, successfully argued the young man down, but the accusation stayed with him. It had been delivered in so casual and even rather affectionate a way. . . . *Bourgeois. You people are so bourgeois.* Could it be possible that students thought of Lewis Seidel as merely one of a group, a faculty member like any other . . . ? Could it be possible that his uniqueness was not recognized, that he might be confused from a distance with such ordinary academics as Warren Hochberg and George Housley and Gowan Vaughan-Jones and old Blaise Perrin and Gladys Fetler . . . ? (He and Gladys were the department's most popular teachers, an embarrassment to Lewis. Everyone loved Gladys, but it was widely known that her Shakespeare course was no more than a superior high school course, and that students enrolled in it cynically, being assured of fairly high grades. Whereas Lewis was demanding; he had a reputation as a difficult marker; his droll remarks often went over his students' heads.) . . . It seemed to him cruel and unjust.

Since that afternoon at the Riverview, however, he has come to hear, in his own words, in his characteristic phrases, a certain queer hollowness, a predictability he had never noticed before. His denunciation of modernist art — of "serious" art — his puckish anomolies and his hearty support of the near-unknown ("Nate Fulmer is the greatest living black writer"; "Geraldine McIvor is the greatest living woman poet") and his dazzling paradoxes ("The highest art is no art at all"), not to mention his outrageous judgments ("*Dracula* is the greatest novel in English literature"; "*Gone With the Wind* tells us more about the American Depression than all of Dos Passos and Farrell"), have come to sound — incredibly, horribly — *bourgeois*.

How has it happened? His rude lusty jocose defiance . . . his

irrepressible high spirits . . . his marvelous sly wit and his fear-
lessness at making quite clear exactly where he "stands" . . . his
tolerance of the opinions of young people and blacks and women
. . . his continuing skirmishes with the administration and with
all forms of authority . . . his casual but intense liaisons with certain girl students (less frequent in the past few years, it must be
admitted: but then he has been very busy with his writing) . . .
his slashing reviews of others' books . . . his notoriously high
standards . . . his flamboyant gestures, his sometimes coarse vocabulary, his frankly ribald anecdotes about famous people he
has known . . . his tigerish playfulness, his unpredictability: how
has it all come to seem predictable? He listens to his own voice as
he lectures to his classes and he begins to tremble, perspiration
breaks out on his forehead, he hears the familiarity, the staleness,
the . . . the Seidel manner: what on earth has happened? The
mirror shows a stylishly dressed man of early middle age, possibly
a little heavy — no more than most of his friends, however —
his face kindly with laugh lines, his pale blue eyes round and
boyish with perverse innocence; he is no longer handsome, but
he is still quite attractive. An expert showman, a jester. Shocking,
really. Scandalous at times. At times outrageous. But —
    Fifty-one years old.
    Phi Beta Kappa in his junior year at City College; prizes as an
undergraduate; high praise and encouragement from his professors. A Woodrow Wilson Fellowship for graduate work at Colum-
bia. High grades, high expectations, a series of articles published
in his twenties, a considerable name for himself before the age of
thirty; an appointment at Brown that had not worked out; a year
in England; more articles and reviews and the appointment at
prestigious Woodslee; the controversial *Cul-de-sac* and more articles and reviews and. . . . He is often invited to give addresses
at universities and women's clubs; surely that means something.
And in their several conversations together he and Albert St.
Dennis have seemed to strike a certain note of accord — an ami-

able kind of discord, it might be said; St. Dennis sees in him someone to be taken very seriously. (Even the dandyish *arriviste* Oliver Byrne takes Lewis seriously: he knows and respects Lewis's position on certain ideological and philosophical issues over which the men have differed.)

But —

In horror he glances at his watch and sees that it is 10:05.

He hurries back inside. What a commotion! Laughter, raised voices, Brad Keough playfully and drunkenly banging on a table, Gowan Vaughan-Jones shouting at Todd Andress, very nearly in tears — what on earth? — vast clouds of smoke — faces — a reeling nightmarish carnival. Trembling, he reaches for a drink someone has abandoned on the cobbler's bench. An inch or two of Scotch, a sliver of ice. He gulps it down. Coughs. Faye is searching for him — he knows that desperate glassy look of hers — *How I hate these parties*, she will scream at him tomorrow, *how I hate your awful friends!* — and he ducks into his study to escape, but there is Leslie Cullendon haranguing a subdued, frightened little group — the Swanson girl, the Jaeger girl, and Babs — wildly and happily drunk, he shouts in a voice like frayed twine something incomprehensible that sounds like *Kidney of Bloom pray for us! Kidney of Bloom pray for us! Sweets of Sin pray for us! Beer beef battledog buybull businum barnum buggerum bishop! BEER BEEF BATTLEDOG —*

His back to the rest of the party, there stands Alexis Kessler, a drink in hand, a cigarette stuck in his mouth as a child might smoke, sucking at it with great concentration. He is coolly looking through some papers and magazines lying on top of Lewis's desk; he has even moved Lewis's quartz paperweight aside. Lewis stares at him. Slowly, with that air of calm contempt that Lewis finds maddening, Alexis turns slightly and raises his eyes to Lewis's face. He says nothing. He does not blush, he is not even mildly startled or embarrassed; he merely returns Lewis's gaze. Lewis wants to rush at him, strike his absurd face, spill some blood onto his elegant clothes. . . . Tear a handful of hair out of his head. . . . He does approach Kessler, his hands shaking; in a lowered voice he says, not wishing anyone else to hear, "So you're fucking Stott, are you! So — !" and still Kessler shows no sign of emotion, he merely sucks at his cigarette and says loudly, loud enough for the others in the room to hear, "Would you prefer that I fuck you, Lewis?"

Lewis retreats.

He hurries along the corridor and pauses at the kitchen door, panting. That noise? Telephone? Doorbell? Another attack of coughing, hard to get his breath, he shuts his eyes for a moment and tries to remember . . . what was he doing, where was he going? Must help Faye with the food. Must go upstairs and change his clothes first: underwear soaking. Sweated through. Then out on the porch, waiting for St. Dennis, sudden chill, a mistake. Flu going around Woodslee. Sweating, shivering. Another drink would help. But if he cuts through the kitchen Faye will get him. But. . . .

That bastard Kessler: impossible.

What had he said . . . ?

Impossible.

Lewis wipes his face on his shoulder, catches his breath, pushes the swinging door open. A blast of heat. Charlotte Haas in one of Faye's aprons, Mona Cuffe on her way out the other door to the dining room, carrying a heavy tray. Lewis helps her; makes a show of being gallant and flirtatious. Mona giggles. Or is it Mona. The younger wives have come to resemble one another over the years. Where is Vivian? Avoided him all evening. Or has he avoided her? . . . He sets the tray down on the table, wipes his face again, trying to catch his breath. Brigit Stott turns from a conversation with Roger Haas and, seeing Lewis, is about to say something amusing and malicious but pauses, suddenly concerned, and asks him if he feels all right? — he's looking rather flushed —

"Is that the doorbell?" Lewis says, cupping his ear.

"The doorbell? I didn't hear anything."

There is an enormous spread of food, a holiday of food, and many of the guests are already eating. They are grouped about the table, partly blocking traffic between the rooms. Noisy cheerful merry group. Friends. Colleagues. There is Stanislaus Chung, grinning his broad "American" grin, picking at the roast beef: he seems to be inspecting it, shaking pieces off his fork that fail to meet his approval, too fatty or gristly, perhaps: he is in an unusually good mood tonight. There is Matt Ryerson, laughing heartily, showing an expanse of gum. There is Faye, smiling her strained hostess' smile, caught in a conversation with George Housley, who is vehement about something — eroding standards at the university, perhaps — and Lewis looks quickly away, not wishing to be drawn to his wife's side. This is a party, after all; *his* party; he wants to enjoy himself. . . . Gaylord Fraser of the drama department is standing in a corner beside a Rockwell Kent lithograph, eating hungrily. His paper plate is heaped high with food and Lewis, flinching, sees that some potato salad falls to the floor . . . but Gaylord doesn't appear to notice. Just then Edie Ryerson sails up to Lewis, arms opened wide as if she were going to embrace him. It is only a gesture, Lewis knows; still, it unnerves him. She asks if she may fix him a plate of this delicious food . . . ? No. No thank you. He'll eat later. The doorbell is ringing. Has the reporter for the *Post* left yet? It's 10:15. He hopes she will excuse him but he must answer the door — there's no time to lose —

"Lewis, you don't look well at all!" Edie cries accusingly.

Lewis grimaces at her and makes his way to the foyer and there, as in a dream, he sees Oliver Byrne and St. Dennis. No: Oliver Byrne and Marilyn. Harry is helping Marilyn with her coat. Lewis staggers forward, disbelieving. "What — what is it?" he cries. "Where is he?"

Oliver Byrne looks around in amazement.

"Where is the old man? What's going on? Is he here? Where is he?"

Suddenly the babble quiets; Lewis's raised voice is a shriek.

"Do you mean — St. Dennis isn't here? You didn't bring him?"

Oliver tries to explain that St. Dennis was too tired to come to the party and is very, very sorry — he isn't a young man, after all, and the hour's reading took a great deal out of him. "He asked Marilyn and me to tell you how enormously sorry he is to miss the party in his honor," Oliver says, "how much he regrets having to go home instead —"

"Home!" Lewis cries. "What do you mean — *home?* Is that where he is? In bed? It's only ten o'clock! What the hell is going on here, Oliver? I want to know — what the hell is going on!"

"Why, Lewis," Marilyn says in a small frightened voice, "what's wrong? You look so angry —"

Lewis ignores her. She is about to touch his sleeve and he brushes her away. "Look, Byrne," he says, "I'm asking you what's going on! What your purpose is! This party for St. Dennis has been planned for weeks — everyone has come to meet him — *everyone* — and you're not going to ruin things! Oh no! I'll drive over there and get him myself!"

"Lewis," Oliver says, "you'd better calm down. I'm not going to tolerate —"

"You're not going to tolerate! Not going to tolerate!" Lewis cries in derision. He half turns to the others, who are looking on in silence; he winks over his shoulder at Gladys Fetler, who is standing nearby, white-haired and aghast. "I know very well what your game is, Byrne — I *know*. You deliberately took the old man home, didn't you? To ruin my plans for this evening? Because you're jealous — jealous and spiteful and — and frightened — You're afraid of St. Dennis's affection for me, aren't you? You've been keeping him to yourself but it won't work — it won't work — I see through your clumsy plotting and I'm going to get him and bring him back here and —"

Afterward, versions of the struggle between Lewis and Oliver varied greatly. A number of guests claimed that Oliver tried to restrain Lewis by touching his arm and Lewis flipped Oliver's hand away and accidentally slapped him; Gladys Fetler is certain that it was an accident. ("Lewis is a good, gentle soul who wouldn't hurt anyone in the world," Gladys says.) Sandra Jaeger, however, who had hurried to the study doorway when the shouting began, claims to have seen quite clearly Lewis Seidel striking Dean Byrne in the face. How quickly it happened! How horrified she was! And then the spurt of blood, the shock of blood on Byrne's shirt front and on his handsome silk tie . . . ! Charlotte Haas, who had come up behind Lewis from the kitchen, was amazed to see Marilyn Byrne staggering back against the umbrella stand as if shoved — but she isn't certain that Lewis really shoved her or if it simply appeared that way. Gowan Vaughan-Jones speaks of the incident in a slow, drawling, distracted manner, pushing his glasses up in order to rub at his eyes, as if he can't quite believe what he evidently saw; he hasn't been able to sleep well in the days following the scuffle. Todd Andress, over-excitable and glittery-eyed and very young, claims to have seen the Dean of Humanities poke Lewis Seidel in the chest before the shouting even began, but no one else supports him; most of the onlookers are uncertain about what really happened. They only know that something happened at the Seidels' party on Friday night in honor of Albert St. Dennis — they aren't even certain if St. Dennis was there or not. (In some versions of the story, repeated throughout the week and radiating outward from the humanities division itself, it will be claimed that the visiting English poet, St. Dennis, was the person who started a fist fight: a tough wiry little bantam of a man, and seventy-five years old! Quite a character!)

But everyone at the party heard Lewis's despairing bawl and everyone who could see him was astonished at his flushed, tear-streaked face. "You can't do this to me!" he cried. "You can't —

any of you! I've waited so long and you can't — I won't let you!
I won't let you!"

A few minutes before midnight Alexis lies in Brigit Stott's bed,
stroking the cat nestled against his side, her head on his stomach,
golden floating lovely notes in his mind, a melody so exquisite he
cannot quite believe in it: he plays and replays it, slows it, expands
it, embellishes it. One of his songs for St. Dennis. His. The third
song of the cycle.

It has come to him, nearly complete, in the last twenty minutes.

Brigit is in the bathroom showering, to get the odor of smoke
out of her hair; Alexis is too lazy to bother; Alexis is sleepy and
drunk and quite content, rubbing the cat's ears and beneath her
chin. The melody plays itself effortlessly. Ah: like that. Yes. Alexis's toes twitch with the rhythm of the piece. Languid and
lovely. Music. Melody. A song for soprano voice, accompanied
by piano. Very simple, almost ascetic. The sorrow of St. Dennis's
words, austere, tragic, no self-pity. How love flares up in the
blood like an infection, raging, carrying all before it . . . how
one's blood is overheated, the brain disturbed . . . how it must
necessarily pass . . . must rise and fall and fade . . . like a principle of nature over which human wishes have no power. . . .
Alexis lies with his eyes open, seeing nothing. The cat stretches
out beside him. In the bathroom the shower door opens and
closes, Brigit calls out to him, Alexis pretends not to hear, listening to the melody in his imagination. Yes: like that. And then
slowing. (But must be careful, since the melody is starting to drift
into something by Fauré, the main theme of one of Fauré's piano
quartets.)

Alexis does not think of the party at the Seidels': those frantic
noisy pathetic people. The ravaged young man in the wheelchair

eating huge slices of baked ham, mustard falling onto his wasted
shanks; the girl in the metallic silver outfit complaining in a small,
pretty, frightened voice that the university had gone back on its
word about something — some part-time job for her; Lewis Seidel red-faced and shouting, a maniac, a fool, having to be restrained by his own son. These images flit through Alexis's mind
but he does not really think of them. . . . And there is Brigit
herself, Brigit of whom he is very fond, sobbing into his shoulder
as soon as they were alone; as upset by the incident as if Lewis
had attacked her and not Byrne, or as if Lewis were her husband
and therefore her responsibility. Why so upset? Why so distraught? He had tried to joke with her. Her breath reeked of gin.
Her make-up was smeared. (Before St. Dennis's reading Alexis
and Brigit had showered together, here in Brigit's apartment.
They had been playful as young animals, kissing and hugging and
soaping each other; Alexis had shampooed her hair, digging his
fingers into her scalp. Then, afterward, he had dried her in a
large bath towel and wrapped another towel about her hair and,
despite her protests, he had examined her face closely . . . had
rubbed cold cream into her skin . . . had taken a tweezers and
plucked at her eyebrows to make their arch more prominent,
raised high above the eye . . . all the while half-scolding her for
not cultivating her appearance more assiduously: didn't she know
her facial bones were marvelous, her eyes marvelous, she was a
woman of beauty who must take responsibility for herself? Brigit
was embarrassed, Brigit wanted to escape. Always so self-conscious! He teased her, kissed her, made her stand obediently still
as he worked on her face. There is nothing pretty about you, he
said, nothing conventionally pretty. You're either beautiful or
ugly. I don't mind you ugly — it's a severe, intelligent ugliness.
Stand still! Stop blushing! . . . But you can be beautiful too, for a
while at least; with those cheekbones you can be beautiful for
another fifteen or twenty years. You're enviable, in fact. I
wouldn't mind being you. . . . Why are you so self-conscious,

Brigit? Do you imagine that your face and your body are your own, your private possessions? Not any longer!

(He had rubbed more cream into her face, and oily lotion onto her body — her small, slightly sagging breasts, her stomach, her hips and buttocks and thighs and legs, even her feet, her small perfect toes that he couldn't help kissing; he had insisted upon cutting her toenails and filing her fingernails and polishing them — he discovered, in her medicine cabinet, an old but still usable bottle of nail polish in a quite attractive shade — opalescent pink-pearl; he put her make-up on for her, stroking the skin of her face upward, gently, while she stood, flushed and subdued, her eyes half-closed as if they had just made love and there was no spirit in her to protest or even to respond any longer. The flesh-colored make-up, faint smears of rouge on her cheekbones very lightly rubbed in, very lightly and subtly, and eye shadow, and eye liner, and inky-black mascara, and her eyebrows penciled in lightly, and lipstick . . . and he had seen, enchanted, a woman's beautiful image emerge from the plain and rather sallow material he had been given: ah, how he loved her! How mesmerizing she was!)

Digging his fingers into the cat's fur, hearing again the melody and moving with it, seeming to rise with it . . . he is pleasantly drowsy, his body satiated, at rest. The party is nearly forgotten; it has no meaning to him. (Brigit, talking to him from the bathroom, is evidently still upset. She uses expressions like "worried," "concerned," "frightened." Alexis mumbles a reply.) A few faces rise again and pop like bubbles: the hard, handsome woman with the mole on her upper lip, the Italian girl with the lovely bright dark eyes, the boy in the denim outfit with the shy, awkward smile — Seidel's son — approaching Alexis in the study to ask if he, Alexis, is the musician, the composer. But the faces disappear, the party itself whirls and vanishes. What does any of it matter to Alexis? He sees again St. Dennis on the stage, behind the podium; a lonely figure. ("Your name is — Alexander?"

"Alexis. Alexis Kessler." "Oh — my dear, yes! Yes. I remember now — we corresponded, didn't we? You sent me that charming picture of yourself.")

The song for St. Dennis shapes itself in Alexis's mind, the loveliest melody he has ever written. He *knows* it is good.

He sits up suddenly. He is fully awake now; a thought has just penetrated his reverie. Brigit's long-haired black cat Minnie gazes at him attentively. Her eyes are yellow. Her small pink tongue protrudes slightly beneath her black nose. She is very fond of her mistress' young lover, she likes nothing better than to nudge and nuzzle him, and purr her hoarse crackling purr, and get him to dig his nails in her hide. But Alexis hardly notices her now. He is thinking that he must get away: must get away to work, to write those notes down, to labor until they are perfect.

Brigit, just leaving the bathroom, is speaking of an odd conversation she had with Roger Haas, the university's chief counsel; denuded of make-up she looks sallow, tired, wan, her severely plucked eyebrows are almost invisible, her expression strikes Alexis as querulous. Had he heard, she says, that someone in political science was actually being sued by one of the big paper-pulp companies downriver because he had said in a lecture that the Powhatan was being polluted by local industry —

"Brigit," Alexis says, "can I borrow five hundred dollars? I'm leaving Woodslee for a few days — for a week. I need to work without interruption."

Brigit stares at him as if uncomprehending. Her robe had come partway open, and now she draws it shut, staring.

"Five hundred dollars," Alexis says, somewhat impatiently. "Could you write me a check before we go to bed? Or do you have cash?"

At

Albert St. Dennis's

and

At the Housleys'

December 31, 7 P.M.

"I can't go there. I can't talk to those wretched people."

"Come on, Sandra, for Christ's sake —"

"I can't."

She is lying in bed, cringing beneath the blanket. The wall is two or three inches from her face; she appears to be staring at it. Much time has passed. Hours. Days. Someone has switched on the overhead light, which they rarely use because it is too bright, too glaring, and now he stands over her, and now he is tugging at the blanket. He wants to pull it away from her, wants to expose her. She is shivering violently.

"Sandra, for Christ's sake, please — You've got to help me —"

She can hear his breathing.

Panting.

In despair, in befuddlement. She stares at the wall but it has no surface — there are no cracks, no patterns, nothing to catch the eye. She might be looking into a depthless substance. Where does it end, where are its limits? Her shoulders are hunched and her arms are tightly crossed. Her bare feet are very cold — her toes hurt with the cold. When she went to bed the other day their thermometer out back read −15° F.

"Sandra, are you sick? Is there really something wrong? Should I — Would you like — Is there anything I can do?"

Her teeth have begun chattering.

Ernest stands over the bed, tall and baffled and outraged. His voice is not familiar. She hears the disgust in it: his astonishment at her failure. Unwashed hair, unwashed body, sleep-encrusted eyes.

"Should I call a doctor . . . ?" he says faintly.

He has spoken of calling a doctor before, when she first went to bed — the last week of November, when the news came; and again a few days ago, when they returned from a three-day visit with Sandra's family in Springfield, Massachusetts. Unwashed, hair in greasy strands, face swollen, eyes puffy. His lovely wife.

But he will not call a doctor, she knows.

"Honey, let me help you up. All right? Honey? . . . I could help you take a bath and you could wear that long dress and we wouldn't need to stay at the party very long; we could stay an hour or so, that wouldn't be too much for you, would it . . . ? Sandra? We've already missed the Hochbergs' open house and Dr. Fetler's . . . and. . . . Why don't you wear that silver outfit, honey, maybe that would be more comfortable. . . . Do you hear me, Sandra? Honey?"

He pulls the blanket away from her shoulders. She tries to clutch at it but her fingers are too cold; it slips away.

She begins to cry.

She cannot remember who he is. A young husband. Her husband. She has not eaten for nearly two days. The bed seems to be tilting, lurching. What if she falls . . . ? But she is safe, someone is holding her, his face buried against her neck and hair. One arm tight around her. The bed trembling with his sobs.

"Oh Jesus I'm so sorry, what can I do, I'm so sorry, so sorry," he cries. "What can I do . . . ? There's nothing I can do."

He lies beside her, hugging her. He is very warm, very agitated. She brings his hand to her face, kisses it, presses it against her cheek. . . . it seems to her that time winks and yawns suddenly, that the two of them slide into an abyss, into the depthless wall, no weight to them; they might plunge like this, in each other's arms, helpless, forever. He sobs that he loves her. He doesn't know what to do — what else to do. This vacation has been hellish because they've had too much time to think, too much time to worry, going over and over again the possibilities — hearing each other say the same things again and again — confined here in this tiny apartment where they have no choice except to talk about it, and then at her parents' where they could not even allude to it but had to tell so many lies: he knows it's been hell for her. But in a week the new semester will begin. Maybe things will change. It may be they are exaggerating it all . . . that they will look back on this in a few years and find it all amusing.

She hears the anguish in his voice. She lies with his warm hand pressed against her face, wanting suddenly to laugh; something convulses in her throat and she has to hold herself still. Amusing. Amusing! Why not reinterpret this hell as amusing, once they are out of it? She has already spoken philosophically and with an admirable degree of control, some days ago, when the first of Ernest's letters of application to other universities were answered, when the first of the form letters arrived, that her feelings were probably exaggerated because of the time of year; she was not really depressed, not seriously depressed; of course she would get better. Isn't there something about December . . . the completion of a cycle . . . a sense of life at its weakest, as the sun is at its weakest, a dull glowering white . . . dusk in the afternoon, the mornings a perpetual twilight . . . the universe filling up with snow. . . . It has nothing to do with their situation, does it, the dreary freezing weather and the gravitational pull toward darkness, toward death, doesn't everyone feel it, the pulse of life growing fainter and fainter until it seems so easy to let go . . . ?

In a few minutes his sobs stop. He is really all right; he is not going to break down. Sandra lies in his arms, feeling the curious weightlessness of their marriage. There is no substance to them, she might drift from his embrace or he from hers, slipping free,

boundless. Their embraces are desperate and their tears are genuine. Their love for each other is genuine. But it has no power to
save them: it is this understanding that has terrified her.

In Cambridge several years ago they had gone to a film festival
and saw for the first time a film by Truffaut called *Shoot the Piano
Player*, which they had liked very much. They had held hands in
the crowded theater, had kissed, had poked at each other when
something on screen especially delighted them. Back in September, however, they had seen the film again when it was shown at
the university, along with a number of other Truffaut films, and
the very first sequence—the first two or three minutes—had
struck them both as transparent and banal and flat; to their astonished disappointment the film, as it moved along, was not the
same film they had admired, but another, lesser, quite unconvincing work that had lost its magic. Sandra had not wanted to
speak of her disappointment to Ernest, but midway through the
film he asked if they should leave? — and she got to her feet at
once.

For some time afterward they discussed that perplexing experience. Had it been the film itself that failed, or had they failed;
had they somehow lost the emotional key to a work of art . . . ?
Or was it possible they mourned not simply their inability to
relive an experience but, in a profoundly disturbing way, their
realization that the original experience had been spurious . . . ?

Magic might depart from every experience: this was the possibility that terrified.

On this freezing, windy, attenuated day, the final day of the year, Brigit Stott prepares herself for a New Year's Eve party and thinks of mortality.

She has been thinking of mortality for some time. The past two weeks, the past several months, the past five years. Mortality, mutability, death, she thinks; what other thoughts are worthy of our attention? — and yet, what other thoughts evoke in us such a sense of luxurious futility?

She is in love and therefore thinks of death: it is a romantic reaction, an instinctive impulse. Wishing to live and wishing to live keenly in the body — as she has not lived for years — she naturally thinks of the body's breakdown, its perverse but inevitable failure. But she is unable to imagine herself aged. There are models and images of age for her — two grandmothers, a grandfather; even St. Dennis; even, at times, at the very end of a school day, Gladys Fetler herself. But Brigit is unable to think of herself in these terms. For several years death wore her husband's face — came to her in dreams and in waking visions with that man's strangely commonplace appearance, his look of being quite ordinary. (Though she lived with Stanley Fifield for more than a decade she isn't altogether certain of what he looks like, and she suspects that she, to him, is a ghostly, maddening presence. Having been so close, so compulsively intimate, how could they have failed to be blinded to each other . . . ? If it did not hurt so much, if the abrasions were not, still, so embarrassingly raw, Brigit would write about her marriage: but she hasn't the courage. She hasn't the distance. Throughout the marriage she was cursed by a sense of his not knowing her and not wishing to know her; not *her*. He fell in love with and married a certain young woman, an image in his imagination, and he did not want this image violated. He fought for it passionately and viciously, as if it were life itself — he fought Brigit for it, in fact. Making love with him in the customary dark she had often thought, though every instinct in her tried to forbid the thought, that she was, at such times, only a physical stimulus for him — a means of stirring his manly desire, his "love" — which thrust itself desperately and wildly and ecstatically into a ghostly image of Brigit Stott, a vapor that had no relationship to the living woman at all. And when she could not respond to his love he had been murderously resentful — as he would naturally be, as any man naturally would be; in a way she could not blame him. She had thought — is all love founded upon such illusions? — is pleasure in the flesh, like the pleasure of art, possible only when the imagination wills the outer world into the form it desires? If this were true it was not a cynical truth, only a truth that must be faced. But she did not really believe it. She could not believe it. My experience is unique, she thought, it doesn't touch upon anyone else's, the world would have collapsed centuries ago if my experience were everyone's. . . . She believed in love, still; she believed in others' beliefs in love. A single failed marriage does not call into question all marriages. A single disappointing husband is not a judgment upon all men. And it worries her that she alone of all Stanley's acquaintances is the one least able to know him. She could describe him only with difficulty — the outward, physical appearance of the man, his deliberate cultivation of certain styles of dress and hair and mannerisms that identified him with the smartly affluent, even the vocabulary he affected, even his tone of voice, at times, seemed strategies of disguise rather than expressions of his unique personality. The public self, the private self, the husband and the lover and the man and the human being with his own raw, indescribable need were all different, always at war. She had been a minor casualty of that war.

But it is Alexis she thinks of, not Stanley; she has not seen Stanley for over a year, and apart from random reports on his behavior from friends (most recently, just before Christmas: a woman friend living in New York telephoned Brigit to talk of various things and brought up, as if incidentally, the subject of Brigit's husband and his continued abuse of her — less slanderous now than in the past but still imaginative and distressing), she knows nothing of his life. She wants to know nothing; she would like to forget. Alexis dominates her thoughts, and if she finds herself thinking of death, of extinction, it slips about her with an air of being, somehow, related to her lover. . . . She wants to live, she wants to live passionately. But it seems to her that it is only through Alexis that she can live; almost, in a way, it is only through his embrace, his awakening of passion in her. She sees through him, through his vision. She hears through him. The life in her arteries and nerves and marrow seems no longer her own but his. He has, therefore, without wanting it, the power of death over her. . . . At the same time she rejects this as grotesquely romantic. She does not believe it at all.

(When her friend telephoned two weeks ago Alexis was with her; it was after dinner and the two of them had been cleaning up in the kitchen. Brigit made the mistake of accepting the call, of talking animatedly within Alexis's earshot, and she must have mentioned Stanley's name, because after a few minutes Alexis came to her and took the receiver from her and put it quietly back down. She had been amazed and rather angry, and he had been calm at first and then angry and then furious and then hysterical: they had ended up screaming at each other. He did not want her to talk to others while he was with her — he did not want her to *care* enough about her husband to even inquire about him. Didn't she know, he raged, what an insult that was to him? Was she so insensitive she didn't understand — ?)

That Brigit Stott could imagine her life dependent upon anyone else, especially upon *him:* it is absurd, really. A grotesque exaggeration.

It is only 7:10. She has been awake since six that morning, thinking about Alexis, about the party tonight, about the direction in which her life seems to be plunging. She can barely recall the days before she met him, back in September; it seems to her, now, that those days were a preparation for their meeting. She cannot imagine this winter without him. She cannot even imagine this party tonight — at St. Dennis's — without him. Last Christmas she made the egregious error of accepting her mother's invitation to visit with them and had returned to Woodslee only two days after Christmas, almost suicidal. Apart from a hectic, totally unpremeditated hour in an ice-cream shop with her sister Janet and her sister's two young children, during which Brigit flinched at the little girls' excitement but enjoyed it all the same — enjoyed being an aunt, enjoyed feeding a one-year-old ice cream in an atmosphere of simulated wrought-iron tables and chairs and peppermint-stick walls, and rediscovered her genuine liking for her sister despite their great differences; and apart from the first night's blissful dreamless sleep (she had driven down from Woodslee alone, non-stop), she had found the experience torturous, and had wondered seriously whether she could ever bring herself to visit Norfolk again. It was not simply her parents' and her relatives' smugness, their complacency in terms of their own lives, and not even their disapproval of her husbandless state; and not even — though this hurt — their indifference to her writing and her university teaching; it was their air of resentment — her father's almost rude rejection of her offer to help her mother and him financially. (Mr. Stott was partly retired from his real-estate business in a Norfolk suburb, having had a mild heart attack the year before. He had been, in his prime, "underfoot" in local politics, though he had never run for public office and had never aspired — had never dared aspire, relatives said behind his back — to anything more than a mayor's aide or a committee chairman for the county. Having complained about money all the years that Brigit lived at home, he had evidently stopped talking or thinking about it at all, perhaps out of shame or dread; at any rate Brigit had annoyed him on Christmas Day, of all times, bringing up the subject of money in the bright gay-girlish manner she had cultivated years ago, which had charmed him once. A terrible mistake: he had been sullen the rest of the day. . . . Alone in her old room she had wept with frustration and dismay. How unfair he was, how ridiculous her parents were! All of them! Herself included! There was to be no overt quarrel between them but she left ahead of schedule just the same, and it seemed to her that no one had seriously tried to prevent her leaving.)

The Christmas before, she had become involved, against her saner judgment, with a Woodslee student, a girl of nineteen with apparently insurmountable problems — a lover, parents in the process of getting divorced, other professors who did not understand her. The girl had been pretty enough, and lively, and intelligent, but there was something alarmingly infantile about her, and once Brigit befriended her — after a stormy, tearful session in her office at the university — the girl became quite dependent upon her. She brought Brigit pages from her journal, talked to Brigit at great length about her apocalyptic dream-visions, her tumultuous love affair with a young man studying forestry at a nearby state university, her parents' hatred for each other and their paranoid suspicions about her, her problems with drugs, alcohol, common aspirin, and Coke. Having received a grade of D− at mid-term from Brigit, she wisely withdrew from Brigit's course in the American novel, but she kept coming to Brigit's office, sometimes twice a day, and was so weak, so troubled, so tearful that Brigit could not turn her aside. Just before Christmas the girl had a crisis of some sort — a "spiritual crisis," she called it — and was afraid she would kill herself if she remained in the girls' residence hall, so she came to Brigit's apartment and was allowed to move in temporarily. . . . Two years later the episode strikes Brigit as merely ludicrous; she cannot believe she was ever so naive. How had it happened, Brigit Stott manipulated so blandly! Brigit, who prided herself on her cynicism! The girl, whose name was Kim, and whose outfit was a single filthy pair of blue jeans and one or two filthy cashmere sweaters, simply moved in with Brigit and stayed for eighteen days. She smoked, she drank can after can of Coke, she walked about barefoot, she crooned to the cat and slept on Brigit's sofa, nude beneath a blanket, and snored so loudly that Brigit had trouble sleeping; she chattered to Brigit or to herself, she was constantly singing under her breath, she pleaded with Brigit to allow her to "help" with her novel — she could type, maybe, or she could provide descriptions or dialogue; surely there was something she could do, her high-school English teachers had praised her "gift for expressing herself" so highly —? Brigit spent more and more time at her office in the Humanities Building or in the university library or walking aimlessly about the campus, homeless herself, spiteful and outwitted, and though she rehearsèd innumerable speeches she was never able, to her shame, to ask the girl to leave. It happened, simply, that the girl left. One afternoon. Brigit returned from the library to find a note on the coffee table: *Dear B., Hate to run out on you like this just before Christmas without even a personal good-by & thanks but I got a chance for a ride all the way to Ft. Lauderdale & he's leaving right now. Thanx a Million for Everything. Love, Kim.*

The girl left Woodslee, and as far as Brigit was able to discover, she never returned. The first week of January Brigit received her telephone bill and was astonished to see that the girl had run up a bill of $240 — telephone calls to Los Angeles; to Madison, Wisconsin; to Baton Rouge, Louisiana; to New York City. There was something frightening about the experience, Brigit thought afterward: not just the girl's placid assumption that she would be cared for, not even her selfishness, but some answering assumption in Brigit herself, that she must allow this victimization, she *must* subject herself to an imposition without charm or nobility. She had known beforehand she would be disgusted with herself afterward and yet, even before the girl had pleaded with her to allow her to stay — "for a few days" — she had more or less acquiesced. It was as if she were too timid to be as cruel as her good sense directed her to be; as if she were acting out someone else's idea of Brigit Stott. But the Christmas holidays had been less burdensome than usual because she had, at least, the fuel of her anger to keep her warm. She had gone to parties, to dinners and open houses and receptions, and to a particularly noisy and drunken New Year's Eve party at the home of a sociology professor no longer at Woodslee, and, in those interstices of social occasions that are so painful because one feels, at such times, doubly alone, she had at least the image of Kim before her — the dread of knowing she would be waiting for her at the apartment, the horror of a halfway serious belief that the girl would never leave, that she was really a daughter of Brigit's and her responsibility forever.

(When a Woodslee student committed suicide last March by taking an overdose of barbiturates, Brigit heard the news with unreasonable horror — she had the idea that the girl must somehow be Kim and that she, Brigit, was guilty of not having prevented the suicide. It turned out she did not know the girl at all; but her first reaction had been one of panic.)

Sixteen years ago. . . .

She does not wish to think of suicide; not tonight.

She switches on the light above her narrow balcony and stands close against the cold windowpane, staring out. That hard-

crusted look of intense cold: must be at least ten degrees below
zero. A certain cruel, gritty radiance to the snow. Beautiful. The
light shows uneven dunes of a few inches on the balcony floor
and on the narrow railing. A thin scattering of seed for the wild
birds, now partly covered by snow. (Earlier that day a number of
hungry birds descended upon Brigit's balcony and she rejoiced in
their fluttering busyness and the surprise of their color: several
cardinals, two mourning doves, house sparrows and slate-colored
juncos and a single chickadee, and the jay with its broken and
now withered left leg, all picking in the seed. That they were
oblivious of her and cared nothing for her admiration made the
experience all the more valuable: they descended like grace, un-
bidden, unearned, impermanent, quite beyond her control.) Past
the railing there is a formless dark penumbra. Lightly falling
snowflakes, again and always, a day and an evening and a night
filling up with snow, a harsh wind from the northeast, from Lake
Champlain, from the future. The temperature has not risen
much above zero for the past week. Each year this long holiday
period seems to Brigit more mysteriously depressing. Perhaps it
is her age — she will be thirty-nine next August — and she has
lived through the cycle too many times. Yet there is always something jarring about the power of this time of year to affect her: a
familiarity that carries within it a sense of profound mystery.
Even when the sun glares in a blankly blue sky and the heaped-
up banks of snow are surpassingly beautiful there is something
tenuous about the world and about her position in it. A physical
organism, of course, a distinct physical entity with sense enough
to preserve her being, and even to persevere — but drawn to
what is not human, what is defiantly not human, in the glacial
landscape and in the pale-glowing winter sun. She yearns for
something, she yearns to surrender to something, that almost
tactile gravitational pull toward dark and quiet and sleep and
death. . . .

Only 7:25. The party Albert St. Dennis is giving doesn't begin
until 9:00; and it isn't clear whether Alexis will stop by for her —
he is going to another party earlier in the evening, given by
someone in the drama department. (He doesn't care to see these
people, he claims; they bore him. But they've invited him to their
home several times and he has always declined and it would be
fairly easy for him to spend an hour in their company and then
leave for a more important, smaller party. . . . He doesn't want
to antagonize them, he says; he has so many enemies at Woodslee already.) Brigit was invited out to the Housleys' and she
halfway regrets now that she declined the invitation, since it
would give her something to do, a way of filling up time before
she walks over to St. Dennis's apartment building. It might be
best simply to walk, rather than call a cab or wait for Alexis; the
walk is only a half mile and she has been unpleasantly inactive
since classes stopped on the fifteenth of December. A few discouraging days spent on her work: looking through graduate students' term papers, rereading *The Wings of the Dove*, writing a
page and a half on her novel and discarding it and returning
again to her students' papers; several social events — a dinner at
the Haases'; a small luncheon given by an unusually agitated and
verbose Marilyn Byrne for women faculty members; a pointlessly
huge open house at the Garretts' which she and Alexis attended
together, and left together after forty-five minutes; Gladys Fetler's usual punch party for members of the English department
and favored students; and there had been something else, hadn't
there, at least one other party . . . ? Yes: an awkward buffet dinner at the Cuffes'. (Joe Cuffe is an assistant professor no longer
precisely young and promising, and Brigit has heard — by way of
Lewis Seidel, who perhaps should not have told her, since the
information is confidential — that the man is not only not going
to be promoted this year but is, very likely, going to receive notice
of termination of contract; there have been rumors, more than

usually hearty, about budget cuts imposed upon the departments from above, from beyond even Dean Byrne's office. Brigit knows her own position to be quite secure but nevertheless she feels a thrill of apprehension. That faintly smiling, guarded look about the Cuffes — poor Mona Cuffe's attempt at talking warmly and sincerely and intelligently with the Hochbergs — and Joe drinking too much and stumbling over Gowan Vaughan-Jones's feet: Brigit noted it all, could not help but observe, and felt the evening to be enormously depressing.)

"Stay home, then," Alexis said. "Why don't you work on your novel . . . ? I work, don't I? I work all the time. I destroy most of what I do but at least I do it; there's some pleasure in that. Then I go out, I've earned the privilege of going out. . . . But you're always going out and always complaining; why don't you stay home?"

Brigit had been irritated by his tone. It was not true that she was always going out, still less that she was always complaining. She liked the Woodslee people quite a bit — she was really fond of them — quite dependent upon them. Her discontent was with herself and she thought it cruel and insensitive of her lover to attack her.

"You don't understand me," she said angrily. ". . . You don't love me."

Now it is 7:30. She realizes she is waiting for Alexis to call; she has been waiting most of the day.

"Bastard," she whispers.

She remembers their first meeting: the boy's filthy hands. The shock of his handsome face, the shock of his too-blond hair. When she brought up the subject of their first meeting and told him of their exchange — "If you think my hands are dirty, you should see the rest of my body" — he claimed she was mistaken: he had never said those words to her. Never. He laughed at the fact of his possibly dirty hands but did not acknowledge that either; he denied everything. "You must be confusing me with someone else," he said. He stretched his fingers wide to show her that he wasn't dirty now, he had washed his hands thoroughly before coming to her.

"I remember it very well," Brigit said stiffly.

"No, you're mistaken: mixing me up with another man."

Impossible, she thinks, to mix him up with another man.

She pours herself a drink, brings it to the balcony window, sips at it while staring at the snowflakes. This evening is far better than last New Year's Eve — incomparably better. She will be with Alexis in a short while, they will probably drink too much and stay too late, and come back here together; last New Year's she was totally alone. She had thought of suicide then, not as a possibility but as a privilege she had not earned — scoffing at herself, talking aloud, her interior harangue surfacing crazily as if, at this dull dark time of the year, the least flattering of one's thoughts demanded utterance. Suicide was not for her anyway: it wasn't imaginative enough. Those of her friends and acquaintances who had committed suicide struck Brigit as having miscalculated the significance of their lives; had they been less fascinated with themselves they might be living still. And suicide seemed to be, now, an option for younger and younger people. There were children as young as ten or eleven, she had read recently, who killed themselves, given the idea by television, perhaps, or by the example of others; the son of a casual friend of Brigit's from the early days of her marriage, certainly no more than thirteen years old, had shot himself in the base of the skull with his father's police service revolver, kept in a desk drawer in his parents' suburban home in Connecticut — Brigit had heard the news only a few weeks ago and had yet to contact her friend, couldn't think what to write, put off not only doing it but thinking about it: there seemed really nothing to say. But such acts of self-destruction could not be considered, by even the most sympathetic survivor, to be intelligent strategies. It occurred to Brigit that in her life span she had witnessed the decline of suicide as a possibility for intelligent people. What was so commonplace was obviously déclassé.

7:45. Her glass is empty.

A pity she hadn't accepted the Housleys' invitation. She is ready to leave, ready to escape this small apartment where in another few minutes she will find herself thinking of the early days of her marriage, sixteen years ago; a forbidden topic. Drinking alone is an embarrassing habit. It gives her no joy, no sense of release. Instead, it seems to loosen her control over herself, so that what has been skillfully suppressed now works its way free and rises into her consciousness. The Housleys' party was to begin at 7:30. One of their large indiscriminate gatherings, probably, at which anyone was likely to appear — Republican congressmen and their wives; elderly bachelors engaged in translations of Juvenal or Catullus, and contemptuous of all existing translations; a couple whose son might have just received a Nobel Prize in biology; administrators whom one never thought of — the Dean of Women, the registrar, the director of food service, the Assistant Dean of Commerce and Finance. Brigit had met at the Housleys' once an old gentleman whose exhaustive study of Melville she had always considered a masterpiece of scholarship and tender, fastidious criticism — the sort of work she had, in a way, once wanted to do, believing it to be less disturbing than original work and possibly more valuable. She had met the New Hampshire poet Howard Flynn at the Housleys' three years ago and had almost — though not quite — made the mistake of bringing him back to her apartment with her (she learned afterward from her friend Natalie Trevor, who lived in Manhattan, of the extraordinary sexual demands Flynn commonly made — and of how disappointing he himself was as a lover); she had met a fascinating woman, a dancer, a non-resident of Woodslee, who was trying to free herself of a husband as bitter and jealous and unreasonable as Brigit's husband was being at that time, and the two talked together for hours in a corner of the Housleys' big living room — in rather strident drunken hilarious voices, Brigit supposed afterward. But there would be, mixed in with fascinating strangers, the usual people — the Hochbergs, the Seidels, Gowan Vaughan-Jones, Gladys Fetler, Perrin Blaise, possibly even Leslie Cullendon. And the Housleys lived too far away — southeast of the university, out on the Valley Mills Drive, halfway to Kittyboro. Too far to go alone.

She pours another drink.

Sixteen years ago tonight she and Stanley Fifield had been married two days. They had set out on their honeymoon, driving down the coast from New York City to Florida; they had been, at the start, quite happy. She is certain they were happy — must have been happy. A young woman of twenty-two, a young man of twenty-eight. They were in love and newly married and consequently happy. On the second-last day of their drive, however, they stayed on the highway too long; Stanley wanted to spend the night across the Florida border. Brigit drove for an hour and a half at a stretch and then Stanley took over and drove for as many as four hours in a row, just above the speed limit. He was reluctant to stop even for gas. In the Jacksonville-St. Augustine area Brigit began to feel nauseated; there was a wet, gassy, sickening stench to the air. She had never been in Florida before and it seemed rather disappointing, not much different from northern New Jersey. Stanley kept them on the road well past sunset, however, and well into the evening. (His paternal grandparents, who were fairly wealthy, owned a house in Palm Beach and it was there Brigit and Stanley were headed; the house was to be lovely — white stucco with its own beach on the ocean — and their two-week vacation was to be conventionally idyllic, though by then the marriage was more or less broken.)

They could not stop in the St. Augustine area because of the odor. Stanley did not comment on it, and Brigit dared not say very much (she sensed that her young husband felt a certain defensiveness about Florida). So he continued driving south on the interstate highway, past Crescent Beach, past Summer Haven, past Marineland and Flagler Beach and Ormond-by-the-Sea; his destination was Daytona Beach. The gassy odor gave way to freer air. It was drizzling, however, and quite dark by the time they reached Daytona Beach — Brigit estimated they had been on the road nearly ten hours.

And then Stanley began to act oddly. He passed motel after motel, slowing a little, then speeding up, always finding something wrong. Brigit was leaning forward in the passenger seat, peering through the rain at the indistinct neon signs. *Vacancy. No Vacancy.* Her vision trembled, she felt nauseated and chilled. She was so exhausted she could not trust her judgment. When Stanley slowed she stared hard at the upcoming motel, trying desperately to see if it had a vacancy, or if its rates were listed; Stanley would say, "This one? Here? How does it look?" and when she didn't reply at once he pressed down on the accelerator and drove by. She began to stammer. She looked from one side of the highway to the other. Motel after motel, neon signs, drizzle, windshield wipers, her husband's peculiar impatience, her own exhaustion. It seemed to her that they had been driving for days. The two of them, like this, driving for days without end. Stanley at the wheel, subtly angry, Brigit beside him staring ahead at the wet highway and trying to think what was going wrong. Motels, trailer courts, neon signs of pink and scarlet and blue and gold and green, the thumping of the windshield wipers, the blinding rain. "What about this one? No, on the other side, Brigit — for Christ's sake — can't you help me? It's hard enough to drive in this fucking weather — can't you at least help me with the signs?" *Vacancies. No Vacancies. Closed. Open. Special Rates. No Vacancies.* There were high-rise hotels alternating with old one-story stucco motels and cottages. There were wild stretches of vacant land. On the shoulder of the highway, in the rain, stood two young people — a boy and a girl, Brigit believed

— hitchhiking without much hope. Stanley sped by them at fifty miles an hour.

When Brigit pointed out a possible motel Stanley seemed not to notice it in time. Or, noticing it, he rejected it at once — it was too old-looking; it was probably too expensive. Brigit's eyes filled with tears. She was tired, so tired, she had come so far from home, she had put her trust in a young man whom she had seen, mainly, in the company of other people, at parties and in restaurants. He had been sweet and charming and witty and she had fallen in love with him, and she had married him, and now it was too late: they were searching for a motel in Daytona Beach on New Year's Eve, it was very dark, it was raining and cold and ugly. She was not Brigit Stott any longer; she was Mrs. Stanley Fifield. She blinked at the neon signs and tried to read off their names and rates but she was never quick enough, and if Stanley did slow down it was Brigit who hesitated, certain there would be something wrong with the motel they were approaching. Stanley chuckled once or twice but did not explain himself. Sand 'n' Surf . . . Daytona Motel . . . Mayan Inn . . . Pirates' Cove . . . Red Carpet Inn . . . Sunshine Motor Inn . . . Boardwalk Inn . . . Surfrider Motel . . . Top o' the Surf . . . Atlantic Inn . . . Whispering Waves . . . Treasure Island . . . Holiday Shores Inn . . . Hawaiian Motel . . . Inlet Motor Inn . . . Harbor Motor Hotel . . . Gull Inn . . . Pelican Motor Lodge . . . Day's End Court . . . Stanley drove through Daytona Beach, past the city limits, and made an abrupt, reckless U-turn on the highway, and headed back again. It was now 8:30. The rain whipped across the pavement. Brigit began to cry softly, so that her husband wouldn't hear. Again the motels, the trembling neon signs, again, again, Day's End Court . . . Pelican Motor Lodge . . . Gull Inn . . . Harbor Motor Hotel. . . . "Here. This one. This is it," Stanley said suddenly, turning into one of the high-rise motels. "Goddamn it, we're not going any farther tonight."

He jumped out of the car without closing the door and hurried to the office and reappeared a minute later with the keys to a room. The two walked through the rain to an elevator and went up, silent and reeling with exhaustion, to a room on the sixth floor that overlooked the ocean, and Brigit stood there, at the window, staring stupidly out into the night, trying to determine what she must say or do. Stanley checked the bathroom, the closet, the bureau drawers. One of the lamps didn't work. The rug was stained. He asked her what she thought — was the room adequate? She said the view would probably be quite lovely in the morning. It amazed her, and rather intimidated her, that the ocean was almost directly below their back window; she opened the door to the balcony but the wind was strong, rain was coming in, she thought it wiser to close the door again. The sea air was marvelous. It was so fresh she felt dizzy. She thought — What did she think, he asked, was it adequate? — or too shabby? The stucco walls were dirty. The rug was dirty. Look at the bedspreads — look at the cigarette burns! Or was it all right? "I don't know," Brigit said numbly. "I think . . . I think it's all right."

"Fine," Stanley said. "Because I can't drive any farther. Not tonight."

"The view should be —"

"I'm not going out in that car again tonight," he said.

He paced about the room, opening the bathroom door, checking the closet again, switching on the television set. He opened the door to the balcony but the ocean wind was too strong.

Brigit hugged herself, shuddering.

He looked at her.

He was young and fierce and handsome. His hair, damp from the rain, fell slanted across his forehead; his lips worked silently. She had never seen him before. She did not know him. His complexion had gone pale with exhaustion, his eyes were bloodshot.

"What's wrong?" he asked. ". . . You don't like the room, do you?"

"Yes," Brigit said. "It's all right."

"But you don't *like* it. You're disappointed."

"I don't know, Stanley. Please. It seems to be —"

"You aren't very enthusiastic."

"I'm tired —"

"*I'm* tired! I've been driving that fucking car for the past four hours!"

"The room is fine," Brigit said hollowly. "Why don't you check in at the office and I can bring some of the things up and —"

"You want to go somewhere else, don't you?"

"No. It's fine here."

She was hugging herself and it seemed to her that this annoyed him. She wore slacks and a heavy-knit sweater but she was still quite cold; she had never felt so chilled and exhausted and helpless in her life. Somewhere in Daytona Beach, in the dark, on New Year's Eve, a motel room that stank of disinfectant — she realized, now, what the odor was — a young man who stared at her without recognition, without sympathy. She had made a mistake to come to this room with him, she knew: he was going to hurt her badly.

She heard herself laughing.

"Really, it's fine! It's fine," she said, laughing. Then she began coughing. She coughed for a while, one hand pressed flat against her mouth as if she were ashamed of herself. What was so amusing? Stanley stared at her in disgust.

"Well," he said slowly, "do you want to stay, then? Will the room be satisfactory for you?"

"Yes."

"You want me to check in?"

"Oh yes. Yes."

Still he hesitated. He pointed out a burn mark on one of the bedspreads, near the headboard. He sniffed the air; he stopped to look under the bed.

Brigit laughed, seeing him in so awkward a posture.

"Yes," he said, coloring, "it's all right for you to stand there judging me. You really don't give a damn, do you, if our honeymoon is ruined? Since we crossed the border into Florida you've been acting strangely — every five minutes you've made a comment about the weather."

"I don't believe that," Brigit said. "Surely not every five minutes —"

"What do you expect, Brigit, on New Year's Eve? On December thirty-first? It isn't summer, you know, it gets cold here in Florida and it rains occasionally, you seem to have had unrealistic expectations about the trip and now you're becoming hysterical, and we haven't unpacked and we haven't eaten dinner and I'm exhausted, I can't see straight, I'm not going to another motel no matter what you think of this one — *I'm not driving that car another mile!*"

"Yes," Brigit said softly. "I know. That's fine. I understand."

But he continued to talk: bullying, whining, accusing. She could not follow the logic of his argument. She sat suddenly on the edge of the bed, the lower part of her face frozen, locked into a foolish gay-girlish smile, a young bride's smile, and while her husband paced about the room opening and closing bureau drawers, opening and closing the bathroom and the closet doors, flinging his arms about, she cast her mind back, frightened, over the months before her marriage, trying to trace the events that led her here — as one might trace, with fastidious horror, the exact movements of two separate parties that came together in a violent collision — and every effort proved futile, every recollection of their meetings was unsatisfactory, for they had seemed, all along, really incompatible: she had never understood Stanley Fifield's innuendoes and she had often disapproved of his more explicit beliefs, but all uncertainties had been more or less swept aside by the fact that she had, evidently, "fallen in love with him" and — more importantly, perhaps — he had "fallen in love with her." And so they were married, and so he was pacing about this stucco motel room, coming closer and closer to the moment at which he would seize her shoulders and shake her violently, maddened by her limp silence, and throw her back onto the frayed bedspread.

"Now — do you love me," he would cry, "do you? Do you feel me, Brigit? *Do you feel me?*"

Her lover, smelling of rum and cologne and cold, embraces her and asks what is wrong — why is she upset? He kisses her damp face. He is fairly dancing with life. Why, why does she sit alone in the dark like this, drinking? Why does she dislike herself so?

"I didn't think you were coming," Brigit says faintly.

"You misunderstood," he says.

He is in excellent spirits because it is New Year's Eve, it is 9:20, it is time for them to leave for Albert St. Dennis's party.

"You're perverse," Alexis says lightly, "with your misunderstandings."

It might be, Mina Housley tells her with sympathy, that she is coming down with the flu.

The flu — ?

This particularly virulent strain now making the rounds of the Woodslee community. Every winter, it seems, people are stricken with varieties of the flu — sometimes it settles in the throat, sometimes it settles in the stomach, sometimes one's entire body sweats and aches and goes cold. Mina herself was terribly ill last year — nauseated for an eighteen-hour period — and George had piercing headaches (a queer pointed ache in one of his eyes that frightened them both but disappeared, then, never to return) and poor Gladys Fetler, who is never ill, who has never missed a day of class in her forty years of teaching, came down with a vicious case not long ago at this time of year (or *had* it been long ago? — in 1968 or '69, Mina thought) and lost at least ten pounds — and everyone was quite worried about her, as Sandra could imagine.

"Yes," Sandra says politely. "I can imagine."

"One of the symptoms of the flu is a sense of — how should I describe it? — I should really ask Lewis, he's so articulate," Mina says, laying a surprisingly cold hand on Sandra's arm and glancing over at Lewis Seidel with a maternal smile (but Lewis is too

engrossed in a conversation with a middle-aged man whom Sandra doesn't know), "an almost eerie feeling of — of disconnect-
edness, of things being not quite real. Oh, it's alarming! It's truly
alarming! To see the marvelous familiar world of ours — and
Woodslee is so lovely, isn't it? — the university and the country-
side, the hills, the river, the *people?* — and of course the Adirondacks — To see this world distorted, all gray, everything pale and
strange and sad and — this shocked me most of all, I remember
it vividly — so *inconsequential*."

"Inconsequential," Sandra says slowly. For a long moment she
stares at her hostess' kindly face; then she says, in a small toneless
voice, "Woodslee is anything but inconsequential."

"Exactly," Mrs. Housley beams.

They talk for a while longer. Sandra sips at her drink and smiles
and nods, and occasionally frowns, and looks grave; then she
smiles again as Mina Housley gets to her feet, smoothing down
her dress — which is wrinkled across her lap — and calling out
to someone, a man Sandra doesn't know, a new arrival at the
party. The party is large but curiously subdued. Perhaps everyone
is tired of the holiday season — Ernest mentioned several parties
he had heard about to which the Jaegers hadn't been invited,
including one given by the Cuffes; and Carol Swanson had alluded to an event of some kind connected with the Tomlinsons
(though perhaps there had been no formal party, and Carol had
brought the subject up simply to annoy Sandra). . . . A figure
appears, summoned to meet young Mrs. Jaeger. Who? History
department? Sandra smiles and says hello: yes, it's amazingly
cold: must be twenty degrees below zero again.

A portly gentleman in his mid-fifties, with pale green eyes and
a courtly, avuncular manner, stinking of pipe tobacco, a specialist
in seventeenth-century England. Bachelor? Widower? Divorced?
Sandra would have cared at one time but now finds it difficult
even to keep her gaze on his face; he is blustery, pink-cheeked,
garrulous and friendly, obviously a nice person, but she cannot

make herself care. If he were Warren Hochberg, perhaps. . . .
Or Lewis Seidel. . . . But Warren has been talking with George
Housley for some time, keeping his distance, Sandra suspects,
from the younger faculty, and Lewis Seidel is telling a lengthy,
convoluted anecdote, punctuated by his and his listeners' bursts
of laughter, that seems to involve himself and — can it be? —
William Faulkner — at a party years ago in New York City.

The professor of history is admiring the Housleys' living room
and Sandra agrees; it is very comfortable, very attractive. Built in
1881, did Mina tell her? — yes, Mina did tell her — this lovely
fieldstone house — a pity the barns had to be razed but evidently
they were rotted through. Fifty acres came with the house. Enviable! Sandra agrees, forcing herself to sound enthusiastic. "It is
enviable, yes," she says. She looks around, smiling. (At that moment Ernest happens to glance her way, which is good luck; he
will have seen her smiling. He will be pleased.) That fieldstone
fireplace, the brass andirons, the logs on the fire — white birch?
— the beautiful little spruce, a Christmas tree decorated with
green and red and golden bulbs and strings of popcorn — aged,
homemade ornaments of the kind Sandra's grandmother put on
her tree. Very comfortable, very attractive. Indeed it is enviable.
Behind Warren Hochberg and George Housley, who have been
deeply absorbed in their conversation for some time — they look
serious, Sandra thinks: are they talking about the department?
— there is a small upright piano with numerous framed photographs on it, old-fashioned, quaint, very charming. There is a
grandfather clock in one corner, there is an antique settee with a
faded red-velvet cushion. There is an enormous braided rug. Da-
mask drapes. A yule wreath on one of the front windows. American colonial furniture. "Yes, it's very attractive," Sandra says
softly. ". . . Woodslee is anything but inconsequential."

Her companion grunts affirmatively, as if he had really heard
her words; he smiles, his gaze skitters across the crowded room,
he is looking for someone else, for a friend. Why is the party so

quiet? There are quite a few people here — twenty-five or thirty at least. Sandra knows some of them, doesn't know others, has forgotten the names of people to whom she was introduced just this evening — including the man beside her. He asks if she would like another drink? — and she says no, no thank you — and he is about to excuse himself when it occurs to him to ask politely how she and her husband like Woodslee. And Sandra says the Forbidden Thing: that she and her husband like the university very much and are terribly unhappy about being forced to leave.

"Forced to leave . . . ? Oh."

For a moment there is silence, and then the man mumbles something sympathetic; but he doesn't ask any questions. It seems to Sandra that he is suddenly very tense, almost frightened, as if he were personally challenged; or as if someone very ugly had thrust herself upon him.

"Forced to leave, yes. Terminated," Sandra says brightly.

The man stares at the floor and then, after a long, awkward pause, asks again if she would like another drink? — no? — well, he believes he would like one himself — so if she will excuse him, please — it's been delightful talking with her —

Alone, Sandra finds herself staring at the floor too. She wonders if she should be embarrassed or not.

Now it is necessary to join another conversation. It is more than necessary, it is urgent. If Ernest sees her sitting alone in the midst of all these people. . . . Only a few yards away is a reasonably merry group; Dr. Stanislaus Chung is talking loudly about something to do with university standards; their erosion in recent years, perhaps . . . ? Sandra stares at Dr. Chung, not knowing what to think of him. He is a square-bodied man in his fifties, about five feet three, overweight in a queer puffy way. He is wearing the same blue-and-green plaid suit Sandra remembers from the Seidels' party, and the same electric blue cotton socks, which are distractingly noticeable between his trouser cuffs and his brown leather shoes. A peculiar man about whom Sandra and Ernest have heard many rumors, some of them too fanciful to be believed: he received his advanced degrees at a remarkably young age from Oxford, published an excellent book on Spenser before he was twenty-seven, and has published nothing since, though he has accumulated two filing cabinets of notecards on the post-Spenserian age (which runs up to and includes Wordsworth and Coleridge); he was born in a small provincial city in China, hardly more than a village, left home as a boy, was taken in by American Baptist missionaries in Singapore, made his way to England, married, attended Oxford, divorced or in some way not known "lost" his English wife, came to the United States and married again, this time an American-born Chinese woman whom (it is said) he routinely humiliates in public and terrorizes in private, though the poor woman (she is sitting with a small group of other wives across the room, smiling, mute) looks ordinary enough, even rather youthful for her age. Ernest reported that he'd been in the departmental secretaries' office late one afternoon when he and the secretaries heard someone shouting in the hall, and they went to investigate, and discovered Dr. Chung chasing a book salesman and calling after him the most extraordinary obscene words — his swarthy face nearly purple with outrage. He limped badly, he was throwing his arms about, saliva flew from his lips. Ernest, of course, was astonished. The secretaries were astonished. "Asshole! Cocksucker! Filth! Dogshit! Insult me, will you? Insult *me?* I will have you fired — I will have you destroyed —" He was quite literally chasing the salesman down the corridor; it was a fact; Ernest had not exaggerated at all. (Afterward Dr. Chung explained to Ernest and the secretaries that the man had been "impudent." He had told Chung that the publishing firm he represented had published a number of very important books the previous year, and Dr. Chung had flared up immediately, pointing out that no important books were being published today, that was a ridiculous lie, and in any case he had no interest in modern or contemporary writers, or whatever they called themselves, there is no literature worth bothering with after the seventeenth century, as everyone knows, why was the salesman harassing him, just what was going on, "important books in your field," what sort of elliptical insult was that, just what did that mean, what was the man's contemptible game — ? And so Chung had ordered him out of his office and forbade him ever to return.)

Now he is laughing, his eyes narrowed to slits. His grin is broad; Sandra thinks it is rather demented. But he is one of the senior members of the department. Since he was hired at a time when the Woodslee English faculty was not nearly so substantial as it is today, when there was no one on it with, for instance, the credits of Gowan Vaughan-Jones, he was given tenure fairly easily, and his salary has increased year by year, and his rank as full professor is unassailable. Students dislike him, and drop his courses in dismaying numbers; but that fact does not appear to upset him, in fact it excites his contempt for them and for the younger, more popular faculty who are, in his words, "fashion-conscious fools." But is he contemptuous of everyone, Sandra wonders. What if she were to approach him and attempt to involve him in a warm, stimulating conversation. . . . His vote on the Promotion and Tenure Committee is an important one.

But she does not move.

Yes? No? Stanislaus Chung, or. . . .

Raucous laughter nearby: ah, Lewis Seidel. Dr. Seidel who insists upon being called Lewis. ("*Lewis,* my girl, don't you let me hear you calling me *doctor,* am I a physician, eh, are you bringing your ailments to me in the hope of being cured?") Bearish, friendly. Open. Frank. Unpretentious. The most calculating person in the university, Joe Cuffe once called him, in the guise of being the least calculating. But is that altogether fair, Sandra wonders. He does appear to carry his importance lightly. He *does* talk to the younger faculty members, and to their wives. . . . Sandra might join him, perhaps. Lewis? How are you, Lewis, on this freezing hideous night, are you as powerful in the department as everyone says, are you simply pretending to be merry, and careless, and very, very young . . . ? One of the nastier rumors about Seidel had to do with someone named Hogan. The incident had taken place years ago, many years ago, and Sandra had not cared to inquire about it; all her life she had chosen deliberately not to listen when people talked of matters that had taken place in the past; for the only past that mattered was *her* past. But she recalled bits. Hogan: Andrew or Adrian. A contemporary of Seidel's who had published a book on Scott Fitzgerald that had been rather poorly received. Though Hogan's degrees were from Yale, he had evidently lost his nerve suddenly, or whatever it was that professors might lose — whatever self-deceptions worked for them in the classrooms and in their graduate seminars — and he began to back down before his graduate students' pointed, aggressive queries. It was Seidel who urged them on, rumor had it. They were his students, committed to him and to certain theories of his about American literature of the twenties, and they were ruthless with Hogan, lying in wait for him not only each week in their seminar but even in the corridor, raising questions of interpretation, alluding to reviews of his Fitzgerald study, asking him biographical and scholarly questions he could not answer. Shaken, he went to the chairman and confessed his inability to control them, or to handle the situation in general. (He had begun to cut classes, even undergraduate classes.) There were rumors, he said, that his contract would not be renewed. He heard them everywhere. And crueler rumors as well. . . . In the end, the man had done something grotesquely foolish: he had parked his car in his garage and turned on the motor and asphyxiated himself.

But rumors, Sandra thinks: how seriously can they be taken?

Seidel was attracted to her back in November, for a few minutes at least. He had seemed to admire her quite openly. Took her arm, her hand. Leaned close to her. Winked, grinned, teased. Later, it is true, she saw him flirting with Carol Swanson, and that was a disappointment; but he had seemed genuinely to admire *her* at the start. So there is always the possibility of. . . .

The bastard, Sandra thinks. To goad someone into committing suicide.

Would he be pleased if she approached him . . . if she smiled up at him as women smile at men, as young women smile at middle-aged men, slyly, hopefully, with a certain air of desperation? (Not always with an air of desperation. Yet if they are not desperate why would they smile in that way, why would it ever occur to them to smile in *that* way?) Or would he be suspicious? After all, she is Ernest Jaeger's wife. And he certainly knows the situation that young Professor Jaeger is in.

Sandra looks away. No, it might be unwise. Poor strategy. Lewis would see through her at once.

Nearly every member of the Promotion and Tenure Committee is here tonight; except Gowan Vaughan-Jones, and Ernest told Sandra that Brad Keough had told him (when they were still on friendly terms) that Vaughan-Jones, the youngest member of the committee, really has little power; he is passionately caught up in his scholarly and critical work, it is said, and leaves university and departmental politics to others. And perhaps he isn't even aware of what is going on most of the time. His own position is secure; unassailable; enviable.

The new division, Sandra thinks dully. The new struggle. Between those who have unassailable positions and those who have not. Between the aristocrats and the stateless. . . . In any case, Gowan Vaughan-Jones would be difficult to charm. He doesn't seem interested in women, he *is* unassailable.

Sandra sees that Carol Swanson is trying to ingratiate herself with Mrs. Hochberg. But how obvious! How ludicrous! Carol has gotten herself up for the holiday season in a tight-fitting red wool dress with a sprig of plastic holly on the collar. Her lipstick is too bright, her patent-leather shoes are years out of style, surely Mrs. Hochberg with her humorless acerbic wisdom must see through her. . . . Sandra wonders what the two are talking about. She wonders if Carol is desperate enough, or drunk enough, to actually have brought the Forbidden Topic up to the wife of the department chairman. But might such a strategy work? Might the Hochbergs take pity on the Swansons? And if Carol is pregnant. . . .

Sandra forces herself to look away. Such thoughts are degrading and she will *not* degrade herself and they are a sign she has had too much to drink and there is nothing to do but drink, it is the holiday season, the party is too restrained, too mild, frankly it is too dull, everyone must continue to drink, what will happen otherwise . . . ? She sees Brigit Stott near the fireplace. Slender fine-boned woman, with her very dark hair in an attractive chignon. Ah, how Sandra envies her! A successful novelist with an unassailable academic position. Unmarried now: rumored to have a beautiful apartment cluttered with books and art objects and several highly bred cats (not Siamese but Himalayan), independent, admired if not particularly liked (but then, who cares about being *liked*, Sandra thinks with revulsion: we're out of high school now), respected, perhaps even feared. She is said to carry a small pearl-handled revolver in her purse. . . . She is said to be merciless with students, and abrupt with flatterers, and *not* friendly to any man who drifts by and compliments her. . . . (What a luxury, Sandra thinks, to be freed of being charming!) Sandra is about to heave herself to her feet and approach Brigit Stott when the woman turns further and Sandra sees that it isn't Brigit Stott after all.

Oh Christ, she thinks. Oh damn.

Yet she must get to her feet, she must mingle, must ease into a conversation with someone, anyone, anyone will do, Ernest has been glancing at her for the past several minutes and will soon approach her, frowning with irritation, "Honey, why are you sitting here by yourself? Would you like another drink? Can't you make an effort to smile, you look so sad and washed-out —"

She rises, smoothing out her skirt. Lightheaded for a moment. Almost gay, before the sickness descends again. But then it *is* only the flu; simple and innocuous as that; nothing metaphysical about her malaise at all. As she turns, several people glance her way. Where in the past she would have felt an immediate secret thrill of pride she now feels a more complicated emotion — near to resentment. Of course she is attractive in this floor-length flowered dress, with her hair recently washed and fairly glowing about her slender face; of course she is — as Ernest will tell her afterward — the most beautiful woman at the party. But it means so little. And it is only the Housleys' party, after all. The eyes of impassive unassailable strangers move across her, appraising her, but then they move on, idly, already forgetting . . . there is no way, really, for her to hold their attention. They like her, they like her hard-working young husband. But it means so little.

She makes her way through small groups of people. Someone is talking animatedly about inadequate snow removal, someone is talking about Alfred North Whitehead, someone is talking about the member of the Oriental Studies Program who is under indictment for embezzlement (of funds belonging to a student travel organization); Faye Seidel is talking about an incident that took place at her son's school, Gladys Fetler about a recipe for mead, an elderly gentleman whom Sandra doesn't know is denouncing vehemently the efficiency of the air terminal at Champlain — but, worse yet, his companion says passionately, is the Kennedy Airport in New York. Sandra is conscious of herself, painfully conscious. She is too tall. She has put on too much perfume. In the eyes of these Woodslee people she is not Sandra Baird but Ernest Jaeger's wife, and since they are embarrassed about being forced to treat that deserving young man so cruelly, they are of course embarrassed about acknowledging Sandra; they shy away from greeting her. *I won't get drunk*, Sandra wants to shout. *I won't get drunk and abuse you. . . .*

Will no one approach her? Not Barry Swanson, certainly. There he stands, slightly stooped over as always, pretending to be interested in one of Mina Housley's anecdotes; showing his gums as he smiles. Poor Barry. A former friend. (Jealous of Ernest and Ernest's relationship with Mr. Atkins, the curator of the rare book room of the library; and he is insanely jealous of Ernest's position in the department in general — though why he should be, Sandra doesn't know; it's utterly irrational on both the Swansons' parts.) Not Brad Keough, another former friend: appears to be drunk already. A pity. Frizzy-haired and raucous and far too cheerful for this atmosphere, drawing attention to himself as he laughs. He does no more than glance at Sandra; he turns away from her. (Once, back in October, Sandra and Ernest invited Brad and the Swansons over for dinner, and they had a long marvelous hilarious evening: they had speculated freely and wildly and irreverently on the private lives of certain of the older departmental members, doing imitations, even, and making predictions; they had gossiped about the Hochbergs — was it true that Mrs. Hochberg was an heiress, was it true that Dr. Hochberg wished to be the next dean? — and the Seidels — was it true that Lewis was having a love affair with one of his girl students? — or the wife of one of his colleagues? — and had he had an affair some time ago with Brigit Stott? — and Gowan Vaughan-Jones — was it true that the man was a genius? — or was he merely eccentric, deep into middle age though only thirty-five? — how peculiar he was, with his poor teeth and his uneasy giggle and his baggy clothes! — and poor Leslie Cullendon, whose students were cutting his classes because they could not bear his hour-long ranting monologues, his sickly intensity, his defiant deathliness — it was true, wasn't it, that everyone avoided him? — Brad had seen dear Gladys Fetler herself duck around a corner to escape

Leslie, and had overheard Lewis Seidel — heartless and witty as he was — make a comment about Leslie's value as a *memento mori* for the rest of them; they had speculated at some length about Brigit Stott and the tales of her legendary promiscuity — Carol Swanson said the woman simply terrified her, that cold smile of hers, those eyes like a snake's eyes, she didn't see how men could be attracted to her; Barry said she *was* attractive, he'd seen her laughing and obviously flirting with men at the Seidels' party — including that young student of hers, Todd Andress, whom everyone thought so highly of but whom he, Barry, believed to be just another spoiled brat; could it be possible that Brigit Stott was having an affair with *him* . . . ? — but Brad pointed out that the gossip was of Brigit Stott and Alexis Kessler, at the moment anyway, and, earlier, when he'd just arrived at Woodslee, gossip had linked Stott and Oliver Byrne; and people alluded from time to time to Stott and Seidel, who were obviously very close friends. . . . So they had spent an uproarious evening. Then, after the letters from the dean's office went out to Ernest and Barry and Brad and Joe Cuffe (and possibly to others: they aren't certain), a storm of unsettling tales made the rounds, and one of the older departmental members took Ernest aside and informed him that certain friends of his had been saying that Ernest and Sandra were contemptuous of Ernest's colleagues — they routinely mocked and ridiculed them. So, for his own good, Ernest should be aware of these rumors; to protect his own position he should, perhaps, apologize . . . or explain . . . or make clear . . . or do something. *But what can I do?* Ernest asked Sandra in despair.) So Brad looks away from Sandra and Sandra looks coolly away from Brad.

Mona Cuffe smiles warily at Sandra but indicates, by a certain rigidity of her body that she does not want Sandra to join her and Christopher Callinan and Edie Ryerson (they are talking about skiing: Sandra has heard that Callinan, a trim, energetic bachelor in his late thirties, a specialist in Old English, is a former Olympics skiing champion) and so Sandra smiles in return, suddenly very self-conscious, and heads through the Housleys' oaken archway to the dining room and the bar, as if she wants nothing more than another drink. Two days without much solid food, only a plate or two of fruit salad and cottage cheese that nauseated her, and several glasses of orange juice — oranges squeezed vigorously by hand, by her attentive, hearty husband — and now a second drink, already a second drink, surely everyone is watching? — Sandra makes her way blindly forward, rather more hurt by Mona Cuffe than she would have anticipated. (Mona is thirty years old and had been very helpful to Sandra and Carol the first weeks of the fall term; being sisterly had seemed a role that enlivened her, that disguised her intellectual inadequacies.) The Cuffes are especially bitter because Joe has been at Woodslee for three years, and his notice of termination of contract was — it is said — as succinct and chilling as those received by Ernest and Barry, who are new appointments, and by Brad Keough, who is rumored to be "disappointing" in the eyes of certain senior faculty members — Hochberg, for one, and Perrin, and possibly even Lewis Seidel; Sandra has heard conflicting stories that leave her confused. (And others say that Dr. Fetler, who is magnanimous about promotions and tenure and raises, always wishing to see the positive sign of a colleague's record, has behaved in this generous, bountiful manner for decades, quite confident that her male colleagues will do the unpleasant task of measuring young faculty members against rigorous standards — she knows very well that, when the committee votes, her own ballot will be outnumbered by the others; otherwise, it is said, why does she show so little distress at the committee's actions . . . ?) The Cuffes have two young children. And a new house in the east end. Joe has been toiling (his expression) in the enormous lower-division courses since coming to Woodslee and hasn't had time to do much writing, hasn't had time even to revise chapters of his doctoral dissertation for publication as individual articles. (The humiliating irony of his situation is, Sandra heard by way of a rather cruelly gloating Brad Keough, that Joe's dissertation was on the "radical political assumptions" underlying the "new avant-garde" — the dismissal of all bourgeois standards of psychologizing and storytelling and linear exposition by several contemporary writers he admired very much; caught up, now, in a scramble for economic safety, he has been forced to admit that either the assumptions underlying the avant-garde are inapplicable to anything other than the avant-garde or that he himself is a hypocrite: hence his bitterness.) It is said of Joe Cuffe that he has talked with Dr. Hochberg on three separate occasions, and that he was seen coming out of the dean's office (which, if Dr. Hochberg knew — and no doubt he was told — would certainly work against him). His drinking, too, would work against him if it were the case (and it might possibly be the case: no one knows yet, not even Dean Byrne) that one or even two of the dismissed men might be rehired for next fall. . . . The fact that the Cuffes have two children and have already bought a house in Woodslee is in their favor, Sandra thinks. The department is likely to pity them. Mona isn't very intelligent but she *is* a mother, and Carol and Sandra aren't; they are merely young wives, adjuncts to their husbands, even rather intimidating since both have applied for part-time jobs at Woodslee — Carol as a secretary, Sandra as a librarian — and there are no part-time jobs, there is no money for part-time jobs, for additional staff. . . . On the other hand, Sandra thinks giddily, hearing on one side a fragment of a conversation about alcoholism among the students and on the other a fragment about someone — an artist? — named Giorgione, the fact that the Cuffes have children and have bought a house might be interpreted as rather presumptuous; she can imagine Vivian Hochberg saying something penetrating and dismissive on the subject of the Cuffes. Still, Joe has been on the staff longer than Ernest, he *is* amiable and intelligent, with an ostensibly harmless big body, soft and shuffling, and impressive credentials from Chi-

cago and the University of London, and . . . and the Cuffes are
evidently established well enough here to have given a party of
some kind over the holidays . . . to which they invited only the
important faculty members. . . . The Swansons and the Jaegers
could not manage anything like *that*, even if Sandra had been
well enough to attempt it. (However: Carol Swanson is aggressive
and vulgar and not very intelligent, and perhaps she will — self-
destructively — actually plan a social evening, and invite the
members of the committee, and everyone will see how crude the
Swansons really are.) . . . Ah, Sandra's head spins. She wants to
laugh aloud. People to her left are quite happily discussing a new
book by Joseph Campbell, a couple just behind her are making
plans to go to Montreal to see the Canadian National Ballet —
and she is a young woman who once, not long ago, wrote fastidious papers on such subjects as Plato's *Meno* and the art of
Donne's religious sonnets and the secret meaning of *Moby Dick*,
before taking up the more practical study of library science; she
is still herself, still Sandra, but her mind is filled with trash, she
can feel it sinking beneath the ugly weight of these thoughts, and
even the early, rather charming naiveté of her aspirations here
in the Woodslee community seems to her idealistic now, pristine
and enviable. But she will never be so innocent again.

(The lies to her parents did it, really. She knows that now.
Without working out in advance — without needing to work out
in advance — the stories they would tell Mr. and Mrs. Baird,
both she and Ernest had lied easily and inventively. Yes, Woodslee was fine; yes, Ernest was getting along very well with his
colleagues. It was much, much better than that dismal extension
in Trenton, of course. . . . But the Bairds would never have
understood. If a man is fired from his job, especially within a few
months, it *must* be his fault: a good man is never dismissed.)

In this part of the house the party is noisier if not merrier.
Sandra finds herself protected by an immense piece of mahogany

furniture — a sideboard that must be an antique, it is so defiantly ugly — and a tight little group of four or five men, arguing about the worth of Dean Byrne; no one will find her here. She is still lightheaded and she finds, oddly, that it does not matter. She does not *care* whether she is sick or well. Eagerness or malaise or indifference: what does it matter, really? (Carol Swanson would be delighted to know that Sandra is breaking down under the tension. A few offhand remarks, queries made to Ernest in earshot of others about "poor Sandra." . . .)

She does not care. Whether her husband finally gets another job (out of the more than two hundred letters of application she has typed for him in the past several weeks — surely *one* will respond favorably?) or whether he is indeed terminated at the age of twenty-eight (as, it seems, certain of his former classmates are; a year's unemployment is a terrible handicap, it is said, both on one's professional record and in one's sense of one's own worth) or whether he is miraculously rehired by Woodslee after all. . . . She does not care, she cannot care. He has worn her out with the intensity of the grief he does not allow himself to feel.

Ridiculous, Sandra thinks: Of course I care.

Efficiently, gallantly, a balding young man in a maroon blazer makes her a drink.

Of course I care. I care very much, Sandra tells herself.

Someone is commenting on the amazing amount of snow they have already had; and the worst is yet to come, evidently — January is always vicious. Sandra agrees. Someone — it is the young man in the blazer — is commenting on the warmth of the Housley's parties. Not like other universities, is it? — Woodslee is famous for its friendliness.

Sandra hears herself agreeing.

Voices float about her, now distinct, now wavering. She feels the rim of the glass knocking gently against her teeth. There is a sharp burning sensation in her mouth — for a moment her

tongue hurts. She coughs, chokes. But then is all right. . . . What
has she been thinking about, what have these people been talking
about? Important to keep her mind occupied.

She wouldn't want it known, the young man says quietly, but
Mina's — that is, Mina and George's daughter is very, very ill. At
the Roswell Clinic in Buffalo. Isn't it brave, then, and generous,
of the Housleys to have this party and to open their home to their
friends?

She is not drunk and will not get drunk. She will not be a
danger to others, or even an embarrassment to her husband.
(Once, in Cambridge, before they were married, she got so pleasantly dizzy, so charmingly silly, Ernest had to carry her bodily
out of someone's apartment — over his shoulder, actually — and
they have, since that night, reminisced tenderly and mischie-
vously about the event; but Sandra hadn't really been drunk,
there was no genuine need for Ernest to carry her out; it had all
been play.)

. . . No formality, no rigid sense of distinctions, the young man
is saying. New faculty, young couples who know no one. . . .
The Housleys . . . genuine interest . . . everybody. Woodslee is
infused with the spirit of democracy, wouldn't Sandra say?

They are joined by a man named Springer. Sandra knows him
only by appearance; she has been told that he is not very important in the department. Hiccupping, he asks her how she likes
the weather. How she likes Woodslee. Is she enjoying the party.
He mumbles something about her hair and sways a little, smiling
damply. He is her height exactly, a man of uncertain age with a
bulbous nose and broken capillaries on his cheeks. Something
damaged, eroded about him. Breaking. Broken. Sandra has the
idea he is divorced — is he the one who was chronically unfaithful to his wife with undergraduate girls, or is he the one whose
wife left him, eloping to New York with an East Indian student?
— she cannot remember. Springer. Pete. Author of — ? A study
of Sherwood Anderson — or Jack London — Or — Possibly a

poet, once promising but now one of the department's disappointments. Of course he is protected by seniority and tenure. Though she knows this and fully resents it and even hates the man a little for it, she manages to smile, and even to blush at his clumsy, mock-flirtatious interest. If there were justice in the academic world a man like Pete Springer would be dismissed and a man like Ernest Jaeger would be kept on, but there is no justice, the situation is insanely unjust, she must accept it, must put off thinking about it for the evening. In the meantime she is, isn't she, a reasonably attractive young woman, not seriously ill, capable, surely, of brightening up the tiny pocket of the evening she finds herself in . . . ?

Springer is talking about Oliver Byrne. At first Sandra listens with genuine interest, then she realizes it is a story Ernest had brought home at least two weeks ago — and subsequently warned her it might be false; the dean had threatened to resign if President Garrett didn't go back to the board of governors and insist that the budget cuts and the positions lost be restored. Springer seems quite certain of the authenticity of the tale. He even imitates Byrne's voice and waves his hands about, as if he had been present at the meeting with Garrett. It seems to him highly significant that Byrne isn't at the Housleys' tonight, and did they know why? Here he lowers his voice so that Sandra and the young man in the blazer have to lean toward him. "Because he's in California at this very minute being interviewed by one of the state universities — Davis, I think — yeh, Davis — being interviewed for the presidency. How the hell do you like that! Huh? Our fair-haired boy! At least *he'll* land on his feet."

Overhearing, another man joins the conversation; he says, rather brusquely, *he* had heard Byrne had been asked to resign by the old buzzard — it seems that Garrett was furious about something Byrne had said in a senate meeting, a comment on the administration's ability to handle the board of governors — It isn't true either that Byrne is in California. He is in — at this

very moment — New Orleans, being interviewed by Tulane.
And not for a presidency either — for another deanship.

Springer shakes his head violently. He seems quite angry. No.
No. That bastard Garrett wouldn't dare speak out against Byrne.
Wouldn't dare. It's common knowledge that the chairman of the
board of governors favors Byrne for the presidency — and the
majority of the faculty, too, would throw its support behind Byrne
— All this is commonly known.

But the young man in the blazer must disagree. Byrne is flashy,
yes, and no doubt impressive, and has brought in some foundation money, and that business about the Performing Arts Center
written up in *Time* — yes, that was excellent, excellent publicity
for the college; but when it comes to solid work, solid achievement —

Shit, Springer cries.

— the allotment for food service expansion has been very disappointing — hasn't kept up with rising costs —

"Hello, hello! Hi! Here we are! Hey! How goes it! Happy New
Year!"

They turn to see a figure in a wheelchair: it is Leslie Cullendon,
wheeled up by Barry Swanson. His is noisy, gay, drunk, even
rather robust; his eyes gleam. He shakes hands with Springer and
the young man in the blazer and the other man and Sandra,
keeping her for last, squeezing her hand in his strong cold fingers
as he kisses it, making a wet sucking noise. It is all a joke, an
overflowing of holiday spirits. Sandra smiles faintly down at the
man's bowed head. "Just in time! Not a minute to lose! Who's
gonna make me a drink? Scotch — and a little water. Not too
much, though! *Not too much!* — Honeygirl, I'm afraid I forgot
your name. Poor Leslie's mind is a sieve these days. What's your
name? Wanta wish you a special happy new year, what's-your-
name!"

Everyone laughs. Sandra, blushing, tries to tell him her name
but he interrupts at once, not listening.

"Can't tell 'em apart! Night or day or other! The only thing about Babs, she's got this one nipple sort of purplish-brown and poking out sideways, 's a distinguishing feature needless to say — needless to say! If you've got your glasses on. If you give a damn. — Look here, honey, don't fidget, Leslie means only to bring cheer, that's what Minnie Mouse squeaked at me when I came in the door, jumping up and down she was, ol' Mousie, saying, *Why here's Leslie our favorite disaster come to bring us cheer* — Hey look, maybe I don't know your name but I know *you*, I can sniff you out, my girl, and in the words of the immortal Pope — also a crip:

> Nothing so true as what you once let fall,
> "Most women have no characters at all."
> Matter too soft a lasting mark to bear,
> And best distinguished by black, brown, or fair.

— By which the little bastard meant public hair, as the footnotes say."

Sandra would escape but Leslie holds her hand tight in his. The others are laughing, Pete Springer is making him a drink, his shoulders rock with exquisite mirth. Sandra tries to smile because it is something that must be done. Must be attempted. She is not drunk herself and she despairs of getting drunk enough, there isn't time, everything is happening too fast and there isn't time.

Fortunately the conversation shifts back at once to the subject of Oliver Byrne.

The dean, Leslie cries hoarsely, is at this very moment in a private sanitarium in Nassau — where his wife is undergoing shock treatment — his wife! The poor dizzy bird-brained idiot —

Sandra is shocked, then realizes it is a joke; then isn't certain if it *is* a joke; but she manages to laugh nervously with the others. Leslie talks and talks, pausing only to swallow large gulps of his drink. His thin, hawkish face is almost flushed tonight; his eyes are very bright. He is dying, it is said, of a rare neurological disorder, related to multiple sclerosis but somehow different. Yet he is charged with life. Frantic with life. Everyone avoids the Cullendons, Babs is said to be very bitter — there she is, Sandra discovers, only a few yards away, staring at her husband's active head and torso but making no move to approach: Sandra smiles at her but the woman does not notice.

It crosses her mind that she and Ernest might become friendly with the Cullendons.

If only she felt stronger . . . !

Ernest told Sandra some time ago that he was really impressed with the work Leslie Cullendon had done on various aspects of Joyce's art in *Ulysses*, before he was taken sick. Ernest had read Cullendon's articles before coming to Woodslee, before he had even known he would apply to Woodslee, and so it would not by hypocritical . . . it would be quite sincere. . . .

If. . . .

It might work out.

The Cullendons and the Jaegers.

Leslie and Babs and Ernest and. . . .

She glances at Barry Swanson, who stands behind Leslie's wheelchair smiling uneasily, not wanting to look at her. In that instant it crosses her mind that Leslie has already been claimed, that Barry and Carol have plotted to befriend him: ah, how obvious!

She is so shocked, she draws her hand out of Leslie's.

He takes no notice, though, talking now animatedly about a small scandal soon to erupt in the philosophy department, having to do with the head of the department falsifying certain records — notably his own evaluations. Everyone listens eagerly except Sandra and Barry, who are both very conscious of each other. Sandra decides to sip at her drink and behave as if nothing were wrong. It is her belief that, in Barry's mind, she, Sandra Jaeger, has always had — during the span of their brief but intense

friendship — a certain luminous quality, a poise and an attitude
of sophistication sadly missing in his own wife. She has caught
his wistful glances, his eager laughter at her clever remarks. A
pity they are no longer friends. . . . He found her bright auda-
ciousness more generally charming than Ernest has come to,
over the months; she used to feel quite marvelous around him.

Now, however, she feels nothing at all.

Regret, maybe. Sorrow.

No. Not regret, not sorrow. Nothing.

He isn't worth an emotion, she thinks, staring boldly at his
face. A competitor of her husband's. A rival. He isn't worth her
hatred any more than his loud, vulgar, unfortunate wife —
whom Sandra believes she can hear laughing in the other room.
. . . Standing like that self-consciously behind Leslie Cullendon's
chair, leaning over to help Leslie wipe up some Scotch that has
spilled onto his trousers, already smiling at an incoherent anecdote Leslie is telling about Marilyn Byrne and a yoga instructor
in town and a potter in the art department: he isn't worth her
concern at all.

Mina Housley has decorated her upstairs bathroom with yellow
wallpaper, white and yellow tile, bright green curtains on large
white rings that put Sandra in mind of something nautical, something to do with ships, she giggles at the absurdity of it, runs cold
water and dabs at her face as if she wished to hurt herself. Should
have stayed home. Not so pretty tonight. Shadows beneath eyes,
really quite discernible. How quickly the face can erode. . . .
Very faint lines in the forehead, those hours of unconsciously
frowning, screwing up her face, grimacing, arguing with herself.
What, after all, is a face? She contemplates her own, which she
has learned, suddenly, to doubt; never before has she been so
struck by the accidental and arbitrary and possibly even mislead-
ing nature of the human face.

She laughs, alarmed.

212 *Unholy Loves*

Must be drunk.

Stares at herself. Sandra this: Sandra that. Not so important after all.

"I care very much," she says, articulating each syllable. She is speaking to Ernest. He leans over her, hands on his knees, his face shadowed. Perhaps his eyes are damp — she sees or thinks she sees that. Love. Husband. "I care very much." Her lips are numb, her worlds are muffled. Cotton batting in her mouth. Packed in tight inside her skull.

"I *told* you I care. . . . I care very much."

In the corridor just outside the bathroom two people are talking and their voices, with Sandra's, make a raucous jarring harmony. It is New Year's Eve, it is a night of festivity. A man is complaining in a slurred, mournful voice that his wife has been insane since Christmas Day: has anyone even noticed? No one has noticed. A woman laughs harshly, clearing her throat. The man says that *her* husband has been no less charming tonight than ever . . . he carries himself so stiffly, is he wearing a brace, or a hernia support?

The woman says something about antibiotics, drinks at the Wallers' before coming here, his persistent sore throat and queasy stomach, pressure on him from above and below. . . . her husband carries himself stiffly: he's a terrified man. If a number of positions are being erased throughout the university his own position is in danger, isn't it? . . . at least in theory?

Hell, her companion says, what has theory to do with reality?

Those young men in the department, for instance. . . .

Oh let them suffer like the rest of us, the man says irritably. You women and your fuss! I'll miss Cuffe, he could be entertaining, but his wife, Jesus, which one is she, I'm tired of those short big-eyed types, I thought women were getting taller. . . . Anyway, the entire situation shows that Byrne isn't omnipotent: which I knew all along. I —

There are plenty of taller women, the woman says. I mean girls.

He thinks he can bully the board of governors because he has the faculty's support, he thinks he can throw his weight around, *he's* going to be Woodslee's next president —

The Jaeger girl, for instance. Surely you've noticed her.

Who? Oh — her. Yes, *her.* Of course I've noticed her, I'm hardly blind.

And what do you think?

What do you think I think? I'm hardly blind.

But she might be rather sour on account of her husband —

Let her! Let them all! I was fired from Brown, you know, my second year there, I've told you about it, all that *I* went through. Let these smart-ass kids get a taste of it. The world isn't a nursery, is it?

Not so loud, Lewis.

Just what do we owe them, huh? They'd love for us to drop over dead so they could climb into our shoes! Some of the jokes Cuffe has been making when he's drunk, by Jesus they *aren't* ultimately funny, and it's going to be us against them one of these days, poison slipped into drinks at the MLA, skirmishes in elevators, guerrilla warfare —

The voices are retreating. Sandra stands, shocked, staring at her pale reflection. Now the man in the corridor is coughing harshly — and then goes on to speak of another matter that evidently angers him. Sandra opens the door a half inch so that she can hear better. Lewis Seidel: his whining drunken furious voice.

". . . damn little ungrateful bastard, has-been, hypocrite . . . like all of them . . . who was it but me drove the old bat to New York, for Christ's sake, afraid he'd get lost on the train, and refuses to fly any longer, he says; a dream foretold he'd die in a blazing holocaust if he took another plane. Yes! And he believes it, of course! The English are all mad — all mad. *All.* They be-

lieve in spirits, they believe in the most contemptible egregious
occult trash, that's why he sits around with Mrs. What's-her-
name at the library sucking tea and probably, for all I know,
reading horoscopes . . . and laughing up their sleeves at the rest
of us. But the lack of gratitude! It's staggering. Byrne has pursued
him shamelessly, from what I gather, but he *is* the man who
hired him, so I can understand him inviting the Byrnes (oh that
God-awful cow Marilyn: if I were Byrne I'd have broken her jaw
by now); and Brigit Stott and Kessler — well, it makes a normal
person shiver just to look at them, I admit there might be something thrilling about the old boy taking them both on — or Kessler anyway — Kessler *will* get what he wants, people say, eventually, and it must be admitted that both Brigit and Kessler are
— well, what are they? — they're failures, they're wrecks, but
they did once have talent and St. Dennis is maybe shrewd
enough to know that; he isn't entirely senile. He's stupid to fall
for them. But I can understand it, I can even forgive it. But —
Vivian — for God's sake — can you believe that he has actually
invited Gowan Vaughan-Jones to his party? — tonight? — to the
first and probably the last party the old miser will be throwing, he
invites Gowan Vaughan-*Jones?* Gowan Asshole Vaughan-Jones,
of all people? — to St. Dennis's New Year's Eve party? Tonight!
This very moment! Gowan Vaughan-Jones — and not me!"

"Lewis, really — "

"And he didn't invite you and Warren either," Lewis says excitedly. "Oh it's fantastic! It's baroque! Of all the people in our
department — *of all the people* — Gowan Vaughan-Jones! The
man who, two years ago, was terribly upset because one of his
students had sprayed 'G V-J Sucks' in one of the men's lavatories
and the poor bastard thought it was some reference to — you
know, you've heard? — he went about broken for days, depressed, almost suicidal, until he explained the situation to Chris
Callinan, he thought the insult had something to do with him
sucking lollipops, or gumballs, or whatever — he told Chris he'd

been fighting a bad cough all week and had been chewing cough drops and the students must have noticed and joked about it and now it was all over Woodslee and he was a laughingstock, what could he do, should he resign, he wasn't accustomed to even thinking about his students having any opinions of him, he wasn't accustomed even to thinking about his students — that they existed, you know — that they had any existence at all. He just lectures! He's brilliant, he's filled with information, he just lectures and they fill up their notebooks! — So poor Chris had to humor him, said it was meant only in play, the kids sucked lifesavers and cough drops too, it was only a gesture of kinship — He figures he might have saved Gowan's life, the poor bastard was so depressed. And that is the man — that half-creature is the man! — whom St. Dennis chooses to elevate over *me*. In full view of the Woodslee community."

The woman murmurs something consoling. Sandra, now peering along the length of the hall at them, recognizes Vivian Hochberg by the dark bunch of hair at the back of her head, and the long floor-length gray and scarlet dress. Seidel is paunchy in a pair of tight-fitting pale green pants and a black turtle neck sweater; he waves his big hands about as he speaks.

They enter the Housleys' bedroom but reappear a moment later, with Vivian now carrying her coat and a man's coat, presumably her husband's. They talk together at the top of the stairs for a while longer, Seidel flushed and earnest, Mrs. Hochberg far more animated than Sandra has ever seen her. She herself has gone cold. She has gone dead. She considers the possibility of stepping out into the hall and demanding their attention and telling them she has overheard everything — that she detests them, she would destroy them if she could. She considers the possibility of stepping out into the hall in a quite natural, unpremeditated way, and of hurrying down to them, in order to say good night to Mrs. Hochberg before she and Warren leave. If she speaks to them at all she will have to use her voice, which she does not remember having heard for a while; the sly babyish drunken slurring of a moment ago isn't really Sandra Jaeger's voice. And the face: which face? Deathly pale, drained and past its bloom. . . . Another used-up wife. . . . No, none of these are familiar. If she confronts the man and woman at all she will have to compose herself anew; she will have to be inventive.

Brigit has been drinking for hours but her mind is surprisingly clear. Remarkably clear. When she hears her own voice it sounds distant; it seems to come from a source outside her head. Ah, it is terse, almost brittle, it is very *wise*. Brigit has always been modest about her reputation here at Woodslee for being witty and cruel — but now, perhaps, it makes sense. She has said some extraordinary good things tonight and St. Dennis's guests — or most of them — have laughed heartily and will no doubt repeat her remarks next week.

Others are witty too. Alexis has been quite inspired tonight. And that explosive joyous laughter of his! — so entirely natural. His eyes narrowed to slits, his beautiful mouth grinning, his fists pounding against his knees. He is elegant, he is slovenly. He has been, from time to time, a little vulgar tonight. But everyone has laughed, Brigit has laughed, she is sick with love for him and cannot look at him, and cannot look for long away from him. She is grateful, absurdly grateful, when Albert St. Dennis comes to sit heavily beside Alexis, and slides his arm about Alexis's shoulders, and asks him how his work is coming along . . . that flash of incredulous boyish delight in Alexis's face is beautiful to see.

Todd Andress has been fairly clever tonight, reciting great

chunks of St. Dennis's early poetry to him, embarrassing the poor old man mightily — but sensitive enough to know, without Brigit's having to tell him, that he should stop; if he wished to demonstrate his eccentric memory he might recite silly jumbled lines from Eliot or Sitwell or Auden, perhaps, and St. Dennis would be more amused. (Todd is twenty-three years old; he has been Brigit's outstanding student for several years, and the English department's most prized protégé — he takes drugs, has taken drugs since the age of fourteen, has been expelled from college and reinstated, has traveled to India, has traveled to Japan, writes poetry that he allows no one to see, is probably — certainly — a genius of some kind: the kind who will not survive. So Brigit has thought, dreading news of his death; so others have thought, fussing and worrying over him. Yet he continues, he returns semester after semester, he appears to love literature as purely and passionately as certain of his professors loved it, in their youth, and he is occasionally malicious, and occasionally manic and embarrassing, but most of the time — tonight, for example — really quite nice: and Brigit adores him. She wishes for him a long, happy life. She wishes for him a *life*, though she cannot quite imagine what that life will be.)

And there is Lee Hawley, the wretched Lee Hawley, he too has been fairly witty tonight . . . though Brigit has resisted laughing at his ugly puns. The woman in the drapery — Brigit can't recall her name — sitting so heavily and impassively at one end of St. Dennis's sofa: she has not been witty but she has laughed loudly at what she must have thought were clever remarks. (She has been especially receptive to St. Dennis's and Alexis's humor.) Gowan Vaughan-Jones is out of his element and is sitting there in that broken-backed chair by the door, the same drink in his hand each time Brigit looks, gawkish, still eager, really an adolescent boy somehow gotten up as a middle-aged man in a bulky blue serge suit with a vest; poor Gowan is looking quite drained and there is a film of perspiration on his grayish-white skin, but he keeps smiling hopefully, and tries to join in the general laughter. From time to time he glances at Brigit as if he wishes to make contact with her, as if he and she are somehow linked, and Brigit smiles only vaguely and looks away at once.

She has been drinking for hours. Before coming to this peculiar party, even. But it has had no effect upon her. None at all. (Which is strange: she wonders if she is, what is the expression, gaining a tolerance for alcohol? — becoming accustomed to it, at any rate.) . . . She is clear-eyed. She sees everything. The dust balls beneath the sofa and the table and St. Dennis's workdesk . . . the cobwebs softly fluttering in the corners . . . the stains on the rug and the cushions . . . the fact that St. Dennis's left sock has ridden down into his shoe. She sees everything and hears everything. Her own voice sails into the dense competition of voices and does amazingly well — she hears herself with pride. One by one others are becoming hazy, woozy, fuzzy. The woman in the drapery is someone's wife and Brigit despises her. Where is the husband? — over in the corner, in that odd chair or whatever it is behind St. Dennis's workdesk. He hasn't moved for some time. Must be unconscious. (A subeditor at St. Dennis's publishers, up here for the weekend to deliver something-or-other to do with St. Dennis's collected poems. Galleys, perhaps. Jacket designs. Brigit wishes St. Dennis would confide in her about his work . . . but he has not, and he will not; he seems embarrassed even to be forced to mention, occasionally, that he has been "working.")

Odd, Brigit thinks, that Oliver and Marilyn weren't invited.

Good, Brigit thinks, that Warren and Vivian weren't invited.

Unfortunate that poor Lewis Seidel missed out. (Within moments of Brigit's and Alexis's arrival, St. Dennis took them aside and asked what had happened to Mr. Vaughan-Jones? — he had thought perhaps the three of them would come together since they were such close friends. Then the doorbell rang and Gowan Vaughan-Jones appeared and St. Dennis's confusion indicated

that St. Dennis had somehow mixed up Lewis and Gowan; he
had meant to invite the chunky red-haired man whose party he
had had to miss in November and whom he was afraid he had
gravely insulted, but he had believed the man's name to be
Vaughan-Jones; he claimed never to have heard of "Seidel."
Gowan, fortunately, was so excited that he seemed not to hear
what was being said by St. Dennis and Brigit, and so the awkward
moment passed. It will make an excellent anecdote but at the
time Brigit was rather embarrassed. Really, St. Dennis is a bit
muddled tonight. . . .)

And fussy and old-womanish, muttering uder his breath as if
scolding himself. Is he drunk? So soon? His perfectly white hair
sticks out about his head in quills, comically stiff; his little potbelly
strains against his shiny dark trousers; the queer purple sweater-
vest gives him the air of a dimunitive thug, a street Arab. He
repeats a few catch phrases again and again: "Ah there! At last!
Good to see you!" and "What can I do for *you?*" and "Are you all
acquainted?" As if to please him everyone is drinking rather heavily.

It is an odd gathering, Brigit must admit. She is highly honored
to be here; she knows she is probably envied by most of the
Woodslee community. Still, it is an odd gathering of people, a
party of strangers. Perhaps in the months to come she and Alexis
will reinterpret the evening but at the moment it is really quite
peculiar.

How strange St. Dennis is . . . ! Whenever he catches sight of
her his face seems to brighten; he smiles broadly and tenderly.
But it is a false smile — it is directed at someone other than Brigit
and it is never accompanied by a remark that makes much sense.
("Are you comfortable, my dear? Are you warm enough? Are you
hungry?") Several times already he has asked Alexis how his work
is and Alexis, blushing, has said it is coming along well. (In fact
Alexis has four of the songs completed and wants very much to

arrange for St. Dennis to hear them — performed, most likely, by several of Alexis's students; but he is too shy to bring the matter up tonight. He has also been working on a slight but charming piece that he says is a springing-off from one of the songs, a trio for violin and flute and harp, but he doesn't mention this either: Alexis is, incredibly, a modest young man where his work is concerned.)

St. Dennis interrupts his guests' conversations, asking if they are comfortable where they are — or would they like another pillow, or a footstool, or a shawl? He spends some time adjusting a space heater; Todd Andress manages to drag it across the room and into a convenient position just below one of the ill-fitting windows. At other times he gets to his feet in the midst of a conversation directed at him and, without excusing himself, without even appearing to be aware of his rudeness, he goes into the kitchen . . . to reappear in a few minutes with a bowl of salted peanuts or a platter of shrimp or cold salmon, though it is far too early for food and no one is hungry. He sighs loudly. He sticks a finger in his mouth to adjust his false teeth. He drinks faster than anyone else — amazing, for a man of his age, Brigit thinks — and laughs loudly at remarks not especially intended to be amusing. (He refers fondly to Lee Hawley as a "wit.") He falls silent in the midst of a remark and, after long moments during which everyone is uncomfortable, he speaks again in an altered voice, abstracted and bemused: a monologue on wines (most of them are tasteless now); on the folly of all learning, especially history (*Eadem, sed aliter.*); on the need to cultivate one's death assiduously ("How does the human animal know *how* to die? It must be learned."); on the hyperborean whimsies of God ("Do you think that old Yeats was right, that God and anni-hilation are *identical?*").

Brigit stares, listens, memorizes.

He is old, he belongs to mythology. She too will be old some-

day, difficult as it is to accept. But she knows, she knows. She
and he know. The others are gross, are too lively, too life-filled.
She knows. . . . It is his mortality that speaks.

He gives off an odor of unwashed clothes, unwashed flesh,
tobacco, liquor and — and what? Grief? (For a moment Brigit is
reminded of her mother's father, who died so suddenly when
Brigit was a very small child. The odor of old clothes, of stubborn
unwashed flesh, of a defiant grief. Who are these old men . . . ?)
St. Dennis's teeth too white. Seemingly too large for his small
narrow face. He fusses, he pads about in his bedroom slippers,
the grape-dark sweater riding up his belly; he is anxious that his
mismatched guests come to know one another and that they eat
and drink heartily. ("More Scotch? More ice? More deviled eggs?
Salmon? Caviar? Stuffed shrimp? Paté? Biscuits?") He is too kind
to Lee Hawley, who must have latched himself on to St. Dennis
at the Riverview Tavern, and who *must* have invited himself to
this party; it is inconceivable that a man of St. Dennis's good
sense would invite Hawley into his home. He is kind, too kind, to
everyone. Poor man, poor lonely man, Brigit's eyes fill with sentimental tears and she rises in the midst of a furious conversation
about contemporary music and follows St. Dennis out into the
kitchen to ask if she may help him . . . and he doesn't seem to
have heard her, he jerks around, obviously startled, and then
explains in a rather formal voice that he never allows anyone to
help, only one person in a kitchen at a time, his mother's saying,
the best wisdom, isn't it? — in fact he has dismissed his housekeeper, there's no need for an old solitary man like himself to
require the services of a housekeeper, he's fully capable of looking
after himself and anyway he isn't that significant: no one is. Brigit
tries not to feel hurt. She smiles, she nods. She appears to agree.
At the same time she cannot help glancing about the kitchen —
which is a discouraging sight indeed. The stove is filthy with
scorched, stale bits of spilled food; the sink smells; the counters

are cluttered and filthy; the linoleum floor is sticky underfoot. Everywhere are dishes, pots, pans, rags, cans, bottles. Bottles.

A smell of — what? Garbage?

"Mr. St. Dennis, would you like me to . . ." she begins, meaning, *Would you like me to straighten up a few things here*, for it seems to her suddenly more important that she get poor St. Dennis's kitchen into some kind of minimal order than that she return to the living room, to the spirited conversation, and to more liquor; but he doesn't hear her, she speaks too softly, too timidly, and he is muttering under his breath as he searches in the crowded refrigerator for another dish. Marinated mushrooms, he says: where are they? In here somewhere. . . .

Brigit stands in her long party dress, nervously turning a bracelet about her wrist. She is wearing several. And several necklaces as well. Alexis looped the necklaces over her head, gaily, and fastened the bracelets, and dabbed perfume on her throat and shoulders and arms. Lovely, he said. Lovely woman. Sometimes I envy you: could *be* you. (From the other room an explosion of laughter — Alexis and Lee Hawley, both quite drunk.) Brigit watches St. Dennis uneasily. Is he well? Is he altogether well? Since his triumph back in November Brigit has seen little of him, though she understands that various members of the university community have been inviting him to their homes; mainly members of the board of governors, and certain administrators, and of course the Byrnes. (Though that may be only a rumor about the Byrnes.) Brigit wonders if Woodslee is really a good place for Albert St. Dennis, after all. He seems somehow altered, less sure of himself than he was in September, even physically smaller, as if shrunken an inch or two. And very distracted. At the moment he is mumbling as if he were alone in the kitchen, scolding himself for not knowing where he'd put something — a wooden spoon, is it? — she can't quite understand what he is saying. The burden of giving this New Year's party seems to have excited and exhausted him so that he is hardly aware of his guests any longer; what is important is the necessity of serving them, of getting the party over. Brigit knows that frantic state of mind well.

"Mr. St. Dennis, maybe I could —"

"No no no no no, not at all, not at all," he says quickly.

Brigit is reminded of a blunder she made once regarding a friend, a woman some years her senior, who lived alone in Manhattan, and whose life was a very lonely one. Never married, a successful editor on a woman's magazine, she was in her mid-forties when Brigit became acquainted with her, and she got into the habit of telephoning Brigit very early in the morning, simply to talk — about literature, mainly, and movies, and theater, and the New York art world. Brigit had been touched by the woman's evident loneliness. She believed it was easy to forget how hellish life was for the lonely (at the time she was married) and so she was patient with the woman's calls and did not mind that they were monologues. She went to the woman's apartment only once — summoned there because the woman had been ill for several days and couldn't go out to do her shopping; and she had been astonished at the mess — more disorderly, even, than St. Dennis's apartment, suggestive in a way of a mind not *quite* right. (There were, Brigit remembers, six-foot-high stacks of Bambi fruit-flavored yogurt containers in the woman's never-used bathtub; the containers had been fitted together with care and had obviously been saved for a purpose. There were several plastic containers of cat litter in various strategic places about the apartment for the woman's three cats, but none of them had been changed for some time.) Brigit, shocked, had offered to do a little cleaning — and the woman had been really insulted; propped up by pillows, she began abusing Brigit so vehemently that she seemed in danger of falling out of bed. . . . There were no more telephone calls after that; the friendship ended abruptly. No more of Brigit's stories were bought for the magazine.

"Brigit, my dear, you shouldn't worry about me," St. Dennis

says gently. "It's New Year's Eve — why don't you enjoy yourself with the other young people?"

"Let me take that heavy bowl from you, at least."

His nearness makes her extraordinarily self-conscious. She is never able to forget who he is, though it is obvious that St. Dennis himself wishes mainly to forget; he has no interest at all in Albert St. Dennis. Brigit sympathizes, she does not want to press his identity upon him, and yet — what a pity! She stands in a kitchen alone with the famous poet St. Dennis and she does not dare ask him any question of seriousness, she does not dare even bring up again one of the subjects that intrigued her earlier, about how to die, about the knowledge of dying, about God and annihilation. Minutes are passing. She is losing him. If only. . . .

When admirers of her writing have spoken with her in the past, she has sensed the folly of her pretensions at knowing anything at all; she has known herself an impostor. But St. Dennis is *not* an impostor. Drunk as he is, distracted as he is, he embodies a certain wisdom that frightens and consoles her — he exists on a plane distinct from her and the others — he *is* an extraordinary man. It astonishes Brigit that anyone should speak of God, for instance. That anyone should speak seriously of God, without being ironic or pious or metaphorical. She wishes to ask him about God: Has he had experience of God? What does he mean by *God?* Is it possible that . . . there is a God of some sort, who truly exists?

She shakes her head to clear it. Suddenly she feels a little unsteady.

St. Dennis is spooning out mushrooms onto a platter. He forces himself to move slowly, for fear of having an accident. Brigit stands beside him. What does it mean to die? — to make an end? — to complete a cycle? He has spoken from time to time, always obliquely, of his wife, his long marriage, the shock of its termination; one of his poems touched upon the idea of dying at the right time, when death is still aesthetically possible.

Brigit wants to ask — wants to know. It is almost midnight. Someone is laughing uproariously in the other room. She believes that this self-effacing old man knows a great deal that would help her with her life, but she is unable to ask a single question. Her own marriage — her love for Alexis — her failure as a novelist — her curious dissatisfying knotted-up life: surely he could help her?

". . . small friendly group . . . large gatherings hateful," St. Dennis is murmuring, ". . . so nice of you to come, dear. Darling girl! And your young husband: charming. You're very, very happy, I assume. . . ."

"I — I — Yes, certainly I am," Brigit says.

"Nothing so comforting as rings of faces lifted in joy," St. Dennis says vaguely, ". . . Least we can do for one another. Tiring but necessary. Must acquit oneself. . . . A religious duty, you know; not social or political. But large gatherings, no! Absolutely dreadful. Hateful. People stepping on one another's feet . . . blowing smoke into one another's faces . . . ogling one another's wives. An affront to one's soul. . . . We have a quite warm, intimate group here tonight, dear, don't we?"

"Yes," Brigit says.

"New Year's Eve is no time to be alone," St. Dennis tells her confidentially. "The planet is about to plunge into darkness and our souls are frightfully sensitive at such times. I'm quite serious! . . . The Explorers, don't you know, set forth with such joy upon their voyages . . . it seemed endless, their passion . . . the universe had no limits, no possibility of being exhausted; ah, how young they were! — how empty of thought! But all along the Mothers were waiting. Observing, don't you know, in absolute silence . . . always in silence. *There is no language to the body!* . . . The Mothers, the Weavers, content to bring all exploration to an end; content to embrace their sons in the end. What they weave they then unweave. The Explorations, the Explorers themselves. Woven — and then unwoven! We come closest to sensing it in ourselves at certain times of the year and this is one of those times, dear, isn't it, haven't you sensed it as I have, don't you sense it even now . . . ? What is woven will be torn apart so that it can be rewoven again . . . but of course it will be rewoven by someone else."

Brigit finds herself shivering. "By someone else . . . ?"

"The risk, you see," St. Dennis murmurs. "The risk. Only someone in a new body can bear it. Otherwise. . . . No, it's impossible. We create ourselves through a torturous activity of the soul but it's necessary that we *not know* when we begin our life's work how very, very difficult it is, how much it will hurt, and how little it will matter, in the end; if we guess this truth, why, the Mothers have us at once, they squeeze us to death in their hot embraces, that's it! that's it! — why, we would never come to know one another, my dear."

He smiles at her. She cannot understand him; she stares at his wrinkled, flushed face, at his colorless eyes, and feels the anguish of being unable to understand.

"It's fortunate for all of us that we're together on New Year's Eve," he continues. There is a strange sheen to his face; it glows in patches, unevenly. Across his nose and cheeks there are broken capillaries. He is smiling, Brigit sees, why is he smiling? — why is he so gentle? He does not know her and yet he addresses her so intimately, so kindly, as her own father and grandfather never did; she is afraid she will burst into tears. Of course what he is saying is incoherent, or mistaken. He seems to be making reference to the group of people in the living room, who have nothing to do with one another, who hardly know one another, and who certainly don't know Albert St. Dennis. Yet he is speaking solemnly. His words are profound. Brigit strains to understand: ". . . as we must be together always, don't you know. You and I and your husband especially. Never again parted! From the very first . . . that first evening. . . . A sense of. . . . Did you too? Yes? Yes. That is the Mothers' touch, the sense of fate. The relief of sinking into an embrace. One struggles, but in the end it's best simply to. . . . But you're young: and so it's wicked of me to talk like this. The young must be kept ignorant for as long as possible! . . . Huxley told me that. They thought he was dying then. More than once. Slipped from his body, you know, and returned, a ghastly look about the eyes, never quite the same again; and now I too. . . . The only duty that remains is completing oneself, tidying up. Very important to go at the right time. Most go too late, you know. Some too early. . . . Is it Nietzsche speaking? Yes. His despair at his own profound ignorance: that he of all men should die too late! Ah, I pity him, I pity him so much. . . . But there was a friend of mine who shall remain nameless who knew it was time for him, who *knew*, and yet he refused to go, he lost all the strength of his legs and then his arms, and he could not control his bodily functions, and had to be fed, my God! — and still the spark of life was stubborn in him, stubborn and cruel, it sickened me to look upon it, oh what selfishness, what wickedness! — he passed into an abstraction at last, being totally blind and deaf and, they said, incapable of smelling or tasting any longer. Can you imagine! The grim mastery of one's own soul. . . . So different from poor Harriet. . . . But, do you know, the poems that have come to me lately are not about death at all but about life: about the life of 1912. It's all so clear, so sweetly clear! I'm halfway embarrassed at Harriet's discovering, after so many years, and others . . . what will they think? Well, they must think what they must," he says, giggling. ". . . in Ealing it was. Living then with my Mum's mother. Across the alley, a semi-detached house, really not half bad for that neighborhood, though they *were* very dark. . . . Marco, his name was. Saucy little brattish thing, my age, black eyes and curls and a raucous jeering voice, a little wildcat he was, six years old, some pounds lighter than I, even, but far far stronger . . . a little demon, really. Of course he had reason. The neighborhood was cruel. I tried to befriend him but. . . . He would have come round finally, I think, but. . . . Ah, he could be so sweet when the spirit moved him! Even his torments were playful. Seeing I meant no harm, he took pity; seeing I wasn't like the others. But his brothers were so violent. . . . Still, I think that . . . gradually. . . . He could scream such obscenities, it was remarkable! Standing there with his knees bent, as if about to spring, a little curly-headed animal, just bristling with life, so very, very different from me and from anything I knew. He hurt me, but he didn't know. He couldn't have known the extent of the hurt or that I would remember it for seventy years and, in this place of snow and ice, at the very edge of the world, I would give thanks to the Fates for having preserved me simply so that . . . so that I can write hymns in praise of him, in praise of his marvelous lost beauty. Perhaps I will justify myself as a poet yet!" he says, smiling broadly. Brigit tries to smile in return; she isn't sure whether he is serious. "All other loves, I see, have been gross illusions," St. Dennis says slowly. "It's a terrible thing to have to admit, but I must be honest. . . . Marco, my dear little Marco; my poor lost vicious Marco; my poor friend, where are you . . . ."

Blinking rapidly, he clutches at Brigit's arm; for a moment she is too astonished to react.

". . . lost broken betrayed child," he whispers.

"Don't be upset, Mr. St. Dennis," Brigit says. "I think you've been — you've been exciting yourself, and — Would you like to sit down?"

"Life conspires to cut us off from one another," St. Dennis says. "We conspire to do so. The Explorers begin as lusty ignorant boys, vessels of flesh, and though they throw themselves into the farthest reaches of the universe it never occurs to them to explore themselves. . . . It never occurs to them to love themselves. . . ."

His legs seem about to buckle beneath him, so Brigit leads him back into the living room. He leans heavily upon her, breathing so hard that the others glance up in surprise. Or is he sobbing . . . ? Brigit goes back for the platter of marinated mushrooms.

She is trembling. Still, she isn't drunk: she is certain of that. Another drink?

The small, cluttered, rather ugly living room with its pale beige walls and its maroon rug and its solid, old-fashioned, styleless furniture is dense with smoke. Brigit's place on the sofa has been taken by Lee Hawley, who is arguing loudly with Alexis about experimental music and theater. (Hawley seems to be in favor of experimentation of all kinds — Alexis is being mandarin and priggish and conservative, and seems to be rejecting all experimentation.) Todd Andress sits cross-legged on the rug, his hair wild about his face, his eyes wetly gleaming, trying without success to break into the conversation. The woman from New York — her name, Brigit recalls, is Edith or Ethel — is paying only minimal attention to the men; she has been eating smoked salmon and anchovies on crackers, and chain-smoking. Her husband still slumbers behind St. Dennis's desk, one arm limp and his fingers brushing against the floor. Gowan Vaughan-Jones is sitting at the very edge of the party, awkward and hopeful, a half-filled glass in his hands; he is watching Alexis and Lee Hawley with an intensity of interest painful to see. (He reminds Brigit of a small boy excluded from his playmates' activities: openly admiring, not at all resentful, not even envious.) St. Dennis has more or less collapsed in a threadbare easy chair, his eyes half-closed, his mottled hands clasped over his soft little paunch.

Unobserved, Brigit pours herself another drink. St. Dennis's words have upset her. She does not wish to think of them — not tonight. A pity, a pity. So old. His hands trembling with excitement. His voice ecstatic at the end. There is so much, Brigit thinks, that he could tell us . . . if only he would. There is so much that might pass between us. All of us. Tonight. Now. If only. . . .

(She half-remembers an incident from her girlhood. An image

presents itself to her but fades almost immediately: a mirror, a mirror coated with grime, her reflection ghostly in it. The attic. A summer afternoon. Suddenly dizzy with the heat or with a sense of apprehension, Brigit had shut her eyes in order not to see — what? The dusty mirror, the ghost-self peering at her quizzically . . . ? But with her eyes shut she continued to see it. A face, vaporous and yet insistent, her own, not her own, familiar and unfamiliar at the same time. *Brigit. Brigit.* She realized that she was Brigit and must answer to that name; she could not escape the fate of being *Brigit*, though, suddenly, she had no idea what that meant. To be a certain person, to *be* a particular human being — what did it mean, really? Did anyone know? She was terrified by the conviction that no one knew, not even the adults of her world knew. They would not help her. . . . Afterward, for days she had contemplated the memory of that disturbing incident. She did not seek out the image in the dusty mirror but she was able to evoke it at will, in her mind's eye; she had always, even as a child, a remarkable visual imagination. The image fascinated her, haunted her, called to her. It was *Brigit*, yet, clearly, it was not *Brigit*: it was something unknown, something she could not grasp. In a dream she advanced to touch her mirror-image but it shook itself free of the mirror and retreated, teasingly, and she followed, she followed, not allowing herself to be frightened by the queer buoyancy of the earth beneath her feet, and the gale-like wind that arose on all sides of her; she whimpered aloud at her own daring but could not stop — there was nowhere for her to stop, no firm ground for her to stand on. Suddenly she realized that the entire dream was alive: a living creature. The world was alive, the universe alive, a creature living in every particle, breathing, trembling, quivering with life. She was *in* this creature. It was not yet aware of her but if she did not turn back it would become aware of her and something would happen. Something terrible would happen. It would wake, perhaps; it would become conscious of her; she would be destroyed.

And so she tried to turn back. She twisted her body at the waist, whimpering, wanting only to turn back, to escape, to wake. . . . She did wake: and within a few hours the dream was forgotten. She had not remembered it now for nearly thirty years.)

Brigit stares at these people. Who — ? Why is she — ? Ah yes: Alexis. Her lover. And St. Dennis half-asleep in his chair. New Year's Eve. Yes. . . . She finishes her drink, forced to realize that she and Alexis have ended up, after all, at the most dismal New Year's Eve party in Woodslee.

It ends badly for Brigit, shortly after 2 A.M.

By then the couple from New York City have departed; they are staying at a motel out near the interstate highway. Gowan Vaughan-Jones has departed, having thanked St. Dennis profusely for the "great honor" of having been invited to his "home." (Brigit, pitying Gowan, and pitying herself for being rather excluded from the conversation between Alexis and Hawley, talked with him for twenty minutes just after midnight, and was impressed once again — as she always is — with the young man's zealousness and the range and depth of his learning. He seems to have no interests other than his scholarly and critical work: he told Brigit that Woodslee was an ideal place for him with its long winter because he would rather be indoors anyway, he would *rather* be forced to stay at his desk for months at a time. Laughing self-consciously, he mentioned to Brigit that following a debilitating weekend bout of the flu in early December (he was stricken only on the weekend, he made clear; he was back teaching at 9 A.M. Monday) he had even lost his ability to taste certain foods. It's a commonplace aftermath of the flu, he knew, yet in his case it seemed to be lingering a long time. . . . He could taste spicy foods, he said, like this mustard dip, and citrus fruits had saved his life, practically, but other, more subtle foods, like the smoked salmon and the shrimp and the caviar, had no taste at all. (He never really developed a taste for caviar, he told Brigit with a childish laugh.) Brigit expressed some concern for his predicament; she suggested he see a doctor. He laughed again, self-consciously, and took off his glasses and rubbed at his eyes, and Brigit could see that he was an attractive young man despite his homeliness; there was something agreeable about the oversized lips, the pug nose, the colorless, weak eyes. Seen on campus, Gowan Vaughan-Jones resembled no one so much as an eccentric, doomed older student of the sort who wears overcoats too large for him and carries a battered briefcase, and whose boots flop about his ankles, unbuckled; he is likely to be unevenly shaved, often with a small Band-Aid on his cheek or Adam's apple; he gives off an odor of confusion and energetic dismay. Yet in fact Dr. Vaughan-Jones is probably the department's most highly regarded critic at the present time, and he is certainly the most widely published. Innocently, he set forth in some detail for Brigit's benefit the contents of his new book on modern poetics, which will be seven hundred pages, at least, upon publication; he gave her a rapid summary of a paper on Hart Crane he will be presenting to the Society of Aesthetics and Literary Criticism in February; he went through the half-dozen book reviews he either had just completed or is working on, all in his area of specialization, for such journals as the *Times Literary Supplement* and the *Partisan Review*. A new project that has occupied his imagination in recent weeks has to do with the Futurists' influence upon the poetics of Charles Olsen. . . . And he wants to talk at length someday soon with Mr. St. Dennis about the circle of poets who published in *Proteus* in the early days. . . . He then paused awkwardly in his monologue to ask Brigit about her work; everyone at Woodslee pauses, at a certain point in his monologue to ask the listener about *his* work. Brigit blushed, taken by surprise, and said that she was working, yes, as always, but not entirely satisfied with the results . . . maybe this would be the year, she said, attempting a reckless smile, when she would come to terms with herself as a failure; after all, not everyone can be a success. Gowan was nodding. His smile was respectful. Either because he was too embarrassed to acknowledge what she said, or because he really did not hear it (Lee Hawley was roaring with laughter), he seemed to agree perfunctorily with her and returned for a final five minutes to the subject of his own work, and then he rose to say good night, expressing surprise that it was so late. Brigit saw him to the door, since St. Dennis was in no condition to get up, and Alexis and Lee Hawley paid no attention to him at all. . . . Strange man, strangely appealing! It is too easy, Brigit thought, to dismiss him as a stereotype, a parody. He *is* a stereotype and a parody, and yet he lives, he breathes, he walks about in the world, he is quite a successful academic and his career has just begun. And he is very nice. Courteous, gentle, perhaps a little silly, and certainly chilling in the innocence of his ambition, and brilliant; but very nice. Brigit wonders why he frightens her so.

1:30 A.M.

Todd Andress has drunk too much Scotch and has eaten too much caviar; he has crept off to St. Dennis's rather depressing cubbyhole of a bathroom, there to be sick at some length. Brigit sits on the arm of the sofa beside Alexis, wishing to leave. But he is talking with Lee Hawley. Has been talking with Lee Hawley all night.

Alexis is quite drunk.

Graceful lean-bodied golden boy, golden-haired boy, a beauty. She stares at him helplessly. He and Lee Hawley are talking about the works of John Cage. ("Silence isn't profound," Alexis says. "It's brutal.") Brigit would like to speak, she would like very much to join them. She is a woman, after all, with opinions of her own; she enjoys hearing herself talk. But she is tired. Very tired. And

they are so absorbed in each other. . . . (What time is it? Only
1:30. It seems to her far later.)

It is the New Year. St. Dennis, his glasses on the table beside him, sits nearby
pretending to listen. He slouches so that his shoulders and chest
appear to have collapsed upon his stomach. His complexion is
parchment-colored; he seems fatigued. Brigit smiles at him but
cannot make contact. She wants to thank him for the party and
suggest they all go home now and allow him to sleep, surely he
must be tired, it must have exhausted him to have prepared so
much food without any help . . . ? He gazes toward her but does
not seem to see her. In a way he seems quite content.

Alexis interrupts Lee Hawley. Lee Hawley interrupts Alexis,
laying a hand on his shoulder to calm him. The two men are very
irritated with each other. What are they arguing about . . . ?
Alexis's drawling voice is rather ugly; he makes no effort to be
charming once he has been drinking for a while. Brigit stares at
him, wanting only for him to break off the conversation, to turn
toward her and smile and say it is time for them to leave. (It
seems to her that at any moment this will happen.) She thinks of
their first night together, she remembers his gentleness, his surprising candor: he had been, evidently, quite upset by the scene
at the Byrnes' while he was playing his sonata. That his work
should be ignored, that it should be mocked — ! She had had to
assure him that no one had mocked him. Certainly, no one had
mocked him.

Lee Hawley is in his early forties, a heavy-set man with a bald
head and a dense curly bronze beard and a small, pink mouth.
He has a habit of licking his lips when excited. His laughter is
explosive and hearty, there is something both congenial and disturbing about him, something benign and at the same time unsettling. He is a very popular lecturer in the psychology department. When, a few years ago, his colleagues in the department
tried to dismiss him, hundreds of students demonstrated in pro-

test. Newspapers throughout the state carried articles and photographs; classes in psychology were boycotted; there was even a
bomb threat.

He is also an amateur musician, it seems. And he has been
involved in something called Action Politics Theater — a movement designed, evidently, to counter the repressive influence of
the Drama School; it's well-known that the Drama School con-
sists of comically sick individuals who can't be trusted with the
responsibility of theater in Woodslee. Hawley is a revolutionary,
a leader, a lover of poetry and music and young people and life,
and he is very certain of himself. Tonight he is wearing a peculiar
outfit: faded blue jeans that are too tight for his full, straining
thighs, a black leather vest, a transparent shirt of dotted swiss.
The backs of both hands have been tattooed: a snake on the left
hand, a white wolf on the right. His eyes are small and babyish
and shrewd. He shouts Alexis down but then allows Alexis to
make his point; his licks his lips happily.

Brigit wishes desperately to leave.

Alexis ignores her.

Lee Hawley smiles at her and winks.

(From time to time, at parties, she has encountered Hawley
and has despised him, without quite knowing why. His insinuat-
ing, sly, presumptuous manner . . . his habit of touching her, of
touching everyone . . . his false, aggressive intimacy . . . his air
of always posing . . . his air of childlike frank open friendliness. . . . *You and I must get together sometime soon*, he has
whispered to Brigit, *I want to pick your brains. Don't be shy!
You're very gifted and everyone knows it, I know it, and I intend
to know you better!*)

But now it is Alexis he wishes to know, and Alexis seems quite
absorbed in him. Brigit half-listens, growing more and more uneasy. She must leave. She will leave. The party has been a disaster, really; there is no ignoring the fact. Still, it was better for
her to leave the apartment, better for her to attend any party,

any party at all, than to remain at home on New Year's Eve, thinking futile thoughts about her husband. If only Oliver and Marilyn had been here tonight . . . ! And Lewis Seidel. . . . And Gladys Fetler: she wishes, suddenly, to become better acquainted with Dr. Fetler. The woman is so strong, so gracious, so confident, so warm and intelligent and admirable. . . . She will be retiring in three or four years and that will be the end, Brigit won't have had the opportunity of knowing her; she must get to know her this year, before it is too late. And perhaps she could befriend some of the younger faculty members and their wives, who are probably lonely here, and uneasy about the future. She must, she will. She will. As soon as the holidays are over she will plan a party of some kind . . . will invite her friends . . . and people to whom she owes an evening or two . . . and of course Albert St. Dennis . . . everyone will be eager to come if they know St. Dennis is also invited.

Yes, she and Alexis will give a party.

In February, let's say.

Mid-February.

She and Alexis. . . .

Alexis in a suit of dark green velvet and an expensive silk shirt from the Montreal trip, the collar unbuttoned; Alexis's voice too loud for this small room. He is angry about something. He is flamboyant, capricious, pouting, playful, dangerous. Sweeping his left hand, he nearly knocks a cigarette case off the coffee table; Brigit catches hold of it; and this seems to annoy him.

"Leave me alone," he mutters.

Lee Hawley, laughs, delighted. He is picking bits of salmon off a plate, using both hands. Again he winks at Brigit.

Brigit is very uneasy now.

She can barely remember the start of the evening. She has had a fair amount to drink — not so much as the others — but she is clear-minded, clear-eyed. She is not at all drunk. . . . What was that business in the kitchen with St. Dennis, something about love and death and poetry and a little boy named Marco in 1912 . . . ? She does not remember. Not exactly. It upset her and she had a drink or two afterward and now she is concerned with other matters, she wishes to dislodge Alexis from the party, from Lee Hawley, she wishes to get him safely home. . . . But when she starts to speak he ignores her; he does not seem to hear.

She touches his arm and says, "Alexis, do you think —"

"For Christ's sake," he says. "No."

He is joking, she supposes. She manages to laugh. Fortunately Albert St. Dennis doesn't notice: he has fallen asleep. Fortunately Todd Andress in still in the bathroom.

1:45.

She pours another drink, a final drink. Her hands are trembling. Either the men are staring at her or they are ignoring her. They do not listen to her. Alexis is feverish, lively, tireless. He can drink all night and sleep a few hours and work the next morning; he is still young. There is something terrifying about his youth. (Brigit thinks cruelly of how, in a few years, he will change: will grow, perhaps, into a form of Lee Hawley, forty pounds heavier. Then no one will love him very much. *She* will not, certainly.) Hawley is so drunk that he is in a space beyond drunkenness; he appears almost normal as a consequence. It was said about him that he involved undergraduates in experiments with drugs . . . that he had sexual relationships with students of both sexes . . . that, when called to President Garrett's office to explain himself, he had sat impassively and chanted a Buddhist sutra as if he were alone, oblivious to the outraged president; he refused to answer any question put to him about his conduct. The university had successfully fired two or three of his associates; had, in fact, so completely destroyed one man's career that (according to rumor) he had fled to Bombay, and had there committed suicide. But Hawley had landed on his feet. Dr. Hawley, much-loved by students — so generous with his grades that eighty-five percent of his considerable undergraduate enrollment

received A's, and not even students who disappeared from Woodslee in mid-semester, or who died, could receive anything lower
than a C+ on their transcripts — always managed to land on his
feet, and had somehow managed to become acquainted with
Albert St. Dennis, and to be invited to this party tonight; and
now he is obviously entranced with Alexis Kessler, and Alexis is
entranced with, or at least very interested in, him, and Brigit
pours herself the remains of a bottle of expensive Scotch, and
wonders what will happen, how much longer she can continue.

She thinks: I am not jealous.

She thinks: I am not drunk.

Alexis and Hawley are laughing loudly together. Hawley's hand
rests lightly on Alexis's shoulder: so lightly that, perhaps, Alexis
doesn't notice.

Brigit approaches them in her long dress. Painterly blotches of
scarlet, of lime, of black; a synthetic silky material that flatters
her slight frame; many bracelets and necklaces; her expression
showing no strain, no exhaustion. She is not upset. She is accustomed to late nights, to excessive drinking, to her lover's willful-
ness. (If they quarrel they will declare, the next day, that neither
knew what caused the quarrel: Alexis will say that "something
came over him" and he seemed to lose consciousness, in a way,
and so began shouting and cursing at her; Brigit will say that
"something came over her" as well. She is reminded uncomfortably of her quarrels with Stanley, which, at the end, degenerated
into ungainly physical brawls she always lost. But there is no
other connection she can see between Stanley and Alexis. There
is no connection between the Brigit of those early years and the
Brigit of the present time.)

Suddenly, abruptly, she sees her arm move, sees the wrist turn;
she has thrown her drink at the men.

It catches Hawley full in the face and splashes onto Alexis.

One springs to his feet, shouting. The other, surprised, remains seated.

Brigit still holds the glass; she throws the glass now, and it strikes Alexis in the chest.

Ah, what confusion! Someone grabs her arm. Hurts her. She struggles, she kicks, there are two men trying to calm her, two men shouting at her. One of them is red-faced and dangerous. She sees that he would like to kill her.

She screams at him to let her go.

He screams at her: calls her a bitch.

A table is overturned. A lamp. Books. Glasses. The plate of marinated mushrooms. Underfoot there are crackers, salted peanuts, cigarette butts. Brigit's face burns. Someone has slapped her and she is very angry. She kicks him — kicks him in the leg just above the ankle. He cries out in pain. The other man, gaping in astonishment, tries to pull Brigit and Alexis away from each other and catches Alexis's cruel elbow full in his belly. He staggers away. He begins coughing. The coughing turns to choking, the choking to gagging, he clutches at his stomach and, doubled over, begins to vomit. Brigit pushes Alexis away and runs to the door. She is frantic, she is angry, she refuses to be insulted by him any longer. She runs into the corridor, she runs to the fire stairs, she struggles with the heavy door and yanks it open, muttering and whimpering to herself.

She will leave him: she will go home.

Suddenly it is very important to get home.

Something terrible has happened but something worse may happen unless she gets back home.

She runs down the stairs, whimpering. It is necessary to watch her feet; otherwise she may fall. (Her grandmother fell, she remembers suddenly: fell downstairs, into the cellar, and broke her poor brittle leg in several places, and was never the same again, and Brigit has forgotten all about it, has forgotten her, and the grandfather too; she has forgotten everything.) Someone is shouting after her. *Bitch! Cunt! Maniac! Madwoman!* She does not dare look back at him. He is red-faced and murderous, she knows him well, she has fled from him many times before.

"I'll kill you —" someone shouts.

Suddenly she is in the foyer of the old apartment building, suddenly she is outside on the street, gasping, panting, alone. What is wrong? — her throat and chest hurt. She gasps in pain. The sidewalk is icy and the sky is very clear and she has only a half-mile walk to her own building, one block along Phoenix Boulevard and a few blocks east on Linwood and she will be home. But something is wrong. She is crying, her face is wet, her skin hurts. Ah, the cold! The cold air! It burns her skin. Flame-like it penetrates her nostrils, her mouth, her throat, her chest. Twenty degrees below zero, is it, or even colder . . . ? She runs slipping along the sidewalk, crying aloud. Ice. Her feet are cold. Her arms, her legs, her breasts, her face — so cold — and behind her someone is still shouting and she wants only to escape him, she turns blindly into a doorway — an alley — she slips and nearly falls — what is wrong? Part of her mind is perfectly clear, as always. Her consciousness of herself and her predicament is perfectly clear. But her feet slip on the ice, her teeth have begun chattering, she cannot control her convulsive shivering. A few cars pass on the Boulevard; otherwise the street is deserted except for Brigit and Alexis. He overtakes her now, he is disgusted with her, he throws something at her that nearly knocks her over. His face too is wet with tears. He is shouting for her to pick up her coat — pick up her coat and put it on — it has fallen to the sidewalk, she's stepping on it. His face looms over her, jeering and frantic. *Bitch! Cunt!* He will show her — will teach her to insult him in front of other people! They grapple together and Brigit tries to push him away. He holds her steady, he shakes her, he is shouting into her face.

A car passes on the Boulevard, slowing. A carload of people. Men and women both, yelling, drunk and merry and yelling; a beer can is thrown at Brigit and Alexis; it rolls noisily onto the sidewalk beside them, splashing beer, no harm. The car's horn sounds in celebration of New Year's. Alexis drags Brigit to his car and opens the door and pushes her inside. What he will do to her! What he will do! He is so angry he would like to kill her. She is so angry — turning now on the car seat, kicking, squirming — she is so angry she would like to kill him; claw at his face, pound and strike at it.

It is 2:10 A.M., January 1.

Hour
of Lead

March 8, 1 P.M.

Today, the day of Albert St. Dennis's death at the age of seventy-one, is a winter day like any other.

The sky appears ravaged. The earth is heaped with snow. When the sun shines everything is blinding: the sky is a blank pitiless blue, the earth is dazzling, white upon white. Winds blow about in little whirlpools. There is no north, no east. People squint, holding their hands before their faces. It has been winter here, they say, forever.

Snowbanks six feet high. Ridges of ice on sidewalks and streets. An uncharted world. . . . Winter, they cry, forever.

No one can remember the earth.

There has been much storm damage this winter: a number of gigantic elms have been split in two. The Housleys' aged spruce was shattered and broken in a storm in late February, and two of the Byrnes' white birches were beaten down. An unusually harsh winter, people say. There are newspaper articles, there are photographs. There are deaths: a retired professor of philosophy, a woman employed in the Student Health Clinic, a twenty-year-old boy from Albany, killed in a skiing accident on Mt. Woodrich. There have been innumerable illnesses.

Lewis Seidel carries a dozen or more tissues around with him, stuck in his pockets. He is in good health except for sudden fits of coughing that leave him weak and angry. And embarrassed: he not only coughs, he spits up ugly clumps of phlegm; sometimes the clumps are threaded with rust. Is it blood, what is it, why is this happening to me, he thinks, vexed, frightened, ashamed, coughing into tissues he immediately crumples and sticks back in his pockets, refusing to examine.

He has given up smoking, he says. Two months, nearly. Which is why his hands shake, why he needs a drink at least by noon, why his dreams are so troubled. Something has been lost and he wants only to regain it.

Does she understand?

No.

Yes, of course.

He coughs, his big shoulders are wracked with the effort of coughing. Something poisonous in him that must be coughed up . . . !

Are you all right, she whimpers. Oh please: are you all right?

At the Tamarack Motor Inn out on Highway 9 one afternoon he retires to the bathroom, half-dressed, shoeless, a tissue held up to his mouth.

His coughs echo in the tiled room.

Sandra Jaeger lies on the bed in her slip, listening, not listening, waiting, motionless. She is very frightened. If he should die. . . . No, she is not frightened: she is empty. It is enough for her to wait.

Here in the motel room, back there in the duplex: she is empty, she is motionless. She is waiting.

One place or another, one Sandra or another. In her champagne-colored slip with the machine-made lace or in her usual blue jeans and a sweater: it does not seriously matter.

She will survive.

The aluminum-framed windows of the motel room are not very tight. The room is chilly. Back home the floors are cold: she must sit with her feet up, tucked beneath her.

Hour of Lead

This winter, people say, has been unusually harsh.

If she should run out into the wind it would tear at her, it would throw her about. The sky tosses itself like the sea, the powder-fine snow lifts itself in thin hissing coils, you must protect your face, there is the danger of breakage. Porcelain-fine skin: easily shattered. At night the wind bellows. There are immense dunes of snow. She sleeps beside her husband, she is a figure sleeping beside him, utterly alone. If he should touch her . . . ! But he does not. He sleeps heavily, wearily, utterly alone. Sometimes they whisper together like children. *Did you hear that . . . ? No. What? . . . Did you hear that, that sound?*

When she is alone she refuses to talk to herself. That would be a sign of derangement . . . .

Sometimes the telephone rings. If she answers it, Ernest's voice may surprise her. (He will be home late today, probably after six. Student papers. Student conferences. A committee meeting. Research at the library. Does she understand, is she lonely, is the apartment still so cold, were there any letters . . . ?) If she refuses to answer the telephone she can sit with her feet tucked up beneath her, safe.

She leafs through her journal. She is too exhausted to make entries.

A one-legged blue jay hops amid the other winter birds, picking at seed scattered by Sandra's next-door neighbor. (The Jaegers can't afford birdseed; it is really quite expensive.) Sandra stares at it, fascinated and repulsed. It seems larger than the other birds. It is far more aggressive: it hops at them, pecks at them, frightens them off.

Once she opened the porch door and screamed at the birds, waving them away. The jay rose at once, its wings beating. The other, smaller birds followed. But they flew only to a barren hawthorn tree nearby and waited for her to go back inside.

I'm too tired, Ernest says, rubbing his eyes. I don't think I. . . .

Yes, Sandra says. That's fine: I understand.

Do you understand?

Of course.

It is difficult for him to wake in the morning, at seven. He works until three or four; she vows she will lie awake until he comes to bed, but she can't stay awake, no amount of hatred, even, can keep her awake. She thinks of Lewis Seidel, she thinks of Vivian Hochberg, of Warren Hochberg, of the others. She is awake but her teeth make a quick bright grating noise and she realizes she has been asleep.

He has not made love to her yet: something is always wrong.

He laughs explosively, he drinks too much, he tells long anecdotes about his meetings with famous people, or about his sons' achievements. She listens intently. She is, after all, an attractive young woman, an attractive young face, it is not expecting too much of her to make him happy for these minutes. A service like any other, sure to be appreciated. He is really quite nice. They are all quite nice once you become acquainted with them. (*When you get to know us . . . you'll see we aren't so bad. A little eccentric maybe.*)

What is the alternative, Sandra thinks lazily, listening to the faucet and the rush of water: is it blue jeans and that fuzzy violet sweater of hers, the baby-doll angora sweater, is it Sandra peering at Sandra in the apartment's several mirrors and refusing to acknowledge what she sees . . . ? If the alternative is the long wait for the mail (presumably delivered at 10 A.M. but not, in fact, delivered on some days until nearly 12) she has no special wish to be there and not here. There she is Mrs. Jaeger, here she is Sandra, she has no last name. (Except, of course, he will be kind to Ernest: that goes without saying. To mention it would be vulgar.) Here she has nothing much to do but lie and wait, trying not to yawn, trying to arrange her features into something pleasant and sympathetic. (A man wants, basically, someone to sympathize with him: that is, to listen to him.) At home there is the card table set up in a corner of the dim bedroom, there is Ernest's old manual typewriter, the pile of envelopes, the plain white stationery they decided upon because it is chaste and unpresumptuous. (To use departmental stationery would be a mistake, they think.) Though she has typed out nearly two hundred and fifty letters by now, there are a few more letters to be typed, a few more addresses still unchecked: *Dear ———, I am inquiring about a possible position in your department. . . . Instructor, assistant professor, several years' full-time experience. . . . My Ph.D. degree is from. . . . Two articles of mine have been accepted for publication at. . . . Cutbacks in the budget here at Woodslee have forced . . . and my chairman, Dr. Warren Hochberg, has indicated his willingness to write in support of my application if. . . . If you are interested. . . . My credentials and transcripts and other letters of recommendation are available if. . . .*

With uncharacteristic emotion she asks Dr. Seidel if it was true that Barry Swanson's wife is pregnant: but he seems not to know.

And Brad Keough, it is said, has been drinking a great deal lately at the Riverview; he has even missed a few classes.

And the Cuffes. . . .

He may send her home. She can call a cab. She isn't helpless. Either she lies on the sofa for long hours at a time, immobile, too exhausted to move her head, or she cleans the duplex in a frenzy of activity, singing at the top of her voice. It occurs to her at such times that life is merely a matter of the arrangement of words into phrases and sentences and paragraphs. If you can master that you are invulnerable.

Whispered or muttered or sung, does it matter?

She types out letters. She stoops to pick up letters from the foyer floor. Quickly she rips the envelopes open: she glances at the paper inside, reading it at once, knowing what is a form letter and what is not. *We are sorry to inform you that. . . . No new openings anticipated for next year. . . . We cannot encourage. . . .*

She yawns, listening to the plumbing in the other room. The Tamarack Motor Inn is quite new but its plumbing is noisy; its

simulated pine walls appear to be solid but are really thin. She is
lazy, she is sluggish, she is terrified. He has not touched her yet,
not really. A few kisses. Damp and groping and somehow pathetic: a boy's kisses. For her husband she is a secretary and a
housekeeper and a cook and a body that lies quietly beside his,
making no demands, wishing only to be neglected; for this man,
her "friend," she is a kind of physical therapist, a listener, perhaps
even a daughter. (He has no daughters, she gathers: three sons.
And a wife whom he doesn't love.) He and she and Mrs. Hochberg had lunch together once in the Arbor House, downtown, an
"accidental" meeting, ludicrous and strained. Sandra drank too
much wine, Sandra was charming and silly. Ah, they loved her!
Doted upon her. Mrs. Hochberg in a cream-colored cashmere
coat with a mink collar, her hair scooped up into a knot, her fine
hard brow crinkling with delight. Sternly she smiled, sternly she
touched Sandra's hand. Lewis pleaded with Vivian not to smoke:
it was unfair, unfair! (Sandra wonders mildly if the two of them
did once, many winters ago, here in Woodslee, here, in this
snowy Eden, fall in love and almost-marry; she wonders if they
clung to each other and wept and made vows and cursed each
other and wanted to die but did not die . . . ?)

A small shiver of fastidious distaste: one should not imagine the
middle-aged in love.

One should not imagine anyone in love.

Sometimes her husband holds her and presses his warm face
against her; his breathing is troubled, she can feel the agitation
of his eyeballs behind the closed lids, she can almost hear him
thinking. It is not of Sandra he thinks. They whisper together in
the dark that they love each other because this is the sort of thing
people whisper in the dark, huddled together, beneath the blan-
kets while the night throws itself about, a merry howling whistling
chaos that would smash their house if it could and bury them in
snow; they whisper together that things will be better, things must
be better soon.

Like a grown-up child at a party Sandra takes a sip from the drink her friend has poured for himself and rises from the bed and smooths the bedspread, readjusts the pillows; the bed has hardly been disturbed, the linen will not need changing, she yawns and stretches her hard, slender body, half-believing that someone is witnessing her behavior, noting how confident she appears. She is not frightened: she dresses without haste. (Obviously he wants her gone; he doesn't care to face her again today. The last time, at this same motel, he arrived half-drunk and proceeded to drink more, nervously, telling her about his sons; his problems with Faye; the invitations he receives from other universities that he declines, for reasons of his own; his work, which is widely read but not adequately understood; his plans for future work; his anger and disgust over the political situation at Woodslee; his many enemies at Woodslee and elsewhere who watch his career closely and would be delighted if something happened to him. . . . He became more and more excited as he spoke and then, finally, he fell asleep. A large barrel-bodied sweating man, his red hair gone gray, his face a handsome creased ruin. . . . *Adultery*, Sandra thought. *This is adultery. This.*)

Now she calls out to him that she must leave: it's late, it's nearly two o'clock, she will call a cab, she's sorry, she can't stay any longer, she must leave.

He shouts something unintelligible through the closed bathroom door. It is a release, she knows; he wants her gone.

Now that she is bereft, strangers approach her boldly. In the A & P on Van Buren a middle-aged woman just ahead of Brigit in the check-out line turns impulsively to tell her about her husband who is in love with a girl at work, a young typist named Molly. The woman's husband has long conversations with Molly, in the bathroom with the door locked, and the woman rattles the doorknob and says *Who's in there with you, old man!* and he clams up of course and the woman rattles the knob again, *I hear you talking to yourself,* she says, *I'm going to have you put away, you crazy old fool . . . !* He hides in the bathroom and in the garage and even goes to seven-o'clock Mass just to be alone so he can talk to the girl under his breath. Forty-three years of marriage, the woman tells Brigit, angry and astonished, and now what will happen? *What will happen?*

And Brigit's dentist, just last Saturday, put down his instrument and rubbed his eyes and, giving off an odor of clammy fear, told Brigit he couldn't continue with the examination: to be quite frank, he had good reason to believe he had cancer. . . . Had he seen a doctor, Brigit asked, concerned, but he seemed not to hear; he was rubbing his eyes with both hands; he mumbled something about bleeding from the rectum, having been unable to sleep for days, he hoped she would understand if he didn't continue with the examination.

Oliver Byrne called to ask if Marilyn had telephoned her earlier that day: she told him no one had telephoned. He had not explained himself, he was uncharacteristically perfunctory, she had been quite hurt by his tone. Shortly after Oliver's call two of Brigit's former students stopped by, both young men who were concerned about a friend of theirs, another former student of Brigit's who was — the story was quite complicated — somehow involved with drugs being brought across the border from the province of Quebec; they talked earnestly, interrupting each other from time to time, and though it was never very clear to Brigit what they wanted from her she listened patiently for an hour and a half. She liked the boys well enough; she had been impressed with their work in her classes. But it was difficult for her to remember them clearly. One semester displaced another, one set of students displaced another, she learned names and forgot them abruptly, she felt unreasonably guilty when confronted with students from the past who appeared to remember her very well, but whom she could remember only vaguely; still she listened, and heard herself giving advice of some kind, which the boys appeared to take seriously. As they were leaving one of them happened to remark that he had "experimented" with death the other night — had walked out along the river to the edge of town and lain in a snowbank for over an hour. He told Brigit about the incident with a bemused, rather childlike smile as he and his friend were buttoning up their jackets, and since the remark seemed to call for no special comment Brigit made no comment; she did not know whether to be astonished or annoyed.

It must be obvious, Brigit thinks, that there is something wrong with her.

The afflicted see in her a kinswoman. She has been wounded, she is in mourning, she is one of them. She is an aging woman despite the attractive clothes she forces herself to wear (since losing Alexis her instinct is to let herself go); she is an aging, sexless creature, the surface of her skin covered with scar tissue.

Her eyes are threaded with blood. They ache from crying and she must wear sunglasses outside: even when the sun isn't glaring the snow is too white.

Everything hurts.

In the mirror there is a woman, an impostor, not remarkably changed. She goes out to parties, she teaches her classes, she meets with people and smiles at them and exchanges remarks, as always. She is a little drained, perhaps, a little wary of others, but everyone has been affected by the winter and Brigit does not seem very different from the rest.

She hates him, of course. She wishes him dead.

(At the moment he is in Nassau, someone told her, vacationing with a friend. Brigit did not comment. — A friend? Who? Not from Woodslee, surely? Probably from New York.)

She tells herself she is grateful for solitude. There is so much work for her to do . . . ! Classes, students, correspondence, books to read and reread (she has been rereading *The Wings of the Dove* for weeks, fitfully; it is one of those odd books in her life to which she keeps returning as one might return to an exquisite, maddening riddle never satisfactorily explained — though reading this particular novel, James's most beautiful work, impresses upon Brigit's mind the disturbing fact that James was not, himself, quite equal to the tragic vision he evoked: the death of poor Milly terrified him so much that he could not approach it), and her own novel to write. Her own life to transmute into art. . . . She is relieved to have ended it with him, really. He interfered greatly with her work; his own work came to him easily and so he could not appreciate the difficulties others had to face. Selfish, he was. Slatternly, unreliable, a cheat, a bastard, perhaps even a criminal. . . . It was said that Alexis Kessler had borrowed money from a number of Woodslee people over the years and was reluctant to pay it back.

Will you lend me . . . ?
Yes, of course. Of course. How much did you . . . ?
She tries to work. Tries to stop her thoughts. Her lover flies
into her head, she breathes in his peculiar odor of cologne and
bodily heat and something not quite fresh. He is garish, he is
ludicrous; he is sneering at her behind his charming smile. A
face, merely. A face and a body. She fell in love with a face and
a body: nothing more.
My lover, Brigit thinks contemptuously.
And her husband. *He* appears suddenly, inexplicably, when
she is at her weakest. He has watched her in Alexis's embrace, he
has watched her all these days when she believed herself alone.
Staring into her head. Into her thoughts. A frigid woman, he
declares. Selfish and secretive and half-dead in her perpetual
virginity. No man could love her except out of pity, she isn't even
very attractive; when men take a second look at her they are
disappointed. In fact she is ugly. She is repulsive. . . . And selfish, yes. And secretive. She always thought more of her work
than she did of her husband; she had not spent enough time
thinking of her husband, which was why their marriage disinte-
grated. How fitting it is, then, that her flamboyant young lover
has rejected her, and that everyone knows about it! — everyone
is talking about it! How fitting, how just!
No, Stanley says suddenly, the ugly truth about her is not
frigidity. It is quite the opposite. Her sexual nature is ravenous.
She is insatiable, she is disgusting, possibly a little mad. In fact it
was the fear of awakening her sexual hunger that inhibited his
lovemaking, the times she did respond to him were violent and
cataclysmic and rather frightening. And for so many hours afterward she had seemed altered, in a queer pale drained drugged
state, like a convalescent. . . . Any man would have been intimidated by her. Any man would have fled. Had she never guessed
how she disgusted him? And certainly she had disgusted her other
lovers as well.

I didn't have other lovers, Brigit says. There was no one. . . .
I had no one. . . . Nothing. . . .

Certainly she has disgusted them all.

And they talk about her, probably. Which is no more than she deserves.

There was no one. Nothing.

The telephone is ringing and she discovers herself stumbling to answer it. She is very nervous. The receiver nearly slips out of her fingers. Yes? Yes?

(It is Alexis calling at last. She hears his drawl, his mildly ironic greeting: *Brigit dear?*)

No one answers.

Yes? Hello?

Hello?

A child's voice, almost inaudible. A wrong number.

Outside everything hurts. White heaped upon white. Layers of eye-piercing white.

Each breath is painful but one must breathe.

Over the snow a fine crust of ice has formed, and it is said that certain winter birds, desperate to escape the cold, have burrowed into the snow and have been trapped by the layer of ice so that many of them will die, unable to free themselves. Brigit finds herself thinking of the birds, imagining their dark suffocating confinement. And in the spring will their bodies be discovered, strewn about the landscape? . . . She finds herself thinking of the birds too often, at too great a length.

She is mourning something. She has had a violent loss, a death. Strangers, glancing at her, see instantly that she is in mourning. A husband? A lover?

Snowflakes of the consistency of sand or grit sting her face.

The voices follow her, sensing her vulnerability. One and then another, and then another voice; they know she has been weakened.

For an hour and a half she wanders aimlessly about the stacks in the library, drawing her hand across the spines of books; from time to time she pauses to take up a book and open it and read a few lines. She has always been absurdly superstitious: she believes that anything she might come upon, in such a situation, could have great bearing upon her life — could alter the course of her life. (Always, when she has been most unhappy, she has wandered into libraries, often into the libraries of unfamiliar cities; she has spent hours like this, rather like a blind woman, drawing her fingers across the shelves, across the books, choosing a book at random to open. After a particularly unpleasant scene with Stanley she fled to a tiny branch library, and by accident came across a book on Mozart, and became so absorbed in it that she forgot the quarrel entirely; when she at last looked up, hours later, she was dazed and disoriented and could hardly believe anything so trivial as a quarrel with her husband could have upset her so. In a world in which Mozart had lived, and written music, and died — died as he did, so cruelly — how could the Fifields' disagreements matter?) But today she is fearful of what she might read. Perhaps it will be too significant, or perhaps it will have no meaning at all — *To live alone one must be either an animal or a God*, says Aristotle; *I hold that God is the immanent, and not the extraneous, cause of all things*, says Spinoza. *All is in God; all lives and moves in God.*

A dreary prospect, such transcendence of duality, Brigit thinks. If she and Alexis are in God, and nothing of them remains that is not God, how was it possible that they had ever loved each other? For they had, she thinks bitterly, they *had* loved each other for a time. . . . The God immanent in them had been a God of erotic necessity, not to be placated or denied.

Their last quarrel: both of them white-faced, trembling, abusive. You want me as a sort of husband, Alexis shouted. But I'm not your husband — I'm nothing of yours!

Brigit pulls another book from the shelf and opens it blindly.

Anything to still her lover's anguished voice. . . . *To Carthage then I came, where a cauldron of unholy loves sang all about mine ears.* St. Augustine. *The Confessions.* Which she has not glanced at since her sophomore year at Smith.

In another part of the library she locates Albert St. Dennis's books. A shelf and a half — a good-sized collection. Some of the books appear to be first editions, quite old and tattered; there is even a chapbook from 1937; Brigit must make a note to inform the curator of rare materials, so that these items can be recatalogued. Most of the St. Dennis books have been bound in the library's bland green binding, however, and look like other books by other authors. (So many books, Brigit thinks dizzily. Shelves and shelves, row upon row, floor after floor: a galaxy. Her own are somewhere among them but she has no wish to seek them out. A friend of hers, a writer, once pulled a book of his off a shelf in a public library and leafed through it to discover that someone had marked nearly every page in red ink, making insolent queries in the margins and even crossing out certain words and substituting others; he had been so shaken by the experience, he said, that he never dared examine any book of his own again, not even those belonging to friends.)

She opens St. Dennis's *The Explorers.* Terse, brittle lines; none of them familiar. She reads, loses the thread of meaning, begins again. *What is the story, the pattern, the myth that I live?* the poet asks. *What is the voice that attends me?* She reads passages and hears the old man's voice drowning out this young man's passionate words.

What is the voice that attends me. . . .

She returns to the apartment and notes its absolute silence, which seems bound up somehow with the winter, with the snow. Silence is brutal: the world will end in silence. (She knows that someone has told her this melancholy truth but cannot remember who it was.)

"Is someone here — ?" she calls.

Her long-haired black cat, silky and lazy and tawny-eyed, glances up at her without much concern. The cat is fairly old now — seven years at least.

She is alone and the voices intrude.

It is only three o'clock.

She might have remained at the library longer; it was a mistake to come home so early.

She might have gone to her office in the Humanities Building. But if the telephone rings. . . .

Fortunately there is a dinner planned for tonight, she need not endure another evening alone. But the dinner doesn't begin until six-thirty and she should plan on getting there no sooner than six-forty or six forty-five.

Hours.

Voices.

"Leave me alone," Brigit whispers.

Her work intrigues her and frightens her. She cannot approach it. She *must* approach it . . . but when she does, when she reads through what she has written, the voices rise jeering and impatient. *Who are you to attempt anything! What do you think you are doing!* She writes in longhand, slowly and carefully, with an almost morbid fastidiousness, in journals bought at old-fashioned stationers' stores. The journals resemble ledgers. (In fact as a child she began with one of her father's ledger books, he must have given it to her to play with.) She writes in dark ink with an old-fashioned fountain pen. The act of writing is sacramental; it must take time, it must be a little difficult, a little awkward. *Worlds Elsewhere* had taken her fours years to write, *Melodies* had taken her even longer. Each sentence written and rewritten and rewritten, paragraphs rewritten in blocks, whole pages rewritten. Again and again. Her present novel has taken an inestimable amount of time: she has accumulated over three hundred pages of a narrative, but notes and outlines comprise at least five hundred pages. Characters — even minor characters, even characters who will not appear in the novel but are alluded to — are described in excruciating detail; their homes, their families, their backgrounds, their interior lives. Brigit looks through her notes, intimidated by them. She is lost, it is hopeless, she can never handle so much material. But the characters are living people, they demand to be heard in their own voices, they are far more real than the people Brigit sees in Woodslee, they *will* insist upon the mad proliferation of details that constitute their lives. (Brigit had noted even as a young girl the curious fact that while "real" people often presented themselves as shallow and not very likable, "fictional" characters of a high order revealed themselves as marvelously complex, no less devious and subtle than Brigit believed herself to be. Her external self, her social persona, *Brigit Stott*, hardly represented her — it was, in fact, an indifferent performance at best, since her imagination was usually elsewhere; and she assumed that the same was true of everyone. The interior life is rich and deep and strange and inexplicable, and the exterior life — the "social" life — is no more complex than it needs to be. *Brigit Stott* is a character she lavishes little skill on: it is a vessel, a means, a transparency.)

The writing of the first novel gave her some pleasure, despite its difficulties; the writing of the second novel was torturous. It was not simply that her husband had come to resent her writing, since the meager success of the first novel, and spoke of it in a certain bantering tone she came to find intolerable — it was the writing itself, the act of writing, the feat of transforming emotions into language, into a coherent structure. (Alexis told her that when things went well he heard his melodies in his head, and then transcribed them; when things didn't go well he had to invent. In a way this was true of Brigit too.) *Melodies* gave her very little pleasure. She had often hoped for illness — for private catastrophe — anything to interrupt her work. Stanley's odd behavior, his alternating pride in her in the presence of others and his jealousy of her or of her work when they were alone, his quarrels, his bouts of silence — these were catastrophes of a kind, and perhaps, secretly, she willed them. (But she had not willed his physical violence: she was not that eccentric.) He had sometimes slapped her during their arguments, as if unable to control himself, and his failure to control himself exasperated him all the more so that he seemed, at times, truly to hate her; he shouted at her, pleaded with her, begged her not to drive him insane. Once, drunk, he had begged her not to force him to kill her. (Brigit fled the apartment that weekend, stayed with a friend, went over and over her husband's words in her imagination until she came to the conclusion that he must be joking — he was too intelligent, too witty a person to have meant such melodramatic threats.) The worst single event of her marriage was not a beating, however, but a display of Stanley's bad temper in public, in a restaurant. While everyone stared, Stanley accused her of not loving him, of being jealous of the fact that he earned so much more money than she, and had more friends than she; he accused her of having been unfaithful to him innumerable times, simply out of spite, out of hatred. Brigit had been crushed with shame, too embarrassed even to leave the table. She had forgiven him the slaps and blows and occasional shoves but she had never forgiven him those excruciatingly awful ten or fifteen minutes. . . . And his jeering, intimate voice: You really think you have something to say, don't you, something of value to say; you really think your work is more important than our marriage — Who are you to attempt anything? *Who are you?*

Now she wants to work but she cannot work.

Stanley is gone, she has fled Stanley, yet still she cannot work. This is the only hell; *this* is more painful than any marriage.

Years of labor. One novel; and then another. Published, her photograph on the dust jacket, a young, hopeful stranger. Presented to her parents and, so far as she could judge, never read. In her letters to Brigit her mother wrote of Janet's new baby, her

cousins' children, her father's Rotarian committee work, their
disappointment that she hadn't been home to visit for a while.
Never any mention of her work, never any queries about her
teaching career. Was it indifference or perhaps a curious sort of
timidity. . . . Was it an expression of their disdain for all that had
meaning in her life. . . . (Why do you want to write such *sad*
things, Janet had asked after reading the first novel, fixing Brigit
with a fond worried smile.)

But perhaps they were embarrassed for her. And of her. The
breakup of her marriage, the first divorce in the Stott family for
generations, no children, a job that is — isn't it? — a man's job,
up there in the North, among strangers. They had probably
known from the first that the marriage was doomed. Brigit was
too selfish, too stubborn, to maintain a role that would draw forth
husbandly love from any man: she hadn't enough sense, she was
always brooding and letting her imagination run away with her.
No wonder, Mrs. Stott whispers, no wonder things collapse
around you, no wonder even that disgusting young lover of yours
has fled, what can you expect when you're so selfish, when you
don't try hard enough to make other people love you? It's work,
my girl, believe me.

And trying to bribe *us*. Offering money instead of coming back
here to live, as you should. The rumors that fly about, now that
you're getting divorced. . . . And I have to contend with them. I
have to face people. Even your Aunt Stella said something cruel
the other day. There's always been something missing in you,
Brigit. . . . What is it?

What is it?

Years of labor at her writing. Trapped in her work, addicted to
it, in love with it as she could never be in love with any man — is
this a sin, is it criminal, will it bring punishment upon her? Her
work is her life, her soul, her destiny; yet might it be sinful just
the same? St. Dennis had said one must not guess at how arduous
the work will be and how little it will seem to matter; Brigit does

not want to hear his voice again, not now; her skin burns with an emotion she cannot understand, she wants to work but cannot, she wants to work but doesn't know how to begin: so many pages, so much material transcribed with painstaking care, with a kind of demonic love — she is exhausted by it, overwhelmed by it. Paralyzed. She can sit at her desk and write paragraphs for hours and then rewrite them, and then rewrite them again, growing with each revision less confident, less certain of what she is doing: her dread of this work springs out of her fear that others will reject it, without sympathy; or does it spring out of her fear that she is unwittingly exposing herself, and will never own herself again . . . ? Or does it spring out of nothing more than her awareness of the fact that however fastidious she is, however hard she works to transcribe her vision, its impact, on the printed page and in the minds of others, will be so much less than it is in her imagination . . . ? So her paralysis these many years is cowardly and she is a coward and it is quite fitting that people whisper about her and that her parents refuse to acknowledge her except as a daughter who has inexplicably disappointed them and will no doubt continue to disappoint them the rest of their lives. . . .

She glances at the clock, suddenly eager to know the time. Only 3:15.

The time is very important. Even as a child she had stared at the clock, mesmerized by the position of the hands and by the possibility that she might see them move if she looked closely enough. And it is important even now that, if the long hand is poised exactly on the hour or the half-hour, she *must* act at once, *must* do something quickly, before it moves. A strange eagerness leaps in her at such moments. The clock is sometimes an ally, sometimes an assailant, like the calendar. There are times of the day and days of the year that, for one reason or another, are highly significant to Brigit; she must approach them with a certain cautious respect, otherwise there might be disaster. Otherwise. . . . It had been against her intuitive judgment, for instance, to take part in a program designed to raise funds for the publication of "creative work" by the inmates of a certain New York women's prison, several years previously: she had known beforehand that the project would fail and that she would regret the fact that her name was used for publicity purposes. (Though she could not have guessed that nearly three thousand dollars in donations would be "lost," and that one of the women involved in the program, a parolee, would be brutally stabbed by another, also a parolee, and that the entire fiasco would be wittily dealt with by a national news magazine.) She had agreed to participate in the program only because her reasons for not participating were so patently foolish — something to do with the timing of the organizer's telephone call, something to do with a vague warning dream about precisely that day, that afternoon. More recently she had had a long conversation with the Andress boy about his "future" since she had misread a name in the *New York Times*, seeing "Andress" where "Ambrose" had been printed in a brief news item concerning an eighteen-year-old's mysterious death (by drugs, most likely) in Manhattan; it had seemed very important to her, suddenly, that she talk to Andress about matters other than literature. Wisely, she had not told him the reason for her concern; but he had appeared rather puzzled just the same, though possibly flattered by her interest. (Todd Andress, like the majority of those students closest to the Woodslee faculty, alternates between admiring his professors indiscriminately and rejecting them contemptuously; Brigit has always suspected that the young man's brilliance is but one side of a complex, cloudy personality, and that she has done him a disservice by reacting always, and exclusively, to his "good" side.) And there have been innumerable other incidents, most of them too ordinary to recall, where a faint superstitious conviction has determined her behavior, though she is fully willing to recognize the absurdity of the situation.

Alexis had gotten into the habit of ridiculing her; he had airily pointed out that her oversensitivity in certain areas was outrageous in the face of her insensitivity in others. She was so maddeningly *blind!* So willful! (One of the things that had annoyed Alexis back in the early weeks of their love affair, and which he had tolerated as long as possible, was Brigit's apparent inability to see herself; to *see* a person who was Brigit Stott in other's eyes, and who must be responsible for that image in every respect. Once she was wearing a very attractive dress of jersey wool, bought in the designer's salon of an excellent New York shop, and he was infuriated by the fact that one of the dress' buttons was missing — though the missing button had been only decorative, not functional, as Brigit tried to explain; why should its loss matter so much? The dress itself was handsome enough, surely . . . ? Another time, at President Garrett's Christmas reception, Brigit had been so plainly uninterested in a tedious conversation with Mrs. Garrett (about the various sorts of wainscotings in the older Woodslee homes) as to have been, in Alexis's judgment, positively rude. Alexis pointed out the fact, which Brigit had not really contested, that such behavior, such indifference to the consequences of one's behavior, could bring about in the world — in the "real world" — events that would hurt her ultimately far more than the murky consequences of a violation of some foolish superstition. How could she be so stubborn, so shortsighted? So perverse?)

But Alexis was the one who was perverse.

But —

No. She will not be drawn into another argument with him, with her ghost-lover. Not again. Not now.

It is her work she craves, it is only her work she loves. She does not hate Alexis; she does not wish him dead. Or broken. Or hurt as badly as she has been hurt. She feels nothing for him. Her body feels nothing. It is empty now of desire and of the memory of desire.

Passion has no memory.

Her eyes are threaded with blood, her head feels suddenly very heavy. Loose, it is, and precarious; it could break like crockery. Otherwise she feels nothing. . . . *I'm going to have you put away, you crazy old fool*: a voice rises in sudden hatred. It is not hers, it is a stranger's, she will not acknowledge it. *We must be together always*, her lover declares, *we must never again be parted. It is very important to go at the right time. Most go too late, you know*. . . . Her lover's hoarse voice, aged and unrecognizable, it frightens her, baffles her. She will not acknowledge it, what claim has it upon her? It is not her lover's. It is an old man's voice. *We must be together always*. Ah, she thinks, a sickening dread in her, he is going to die, he knows he is going to die, he is reaching out to me to save him. . . .

She listens but now the voices are silent.

There is only silence.

3:20.

. . . either an animal or a God. But neither: she is exhausted, she is overcome by fatigue, she wants to work but cannot. A mountain of papers, a snow-glaring wasteland of words. Bereft. Years have passed. She is no longer young, she can no longer reasonably expect to be desired: no longer the bright promising girl who fled Norfolk. It does not matter, it should not matter, others have grown old, why is she empty now of desire and anger, why does she remember so little? Her body is bruised and broken and empty; it should not matter. This exhaustion! This fatigue! She is mourning something but does not know what it is. There are certain thoughts she wants desperately to pursue but perhaps it would be better for her to surrender to the exhaustion, perhaps she should lie down, it is only 3:20 and she has hours ahead of her, hours of unbroken solitude, a small lifetime, a wilderness. Her eyes ache. Snow glares outside her window; everything is too bright. It is so difficult, this struggle to remain herself. . . .

There is a consciousness, Brigit thinks sleepily, that permeates language and is somehow given birth by it, and it is always with us, we are never free. From birth onward we are surrounded by it . . . a cocoon of words . . . a living web of language. The world is filtered through it. There is no world except what is filtered through it. A living web! And there are narrators: sometimes one narrator dominates, sometimes another. As in old-fashioned novels we are guided by a presence we never see; it is always commenting, interpreting, predicting, directing, passing judgment. She cannot fight the narrators, cannot compete with them, she hears them distinctly at times and would isolate them from her but she is too tired, she is deathly tired. She thinks groggily: I will know the nature of this consciousness, I will know its language. . . . I will set my own in opposition to it. . . .

Her senses reel with fatigue.

She has been wading in the surf. And now the waves are coming in brusquely, violently, surprising her. And the wind — how strong, how cold! She is stubborn, she wants to remain where she is. She is very stubborn. But the wind has driven the waves into a frenzy and they are crashing madly about her, she is about to lose her balance, she is about to be knocked off her feet. She cannot remember why she is here, what her recklessness means. but she knows she is in great danger; she must retreat.

"Where is Brigit Stott? Isn't she coming? Do you think anything is wrong?"

"She'll be along," Oliver says irritably.

"But it's already after seven. . . ."

"I'm reasonably certain she'll be here," Oliver says. "I talked to her just this morning."

The dinner party at the Wallers' is in honor of a visiting lecturer from Oxford, a specialist in Russian ecclesiastical history. Like Albert St. Dennis, with whom he seems to be having an excellent conversation, he is wearing a dark blue three-piece suit and he is probably in his late sixties or early seventies; he is quite tall, however, and his hair is brown — rather stiffly brown, Oliver observes, as if it were artificial. That afternoon in Blandford Hall he gave a slide-lecture on the religious art of northern Russia. (Oliver was disappointed with the number of people who turned up. So many empty seats at the rear . . . ! The Russian department had publicized the lecture throughout the university and Oliver's office had been quite generous with funds. Even so, few faculty members had attended, and certain people who were invited to this party in honor of Professor Cahill — like Brigit Stott — hadn't even bothered to show up. Which was rude, Oliver thought, and inexcusable.)

Oliver himself had had to leave the lecture after twenty minutes because he had a meeting elsewhere. He had been impressed, however, and even rather moved, by the photographs of icons from Vologda — fourteenth- and fifteenth-century works, virgins and crucified Christs and martyrs and crowded apocalyptic scenes, remarkable for their vivid colors: red, red-orange, blue, bronze, gold. Such passion in that art, such ferocity of certitude . . . ! Some of the human figures were childlike, some were astonishingly sophisticated in their delineations; all were powerful. There was a painting of the Virgin of Vladimir bordered by saints that especially intrigued him — the mother's face and the infant Jesus' face were pressed close together, both a tawny bronze-gold; their expressions were inscrutable, even secretive. Uncanny, Oliver thought, how beautiful the icons were, and what power they had to move the observer, so many centuries later, in a part of the world so very distant from northern Russia. . . .

He accepts a drink and places himself on the periphery of the conversation between Professor Cahill and Albert St. Dennis and Leonard March, the head of Russian studies, and Lewis Seidel, who seems to know more about Vologda than one might have suspected. Oliver appears to be at ease; he is wearing a camel's hair sports coat and a beige-and-white-striped tie and new, sharply creased trousers. He thinks of the icons and their marvelous flaming colors, he thinks of the emergency meeting he must attend tonight at 8:30, he thinks of his wife, and of tomorrow morning's hearing on the subject of the library budget, and of the interview he will have this weekend at Cornell — where he is being considered, along with three or four other men, for the presidency of that university — and he thinks of Brigit, who is now forty-five minutes late. (He intends to accuse her of having cheated herself of a very rich and rewarding lecture this afternoon. Had she forgotten? Wasn't she interested? . . . He intends, too, to bring up the subject of his wife, as casually and discreetly as possible: Marilyn hasn't been altogether well for the past several months and one of the manifestations of her distress has been, in recent weeks, a conviction that Oliver and Brigit are having an affair and have been having one for years. She has threatened to telephone Brigit to accuse her directly, but as far as Oliver knows she hasn't actually called Brigit . . . though he suspects, uneasily, that she has alluded to this "affair" to friends and acquaintances of hers in the university community. It seemed to him this evening that Lewis Seidel, greeting him with a handshake and his customary overloud hello, gave him a peculiar winking look; and Gloria Waller, the vice president's wife, seemed to think it quite natural that he would know if Brigit was coming tonight or not. And there have been other inexplicable remarks. . . .)

Cocktails and hors d'oeuvres and Milton Conroy — Judge Conroy, retired — asking him neighborly questions about storm damage to his trees this winter: maybe they could use the same tree service, get an estimate from several companies, have all the work done at the same time. Oliver agrees. It is an excellent idea. Judge Conroy is one of the members of the university's board of governors, a tacit supporter of Oliver Byrne though he is always cordial to President Garrett; he is here without his wife (she is visiting relatives in Naples, Florida) as Oliver is here without his wife, and seems unusually talkative. Clay Waller joins them. Bovine, good-natured, slow. Not an enemy of Oliver's; not important enough to be an enemy. In senate meetings Oliver has been quite critical of this man, and has even aroused laughter against him, but he seems friendly enough tonight, as his wife always appears to be friendly to Marilyn. Oliver hears himself talking. Laughing appreciatively. Roger and Charlotte Haas join the group, carrying drinks, smiling broadly in expectation of — of what? — of a purpose for smiling? Everyone appears to be friendly. The party is a success.

Dinner. They file into the dining room and Oliver looks about as if seeking someone: isn't there a woman he is responsible for? But his wife isn't here. She is at home, possibly out of bed now; but not well enough to attend the party. ("I'm sick of those people. I'm sick of them and you. The mere thought of enduring another evening with them turns my stomach. . . .") For days she hasn't dressed, she has been lying in bed in a kind of trance, refusing to eat, drinking only herb tea and fruit juice. Sometimes her door is locked against him. She was improving for a while in February, it seemed, after a terrible two weeks around Christmas when it crossed Oliver's mind, from time to time, that his wife had gone insane; but last Thursday she fell into a depression again and refused at first to talk with him and then began to accuse him of having been unfaithful to her . . . not only here at Woodslee with Brigit Stott, but elsewhere, with other women, even with girls. Of course she is sick: it is the long winter, Oliver knows, and the peculiar pressures of his deanship. He forgives her. He does not blame her. There is no question of his loving her any longer; he has not loved her — has not felt the slightest sensation of desire for her (or for any other woman, it must be sadly admitted) for three or four years now. The dean of the Law School, with whom he used to play handball some time ago before both men were overwhelmed with work, confided to Oliver that *he* had been more or less impotent for eight years now, since having become dean; it was a psychological or an emotional impotence, he said, rather than merely a physical impotence — he could not force himself to care enough about sexual matters even to think about them, and if one does not think about them one cannot feel desire for any woman at all, however attractive. Did Oliver agree? Yes, Oliver agreed.

A handsome table, a handsome dining room. The Wallers are conventional but reliable; they have seated their guests sensibly, knowing that Oliver and Lewis Seidel should be kept apart. Oliver is content to be seated beside Charlotte Haas and the middle-aged wife of the area's state senator, an attorney who lives in Phoenix Heights and whose thirteen-year-old daughter is a friend of Oliver's and Marilyn's daughter, and he is pleased to be seated across from Professor Cahill, and not far from Albert St. Dennis, who is in fine form tonight, reciting poetry for Professor Cahill's benefit — translations he had done of Pushkin, evidently, many years ago. St. Dennis has worked out well at Woodslee. Oliver is relieved. The old man is touchy, of course, and certainly has a drinking problem, but in general the students appear to like him, and even the English department — notoriously hard to please, and almost pathologically fickle as a group — seems satisfied with him. If Marilyn weren't so unstable Oliver would have him to dinner more often; he regrets not having become better acquainted with him. And the year is passing so quickly . . . ! So quickly.

Brigit Stott appears, escorted by Clay Waller. She sits at once, obviously embarrassed; she seizes her napkin, her eyes lowered, and Oliver cannot get her attention. He is happy to see her. Really, he is very happy; perhaps he should call down the table to her . . . ? She is seated between Lewis Seidel and Roger Haas, almost hidden from Oliver's view. How pale she looks, how peculiar . . . ! Oliver wonders if the business with Alexis hasn't affected her considerably; he wonders, with a tinge of distaste, if he should ever bring up the subject to her. . . . Perhaps she would like to talk about it; perhaps she has no one to talk with. Marilyn used to pity her, in the past. The woman must be so lonely, Marilyn would say, she *looks* so lonely, so very much alone; she will never fit in at Woodslee. (And Marilyn could not resist talking about Brigit behind her back, to other women, and even to Oliver: relaying anecdotes and speculations and outlandish rumors about Brigit's private life.) Staring at her, Oliver recalls the abstracted face of that virgin in the painting — the expression of melancholy, of secrecy, of utter strangeness. One cannot ever know that person. One cannot ever *know*. . . . Then she glances up at an apparently jocular remark made by Seidel, and grimaces, and laughs loudly; and Oliver is faintly offended.

He has little appetite tonight. He keeps glancing at his watch obsessively — must remember to excuse himself well in advance of eight o'clock so that he won't be late to the meeting. The roads are icy, it is snowing again, he must drive five miles back to town. Professor Cahill and St. Dennis are talking about a Czechoslovakian poet of whom Oliver has never heard and he tries to listen but his mind is crammed with thoughts — thoughts like gnats, like mosquitoes, like flies. He cannot concentrate. He wants to hear, to respond, to learn; it depresses him to realize how very long it has been since he has learned anything at all — since he has read a book of merit all the way through — since he has had an intelligent conversation. As soon as he gets through this crisis at Woodslee he will change his life; he will set aside blocks of time for his own personal use. If the presidency at Cornell comes through (and he has been told unofficially that it will) he will move to Ithaca with an entirely different conception of his role as an administrator, and he will protect Marilyn more successfully from the pressures that seem to have weakened her. If the presidency is offered and Woodslee's board of governors counters with an offer of its own (and he has been told unofficially that there is a good chance it will), he will remain here with an altered sense of himself and his responsibilities. It isn't clear yet how he will manage but he is confident that he will. As soon as the present crisis is over. . . . Power has been shifting since last September from President Garrett to Oliver Byrne, and when enough power shifts the crisis will be over; his position as dean will be strengthened; and Garrett will be forced into retirement a few years earlier than he had planned. And the presidency of Woodslee will be a marvelous position, a truly enviable job: in a way it is Oliver's highest hope.

(He is certain that Marilyn would be very happy if the presidency were offered him. She has always been very ambitious for him; she has shared his contempt for the Garretts and for the older Woodslee administrators, and has talked for long hours with him about *his* plans for the university once he is in a position to implement them. As soon as the crisis passes, Oliver thinks, his wife will probably recover.)

Little appetite for Gloria Waller's thick salty ham. And these creamy potatoes with too much parsley in them. He glances at his watch surreptitiously while talking with Mrs. Haas about what a shame it is, the difficulties the modern languages department is having — they cannot choose a new head because the three factions into which the department has divided will not speak to one another; in the meantime it is Oliver, Dean of Humanities, who must act as surrogate head. Isn't it a shame that people can't get along? Oliver agrees that it's a shame. . . . And the drinking among the students, what of that? Roger has been telling her such extraordinary things! Students showing up drunk for classes, a boy actually expelled from a math class for drinking out of a pocket flask. . . . What does Oliver, as dean, think of such things? Isn't it a bit demoralizing?

Oliver says that the issue has been exaggerated; he checks the time and sees, relieved, that it it nearly eight o'clock.

He must begin extricating himself from the company. It has been a fairly pleasant evening, the food satisfactory, the wine a little sweeter than he likes, and Charlotte Haas more intimidating than usual; but he has enjoyed himself as much as he expected to and it is a relief, he must admit, to be alone, without his wife, without the uneasy responsibility of looking out for her. (At the Ryersons' in early March Marilyn disappeared just before dinner and Oliver had to search for her, with Edie Ryerson's help: they found her sitting on a bench near the Ryersons' washer and drier, in the basement, alone in the dark.) Unfortunately he has so much on his mind, so many things to deal with, meetings and people and telephone calls and petitions and correspondence, the evening has passed like a dream, he has participated in it at several removes from his own being, and he regrets it, but . . . but he did enjoy overhearing snatches of Professor Cahill's conversation with St. Dennis . . . and if he weren't in such a hurry he would make it a point to speak with St. Dennis, whom he hasn't really talked with since December . . . and he regrets not having had a chance to speak to poor Brigit (who has been unnaturally quiet throughout the dinner, subdued and pale, and a little haggard in a black dress that seems too large for her) . . . and he should have spoken at greater length with Roger Haas, whose opinion on a certain threatened lawsuit he very much wants, and quickly; and he should have been more attentive to Judge Conroy, and Gloria and Clay Waller, and even Lewis Seidel, whom he does not detest so much as pity. (It is important to Oliver to demonstrate in public his total lack of ill-feeling for Seidel. He wants the community to be aware of his generosity, his forgiveness, his good nature. He and Seidel have disliked each other, in fact, for three years now: they became enemies one afternoon at a meeting of the university senate when a faction noisily headed by Seidel contested the adoption of a new official stationery proposed by Oliver — pale blue paper in place of the customary creamy-white, with a letterhead in midnight blue instead of black. Oliver had won the issue after some very bitter debating; he had been puzzled and stung by Seidel, whom he knew only as an aggressive member of the English department with a minor national reputation, and whose sarcasm on the stationery issue had provoked malicious laughter against Oliver. However, the triumph *had* been Oliver's, and since everyone knew it, he must take care at all times to be inordinately gracious to Seidel: nothing infuriates the man more. If only Seidel would resign from Woodslee . . . ! It would be very difficult for Oliver to fire him, since he has tenure, and since his colleagues in the English department appear to like him — or to fear him; if Oliver ascends to the presidency, however, it will be well within his power to make life at Woodslee so unpleasant for Dr. Seidel that. . . .)

"Good night, Dean Byrne!" Seidel calls after him merrily.

As he is slipping into his coat in the foyer Brigit hurries up to him. She is smiling anxiously, she puts out her thin hand by way of a greeting, or a farewell; Oliver takes it, a little startled by her urgency. Like a steel spring, she seems at such times; the pupils of her eyes appear to be unnaturally dark. For several minutes they talk together — Brigit asks Oliver about his wife, Oliver replies that she is fine, fine, she sends along her very best wishes to Brigit, and regrets having been unable — because of their daughter Eunice's bad cold — to come to the party tonight; Oliver asks Brigit about her classes and her work and how she has been, in general, and she replies with a high, tense laugh that things are going very well indeed — her life is less complicated these days, as he probably knows, and so she has time for important matters.

"A pity," Oliver can't resist saying, "that you missed Cahill's lecture."

Driving back to Woodslee he thinks of Brigit and of Marilyn and of the Russian icons — the Virgin's face especially; he thinks of Seidel's taunting farewell and the fact that Garrett is out of town again this week, in Washington, D.C. He is uneasy about something. Why did Waller look at him so oddly? Why did St. Dennis say only a few perfunctory words to him? It is snowing again. Large wet blossom-like flakes: he turns on his windshield wipers.

He thinks of Brigit and of the possibility that he may be leaving Woodslee.

He thinks of the hearing scheduled for tomorrow morning, and of the difficulties he is having with the modern languages department, and with one of his vice-deans; he thinks of the unpleasant scene he had a few days ago with a senior member of the history department who routinely gives his students A's and B's and requires no written work other than exams — the man defended himself by claiming that it is widely understood, not only at Woodslee but everywhere, that professors draw their salaries largely for humoring their students these days, and that anyone who is known to be difficult simply won't have any students.

The time . . . ?

He doesn't want to be late for the meeting.

From earliest childhood Oliver has sensed that the world will oblige him when properly approached. Doors will open, people will step forward to greet him. All the pieces of the jigsaw puzzle are in his possession; he is in control. He is still fairly young. He *is* young. Doors will open, people will step forward. . . . He thinks of Marilyn's accusations. But you don't love me, you don't make love to me, you don't look at me, I don't exist for you. . . . He thinks, oddly, of the mole on Vivian Hochberg's upper lip. Vivian and Warren. Vivian and Lewis. An old story. And they *had* loved each other (or so Oliver has been told, it all happened long ago, before he came to Woodslee) and were on the brink of suing their spouses for divorce . . . and then something went wrong . . . someone's passion must have ebbed . . . or someone's wife or husband threatened a breakdown, or revenge, or. . . . However the details went, the story, in essence, is a familiar unhappy one, and from time to time Oliver almost pities Lewis: but then, why pity Lewis, who ridiculed him so viciously about the blue ("Sky-blue! Powder-blue! Ladies' lingerie-blue!") stationery before the entire university senate? Seidel is a bastard, a criminal mentality; when Byrne ascends to the presidency he *will* force him out of Woodslee. . . .

For some reason he finds himself thinking of an altogether incomprehensible anecdote someone told him about Gowan Vaughan-Jones and some candy — lifesavers? — and cannot remember why the anecdote was supposed to have been amusing.

He laughed, of course, since laughter seemed expected; he has always been a gracious, agile, highly sensitive social person. But was the implication that Vaughan-Jones was immature, or unworldly, or addicted to sweets, or — ? A puzzle. He finds himself thinking again of Cahill and the vivid reds and bronzes and golds, and of another — yet another — dinner party he must attend on Saturday, and of the deathliness of this masquerade, and how he hates it all, this imposture, and what had they spoken of, Brigit and he, when they first met — ? The extraordinary scenery in this part of the world, and of Oliver's ambitious plans for the expansion of the arts division, and — But there was something further —

Brigit. Brigit Stott. If the presidency at Cornell comes through, he will leave Woodslee and he will leave Brigit and there is the possibility that he will never see her again. . . .

If he leaves. But then perhaps she might come along with him, if he arranged to have her hired there. Or: if he spoke to her quite frankly. . . .

There is the possibility that. . . .

He must talk with her at once, this very evening. Should he turn the car around and return to the Wallers, or should he get to his office and make a call immediately . . . ?

Then the car begins to skid. Oliver applies his brakes, quickly but with caution. Mustn't slide. Mustn't go into the ditch. The car is still skidding, he is going to die like this, so suddenly, so stupidly, with no preparation. . . . But then the brakes hold: the tires hold and the heavy car rights itself and all is well.

Jesus, Oliver murmurs. For a moment he feels faint.

For the rest of the journey he drives at no more than twenty miles an hour, his foot hovering above the brake. What on earth had he been thinking of to so distract him. . . . Something quite important, was it . . . ? He will be presiding at tonight's meeting, which is sometimes tiring, but ideal because then he needn't listen to another chairman's ramblings and political circumlocutions. What is the issue tonight? Parking. Once again, parking. Oliver is deathly tired of the subject but it is important, all issues are important, small political skirmishes that add up to significant battles with their necessary winners and losers. Parking and parking-lot assignments and the shortage of space. And bitter, bitter feelings between the divisions and the departments, between the faculty on one side and the administration on the other, and then one must consider (more and more one *must* consider, reluctantly, since they are so powerfully unionized) the angry complaints of the university custodians, maintenance crews, grounds-keepers. There has been, he believes, more passion on the subject of parking-lot assignments in recent years than on salaries, and certainly more than on academic principles. Faculty members as well as irresponsible students have, upon occasion, not only parked illegally and blatantly in places clearly reserved for administrators; they have even driven their cars through gateposts, deliberately breaking them. There have been fist fights in the parking lot nearest the library, which is generally considered the most desirable. Tickets issued by university police have been ripped to shreds and mailed to his, the dean's, office; a highly regarded professor of mathematics once accosted the president of the university on the street and shouted at him, before astonished passers-by, on the matter of his having been assigned to a remote lot, over by the physical education building. . . . The most crucial issue in recent weeks, apart from the ongoing agony of the budget, is whether certain acres now given over to woods should be razed and paved and turned into parking lots. Oliver is certainly a lover of nature: no one loves trees more than he. Yet one must be practical. The outrage of the alumni and the sentimental squabbling of the students notwithstanding, quite clearly the faculty wants more parking lots, more parking lots, more parking lots. . . . What strategy should he use tonight? He isn't altogether certain how many votes are with him, how many against. And of course someone will call for a secret ballot:

a seemingly offhand ploy that, upon other occasions, he himself has used. No harm. But. If. On the other hand. He might open the meeting by saying, as if incidentally . . . and this will stir one of the committee members into a too-heated response . . . and then. . . .

He arrives, quite safely, at the meeting; by 8:28 he is ready for business.

"Too many people . . . too many houses. . . . Time for bed," St. Dennis mumbles. "Where's the bloody key? . . . So tired."

Lewis takes the key from St. Dennis's fingers, unlocks the door and helps the old man inside. Switches on the light. God, what a clutter! As if not cleaned for weeks. Books, glasses, cups, plates with dried food on them, knives and forks and spoons, bottles, towels, underclothing, tissues, jigsaw-puzzle pieces, scraps of paper. . . . A Dorothy Sayers novel on the floor behind the sofa; a very wrinkled white shirt on the coffee table. Whitehead's *Modes of Thought*, a used tea bag, dried orange rinds, sheets of stiff paper covered with St. Dennis's tiny crabbed handwriting, in pencil, *The New Statesman*. An ashtray overflowing with cigarette butts. The apartment is rather chilly and oppressive.

Lewis helps St. Dennis to the sofa and he sits down heavily. There are sheets and a blanket, folded, at one end of the sofa, as if it were used for a bed.

". . . 'self to a drink, eh? And one for me too. . . ."

Lewis hesitates. He really should get home. He hasn't felt well today and the Wallers' party was unusually tiring; and there was that unfortunate incident at noon of which he tries not to think. He is really quite tired.

"Damn long winter, isn't it?" St. Dennis says with a ghastly smile.

Lewis forces himself to move briskly. He locates two reasonably clean glasses in the kitchen, finds a bottle of Scotch, half full, on the stove, and returns to the living room to sit facing St. Dennis. At last . . . a private, intimate conversation with the old man . . . a conversation uninterrupted by others. It has turned out that St. Dennis likes him, evidently; thinks highly of his work.

"Match?" St. Dennis says, slapping at his pockets.

"No, sorry, I gave up smoking a few months ago," Lewis says apologetically. "I. . . . Is this a box of matches here . . . ? Yes: here."

Frowning, the old man takes the box from him and, with shaking hands, manages to light a cigarette.

There is so much Lewis wants to ask St. Dennis, he hardly knows where to begin. Must be careful, of course, of offending him. His moods are notorious: he has been gracious and patient with some of the young poets who have given him their work to read, and he has been unaccountably rude to others. It is said that he answers many strangers' letters in longhand, that he spends hours of his time each day on his correspondence; on the other hand, Lewis heard that he once directed the departmental secretaries to throw away a week's accumulation of mail because he hadn't time even to open it.

". . . is it?"

"What?"

"Snow?"

Lewis leans forward, cupping his hand to his ear. "I didn't. . . ."

St. Dennis waves in dismissal.

"Did you ask if it was snowing?" Lewis says uneasily.

"No matter. Tired."

He drops the cigarette and fumbles for it and picks it up again. A few sparks fall to the carpet and go out. How tired he looks . . . ! All evening St. Dennis was unusually charming; riding back to town with Lewis, however, he said very little, and lay slumped against the seat and the passenger's door as if asleep. Pale hooded eyes, skin so pale as to look powdered, mummy-like, parched. . . . He is a peculiar old man, a stranger, whom Lewis doesn't know at all and whom he halfway fears.

But there is so much to ask him!

Questions of death, love, fame, old age. Poetry. Life.

". . . people. Continent of them. So tired."

"Yes?" says Lewis, cupping his ear again. "I didn't hear. . . ."

St. Dennis has swallowed half his drink.

Lewis hesitates, not knowing quite how to begin. He wants to ask St. Dennis about his relationship with the Huxleys, and with Robert Graves, and with Auden: hadn't they disagreed violently on political matters? And how had he managed to remain friendly for so long with Arthur Koestler? But it is difficult to begin. Easier, perhaps, to ask him about his plans for next year (there is a rumor that Berkeley has offered St. Dennis a handsome position as poet-in-residence) . . . and about his *Collected Poems* (due out in May) . . . and about a certain essay just published in the *Times Literary Supplement* (said to be a blistering attack on St. Dennis — a dismissal of the poor old man's entire lifework). Easier, even, to ask him if he had enjoyed the Wallers' dinner . . . if he liked talking with Cahill . . . or wasn't it all a little strained, a little too intense . . . ? The Wallers try to make their evenings intellectual because Clay Waller is notoriously ignorant; he has only a Master's degree in business administration and is something of a joke in the community. . . .

St. Dennis yawns rudely.

Lewis stares at him. This peculiar mummified old man . . . ! Why does he have the power to reduce Lewis to an awkward boy? And damp with perspiration too. And a little sick to his stomach.

Why does everyone, even Faye, have the power to upset him now?

St. Dennis raises his glass to his mouth slowly, with care; even so, his hand is trembling.

". . . I wonder if you should go to bed," Lewis says hesitantly.

St. Dennis doesn't hear or is ignoring him. It crosses Lewis's mind that he has lived through this moment many times, he has been here in this depressing room with this old man many times, an eternity of times, and he must escape. It is unbearable! Unbearable.

". . . help you undress . . . ? Bed?" he says.

"Another drink," says St. Dennis.

"Mr. St. Dennis, I don't think . . ."

"Albert. *Albert.*"

"Albert, I don't think. . . . It's late, isn't it, aren't you ready for. . ."

"Hell. Where's the bottle? . . . myself."

He tries to get to his feet but falls back, helpless. His glasses have ridden down his nose. When Lewis stoops over him he draws away irritably, as if revulsed, and even makes a slapping gesture at Lewis's arm. He mutters something Lewis can't make out.

(Was it *Jew* . . . ? Or merely *you?*)

"I think you should go to bed," Lewis says nervously. "As long as I'm here I might as well. . . ."

"*Here.* Right here," St. Dennis says, patting the sofa. Evidently he sleeps on the sofa. "No fuss."

"Mr. St. Dennis . . ."

"Go away, for the love of Jesus," St. Dennis says in a singsong voice. "Leave me alone. . . . Big ruddy faces, face like a pie. Pumpkin pie. So many. Faces. Continent of. Planet. *Leave me alone.*"

Lewis is suddenly lightheaded with rage. How unbearable this is, this scenario! The craven words he hears himself say! He hates St. Dennis savagely and he has nothing to ask him, nothing, he wants only to escape, to be free, to burrow somewhere deep into the snow and put an end to it, to this masquerade. . . . But he hears another plea of his, a plea for St. Dennis to be reasonable, and he observes himself attempting, even, to take that lighted cigarette out of the old man's trembling fingers; he wants to scream aloud with the futility of it — since St. Dennis is resisting, and even appears to be getting angry.

"No. Leave. For sweet Jesus' sake," St. Dennis cries. "This is . . . you are . . . all . . . intolerable!"

"But —"

Lewis hovers above the old man, his own hands trembling. He is sick with outrage at the injustice of . . . the colossal unfairness of. . . . He grinds his teeth, he is so upset. Sweat is trickling down his sides. Unbearable! God, this is unbearable! Albert St. Dennis grimaces and draws away from him, from *him*; everyone will know, everyone will laugh and jeer and. . . . What has any of it mattered, Lewis's offer of friendship, his kindness, his wish to help? — his presence here in this filthy place? — his very existence? He is not well himself; was quite frightened at the motel this noon, coughing so violently; yet he went far out of his way to drive St. Dennis home and has only meant well, has only meant to help. . . . But none of this matters to St. Dennis. Not at all.

"I implore you to leave me. To have mercy and leave. *Leave*," St. Dennis whimpers.

Lewis sets down his glass suddenly. He grabs his overcoat and walks out.

He slams the door behind him.

Slams the door — !

He walks out on St. Dennis, simply walks out. . . . Is walking quickly down the corridor to the fire stairs, too upset to wait for the elevator. Why, he walked out on St. Dennis! On the famous Albert St. Dennis! Grabbed his coat and strode to the door and walked out! The old man was drunk, you see, and babbling stupidly, and insulting him, so Lewis simply. . . .

If something happens to St. Dennis . . . ?

But nothing will happen. The old man must drink every night like this, and smoke cigarettes, lying on that stained sofa amid the papers and bedclothes; he must know what he's doing.

And he did order Lewis to leave, after all.

Leave, he had whispered. *I implore you.* . . .

Lewis trembles with an emotion he can't comprehend, thinking of the queer hooded eyes, the parchment-like skin, the small shower of sparks that fell to the carpet and went out.

It would serve that bastard Byrne right, Lewis thinks on the way home. If something *did* happen. . . .

For all good poets, epic as well as lyric, compose their beautiful poems not by art, but because they are inspired and posses-sed. . . . The poet is a light and winged and holy thing, and there is no invention in him until he has been inspired and out of his senses. . . .

A lie, St. Dennis thinks, a filthy bloody lie.

Thousands of years of that lie.

He is refuting Plato as he walks along the crowded sidewalk, not watching where he goes. He has not dressed warmly enough and he has forgotten his umbrella or lost it. Knees weak, ears ringing, what is that sound? — his interior monologue ceases; what is that sound? He is in Paddington; it is raining; the rain is very cold. Before him several girls in school uniforms are staring in the window of a news agent's shop. One of the girls has shoul-der-length hair, she wears tortoise-shell glasses, she happens to glance over her shoulder at him just as the bomb strikes.

Rain. Mist. The whistling noise and the explosion and the screams. Heat: shimmering waves of heat. From where? — from what? St. Dennis is thrown backward. Something propels him backward as if he has no weight, no substance at all. He falls, his leg is twisted beneath him, he screams at the extraordinary pain in his left knee.

Bricks are falling. A lorry is overturned in the narrow street. There is a fire, there are many fires. Close about St. Dennis people lay stunned. Flames in a building ahead — flaming people — a great resplendent display of fire — the earth itself has burst open in rage. He must get to his feet! Must escape! Must get home! Where is Harriet — is she with him or is she somewhere else, is she hurt, is she dead, is she safe? He calls for her. He tries to stand but the pain is too great and there is something wrong with his head and everywhere there is flame, all individuality is lost, the world has collapsed into flame. He must survive: must carry this knowledge back with him.

Like the aging Turner who spent hours in silence staring at the phenomenon of light playing upon water, so St. Dennis has spent hours of his lifetime whispering words to himself over and over, words that are incantatory, sacred, without meaning, beyond meaning. And now the words and the light and the fire blend; are one; flare up and flame about him as he stares, feeling no terror now, not even much alarm.

In the Founders' Room

May 10, 12 noon.

"Not quite. Not *quite*," Leslie Cullendon is saying merrily.

"Of course not, I only meant that we'd heard —"

"Eight days in Intensive Care but not quite, not *qui-ite* dead: not *quite*. Not yet."

"Leslie, please. You know very well that I — I only meant —"

"Caught a minuscule head cold from Babs and the next morning I could hardly breathe, was practically choking to death, and she called the ambulance, and it was pneumonia, yessir, good old pneumonia, it certainly did look as if Leslie was on his way out — my heart is weak, you know — or didn't you? — yeh, weakened from being sick so much — and it was quite a strain, as you can imagine, coming down with fucking pneumonia on top of everything else — not to mention that sleet or ice storm or whatever the hell it was, the freakish weather that day — last week in April and what the hell? — ice storm! Anyway the ambulance came and poor old Leslie was shipped out and woke eight days later in excellent spirits: so all's well. Any news you heard of my death was therefore premature — mere wishful thinking."

Gowan Vaughan-Jones giggles, shocked; Chris Callinan stares at Leslie in astonishment; Brigit, who is seated far enough away so that she need not acknowledge having overheard, makes it a point to say something to Vivian Hochberg, who isn't talking with anyone at the moment — she asks Vivian if she and Warren have any plans for the summer. Vivian gazes at Brigit for an instant without seeing her. She is quite handsome today in a plain, almost severe dark-brown dress, a small cameo brooch — an antique? — near her collar, her thick, graying hair arranged in a knot at the nape of her neck. Such stern dark eyes — ! She blinks at Brigit and then, having heard Brigit's question, smiles at once and replies that, because of Warren's responsibilities in the department, and because of his new position as acting dean — though that won't go into effect until next fall — it doesn't look as if they will be able to get away for more than a week or two. "We'll probably just drive out to my family's place in Bar Harbor," Vivian says. She smiles again, making a genuine effort to be pleasant to Brigit. "And what are your plans, Brigit?" she asks.

Brigit replies that she doesn't know yet.

By now the Leslie Cullendon danger is past and Brigit can relax and turn back toward Gladys Fetler, who has been reminiscing about the early days of the department with Blaise Perrin and George Housley; Brigit is quite moved, overhearing the three of them talking and laughing together. This luncheon has been a rather formal, awkward affair so far — it is much too early for Brigit to eat a sizable meal, certainly, and her cocktail doesn't taste right — and so it is agreeable to observe people enjoying themselves. Gladys Fetler is wearing a lavender suit with a sprig of lily of the valley at her collar, and her hair has been newly styled and rinsed: it is a very delicate silvery white, a bluish-silvery white, really beautiful. Her face is strong, rather tough, her teeth are irregular and a little stained, her eyes are a remarkable green-gray, almost too striking. When she looks at Brigit, even warmly, Brigit feels uncomfortable. (It was a most embarrassing, clumsy half-hour, that session in Brigit's office some weeks ago when Gladys Fetler first received notice from the administration that her early retirement was strongly advised. Brigit had been correcting papers at her desk late one Friday afternoon when Dr. Fetler entered without knocking, in tears, and asked if Brigit knew what was going on? — if Brigit had had a part in it? Of course Brigit knew nothing; she had not even heard any rumors; she was quite shocked, and asked Gladys to please sit down. . . . The poor woman complained bitterly about the way the department was treating her. She was being betrayed, she said, by the executive committee, which professed to be innocent and helpless over the situation — how that hypocrite Hochberg could lie! — it was chilling, it was suprahuman. — And Brigit knew nothing? She sat in Brigit's chair, pressing a handkerchief to her nose, an enraged, stunned woman, and for thirty minutes talked to Brigit about betrayals, promises, lies, enemies, Machiavellian political maneuvers, how she had been cajoled into supporting Hochberg years ago for the headship against her better judgment (but her colleagues had been so persuasive and it was true, it couldn't be denied, that the head at that time, Dr. Burstyn, was under severe emotional stress and wasn't capable of continuing with his administrative duties), and how she had regretted it afterward, and had felt sick with guilt when Dr. Burstyn ended as he did — had Brigit known the poor man? — no? Well, he was before Brigit's time and it was pointless to attempt to explain, younger faculty could never quite understand the machinations of the department, the subtle interrelationships among people, not only those who are currently on the staff but those who are no longer here . . . in some cases no longer living. Ah, it was so complex, so heartbreakingly complex! All Gladys knew was that she had been betrayed by her colleagues: they wished her to opt for an early retirement though they knew very well that her teaching, her relationships with her students, kept her alive, were life itself to her — *life itself.* "I won't be able to survive, Brigit, without my job," she said wildly. "Even the summer will seem interminable. . . . And next fall, next fall. . . . It will be the first time in forty years that. . . . Brigit, what will I do?" There was little Brigit could say; she tried to comfort her, and promised to speak to Warren on Monday, but she was really quite powerless — when she did manage to make an appointment to see Warren he was on the telephone most of the time, talking to someone in administration, and he insisted to Brigit that he "knew nothing" about the Fetler affair except that the decision had come down from a higher committee and that it was "out of his hands." He seemed sincere enough. He even stammered once or twice, and kept arranging and rearranging papers on his desk. "It isn't that unusual," he told Brigit, "there are quite a few early retirements this year throughout the faculty." But — wasn't it a shame, Brigit said, that a professor as popular as Gladys was being forced out? — an excellent teacher, a woman whom everyone admires? — what a pity! "It is a pity, yes," Warren said slowly. He seemed, as always, sincere.

But today Gladys Fetler is in better spirits. For one thing, she is going to be honored by her colleagues. This luncheon is a kind of farewell party for her, as well as a way of officially acknowledging the Albert St. Dennis Seminar Room. There is to be a scholarship fund established in Gladys's honor that will provide full tuition grants to upperclassmen majoring in English, and Gladys's rank of emeritus will allow her to use the library and its research facilities. And she can, as she has said, return to visit her colleagues whenever she wishes, and have lunch with them; it isn't as if she were being exiled. (Oddly, she has never alluded to her hysterical outburst in Brigit's office. She appears to be no less friendly than ever to Brigit, but there is a peculiar glassiness about her smile and a shrillness to her voice that Brigit has never heard before. . . .)

The luncheon begins almost precisely at noon. Shrimp cocktail for a first course: four rather tasteless shrimp arranged in a pudding or Jello bowl atop some cracked ice. It is too early to eat, Brigit thinks, but one must eat, one must go along with whatever ceremony is being performed. . . . Someone addresses her and asks about her plans for the summer. She then inquires about his plans for the summer. Farther down the table Leslie Cullendon is speculating aloud about whether he and Babs will do any traveling: he wants to go to Italy before it's too late, wants to see Rome and Florence and Venice, but Babs is frightened, Babs is a coward, he is beginning to wonder if he married the wrong woman. His voice sails gaily up and down the length of the room; there is no escaping it. To Brigit's left Mina Housley is talking with Ernest Jaeger and Mona Cuffe about the weather: isn't it wonderful, after that long, destructive winter? It seemed never to end! And the tragedy of Mr. St. Dennis. . . . A terrible, terrible year. Incomprehensible. But. . . . But life is a mixture of good and bad, isn't it, death and life, here they are all together and it's spring, just smell that air through the window! — lilacs, so lovely — so lovely. (She is very moved; Brigit notes that Ernest Jaeger is blushing.) Whatever has happened is past, belongs to the past. And we must live in the present. And the future. Isn't that right? . . . It's a profound wisdom, earned only after bitter experience.

"Yes, that's right, Mrs. Housley," Mona Cuffe says in her small, reedy voice.

Brigit glances at her to see if she is possibly being ironic, but she seems sincere. A pretty woman, hardly more than a girl; something drained about her, a certain hollow-eyed look. There has been the pressure on her husband this year, about which Brigit knows very little except that Joe Cuffe is leaving Woodslee. . . . He has a reasonably good job at a small college in Kansas, however, which (it is said) Dr. Perrin helped him get, since the head of the department there is one of Dr. Perrin's former students. Brigit halfway regrets having failed to become acquainted with Mona and Joe. And the others. Most of the others.

She and Alexis stayed up late one night planning an immense party to which they would invite nearly everyone they knew at Woodslee — people they liked very much, people they didn't par-

ticularly like, people they owed parties and dinners, people whom
they admired but had never really approached; at one point the
guest list included sixty-five names. Since neither Brigit's nor
Alexis's apartment could accommodate such a crowd they were
forced to consider two parties, or perhaps three; or even four.
Brigit had not given a dinner party for more than a year, though
the most recent one she did give — in honor of a young poet
who had given a reading at the university — had been quite successful. (Though someone had walked off with a small marble
ashtray she had always liked — a wedding gift; the outrage had
thrown her into a fury of speculation that lasted for weeks, as she
tried in vain to determine who among her friends, who among
the English department faculty, would have stolen from her.)
Alexis claimed to love giving parties and found it remarkable that
he hadn't, in fact, actually given one for several years: he was
always being invited to other people's parties. So they talked excitedly about a party, or parties, they crossed names off the guest
list, they added other names, they discussed the kinds of food
they would have, how many bottles of Scotch and gin would be
necessary, which weekend would be a good idea . . . and then
they began to argue about something, an inconsequential point
or two . . . and Alexis was unreasonable and his unreasonable-
ness had the unfortunate effect of making Brigit less reasonable
than usual . . . and so, in the end, they had dropped their plans;
and then their relationship suddenly deteriorated and there could
be no question of a joint party.

Still, Brigit regrets having done nothing on her own. And now
it is too late. The Byrnes are leaving, the Cuffes are leaving, the
Swansons are leaving, one or two others may be leaving, and St.
Dennis is dead, and. . . and Lewis Seidel is seriously ill. . . . And
there are undercurrents of hostility in the department that Brigit
doesn't entirely comprehend.

(Barry and Carol Swanson are sitting together at the far end of
the table, eating in silence, unsmiling. They appear to be quite

oblivious to the general conversation. Carol is wearing a pale green smock; she is about three or four months pregnant and already quite heavy. Even her face is heavier. A sweet girl, Brigit once thought, so vivacious and enviable — at the Byrnes' home in September and then again at the Seidels'. Brigit had admired her at the time. Had been a little jealous, even. Her tall big-bodied gentle husband had seemed so proud of her. . . . Brigit had made a note to become acquainted with her and the Jaeger girl both, she had wanted to take them to lunch, perhaps, and it wouldn't have been out of the question to have invited both couples over to the apartment for dinner; during her first year at Woodslee quite a few people had had Brigit to dinner, wishing to make her feel comfortable, and she had been grateful for their hospitality. But she had never gotten around to it. Every weekend was filled and there was Alexis, always Alexis, and then the St. Dennis disaster, and Brigit herself hadn't been altogether well this year, and perhaps the young people would have declined her invitation anyway . . . perhaps they would have resented her interest in them, after the university had treated them so cruelly.)

Without Lewis around to tell her things, Brigit doesn't quite know all that is going on. She is aware that a number of young faculty members have been "non-renewed" this year, and that Oliver Byrne was extremely displeased by the board of governors' behavior; but there are conflicting rumors about restorations in the budget, about certain programs — in athletics and in communication arts particularly — that have been given, secretly, a great deal of money; there is talk, so far unsubstantiated, that Ernest Jaeger has been unofficially informed that he will be kept on at Woodslee after all — despite the fact that poor Gladys Fetler is being retired and the department is having financial problems. An odd decision.

Brigit misses Lewis. She has the idea that everyone misses him. The gathering seems incomplete without his lively garrulousness, his self-serving anecdotes, even his habit of interrupting other people. He would know whether Carol Swanson's pregnancy is deliberate or whether it was an accident; he would know, certainly, if some sort of confidential arrangement has been made with Ernest Jaeger, which will be made official during the summer when no one is around to contest it. Unfortunately Lewis is in the Burlington hospital for a week of tests, and it came to Brigit by way of Gowan Vaughan-Jones, who heard it from one of the departmental secretaries, that the diagnosis is very likely emphysema — not bronchitis as some had believed, and not cancer as some had feared. Brigit hopes he will recover soon. She really misses him quite a bit; though they have never been friends, are fond of each other. She had always thought . . . had always thought, in a way, that Lewis was attracted to her . . . but possibly she was mistaken . . . she had never been certain . . . and she dreaded becoming the sort of woman who imagines that men are interested in her when they are not. Still, she is fond of Lewis. The poor man had been coughing all winter but after St. Dennis's accident he seemed especially ill, and very nervous, not himself at all. (Brigit had come upon him in the corridor one day, outside his classroom; he was coughing violently, a hideous wracking noise, a tremendous effort that must have left him exhausted.) Perhaps he had been closer to Albert St. Dennis than anyone had guessed. . . .

"It's a shame about Lewis, isn't it," Brigit murmurs.

A few seats down, Stanislaus Chung overhears her and says sharply (for he and Lewis are old rivals: both wanted an enviable corner office some years ago that was assigned to two of the younger staff members) that the man brought it on himself — "All that smoking and drinking and making an asshole of himself around town." Brigit chooses not to reply, pretends not to hear, and if anyone else is startled or upset or annoyed he says nothing, Dr. Chung's remark is allowed to fade, someone else speaks up, quickly, deftly, and the moment passes.

Leslie Cullendon is noisily requesting another cocktail —

"*very* very dry this time." Gowan Vaughan-Jones is frowning over his notes for a speech he will be giving. Warren Hochberg, at the head of the long table, is sitting at attention but appears to be abstracted, the third finger of his right hand pressed tight against the bridge of his metal-framed glasses if he fears the glasses may fall off. His hair has been recently cut and his new spring suit is a pale heather shade, surprisingly attractive on him; his wife's choice, no doubt. Beside him sits little Mina Housley. She is chattering as usual, marveling over the warm weather and the handsome seminar room and how fortunate they all are — just look at the walnut paneling, and the quality of those leather chairs, and the carpet. And the portrait of Albert St. Dennis above the mantel. Though it was done from photographs by an artist who had never met Mr. St. Dennis, isn't it a remarkable likeness? — isn't it striking? — beautiful?

The portrait is not of Albert St. Dennis but it is, Brigit must admit, an appealing work of art. A kindly smiling grandfather, with white highlights on his chocolate-brown irises.

St. Dennis's death had shocked and upset Brigit profoundly.

And there was the ugly irony of her initial response to the fire: shortly after midnight she'd been disturbed by sirens but hadn't known where the fire was and had not cared. Certainly she had not cared. The sirens had merely annoyed her. Oh Christ, she'd muttered, let me alone. Having had too much to drink at the Wallers, she had returned to her apartment and fallen into bed without completely undressing.

The party had been disappointing. She had wanted to talk seriously with Oliver Byrne but he had eluded her and had rushed away early; she had wanted to talk with St. Dennis but he spent most of the evening with Professor Cahill, whose company he clearly preferred to anyone else's; even Lewis had been less flirtatious with her than usual. They saw her as a rejected woman, disfigured as if with a physical deformity. That cruel little bastard Alexis Kessler, to have insinuated himself so deeply into her life, to have wounded her more cruelly than her own husband. . . .

Fortunately, St. Dennis had not inquired after him. But then no doubt he had had enough of Kessler.

Before going to the Wallers Brigit had steeled herself to behave in a gracious, poised manner, to resist ironic statements, above all to resist excessive drinking, which was really getting to be a problem with her since the Kessler business. But midway through the evening something happened: a kind of manic fatalism overtook her, she found that it did not matter if she drank or not, if people respected or admired or liked or merely pitied her, how could it possibly matter . . . The murmurous voices of the Wallers' guests enveloped her, eddied about her, rose and fell, fell to sudden pockets of silence, and then rose again, independent of her, seething, flowing, relentless . . . and she was left with the dazed impression that the living of one's life (however serious it seemed) was a perfectly harmless and inconsequential diversion, a way of passing the time.

Take your place in the masquerade, don't raise your voice, don't call attention to yourself or take yourself too seriously . . . !

She stared over at Albert St. Dennis, deeply absorbed in a conversation with Cahill. Did he know? Did he share in this wisdom? She remembered the old man's incoherent but touchingly frank confession on New Year's Eve in his filthy kitchen . . . she remembered the way he had looked at her, tears shining in his eyes. . . .

Take your place in the masquerade.

But how painful it was, how wearying, this ceaseless task of presenting a self to a circle of selves — a ceaseless creation, offered out of the stubborn bitterness of her own nature. With Alexis she had been herself — she believed she had been herself — she hadn't lied or dissembled or — though perhaps she had at times *somewhat* misrepresented herself — hadn't told him about the bouts of fatigue, or certain complications with Stanley, or her own doubts about their relationship — but — in general she hadn't lied, she had been utterly truthful: and it had failed.

So, now. Begin again. Creating oneself again. The effort reminded her of the Creation itself as it was imagined by certain philosophers: God creates it anew each moment, each instant, there is no necessary connection between one moment and another (in human terms), the universe is a raw, continuous, perversely soulless present, a dream of God's that has nothing to do with man though man must, of course, take his place in the scenario. . . . If for an instant this will gave out, then all of Creation would sink into oblivion; the material universe would come to an end. Like a steel spring, she felt herself, ever more tightly held back, more ruthlessly restrained: sheer nerves, sheer will. She must imagine herself into being, she must invent herself anew at every instant, only her brazen, deathly will sustained her, she could never surrender Brigit to the others — could never stand mute and terrified, utterly alone, humiliated by failure.

Was her nature so cunning, so harshly intolerant of the rhythms of her own being, or had she learned these gestures from the others? — did they mesmerize one another, like performers who continually sought to outdo themselves? . . . She did not know, she did not care. She was one of them. She was theirs. She drank, and heard her voice go thick and foolish, and accepted a ride home with the Haases, and went to bed at once.

In the morning when she learned where the fire had been, and whose apartment had been gutted, and who had died in the hospital — she had been speechless with shock.

"Albert St. Dennis is dead? Dead? So quickly? — overnight? *Dead?*"

For days afterward she wept. She did not even attend the memorial service for St. Dennis in the chapel; she wanted only to hide from the others, from their grief and shock and chagrin, which would mirror her own. (What a tragedy, they would say, what a terrible thing to happen, that poor old man, that poor lonely old man — to die here, so far from home — to die in that ghastly way —) She did not leave the apartment, she wept herself into a trance, far more moved than she could have anticipated: she had often thought, cynically, that no one's death would have the power to move her very greatly, not any longer. But she had been mistaken.

The irreparable nature of it! — the crudity, the clumsiness, the stupidity! — the probable cause, after all, was a lighted cigarette: a mere accident. An accident of drunkenness. Antithetical to the man's deepest self, to the marvelous subtleties of his art, his genius. Antithetical to all he represented. Death was hideous in any case, and irreparable, a breaking-off of speech — but this particular death struck her as awful. It was unnecessary, it was unbearable. It was a scandal. It hurt.

She was weak and sick and a little unbalanced by what had happened. It might have been a comfort to slip into madness, but she was, for better or worse, far too conventional to go mad; it struck her as merely distasteful. She was sane, and in her relentless sanity she asked herself why the man had died in that way — why anyone dies in any particular way — is the death matched to the personality, is it part of one's destiny, or merely a foolish accident? "I can't believe it," she said aloud. "It can't have happened. Not yet. Not like that. I don't accept it. . . . He can't leave us."

She wept until her head pounded with a bright, scintillating pain, and her eyes ached, and still she could not believe it, she could not accept it: In his stubborn, private way St. Dennis had seemed the most aggressively alive of them all. And he had slipped from her. He had eluded her. (The body had been sent home to relatives in England: there was not even the minimal consolation of knowing that the man's grave would be here in

Woodslee. . . . In a short while it would seem he had never been
here at all.)

A week after the accident Brigit awoke before dawn, covered
with perspiration. Something had frightened her. She imagined
she heard sirens, a faint unearthly wailing. . . . Was someone
calling her name? Confused, she turned to her lover, seeking his
arms, the sleepy warmth of his embrace; she turned to her husband, who would not deny her, not now, not after she had suffered so much. Help me, hold me, Brigit murmured, reaching
out to discover she was alone: and the bedclothes were damp and
unpleasant to the touch.

"Did I kill you?" she cried.

She awoke; she sat up, her heart pounding; she tried to think
where she was.

She turned on the bedside lamp. 4:20. A winter morning. It
was March, still; groggily she remembered the long winter, the
perpetual snow, the fire, the loss, the death. It was quite real,
that death. Pointless to attempt an affirmation of it. (He had had
a long life, people said; he had achieved recognition, even fame;
he had been happy, hadn't he? Happy? Here in Woodslee, here
in the world — *happy?*) The administration lowered flags to half
mast round the campus for several days and students glanced at
them and wondered, or did not wonder, who had died; whose
death was presumed significant to warrant this public gesture.
Now it was over, the ceremony was over, but Brigit felt her throat
aching unreasonably as it did when she was about to burst into
tears; she was still trapped, she was weakened with sorrow, the
ceremony of death was over but she was not free. A trickle of
perspiration ran down her forehead. She was trembling with anticipation, with anxiety. It was over: but nothing was over, nothing was accomplished. There was someone she must talk with
. . . someone she must contact. She would explain herself to

him, she would weep in his embrace, she would beg forgiveness
from him. . . . It came to her, then, that she had been frightened
awake by a dream of her grandfather. St. Dennis had appeared,
very much as he had been in life; he had smiled at her in that
sweet, rather infuriating way, as if he did not really see her; she
had forced herself to smile in return, disguising the impatience
she felt, and as she approached him — to embrace him, apparently, or to take his hands in hers — he had been transformed
into her grandfather and she had flinched away, she had thrown
herself aside with such desperate violence that the gesture had
awakened her. She remembered: her heart beat with the memory: her skin burned.

She was besieged, then, by memories of her grandparents. She
remained sitting up in bed, hunched far forward, her hair fallen
into her face, her eyes half-shut, her fist jammed against her
mouth. She murmured aloud in protestation. She moaned, she
sobbed. It was not fair, it was not just, they too had died, they
too had been alone in their old age, and lonely, and Brigit had
not liked them, neither she nor her sister had liked them; Brigit's
mother had scolded the girls and threatened to punish them, but
they had not liked their grandparents, the visits had been awkward and torturous, bad enough at the old farmhouse but worse,
far worse, grotesquely worse, at the nursing home. . . . The odor
of medicine, the odor of aged soft helpless flesh; mouths collapsed inward; eyes gone milky-blind. The grandmother had died
first and everyone said it was a blessing. In the coffin she had
appeared frail and doll-like and feminine . . . pretty . . . *charming*. (Isn't she lovely, haven't they fixed her up lovely, everyone
cried; why, she's the very picture of herself as she used to
be. . . .) A blessing, people whispered. First she broke her leg so
badly and then her kidneys were affected and then. . . . But her
grandfather: her grandfather. He had not died. Had *not*. Refused
to leave the farm though he could hardly walk, refused to talk
with Brigit's parents when they came to bring him supplies, ac-

cepted no money from them, seemed to despise them all in the end. Senile, cranky, stubborn, droning and mumbling and coughing, and upon occasion (ah, how the memory hurts! — Brigit flinches in pain) turning up in town, in town, strolling along Main Street like any old farmer in his filthy overalls, a straw hat jammed on his head, beard stained yellow, mumbling and laughing to himself: in town, on Main Street, at noon when Brigit and her friends were out of school. She sees him again, she hears him. Brigit! Brigit! Sharp-eyed, that terrible old man. How she fears him, how she hates him. . . . If she crosses the street surely he cannot see her. He stumbles along in a dream, obviously a little drunk; surely he cannot see her. (Sometimes he carried a flask of whiskey in a paper bag and went to sit in the park with other grimy men, some old, some young, all bemused and solitary, inhabitants of dreams who were nevertheless dangerous — they might call out to Brigit at any time. Sometimes he spent an entire afternoon in a certain tavern on Canal Street and would be seen, just at dusk, staggering along Main Street, his clothes often disarrayed, his fly not buttoned quite right; and Brigit's father, red with shame and indignation, had to drive along near the curb and beg the old man to get into the car — Hey Pa, please! Hey look! *Pa!* You know you can't possibly walk nine miles home —) Then he had a stroke. And another. He was old, nearly eighty, but his heart was strong, he was himself cranky and stubborn and did not much want to die, perhaps because he sensed the wishes of his family; he put up quite a struggle, they said, exhausted, and halfway admiring, but in the end exasperated with him — he put up quite a struggle, your grandfather. There'll be nobody like him left — !

Hospitalized in Norfolk against his wishes, he had died one day, suddenly, in the middle of the week, a Wednesday, Brigit remembered, August 5, and she had been going to visit him in the hospital the next day, her parents had wanted her and her sister to come sooner but the girls had been frightened, Brigit had even thrown a kind of tantrum, not wanting to go, not wanting to go, weeping in rage that they should force her to go see that old man: Brigit, he would say, reaching out to touch her, possibly to stroke her hair (which she hated), Brigit, Brigit? He loved her, everyone said; she mustn't mind him being so cranky; he was sick and old and not himself any longer but he did love her, he loved them all. . . . He died, then, suddenly. Brigit had been in school at the time. Seventh grade: twelve years old. Social studies class. Or math. When had he died, what time . . . ? It was very important to know the exact time. The day was August 5, it was a Wednesday, she had pressed her hands against her mouth and vowed she would not visit him in the hospital, no she would not, would *not*, nobody could force her to go. And then he died, then it was over. So suddenly. Abruptly. He died, he was dead, there was no need to keep away from the hospital, no need to shout her defiance at her mother — no need to risk being slapped. Her grandfather was dead and she would no longer be ashamed of him.

Remembering, she wept with the pain of it: the sense of irreparable loss: the knowledge that she had stayed away from a dying man who had loved her in his own way; she had been selfish and cowardly and despicable. . . . Now she wept, rocking from side to side, her fist against her mouth; it isn't fair, none of it is fair. Louellen moved away and had not answered a letter of hers and she had never written another, she had been too proud and too hurt to write, even to send a birthday card, she had lost Louellen, she had lost them all, her grandmother, her grandfather with his stained beard and his disheveled clothes and his manure-stained boots, she had denied them, she had lost them, at the very time of losing them she had somehow known (for even as a child Brigit had been chillingly perceptive) that she would regret it later: but she hadn't cared. It was the same way with her parents now, with her sister and her cousins and her aunts and uncles, and Stanley, and Alexis. Let them go, let them die, let them be lost. That was her voice and she heard it distinctly.

Exhausted, she rose and showered and made coffee and fed the cat, who brushed anxiously against her legs, sensing something wrong. She walked about the apartment, edgy, nervous, highly charged, then went to her desk and worked for a while, at first experimentally, then in earnest. From 5:30 until 9 she worked, writing in longhand in her ledger. The aching in her eyes gradually faded. She forgot her exhaustion, she forgot her situation — she was writing about her grandparents, about their farm in the hills south of Norfolk; she forgot about herself entirely.

Later that day she worked again, and the next day, and the next. She returned home from school eager to look through what she had written the previous night, and to continue with what she was doing. She had never been so absorbed in anything before; she was sometimes so moved, her eyes filled with tears. It was upsetting, it was draining, it demanded her entire attention, yet she rather enjoyed it — she could not remember, in fact, having enjoyed anything quite so much. If the telephone rang she was reluctant to answer it. (The Bradys were having some people over for brunch next Sunday — would she like to join them? And the first Saturday in April the Tomlinsons were having a party; could she come? . . . She stammered replies, she was distracted and evasive. It wasn't certain whether she could come or not; she was very much caught up in her work; she hoped they would understand.)

"Should we get married?" Alexis asked.

Brigit laughed uneasily.

"You were never serious about me. You were married all along," he said. ". . . Someone's wife all along."

He had come back from Nassau two weeks earlier than he'd

planned because of St. Dennis's death, he said; he had supposed
Brigit would be upset. Strangely, he had not telephoned beforehand. He merely showed up one evening at eleven and knocked
on her door, only a little embarrassed, as if they had not parted
in anger nearly two months previously; as if it were quite natural
that he should drop in so late. "You look surprised," he said.
"You look disapproving. Aren't I welcome any longer?"

"Certainly you're welcome," Brigit said, staring at him. At first
he had seemed unchanged, though deeply and handsomely
tanned. Then it struck her that he was thinner, he had not his
usual buoyancy, his customary aplomb. The sun had bleached
his hair bone-white but he had unwisely cut it so that it fell only
to his shirt collar; from certain angles he looked almost ordinary.
An attractive young man, surely — but not exceptional.

Though he had come to comfort her it was she who ended by
comforting him. St. Dennis's death had been a shock to him too,
and it disturbed him that he should be so shocked: really, he had
not known St. Dennis well and St. Dennis certainly hadn't
known *him*. Yet when he read the brief article in the *New York
Times* he had been tremendously upset. He had left the house he
was staying in, hadn't explained to his friend where he was going,
had spent a day and a night away, simply drinking, as if determined to make himself sick. He would never see the old man
again; he had never gotten around to apologizing, even, for that
dreadful New Year's Eve; he had never finished the cycle of
songs. (Running through them again in his imagination he knew
they were no good. They were arch, strained, meretricious.
"Meretricious" — a cruel word used to describe Alexis by one of
his mentors at the New England Conservatory: he had carried it
about in his head for fifteen years. Only one of the songs was
halfway acceptable and that song suddenly struck him as distress-
ingly similar to Samuel Barber's "Dover Beach." No, the songs
were a failure, he was a failure, he must destroy them all and
begin again. Return to zero and begin again. The music he would

create must do justice to St. Dennis's poetry; it must not intrude, must not call attention to itself.) And he was sorry about the way he had treated Brigit. He missed her. He was lonely, he hadn't been well, he fought with everyone, he was in trouble here at Woodslee — had she heard? — he missed her very much, very much indeed.

"I have no one to talk to," he said.

They lay in each other's arms and he hid his face in her shoulder, sobbing. He despised himself, at times he wanted so powerfully to die that he was frightened, he was frightened he would try to hurt himself, he didn't truly want to die — didn't want to be dead; did she understand? She understood. She understood very well. But it was hopeless, their love. Wasn't it? Yes. They didn't love each other. She was married to another man and seemed incapable of divorcing him. She lied; she avoided telling the truth. And he lied as well. He doubted that he could be faithful to her. A husband, Alexis Kessler . . . ? No, it was impossible; it was ludicrous. They laughed together, stricken.

"Still, we could be married," Alexis said slowly. "We feel something for each other. We feel *something*. . . . I don't believe, frankly, that I'm capable of feeling as much for anyone else. Not any longer. When I was young, when I was nineteen and twenty. . . . I suffered a great deal, I went through those exquisite phases of suffering St. Dennis wrote about, but I survived, I outlived myself, and I'm not really capable of feeling very much. It's so draining, it's so predictable, isn't it? Passion . . . jealousy . . . the happiness of reunion . . . guilt . . . the need to tell so many lies. When you're in love you can't tell the truth because you would hurt your lover: automatically, unconsciously you lie. In the past few years I've become very sensitive to these lies, I despise myself for telling them, but I can't stop. My friend in Nassau. . . . He's separated from his wife, they've been married twelve years and I've always been a friend of his, in a sense, always a shadowy figure in their marriage (the expression is his wife's: she has written me dozens of letters in those twelve years), someone they talk about late at night when they feel the need to torment each other. He lies to me about his feelings for his wife, she lies to him about her feelings for him, saying she isn't hurt, she doesn't mind, I lie to them both. . . . I pretend to be much more agonized by the situation than I am. In fact it means very little to me; when I read about St. Dennis everything shifted, the world seemed to go flat, to lose its perspective, nothing meant very much. I walked out. I flew back here. I can't get up the moral strength, even, to make a telephone call. . . . But I know you don't love me, Brigit, so there's no point in my making a fool of myself like this. You're too intelligent to marry anyone again. Isn't that right? We can't be anything more than friends."

"But that's a great deal," Brigit protested.

Alexis lay without speaking for a while. He was quite warm; he seemed to want to burrow into her, pressing his face against her throat and shoulder. His cheeks were damp. He was sullen, he was childlike, he was very touching. She did love him — in a way; she loved him very much. Stroking his hair (which was not in very good condition — it was dry, strawlike, the ends were badly split), she comforted him as she might have comforted a child, urging him to be calm, to sleep. They were not lovers. They would probably never be lovers again. She felt no desire for him though she could remember perfectly well having felt desire some months ago — having been stricken by it, in fact, overcome and humiliated by it. She had outlived that desire, in a way she had triumphed over it. . . . Should they marry, should they continue as friends, should they try to live together? . . . or would it be better, saner, to break off their relationship entirely? They suspected that all of Woodslee knew about them; it would probably be general knowledge that Alexis had returned, that they were together again tonight. All of Woodslee knew and offered opinions and judgments and predictions. Alexis laughed sadly, alluding to a difficulty he was evidently having at the present time, but Brigit did not press him to explain; it had something to do with his position in the music department and she supposed he would tell her eventually. All of Woodslee watched, all of Woodslee knew. Alexis and Brigit. Brigit and Alexis. It might be a good idea, Alexis said, for them both to leave.

"If I left I would go back to Virginia," Brigit said.

But he seemed not to hear. He spoke sleepily of their going to Rome together. He loved Rome: in his mid-twenties he had done his finest work there. A ballet, an oratorio, many small pieces, part of a symphony. They must go to Rome together. . . . There was some possibility of his getting a Guggenheim for next year, he believed, or at any rate a commission for another ballet; there were people who still had faith in him; not very many, unfortunately, but still a few. Perhaps they would take pity on him. If only he could begin again, in another part of the world . . . ! He supposed he was a failure, he supposed his talent had drained away, but perhaps with Brigit's help. . . . He had missed her, had missed her very much. She ought not to have rejected him as she had. Certainly she was justified, he knew what a bastard he had been, he had meant . . . had meant to apologize . . . to repay some of the money he owed her. . . . Brigit, he said, do you forgive me, are you listening? Yes, she said; why don't you sleep; you sound so exhausted. He made a sound that was midway between a sigh and a laugh. It was true he was exhausted: he hadn't slept well for over a week. Before flying to Nassau he had become involved in a very nasty situation at Woodslee and it exhausted him even to think about it. Had she heard, he wondered. She told him no: she hadn't heard. She stroked his hair, held him close against her. I can't keep fighting them, Alexis mumbled, they hate me and they've worn me down . . . and Byrne will be gone next year, there will be no one to protect me . . . I'm not the fighter I once was . . . I get tired so easily . . . anonymous calls and an obscene photograph in my mailbox at school and people like Bannon smirking at me . . . telling lies to my stu-

dents. . . . I can't keep fighting them, he said wearily, and drifted
into sleep while Brigit held him, thankful he had come back to
her, thankful he did not love her any more than he did; thankful
too that there was someone who trusted her so much that he
would fall asleep in her arms.

He squirmed and twitched in sleep. He too was troubled by
dreams. She was happy to lie with him like this, absurdly happy
to be holding him as she was, knowing that in the morning he
would leave; she would want him to leave; she had her own work
to do, and her attention would shift violently to it. (She was
rewriting the novel entirely: had discarded the original three
hundred pages and was beginning again, beginning fifty years
earlier, locating her narrative outside the consciousness of the
young girl who was to live out Brigit's early life, and dealing
instead with her parents and her grandparents and a single
great-grandmother.) But it was marvelous to be holding Alexis
like this. To have offered him some comfort, however minimal.
To have said Yes, I understand, yes, yes, now please forget,
please sleep, I have no more ambition for the two of us than that
you should sleep with me like this, that we should be entirely at
peace. . . . We want nothing from each other now: we must be
at peace.

(In recent weeks she has been thinking not only of her grandparents and her parents and her sister, and her own childhood,
unexplored, unacknowledged, but of that other world as well —
the world of her dream, through the mirror, across the threshold,
into a realm of ghost-images, ghost-selves, utter mystery. She has
been subject to sudden, piercing memories, almost entirely visual, that come to her with the force of cards being held up before
her eyes. She cannot not see. She cannot resist. There is a mirror
coated with grime. There is a being in it, alive. She approaches it
and the being or image shakes itself free of the confines of the
mirror and retreats, and she follows, she follows as if entranced,

though it is dangerous for her to do so: why, she does not exactly know. She is entirely alone. There are no people around to help her or to warn her or to scold. She is a child; at the same time she is an adult. She is *Brigit* but there is some danger . . . there is some danger of her losing *Brigit* if she does not turn back. . . . Suddenly the world about her is alive. It has always been alive. The world, the universe: a gigantic living creature. She is drifting within it and there is great danger, she knows there is great danger, she must turn back before the creature becomes conscious of her, before it awakes. It is oblivious of her at the present time. But if she continues to press forward. . . . She must not press forward, not at this time. She must turn back. This knowledge is not to be hers yet; she is too young; she is too ignorant. She must turn back to her own life, to her own work. She is *Brigit* and must live out that destiny. . . . And so she turns back, wrenching herself awake. She is fearful of that other world, she does not want to cross into it, she knows very well that it exists, simultaneous with this world; but she is not ready for it yet. Not yet.)

"I have felt the wind of terror stream many a time across my upright hair," Leslie Cullendon says wittily, raising his wine glass to Pete Springer, who laughs, gulping at his food, "yet . . . still . . . it cannot be said that I am brought low, let alone feel despair. And you? . . . And the rest of you?"

Up and down the table they acknowledge his question with small nervous smiles, or pointedly ignore it; Brigit, gazing at him with interest, cannot determine what attitude to take toward Leslie — he is a dying man, after all, and therefore absolved of some of the social restraints that vex the rest of them. His wife Babs sits as far from him as possible and is trying, without much success, to talk to Vivian Hochberg (who has been unusually quiet today, distracted, often glancing around the table as if seeking someone not present); the only people who make a special effort to deal with Leslie are Pete Springer, who is slightly drunk, and Chris Callinan, who is nice to everyone, and Gowan Vaughan-Jones, who seems both shocked and intrigued by Leslie's gaiety. Fortunately, Leslie has never attacked Brigit directly; she has heard that he has mocked her behind her back upon occasion — in a droll manner, she was assured; nothing malicious. (Leslie cheerfully echoes Robert Graves's statement that a woman cannot be a creative artist: she is a Muse or she is nothing.)

The main course is coq au vin, served by student waiters who
appear to be somewhat ill at ease. It is Leslie's noisy exuberance,
perhaps, or the mere fact of so many professors seated together;
Brigit wonders how the department appears to outsiders. She
supposes it looks like a friendly gathering: there is a great deal of
smiling, a fair amount of laughter. Gladys Fetler and George
Housley and Blaise Perrin are enjoying themselves immensely,
talking of the old days of the department, twenty and twenty-five
and thirty years ago. Sometimes the mere mention of a name
sets them off into gales of laughter. Do you remember Denton?
— who shared an office with old Fairfax? Do you remember —
what was his name — ah yes: Conrad Botnivick, who changed
his underwear in his office, who left dirty underclothes and socks
behind in his desk drawers? What a terrible man! There's never
been anyone like him since! Ernest Jaeger and Warren Hochberg
are talking about a new study of *Hudibras*, just published by Oxford University Press; neither thinks the scholarship is really very
sound, and certain of the critical conclusions are indefensible.
Vivian Hochberg is telling someone about an extraordinary incident that happened the other day at the Hoffmans: it was well
after nine, everyone was seated at dinner, and the doorbell rang
and one of the Hoffman children went to answer it before Mrs.
Hoffman could get there and who should be on the front stoop
but a disheveled man, a complete stranger, very drunk, asking if
he could use the telephone. Unwisely, he was allowed in the
house, he went into Henry's study to use the phone, but once
there he behaved so oddly it was obvious that he was dangerous
— he didn't want to make a telephone call, he really wanted to
see the inside of the Hoffmans' house. It took Henry and two
other men to get him to leave — to threaten him with the police
if he refused. The dinner party was nearly ruined as a consequence; no one talked of anything else except the intruder. Such
an ugly, desperate man! — and clearly not quite sane. Brigit and
several others have been talking animatedly about the probable

unionization of the faculty at Woodslee and how it would alter, forever, relationships between professors and students, and relationships between professors and their professions — nothing will ever be the same again, they say with feeling. Yet it must happen; it is merely the next step; even individuals who oppose it on principle, like Brigit, acknowledge that it is the next, inevitable step in the mechanization of the profession. Just as well that Dean Byrne has resigned, they say. He would never have been able to adapt to so radical a change. . . . Yes, Brigit supposes they appear to be a unified group. They know one another's jokes, one another's mannerisms. Their subtle allusions are rarely lost on one another. Perhaps they even look alike to their students.

She has been thinking in recent weeks, since St. Dennis's death especially, that life is a very serious matter. But perhaps it is not serious at all, perhaps it is only a kind of luncheon . . . ? Time shared among colleagues who are not exactly friends; conversations that go nowhere but are mildly entertaining; a way of affirming one's common humanity, one's communal place. Nothing tragic about it; nothing heroic. Never larger than life but merely life itself: ceaseless.

Certainly it is something of a surprise to discover, as one gains access to inner circles, that the distinction of "inner" so rapidly alters. One is allowed into a certain group and begins to see, almost immediately, that this group is peripheral to another, more central group, a far more desirable gathering of individuals. One may peer in the window eagerly, one may scratch or pound at the door; or one may be — finally and miraculously — invited in. And then at once one sees that even this group is not a true group, it is merely another conglomerate of individuals, linked only by the frail bond of their having excluded certain others and their being excluded, in turn, by a most prestigious group . . . a true elite. Again one yearns to be taken up by this elite, one wants only to be noticed, to be invited in, to be loved; one's colleagues are equally anxious to be allowed into that special society; there is no comfort in this outer circle, this hellish exclusion from grace. And then . . . and then. . . . It may happen that one is taken up yet again, and invited into the innermost circle, and almost immediately one realizes that even this circle is peripheral to another circle of more powerful, more blessed individuals whom everyone envies. Again and again, and again. . . . (Was it true, as someone said, that St. Dennis's last years were spoiled by his bitter wish for a Nobel Prize? He had kept this secret desire hidden from Brigit but she did not doubt that it might be true; it had the ring of a melancholy truth.)

Circles within circles, Brigit thinks, and all of them so foolish, and all of them so painfully real.

The coq au vin is overcooked, hardly more than a stew, but Brigit finds it quite good. Her appetite is improving as she eats. Others complain of the slightly stale rolls, the slices of pulpy hothouse tomatoes, the doughy noodles, even the fact that the tablecloth is creased and scorched in odd places; yet Brigit notices that they are eating heartily. They have finished several bottles of wine and are calling for more. Brigit is uneasy when she happens to glance down at the table at the Swansons, or at Leslie Cullendon, or over at St. Dennis's portrait (which does resemble him yet is excessively benign and gnomish, a slander upon the man's acerbity), but for the most part she has begun to enjoy the luncheon. It may, after all, be the last social event she will attend at Woodslee; there is some probability she won't return next fall. The food is satisfactory, the food is really quite good. Her colleagues are jovial and witty. There is Pete Springer reciting lines from a laughably mawkish O'Neill tragedy though he is, Brigit has heard, rather like a character in an O'Neill tragedy himself; there are Chris Callinan and Brad Keough passionately arguing the merits of the film *Barry Lyndon*, Chris preferring the film to the novel, Brad perversely preferring the novel to the film, though Chris has been promoted to full professor and Brad has been fired and hasn't, as far as Brigit knows, a job for next year. Yet in their words they are equals, for the space of their discussion they are equals, they are brothers. They are quite happy. Sandra Jaeger, lovely Sandra, joins their conversation to offer her opinion. They pause, they turn to her, they are wondrously attentive. A beauty, that girl: in a peach-colored dress, her pale hair swinging about her face; lithe, eager, keen-eyed, almost breathless in her desire to please. She speaks softly, she lifts her perfect chin, both men stare at her, momentarily silenced, and Brigit cannot help thinking — but surely she is mistaken, surely she is too suspicious — that Chris's recent election to the chairmanship of the Promotion and Tenure Committee has given him a new attractiveness in the girl's eyes — but *surely* she is mistaken because Sandra looks so innocent, so absolutely without guile. And perhaps Brigit is merely jealous. She knows no man will ever look at her that way again; it will never happen again. That part of her life is over.

Still, she reasons, eating the chicken (it *is* overcooked but delicious just the same, she has not felt so hungry for months), she had had enough of that sort of thing as a younger woman: a man's rapt gaze, a man's *involuntary* admiration: it would be a strain if it went on much longer. Stanley had gazed at her like that, desiring her, and it had been his desire and not Brigit he had loved, and both he and she had suffered as a consequence, and were suffering still. Really, she had had enough of it. Sandra Jaeger's laughter is high, girlish, unconvincing. She wants the attention of men but cannot quite handle it; she grows flushed; she waves her hands about. (Down the table her husband Ernest looks away; he is continuing his conversation with Dr. Hochberg.)

Again there are genial complaints: the pecan pie is too sugary. The student waiters reappear, Gowan Vaughan-Jones rises to make a brief speech, cigarettes and pipes are lit, Brigit folds her arms and listens, hoping she won't be upset. But there is no

danger. Gowan Vaughan-Jones is speaking of Albert St. Dennis
the poet, he is drawing liberally from his own review of the *Collected Poems* that appeared just last Sunday on the front page of
the *New York Times Book Review* — a marvelous review, a forest
of allusions, an almost impenetrable paean to the "one poet of
the twentieth century who may be said to rival Yeats"; but it is
not the poet St. Dennis of whom Gowan speaks so much as his
own invention, a masterly "satirist" of the first rank, and it is
certainly not the man St. Dennis of whom he speaks — not the
man Brigit knew. So there is no danger of her being upset.
Gowan speaks well, in a clear, ringing voice, evidently his classroom voice. He must be a superb lecturer. His corduroy coat is
too large for his narrow shoulders but his red tie is attractive and
he looks healthier than Brigit has seen him since last fall. A fine
man, really. A formidable man. (Honors have fallen upon Gowan
this spring: a Guggenheim grant so he can go to England next
year to complete his book on poetics; an offer of a chair in the
Department of American Literature at the University of London;
a counteroffer, rumored to be unusually generous, from Woodslee.) He concludes his speech by quoting from one of St. Dennis's poems — elliptical, enigmatic lines about "immortality"; he
sits down, blushing, boyish, obviously quite pleased with his own
performance, and as everyone applauds quietly it occurs to Brigit
that *here*, among the world's population, is the individual who
will most benefit from St. Dennis's life and death.

Now Warren Hochberg rises to speak of Dr. Fetler and her
many years of service to the department and the university. He
is, or appears to be, an almost clumsy speaker; the lower half of
his face seems somehow disjoined from the upper; Brigit notices
that he is shredding something in his fingers — one of the paper
napkins most likely. Dr. Fetler is staring into her coffee cup. She
is a large woman, her profile is full and generous, she strikes
Brigit as neither female nor male, really, but simply an individual,
a marvelous presence. The department without her will seem

incomplete, unbalanced. What is happening to her is unfair, Brigit thinks helplessly, and though everyone knows it, nothing will
be done: after today Dr. Fetler will no longer be a member of the
department. Her colleagues appear to be moved, listening to Dr.
Hochberg's recitation of her many achievements — George
Housley is wiping at his eyes, perhaps because, at sixty, he suspects he will be the next to be retired; Ernest Jaeger sits with one
hand pressed against his mouth, gazing at the tablecloth; even
Leslie Cullendon, who is eating the remains of his wife's pecan
pie, glances up now and then, nodding and frowning severely.
But though Dr. Hochberg's manner seems ingenuous, his words
are graceful and effective, and when Dr. Fetler rises to thank
him and to accept the department's gift (a calfskin attaché case
with her initials in gold), and even, tearful, to move into his ritual
embrace and allow him to kiss her cheek, everyone begins to
applaud. It is a full, rich moment; it is the perfect conclusion of
the academic year.

Yet it is not quite the end. Before the first person rises and
the situation is altered, Leslie Cullendon raps on his water glass
for attention. He makes a comic effort to lift himself from his
wheelchair. "A moment, a moment, my friends!" he cries. For
an odd instant Brigit believes the young man's shoulders and
arms have become muscular; weren't they thin, bone-thin, in the
past . . . ? His face is emaciated, his hips and thighs are wasted,
but his shoulders appear to be. . . . No, it is an illusion: simply
the way his tweed coat is bunched up. Everyone looks toward
him, smiling uneasily. He grins, raises his water glass, presses it
against his overheated forehead, and begins a garbled, excited
speech of some kind, a toast: "My friends — a moment — wait!
It's a lovely today, isn't it? Winter is over! Over! My friends —
Signatures of all things, I am here to read — eh? Right? A speech
is in order that celebrates *us*. Not always *them*. St. Dennis is
gone and easily forgot — there's a rumor of another St. Dennis
arriving in the fall — another 'great man'! — but until then it's

us, it's just us, don't we deserve applause? I think we do, by God, by Christ, by blood and bones! — leave me alone, Babs, mind your own business — My friends, wait — Wait — Where are you going, why do you want the luncheon to end so quickly? It's only one-thirty, it isn't late, surely we have time for — time for — My friends, my colleagues, my brothers and sisters, wait, *wait*, don't rush our lives to a close — where are you going? I propose a toast. A final toast. A toast to *us*. Pete, yes, you're my friend, and Chris, and Warren, and Gladys, and George, and Brigit, and what's-your-name, you, and Joe, yes, and Brad and Gowan what's-your-name, oh Christ, wait, my brain's like a sieve, Vaughan-Jones it is, you're my friend too, our offices are next to each other, right? — and Dr. Perrin, and — uh — Nasty selfish things! Always edging away! You'll regret it! I — I — I am proposing a toast — a toast to *us* — I insist that — To *us*. See? *Us*. Nobody else. Just — us. *Us!*"

But the luncheon is over. Though Leslie's voice rises in a near shriek, they are able to ignore him under cover of the activity of rising from the table and drifting into the hall outside the seminar room. Leslie remains behind, in his wheelchair, calling after them while Babs tries to quiet him; Brigit cannot make out exactly what he says, hearing principally the word *Us*.

In the top drawer of the maple dresser, partly hidden by miscellaneous items — stockings, head scarves, gloves, a pair of thick woolen socks — is Sandra Jaeger's ledger-journal; its two hundred pages are now nearly filled with entries. Sandra checks the drawer and the ledger every day, sometimes twice a day, but nothing is ever disturbed.

Tonight she finds herself drawn to the diary. At first she believes she will write in it, a few hurried impressions of that interminable luncheon for the old woman, perhaps a brief recounting of the embarrassing episode that followed, in the parking lot — when the Jaegers inadvertently overheard the Swansons quarreling and were unable to back away before being discovered; then she decides she has no interest in the ledger any longer. (The last entry was three weeks ago and is very brief: telephone calls to their parents to inform them, triumphantly, that Ernest *will* be kept on at Woodslee.) She leafs through the ledger and is filled with astonishment, almost with alarm, at how little she recognizes. The exclamatory entries of years ago, the little-girl handwriting, the names of former friends and classmates and professors, winter summer spring autumn, new clothes, books, movies, restaurants, boy friends, holidays, relatives, grades, *Very sad today*, roommates, dances, *Had marvelous time*, Mother and

Father and home, the first evening with Ernest, *Ernest Jaeger*, Boston, engagement, wedding, Trenton, marriage, borrowing money, acceptance from Woodslee, move to Woodslee, the rented duplex, the Faculty Wives' luncheon, the first party in September. (*The Byrnes are such warm, wonderful people*, the handwriting exclaims, *so friendly all evening.* . . .)

And so on. Into winter, into spring.

Sandra studies the journal for a while and then goes into the living room, where her husband is working. He glances up at her, blinking. He is very tired: after the departmental luncheon he worked all afternoon and since dinner he has been working, transcribing innumerable notes onto note cards. He is wearing a sweatshirt and jeans and bedroom slippers. Hunched over the table he appears, for an instant, to be much older than he is; his glasses have slipped partway down his nose.

Would you like to see my diary, Sandra asks.

He stares at her, as if not comprehending. Then he sees the ledger in her hand; he recognizes it. He has never opened the ledger but he knows what it is.

What — Why do you — Are you joking? he asks.

She isn't joking: she is finished with the ledger and doesn't intend to get another one. In fact, she is going to burn this one. But would he like to glance through it first — ?

Ernest laughs uneasily.

— There might be a few entries that would interest him, Sandra says. Recent entries.

But diaries are private, Ernest says, as if slightly offended by her offer. He would never dream of —

She intends to burn the diary in the morning, so if he has any curiosity at all —

— would never dream of violating another person's privacy.

And he has a long night ahead: hours of painstaking work.

Sandra nods slowly. She understands. It simply crossed her mind that he might be curious about the sort of diary she'd been keeping all these years. But of course he's busy and she shouldn't be interrupting him.

Any husband would be curious, Ernest says. But it would be a violation of — of the spirit of a diary — a violation of their marriage, even. He would never dream of — It wouldn't be right to —

I understand, Sandra says quietly.

Brigit's silken-haired black cat, though neutered years ago, is behaving very strangely tonight.

She leaps and skids and rushes about the living room, and then out into Brigit's tiny kitchen, in a wild figure eight. A chunky, good-sized creature — she must weigh eight pounds — her ears are laid back in mock terror, and her immense plume-like tail is swollen and twitching. "My God," Alexis laughs, "your cat has finally gone completely mad." Minnie, as if excited by his voice, whirls and leaps in his direction and runs across his shoulders; he beats her away, wincing. She then leaps, or falls, heavily to the floor, flops onto her back and, clawing at the bottom of the sofa, propels herself along the hardwood floor on her back in wild spasmodic strokes. What on earth is wrong? — why such excitement? Alexis laughs in bewilderment, rubbing at his neck. It may be the spring evening, the prematurely mild air; it may be the scraps of corned beef they have fed her, a spicy supper for a cat. Or his presence.

Alexis and Brigit watch the cat, astounded. She is now dragging herself along beneath the sofa upon which they sit; she knocks her head against the wall quite hard; she lies there panting, her eyes wide and glaring, an eerie yellow-green.

"I suppose she *is* a little eccentric," Brigit says.

"Well," says Alexis.

"A good thing, your never having moved in with me," Brigit says.

"But Brigit, you never asked me!" Alexis says.

He had stopped by with food from a delicatessen, around seven, and now it is after ten; they have been talking for hours of innumerable disjointed matters. Should Alexis quietly resign and leave Woodslee, should he leave this part of the world altogether; should he leave by himself; should he stay and fight? (For the last several days he has done no composing, not even the sketchy experimental diary-like work he usually does every day, whether he is inspired or not; he has been playing Ravel's *Pavane* and *Jeux d'Eau*, and some pieces by Fauré and Satie and Ives, playing for hours, in a trance, in a stupor, carried out of himself. The piano is joy, Alexis has always known, the piano is bliss, it will save him, it has saved him in the past, if only he could remain at the piano forever . . . ! When he stops playing, however, he starts thinking. He feels then the desperate need for Brigit: the need to talk to her.)

Should he stay at Woodslee. Should he leave. Should Brigit leave? She is considering a position at a small college in Norfolk, and it upsets Alexis to hear her speak so calmly about moving back home, about re-establishing herself with her family. Her mother isn't well, evidently, and her younger sister would love her to be near . . . and her father is rapidly aging. . . . "You can't mean you would bury yourself in that part of the world," Alexis says incredulously.

"I haven't decided," Brigit says.

He is not jealous, he is merely disturbed. Nor is he jealous of her work; it pleases him, in fact, he has said so several times, that she is working again. He has never respected people who don't work, who haven't their own private labors of creation, who are not, in short, individuals; all his life he has been contemptuous of "ordinary" people — the consumers, the non-creative. The tone-deaf, the illiterate, the smug, the boorish majority. . . . He is contemptuous of them, he is possibly a little frightened of them.

"Should we leave Woodslee together?" Alexis says.

His lease is expiring at the end of May and the building super-intendent wants him out (for unconvincing reasons), so he must move anyway. The chore of moving his furniture, his piano, his hi-fi equipment and his eight thousand records and his several thousand books, will nearly break him, he supposes; his nerves have been raw lately. Ever since the death of. . . . Ever since the surprise of that death.

"You don't love me any longer, do you?" Alexis says. "But you *are* still fond of me?"

He can see that she is waiting for him to leave. There is a casual, capricious air about her now that is both intriguing and annoying. For a while he believed it was another mask of hers, just another experimental role; he had faith in his own capacity to break through it. (Though he does not love her he *is* extremely fond of her.) But days passed, weeks passed, she was happy to see him but not unhappy when he left, and no longer anxious, no longer so desperate and intimidating. She did not *want* him; he knew that perfectly well. He was relieved but also a little hurt, a little perplexed.

Still, he could understand. He supposed he could understand. When, at the age of fourteen, he had heard a certain piece by Schoenberg for the first time, he had been excited and upset by the eeriness of what was left unstated . . . what was deliberately omitted by the composer . . . so excited, in fact, that he had begun shivering convulsively and had even been sick to his stomach. Precocious Alexis, so high-strung as a child that his parents believed he might go insane — ! He remembers that experience well. But the child Alexis is gone, lost. The Schoenberg piece remains and Alexis can play it now himself if he wishes, he can play it in his head at any time, it is beautiful still but no longer uncanny, no longer terrifying. He understands the omissions, he understands the structure, the spaces between sounds. The piece of music is the same but Alexis is irreparably altered, no longer fourteen years old, no longer so savagely and beautifully innocent. There is no piece of music, he thinks, that could upset him so violently that he would be physically ill; the child who felt music that passionately is gone.

So Brigit, this evening, is fond of him but does not love him. She is comfortable with him. They eat dinner together here in the living room, lazily, they talk of local, trivial matters — today's luncheon in honor of Dr. Fetler; Brigit's having sighted Lee Hawley on the street with a diseased-looking young man in a cape; Oliver Byrne's rumored acceptance of a deanship at a very third-rate university in New Jersey; the probability of Garrett's resignation and Clay Waller's ascension to the presidency. (Brigit is unhappy about Oliver's resignation but not really surprised, since everyone has been predicting his fall for months: The man had seriously overestimated his own power and had underestimated that of his enemies. He had made several tactical blunders even before the catastrophe of St. Dennis's death, which did him in completely; after that death, and the lurid details surrounding it, Oliver was finished at Woodslee. It is a pity, though, that he must leave. Brigit will miss him immensely. Yet in a sense he is already gone — he has seemed, in the two or three hurried conversations Brigit has had with him recently, already distant from her, already estranged and rather bitter.)

And is it true, Alexis wonders, that Marilyn Byrne is filing for a divorce, or is she instead undergoing electroshock treatment at a private hospital in Albany, or is it New York? — or is she both filing for divorce and undergoing therapy? — and what about the Byrnes' children, and what about their house in Phoenix Heights? — is it already listed with a real-estate broker? — what price are they asking? (There is one rumor to the effect that the price is shockingly low.) . . . And is it true that the Andress boy, of whom everyone in the department is so proud, is declining the offer of a Woodrow Wilson Fellowship for graduate school in order to marry a girl no one seems to know, a student nurse at the local hospital, and to take a full-time job as a counselor in a county home for delinquent boys? Are Brigit and his other professors disappointed? Angry? Jealous? . . . And is it true that . . .

And is it true that Lewis Seidel and Mona Cuffe were found out to be having a love affair, and Faye intervened, and Joe threatened to kill Lewis, which led to Lewis's taking sick as he did?

And is it true, Alexis asks Brigit candidly, that she and her husband are going to attempt a reconciliation this summer?

(Brigit is astonished at this rumor; she asks Alexis angrily who has been spreading such nonsense. In fact Stanley wants a divorce now, he intends to marry someone else, mutual friends have said that the girl is a twenty-three-year-old version of Brigit, very pretty, but very unstable, just graduated from Radcliffe and already published in *The New Yorker* and *The Atlantic*. The divorce should be final sometime this summer.)

And those amazing poems of St. Dennis's that have turned up in an underground magazine in New York, stolen or pirated love poems about a child named Marco — are they genuine love poems, or are they parodies of such poems? Hideously embarrassing and mawkish. . . . What will they do to the poor man's reputation?

What does everyone think?

And what does everyone think about *him* — what is everyone saying about Alexis? He takes Brigit's hand and asks, casually, and she tells him she has heard very little; partly because people know of her connection with him, partly because she has gone to so few social events lately. Only two or three parties since March. And with Lewis sick. . . .

Alexis laughs. "*Lewis* — !" he says in contempt.

Brigit looks at him, uncomprehending.

(In fact it was Lewis's son Harry who came to Alexis's studio

the first week in March, very late one night, to talk of his hopes
for a career in music. He wanted to compose — not popular
music exactly, but ballads, blues. He was very serious; there was
nothing else in life that interested him. Could Alexis give him
some advice? He talked rapidly, he could not sit still for more
than a few seconds, his forehead gleamed with perspiration. Alexis believed he was high on drugs and wanted him gone but the
boy begged to be allowed to stay; he complained bitterly of his
parents' loveless marriage, and of the narrowness of Woodslee in
general. He wanted to live in New York City or San Francisco or
Rome. . . . For an hour he talked, for an hour and a half, staring
at Alexis, pacing from one end of the room to the other. It gradually dawned upon Alexis that the boy wanted something from
him, a gesture of some kind, a sign of recognition; he became
increasingly nervous; and Alexis too became nervous, wondering
how the incident would end. "It would mean so much to me
if. . . . If. . . ." he kept saying, his gaze damp and veiled, his
manner frantic. But Alexis, sitting on the piano stool, his arms
folded, made no gesture, no sign at all. Was it love the boy
wanted, was it merely a blessing of some kind? A sense of kinship?
He was attractive enough despite his blemished skin, but Alexis
felt nothing for him, was capable of feeling nothing except apprehension and impatience; he wanted him gone. Finally the boy
began to cry. He stammered something about having no one to
talk with, no friends, no relatives, no classmates. He had begun
to talk to his father about his problems once, a few years ago, but
his father had cut him short, embarrassed and jovial; he said only
that Harry would "grow out of it." But he hadn't grown out of it
— it had grown worse. Sometimes he thought he would go insane. Would kill himself. There was no one to talk with. . . . He
had seen Alexis at his father's party back in November and had
the idea that Alexis had looked at him in a certain way . . . hadn't
he? . . . and during all those months he had been thinking of
Alexis, dreaming of him, he'd walked by his apartment building

a half-dozen times trying to get up his courage to come here . . . and now he was here, at last, and . . . and. . . . For a moment Alexis hesitated. If the boy wanted love, why should Alexis deny him love? Forty-five minutes or an hour of love? It would be an easy enough gesture, it would cost Alexis very little. The boy stared at him, his face wet with tears. Alexis stared back. And then — Alexis wasn't sure exactly what happened, afterward — and then the boy made a frightened yelping noise and bolted to the door, and Alexis remained sitting on the piano stool, utterly amazed. He had said nothing, had made no movement at all, yet the boy had run out in terror. . . . Unfortunately this was not the end of the incident. Evidently the boy went home and accused Alexis of saying certain things to him and touching him, and inviting him to spend the night. And he gave him several pills, the boy didn't know what they were but their effect was speedy, hallucinatory, awful. Alexis Kessler had done these things. Alexis Kessler! The Seidels called the police, the university intervened, Alexis spent several distraught hours with Roger Haas, the university's chief attorney, explaining what had happened, going over and over the innocuous events of that evening, declaring his innocence, even begging at one point to be allowed to take a lie detector test. "And make the little bastard take one too," Alexis said. He was close to tears, he was exhausted, he saw that it was a plot of some kind to force his resignation, but how could he defend himself? Haas avoided looking him in the eye, as if he were diseased, and Haas's secretary watched him covertly, her skin drawn tightly over her forehead. A leper! A depraved degenerate creature! Garrett refused to grant him an audience but Waller saw him briefly, and Matt Ryerson appeared to listen sympathetically to his side of the story, but Alexis sensed that no one believed him, no one wished to believe him — they wanted him gone. He had not exactly been dismissed from his position but he knew very well that the administration expected him to resign.)

Once beautiful, now merely pretty.

Not very pretty.

Rather tired.

Once easily excited by desire, by the prospect of desire. . . .
Excited also by certain sights, certain sounds; a violent flowering
of passion in him that could not be controlled, its object never
entirely physical, never entirely human. One of his first songs
was a poem of Baudelaire's that spoke for Alexis's deepest self —

> A world of dazzling stones and of precious metals
> Flinging, in its quick rhythm, glints of mockery
> Ravishes me to ecstasy, I love to madness
> The mingling of sounds and lights in one intricacy.

Now —

Now a woman sits beside him in a pair of dark trousers and a
shapeless gray sweater with stained cuffs, smoking a cigarette, an
ashtray on her lap. She does not love him and does not mind that
he has been, and will continue to be, unfaithful to her. She is
sympathetic, certainly, but at the back of her mind she is waiting
for him to leave. She has work to do; she wants to sleep alone;
she does not love him, does not want him, there is nothing for
him to do but pour another drink.

It occurs to him that no one will ever wish to murder him
again.

"We could leave together," Alexis repeats. "You must have
some feeling for me, after all."

Brigit says nothing for a while. He watches her covertly, he is
thinking of having loved her, of having been her lover for so
many months; and now they are estranged and he cannot quite
regain her. He is bewildered and hurt. And angry, too, though he
is too clever to show it. (Did he ever love her, someone asked
him not long ago, and he had said contemptuously that he had
not loved her — not at all. Something about her had fascinated
him. A strange, perplexing woman, eerily unconscious of herself:
as he feels, at times, he is unconscious of certain aspects of him-

self that others know very well. . . . But did he love her, had he
ever loved her? Had he wanted her as a man wants a woman?)

It is not her body he wants but something else he cannot name.
In a sense there is no Brigit, there is no Alexis; they are a relationship, a slightly discordant harmony. He *hears* them but cannot
see them. Cannot touch them. It is not her body he wants but it
is only through the body that he can take possession of another
human being, so he must labor upon her body, he must enter her
body, to make his claim. I love you, he will whisper; only you.
Don't reject me! Don't kill me! There is no way into the soul of
another except through the body, Alexis thinks, saddened, uneasy, wondering if Brigit knows what he is thinking.

". . . must have some feeling for me," Alexis says. "It hasn't
been that long."

His body and hers.

There are, he thinks, no men or women; neither male nor
female bodies, but only other personalities — other selves — for
which he feels, at certain times, a mysterious, almost overwhelming lust. He cannot control his desire. It is so brutal, this desire,
it sometimes threatens to unhinge him. Perhaps it is a comic
predicament: he will try to laugh at it someday. But not for a
while.

"You *must* have some feeling for me," Alexis says, his voice
beginning to tremble.

Brigit looks away. "Certainly I have some feeling for you," she
says. "How could I not? I've been closer to you than to any other
person, even my husband. I trust you more than any other person. But there isn't any urgency in our relationship now, is there?
I mean, there's no need to insist upon anything, there's no need
for emotion, for —"

"You bitch," Alexis whispers.

She says nothing.

". . . bitch."

It is not her body he wants: not this woman's body, not this woman at all. But he wants something. Something he cannot name. He *wants* it, he will have it. He will make his claim and she will not be able to resist.

A flame-like sensation of joy rises in him and he reaches out to take hold of Brigit. She moves away, cat-like: he strikes the side of her face with his opened palm: he hears himself panting.

Brigit jumps to her feet and turns to hit him, her small fist awkward as a child's. "Goddamn you! Get out of here!" she cries.

Alexis flinches away. Her fist grazes his forehead, strikes the very tip of his nose.

"Get *out*," Brigit says breathlessly.

Alexis finds himself pressed against the arm of the sofa, grinning, and yet quite frightened. His heart is pounding: he is terrified.

"I'm not going anywhere," he says.

"You son of a *bitch*."

Something drips onto his shirt front. Onto his chin, his lips.

"Oh, your nose is bleeding," Brigit says in alarm.

"Because of *you*," Alexis mutters. He paws through his pockets in search of a tissue but finds nothing; Brigit has to get one for him. ". . . because of *you*," he whispers, his face flushed hotly.

They sit in silence. He holds the tissue to his nose and tilts his head back, trying to breathe evenly, trying to calm himself. He should not have touched her, that was an error, he does not believe in physical coercion, in violence of any kind. That was an error and he deserved to be struck in return. But he *will* have her. The evening is far from over, their relationship is far from over, he does not intend to leave this apartment in defeat and disgrace: no matter if he loves the woman or dislikes her or feels nothing at all.

In a few minutes the bleeding lessens. With an air of subtly offended dignity Alexis says, "You were saying, Brigit, that you felt closer to me than to anyone. . . . You said that you trusted me. . . ."

"Yes. But there's no need for emotion any longer. We're past that. We can't go back. We aren't lovers."

"Not lovers . . . ?" Alexis says, hurt.

Brigit stares at him. A long, uncomfortable moment passes. She too is agitated: he believes he can feel the gentle urgent pulsing of her blood.

But she says finally, "Not lovers. It's over. I feel a curious sort of peace or suspension. I may leave Woodslee and return to Norfolk, or I may leave Woodslee and go somewhere else, I can move in one direction or in another, or in another. . . . It's so difficult to explain. But whatever happens to me for the rest of my life," she says slowly, "won't be inevitable. I think that's why I feel so optimistic."

"Not inevitable . . . ?" Alexis says, dabbing at his nose.

He glances at her quizzically.

"But surely, my love, that can't last?" he says.

Date Due